You're invited to a…

White Wedding

Everyone loves a wedding and in this special
collection you'll meet blushing brides and
gorgeous grooms who all have one thing in
common: for better or worse, they're
determined the bride should wear white
on her wedding day…

*Three of your favourite authors bring you these
classic love stories – when true love really
waits…until the wedding night!*

D1335229

Margaret Way takes great pleasure in her work and works hard at her pleasure. She enjoys tearing off to the beach with her family at weekends, loves haunting galleries and auctions and is completely given over to French champagne 'for every possible joyous occasion'. She was born and educated in the river city of Brisbane, Australia, and now lives within sight and sound of beautiful Moreton Bay.

Jessica Steele lives in a friendly Worcestershire village with her super husband, Peter. They are owned by a gorgeous Staffordshire bull terrier called Florence, who is boisterous and manic, but also adorable. It was Peter who first prompted Jessica to try writing, and after the first rejection, encouraged her to keep on trying. Luckily, with the exception of Uruguay, she has so far managed to research inside all the countries in which she has set her books, travelling to places as far apart as Siberia and Egypt. Her thanks go to Peter for his help and encouragement.

Judy Christenberry has been writing romances for years because she loves happy endings as much as her readers. She loves traditional romances and is delighted to tell a story that brings those elements to the reader. She hopes readers have as much fun reading her stories as she does writing them. She spends her spare time reading, watching her favourite sports teams and keeping track of her two daughters.

You're invited to a…

White Wedding

Margaret Way, Jessica Steele, Judy Christenberry

*MILLS & BOON and MILLS & BOON with the Rose Device
are registered trademarks of the publisher.
Harlequin Mills & Boon Limited,
Eton House, 18-24 Paradise Road, Richmond, Surrey, TW9 1SR*

YOU'RE INVITED TO A...WHITE WEDDING
© by Harlequin Enterprises II B.V., 2004

Gabriel's Mission © Margaret Way, Pty., Ltd 1998
A Wedding Worth Waiting For © Jessica Steele 1999
The Nine-Month Bride © Judy Christenberry 1998

ISBN 0 263 84499 4

024-0804

*Printed and bound in Spain
by Litografia Rosés S.A., Barcelona*

GABRIEL'S MISSION

by

Margaret Way

PROLOGUE

HEAVEN

Titus and Thomas came tumbling down the grass, rolling ecstatically across the cushiony emerald sward, hurtling onwards to the stream that flashed silver in the all-pervading shining light. They often played this tumbling game. They loved it. Rolling from the very top of the undulating hill with its thick sprinkling of wildflowers, into the translucent water below. With their wings tucked back they dived to the bottom where gorgeous little fish, lovely little things, came to the hand, and flowers like jewels opened and shut amid the green reeds that grew out of the sand with its rich dusting of gold. Afterwards they floated with the immortal white swans that gently made way for them, bending their beaks to the still water that mirrored their snowy reflections. Afterwards they could ride the silky softness of the clouds calling on the Sky Wind to blow them to heaven's brink or perhaps play with the cherubs who loved to fly through the great soaring trees of the forest on pretty little dragons, beautifully caparisoned. It was all marvellous fun! But sometimes Titus wished he had a *job* to do. He was bursting with love and miraculous energy so sometimes his aura flared like the sun.

They were almost at the bottom of the slope and into the crystal fountain when a voice like a golden trumpet echoed across the hillside and a great beam of pure white light approached them at enormous speed.

"Titus, Thomas, I haven't seen you all day. A meeting

5

at the Archives Building, if you please. Titus, Thomas, hello…hello…''

Mr. Bliss, Titus thought in surprise. Archangel in charge of recruitments for guardian angels.

Immediately Titus popped out his wings. Thomas followed suit, both soaring high in the air above the tops of the eternally blossoming trees.

''Ah, there you are, boys. A busy morning ahead,'' Mr. Bliss said as soon as he saw them. Mr. Bliss stayed in place with a whirring of great wings, while Titus and Thomas flitted around him, all of them hundreds of feet off the ground.

Titus's radiant blue eyes shone with excitement. Just maybe one day he would get to be a guardian angel. ''What's the meeting about, Mr. Bliss?'' he asked with an eager inflection.

Mr. Bliss lifted his hands, light streaming from his fingertips. ''Surely you can guess, Titus? Guardian angels have to be elected. We have to help our earthly friends. Poor souls, what would they do without us?''

What indeed!

The Great Hall of the Archives Building spired to God's glory, its walls sculptured of sparkling crystal inlaid with silver and gold. Today it was filled with luminous beings wearing exquisite flowing robes, rose, saffron, azure, rich emerald and crimson and a wonderful violet, so that everywhere one looked there was rainbow upon rainbow of rippling colour. The higher one went through the nine angelic ranks the more the myriad colours gave way to an extreme white radiance like that of Mr. Bliss who now stood before them in a blinding flash of light and a great rushing whirl of majestic white wings. Wings they all had in common, from the cute double and triple wings of the adorable little cherubs to the six-foot splendour of the most awesome angels of all, the Cherubim and Seraphim, the highest-ranking heavenly beings who guarded the Divine Throne. These exulted angels, naturally, did not attend staff meetings.

Mr. Bliss lost no time getting things under way. Angels were encouraged to speak of their experiences; looking after their earthly charges, leading them to the realm of Heaven, a place of such joy and beauty no human mind could encompass it; or sending souls back through the long tunnel between near death and eternity to fulfil their destiny. Guardian angel roles were renewed, legions more appointed in the twinkling of an eye. A few angels spoke of exhaustion, a state rare among their ranks, although it *was* known. One angel in particular, Lucas, told the most wistful tale of all. For twenty-four years he had been the appointed guardian angel of one Chloe Cavanagh who was proving such a handful Lucas feared he had suffered a temporary burnout. In fact he was feeling a loss of power in his lower right wing.

"It's not as though Chloe isn't a fine compassionate young mortal with considerable spirituality, but she's becoming something of a danger to herself," he told his brilliant audience. "She has a tragic history you see." Lucas went on to tell them Chloe had lost a sibling, a brother, Timothy, when she was six and the child barely eighteen months, leaving the family desolate. Then some two years ago tragedy struck again like a lightning bolt. Chloe's parents were involved in a car crash that killed her father and put her mother into a coma from which she hadn't emerged for months on end. The mother, still locked in a waking dream state, was now in a nursing home being cared for while Chloe tried to balance her career as a journalist in the high-powered world of network TV with being there for her mother.

Mr. Bliss was faced with a decision. To counsel Lucas and allow him to continue? Or allow Lucas a long rest and appoint a replacement. There were many positive angels he could rely on to do the job. Angels who wouldn't collapse under the strain.

As Mr. Bliss looked around thoughtfully a glowing young face distracted him. Titus, of course, his garments radiating a flawless blue light. Angels' beautifully sculptured tranquil features were seen mostly through a luminous haze rather like a vapour, but for some reason Titus's sparkling face was almost flesh and blood. He glowed, with his burnished rose-gold curls, brilliant blue eyes and a tracery of gold freckles that danced across his nose. Curious to have freckles in this perfect realm where the sun spilled only *adoration* onto God and His heavenly kingdom. Mr. Bliss had the feeling there might be much to learn about young Titus's past. Was it possible he had had an earthly life?

Even as Mr. Bliss considered a dip into Archives, Titus spoke up. "Please, Mr. Bliss, can't you give us little guys a go?"

There it was again. Those unusual words. *Guys?* Of course Titus liked reading about life on earth. Didn't they all!

Mr. Bliss folded his long, beautiful fingers together, the expression on his wonderful classic face not without sympathy. "Hmm. Not possible, young Titus, I'm afraid. I'm not saying not *ever* but not just yet."

"It could be the answer," Lucas suddenly interjected in a very deep mellow voice like a gong, reminding Mr. Bliss Lucas must be many thousands of years old. "I do realise Titus has had no experience but he's so full of pep he just might be able to keep up with Chloe."

Mr. Bliss's singular eyes that were very dark but sparkled with light, began to sharpen and glow. "I rarely if ever send anyone so young, Lucas," he pointed out gently.

"*You* started young, Mr. Bliss," Titus piped up.

Another thing that struck Mr. Bliss as odd. How did Titus know? "So I did," Mr. Bliss admitted.

There were chuckles all 'round, tender smiles for Titus.

"What joy it must be to be a guardian angel!" Titus exclaimed, bright curls abob. His expression was one of radiant hope.

Mr. Bliss pondered. Titus was an extremely helpful and cooperative young angel, given to playful games perhaps but excellent at supervising the cherubs. The experience of taking charge of a mortal life might catapult him into real responsibility, earn him his three-quarter wings. Really Titus wasn't all that different from himself at the same state of transformation.

"All right, Titus," Mr. Bliss announced to a rippling wave of applause and a familiar swishing of wings. "The position of guardian angel to Miss Chloe Cavanagh is yours as of now."

Titus strove to control the great flame of excitement that sent far-distant memories raying through his mind.

While the cherubs played ball with the low-hanging silver stars, Titus embarked on his great flight to earth, accelerating through the vast sea of clouds with a rhythmic swishing of his wings, revelling in the freshness of the wind, the extraordinary smell of earth's atmosphere as he entered it. While he watched the play of glittering golden sunlight on the near side of the planet, he was conscious of being happier than he had ever been in his experience. Maybe he had overdone the surging speed of descent. Even Heaven didn't seem real.

"Hold on, Chloe," he called in a sweet ecstasy, his glowing blue garments suddenly reflecting a white light. "I'm your guardian angel now. You can call upon my power."

To keep Chloe safe would be his great mission.

A great wave of love engulfed him. Not so much glory, but something of a different lustre; warm, human affection.

The soul remembers.

CHAPTER ONE

IT WAS well after nine-thirty when Chloe finally made it back to BTQ8, thinking she mightn't have a job at the end of the day. In the year since he had become Managing Director of the Brisbane link in the national network, McGuire had been reducing numbers at the drop of a hat. Downsizing, he said, in the quest to achieve better results. Not being a fan of McGuire's, Chloe chose to ignore the fact the TV station had been staging a remarkable comeback from near disaster under her old mentor, Clive Connor, who had since been moved on with a very generous redundancy package. She had never taken to McGuire, Clive's successor, but the Big Guys loved him. He was the Golden Boy with a big future in the industry. The man who could do no wrong. This might very well be her day to get the shove. The third monthly meeting she had missed in a row when she always started out with the very best intentions.

Hunching her shoulders against the heavy tropical downpour, Chloe dashed across the station car park and into the main building, struggling with her brolly which, being cheap, was playing up. When she looked up, McGuire was coming towards her. Six foot three of raw animal power. He had shoulders like a front rower which he had been apparently at University. She wouldn't have cared to be his opposite number. She didn't like men who were so dark, either. So in-the-face uncompromisingly male. For a man of Irish ancestry he was almost swarthy with thick jet-black hair he wore short to discourage the curl, a bronze skin and, it had to be admitted, rather fine near-black eyes with eyelashes most women would die for.

Chloe raised her hand and before she could help herself gave him a cheeky wave. Where for the love of mike was her sense of survival? Gone with the great wind from Hell that had blown away her entire world.

"Cavanagh, you're late," McGuire said with a touch of gravel, amused and irritated by the sort of cockiness she usually exhibited with him. He moved to join her, watching her fiddle with a floral umbrella that looked more like a child's sunshade, then flip back her trademark mane of red hair. It was pouring outside and her hair curled extravagantly in the humid heat. Corkscrew locks spilled forward onto her forehead and flushed cheeks. She looked ravishing, like a heavenly illumination in a Medieval manuscript where the artist used precious pigments and gold inks. All that was missing was the bright halo and she sure didn't deserve that. Three missed meetings in as many months. It made him so damned mad. Exaggeration. Exasperated. For some reason that evaded him, he had a soft spot for Cavanagh. Maybe it was the look of her, the finely constructed frame he would like to give a good shake. She appeared so light, so fragile, so feminine, the tender curves of her breasts, the willowy waist and delicate hips, the ballerina legs. Yet there was something strong about her, something supple and resilient that shone through the lightness. Of course he knew her tragic background, and that smote him. Not that she would ever confide in him. He was well aware of her hidden antipathy. Almost a revulsion, he sometimes thought, like a princess under siege with the barbarian at the gate. She had been ready to dislike him before he had ever been given the chance to open his mouth. He had no hand at all in Connor's sacking. Poor old Clive had brought it all on himself.

Chloe looking up at McGuire towering above her suddenly coughed, making him aware he had been staring. "In my office in ten minutes," he clipped off.

"Right, Chief." She just barely refrained from saluting him. What had stopped her? Perhaps because McGuire had swung back on her. Lord, for a big man he was remarkably light on his feet. A sudden vision of him in a tutu almost made her laugh aloud. "I'm so sorry I missed the meeting," she found herself saying hastily, "I do most humbly apologise."

It was so sweet he damn near lifted a hand to toy with her rain-sequined hair. Instead he asked sarcastically, "Another hot story breaking?"

"Could be a real scoop." It was a fib. She had made an unscheduled early morning visit to see her mother then got caught up in road works. No use to tell McGuire that. She could see the flint in his all-encompassing dark eyes.

"Sure you're not getting overly ambitious?" he challenged her, worried it might be the case. She had taken so many risks of late, even if they had managed to come off.

"It was you who persuaded us to lift our game, Chief," she pointed out innocently.

"Then I'll have to dissuade you from placing yourself in danger, as well. Get rid of these wet things then we'll have a nice chat."

Chat? Ha! As if she needed a chat with McGuire. Communications between the two of them were becoming increasingly edgy. She didn't know why she disliked him so much. Every other woman in the building fell in a swoon as he passed. Hers was a feline reaction, much like her marmalade cat confronted by a very large Doberman. Chloe raced on, greeting fellow workers to her left and right in her bright, friendly fashion, beaming at Mike Cole, senior sports writer, as he held the door of the outer office for her.

"Chloe, damned if I've ever seen anyone look so pretty in the rain," Mike exclaimed. "You've got messages, kid. They're on your desk. Better warn ya, Gabe was browned off when you didn't show up for the meeting."

Chloe looked up at Mike with a little grimace. "Don't I know. I saw the dear boy in the lobby. I started out so early, too, but I got caught up a traffic jam. Road works at Lang Park. Hopeless. They do everything right before an election. Fact is I called in on Mum. I had the weirdest dream last night. Mum was trying to tell me someone was coming. Pathetic isn't it?"

Mike shook his head in sympathy. He had been on his way out but decided to walk back with her. He and his wife, Teri, were very fond of Chloe. A frequent visitor to their home, she was the godmother to their newest baby, Samantha. Chloe had been given a very rough deal in life. But she was such a fighter. "What about a coffee?" he suggested.

"Love one. A rushed one," Chloe said. "I didn't have time for breakfast. McGuire gave me a drop-dead invitation. In his office in ten minutes." She glanced at her watch. "Correction, eight. He was looking at me so queerly as if he couldn't figure me out."

Mike snorted. "For such a tough guy, he's mighty easy on you." He walked to the coffee machine, came back with two steaming cups of black coffee. "And how is Mum?" he asked. He and Teri had accompanied Chloe to her mother's nursing home on several occasions. Delia Cavanagh was still a beautiful woman but the life switch had been turned off. Probably for good, Mike thought sadly.

"She looks so serene, Mike," Chloe said, a bright glitter of helpless tears in her dark blue eyes. "For all that has happened to her she doesn't seem to have aged a minute. It's like she's locked in time."

Mike shook his sandy head, receding rapidly at the hairline to his distress. "It's been hard on you, Chloe, but you're a daughter in a million." Chloe visited her mother on almost a daily basis when Mike knew her packed schedule. No wonder she looked like a breeze could blow her out of town.

Chloe gulped her coffee, too hot. "Why did it have to happen, Mike? Isn't it enough to lose your husband and child? I try, but I don't know that I believe in God anymore."

"Well, he sure isn't selling this world," Mike observed with a wry expression. "Maybe it's the next we should be aimin' for, kid."

"I think McGuire is of the opinion I'm trying to get myself killed."

Mike took a while to answer. "It makes sense, Chloe. Goodness knows Teri and I think you're the bravest girl in the world but you haven't quite come to terms with all the blows fate has dealt you. That's what worries Gabe."

Blue fire flashed from Chloe's beautiful eyes. "What would McGuire know about it? He knows nothing about me."

"Of course he does, Chloe. Don't take it so hard." Mike leaned back against Chloe's desk, a gangling attractive figure. "Your father was a well-known physician. It was in all the papers. Gabe has access to anything he wants to know."

"I wouldn't put a great deal of faith in McGuire's kind heart." Chloe started to push her coffee away. "I don't want him to know anything about me. I certainly don't want his pity."

"Chloe, love, settle down." Mike's voice carried a fatherly note. "I know you can't see this, but Gabe's a great guy."

"Who gave our good friend, Clive, the push and laid off Ralph and Lindsey," Chloe retorted.

"Connor had it coming. Be fair, in fact they all did. You have to admit Clive had lost his drive. I know we all liked him. You saw him as some sort of a father figure, but he totally lacked Gabe's skills, let alone brilliance."

"Gabriel McGuire, the one-man razor gang?" Chloe mocked, twiddling her fingers at a junior staffer.

"Everyone is cost conscious these days, Chloe. The shareholders want an adequate return and Gabe has to satisfy our national bosses. He's single-handedly pulled us from disastrous near-bottom ratings to giving Channel Nine a run for their money."

"All right, all right," Chloe sighed, wishing she had a croissant. She was hungry. "He's a dynamo but there's something kind of ruthless about him. I don't like men who look like that. So dark and overpowering."

"You just cut your teeth on poor old Clive," Mike pointed out gently.

"At least he was a gentle man."

"You just don't like Gabe, full stop."

"I told you. Something about him frightens me away."

"Hey, Chloe, like a muffin?" someone called. "Nice and fresh."

Chloe looked up as a young production assistant sauntered up to her, holding out a white paper bag.

"Gee, thanks, Rosie. I'm hungry, missed breakfast."

"Just popped into my head." Rosie smiled and moved off.

Chloe made short work of the delicious apricot muffin, wiped her mouth and fingers, then adjusted the collar of her yellow silk crepe blouse and stood up. "That's it, then. I'd better see McGuire."

"I'll walk out with you," Mike said. "I should have

been over at the Broncos training session ten minutes ago.''

McGuire was watching her approach through the glass wall of his office, motioning her in with a near pugilistic lift of his arm. Needless to say he was on the phone, one hand riffling through some papers, the other holding the receiver slotted between his aggressive cleft chin and his broad shoulder. Chloe took a seat, sitting upright, slender legs neatly locked at knee and ankle. She wished now she hadn't worn the yellow outfit, a favourite because it brightened her mood, but the short skirt was undeniably short. McGuire must have thought so, too, because his eyes moved slowly over her legs before settling on her face.

Drat. Why did he have to do that? He was carrying on a high-powered conversation while his near-black eyes almost bound her to the chair. He was openly studying her. Not politely, formally, but with confrontational male interest. Chloe couldn't help knowing she was pretty—other people said beautiful—but Chloe, at twenty-four, was still a virgin with a very fastidious mentality. Having sex, for Chloe, involved falling in love, and Chloe knew better than anyone that love and the loss of it meant terrible suffering. She had friends, of course. Lots of friends. Male and female. But she couldn't play the jump-into-bed game. One of the things about McGuire that bothered her was his sexual charisma, the certain knowledge that he would be a passionate maybe too demanding lover. She had known the second she had laid eyes on him, felt his eyes on her; recognised the looming battle ahead. She had readied herself, immediately raising her defences against such a threatening aura.

Now inexplicably she knew a bleak moment. She was a mess. Had been since the fabric of her life had been ripped apart. No man could ever put his heart in her hands. She wouldn't know what to do with it.

McGuire slammed the phone down and leaned across his massive mahogany desk, causing Chloe to audibly exhale.

"Tell me why you couldn't make the meeting?" he asked, almost gently for him.

For an instant, to her amazement, she considered telling him about her visit to her mother. What was the matter with her? "I was held up in traffic, Chief. They've decided at long last to do something about Lang Street."

His sensual mouth so clear cut, compressed. "Our meeting was set for 8:30 sharp. Road works commenced at 9:00 a.m. I heard it on early morning radio."

He would. "I'm sorry. I apologise." Even to her own ears she sounded sincere. "I know it's my job to attend. I fully intended to but I couldn't make it through the traffic." Heck, usually she threw down the gauntlet.

"Why can't you talk to me, Chloe?" He leaned back in the leather armchair, powerful body languid, two seeing eyes trained on her.

She got some kind of a mad rush just hearing him speak her Christian name. She flushed. "There's nothing to talk about, Chief. Outside work."

"We'll settle for that. You have a lot of potential, Cavanagh." He could see she was more comfortable with the surname, the odd, sweet, prickly little creature. "How long is it now since you joined BTQ8?"

"Of course you know. Four years. I came straight from University to cadet reporter. Clive taught me everything I know."

"I know he took you under his wing." Why not? She must have looked like a cherub. "Clive in his heyday as anchorman never had your flair. People are starting to get riveted to your on-camera reporting. That was a good piece you did on the Fairfield tragedy. I got a phone call from upstairs. Sir Llew was very pleased with the way you handled it.''

"Maybe, but I hate covering tragedies," Chloe said.

"We all do but it's our job. The public appetite for news is voracious. What sets you apart from many others is your compassion.''

Chloe looked down at the hands locked in her lap. "I didn't feel too compassionate staging a wait outside his house. I felt more like a vulture.''

"That's understandable but we all know about real life. A prominent politician about to be investigated for corruption. Not even his widow guessed he was going to commit suicide. I marvel she could talk at all.''

"Only to me,'' Chloe said, shaking her head sadly. "Only to Chloe Cavanagh. I don't know why.''

"I do," he said briefly. "You have a special knack for communicating with grieving souls.''

Why not? Chloe thought. I have a troubled soul myself.

"The only problem is, you're putting yourself too much in the front line.'' His voice switched suddenly, rasped.

"But this is a tough industry, Chief. No need to tell you that. I'm after the best story for the channel.''

He continued to appraise her as though seeking to see through to her soul. "You're not taking enough care and you know it. I know for a fact Rob has concerns.''

She was utterly taken aback. "Did he speak to you?''

"Most people outside of you, do.'' He smiled, a little tightly. "He's entitled. He's your sidekick, your photographer. He's very protective of you, like your mate Mike. But that was a very expensive camera that got wrecked. It's not your job to beard international con men in their den. You can leave that to our top investigative reporter.''

''But he didn't get the story, did he?'' She spoke with a light note of triumph.

''No, but he has a black belt.''

''Are you suggesting I learn karate?'' she asked sweetly.

He shrugged a broad shoulder. ''I'm suggesting you learn a few moves if you're going to continue to get yourself into situations where angels might fear to tread.'' His tone, tough and uncompromising, suddenly changed. ''What would you think about taking over as anchorwoman at the weekend?'' Hell, what a good idea. It just popped into his mind.

Chloe, too, was startled and looked it. She didn't want to take anyone's job but the thought excited her. ''I don't know that I'm ready for anything like that,'' she evaded. The weekends gave her extra time with her mother.

''That doesn't sound like you, Cavanagh. Too boring?''

''I suppose you could say that,'' she sighed. ''My talent is for getting a story, getting to the bottom of things. I'm not a talking head.''

''You will be if I think you fit the bill.'' He had to think this thing through.

She sat very still. ''You're the boss.''

''And that continues to enrage you.'' There was a slight bunching of the muscles around his hard jawbone.

''Not at all.'' Her answer was surprisingly, disarmingly soft.

''So why look at me as if I'm a woman-eating tiger?''

Because you are and you'd better believe it. ''You did send Marlene Attwell on her way,'' she pointed out.

''You admired her, did you?'' His expression was cynical.

''Not quite. She was too bitchy for any of us to like her, but she's a professional. She looked good in front of the cameras and she has credibility.''

He quelled a little rush of anger. Like some other people, he wasn't a forgiving soul. "She insulted a lot of powerful people once too often, Cavanagh. Not to set the story straight but to establish her own questionable style. Then as you say, her in-house standing was far from good."

Chloe nodded, looking suitably chastened. "I knew I wasn't going to leave your office with a big smile."

"Why so sure?" His black eyes sparkled with sardonic humour. "Mel Gibson will be in town the beginning of next month," he found himself saying. "A quick trip home to promote his new movie. He's willing to talk to us. I've had it confirmed."

Chloe looked back at him in astonishment. "You're surely not handing the job to me?" Her melodious voice, one of her big assets, took on a decided lilt.

"Can't handle it?" One black eyebrow shot up, giving him a rakish look. Surely he should be handing the interview to Jennifer?

"I'll have you know I once sat a few seats behind Mel on a plane." She smiled.

"Is that so? Then you won't want to miss this golden opportunity, either. He's happy to talk. Keep it short and keep it light."

"A pleasure." She totally forgot herself and beamed at him. Gosh, what was in that muffin? "It should be fun. They say he's the easiest person in the world to talk to. None of that Big Star ego. A down-to-earth Aussie. Won't Jennifer have her nose put out of joint?"

He held up a large palm. "There's no law against passing over our senior female reporter. Though Jennifer is never late, never misses meetings, and never gets herself involved in ongoing brawls."

"She'll certainly have something to say to me." Chloe smiled wryly. There were big jealousies abroad. Grudges. Undercurrents.

"That's your problem, Cavanagh." He stared at her for a minute or two. "I had intended to bawl you out, but I seem to have surrendered to your charm. You can go now. I'm busy. By the way, Sir Llew is giving a small party, which means roughly a hundred people, Saturday night. You'd better go out and buy yourself a new dress."

Anyone else but McGuire, she would have rushed to kiss his cheek. "You mean, I'm invited? That's a first."

His eyes sparkled sardonically. "Cavanagh, you're well on your way to becoming a high flier. I'm in a position to provide you with wings. Sir Llew wants four of us for company. Bright, engaging people, he said."

Chloe suppressed a snort. *Sure!* McGuire was brilliant. Engaging? *Never.*

He had to be a mind-reader because his dark eyes flashed. "Cavanagh, your face is so transparent you ought to wear a mask. The party's for Christopher Freeman, by the way." He named an international businessman of legendary wealth. Australian born, but currently residing in the U.S.A.

"The wild one." Chloe feigned a gasp. "Freeman has quite a reputation as a womaniser."

"Don't worry, I'll be there to protect you."

"No problem," Chloe responded blithely. "The likes of Christopher Freeman would get nowhere with me." A professional virgin with ice cubes rattling in her veins.

"I like that, Cavanagh," he said. "By the way, I'd like you to know our present weekend anchorwoman is looking to retire."

Chloe, walking to the door, turned back in surprise. "She never said so."

"She hasn't seen much of you of late," McGuire pointed out dryly, bewitched despite himself at the image of her. "For a girl who doesn't run with the crowd, you keep yourself mighty busy."

"I have a wonderful garden," she quipped.

"I admit you're a bit of a puzzlement, Cavanagh." He seemed to lose interest in her, reaching for a pile of papers. "Get Farrell in here, would you. I wish he had a few of your daredevil qualities." He glanced up casually. "I can give you a lift Saturday night if it would help. Drop you off home afterwards. The party's at Sir Llew's so it's going to be difficult getting parking near the house."

It sounded so simple yet it took her by storm, McGuire at close quarters? How claustrophobic could one get? Her moods were shifting madly back and forth. She couldn't account for it. "Thanks for the offer, Chief, but I'll be okay. I know my way around that neck of the woods."

"Well, the offer's open in case you change your mind. Oh, there's something else, too. I want a piece on Jake Wylie, the writer. I don't suppose you've gotten around to reading his book, *One Man's Poison?*"

Chloe's expressive face brightened. "As a matter of fact I have. I bought the hardback to see what all the fuss was about. A mite strong, but a cracking good story, very funny in places."

McGuire nodded. "He has all the makings. Our new great white hope, though he could pare down a bit on the sex. We don't need a potted course in how and where to do it."

I might, Chloe thought. "When would you want the piece?"

"Couple of weeks." His eyes were already on some newspaper clipping on his desk. "I'll give you time. Talk to him first. If you think he might have some on-camera potential we can find a spot for you both."

Just when she thought miracles were for someone else! "That's great!" From such a shaky start she thought a soft billowy cloud was beneath her. She could almost have gone skydiving. Sans parachute.

"Well?" He glanced up. For all his black eyes could bore a hole through her, their expression was almost kindly. "Everything okay, Cavanagh?" he jeered. Why did she have to look so beautiful, so delicate, so refined? It pierced his heart. She was usually such an uppity little devil, as well, with a lot of aggravation. Hair like flame, and a spirit to match.

"Everything's fine, Chief." Chloe tried to move off but she seemed stuck to the spot. "I suppose about Saturday it doesn't make sense taking two cars?" She *didn't* say that. She *couldn't* have said it. She began to seriously wonder what had befallen her. Maybe she should rush out and see a psychiatrist. This was McGuire, remember? The Wolf Man. Rumour tied him to Sir Llew's nubile daughter, the very attractive, high-profile party-goer, Tara.

"No sense at all," McGuire casually agreed. "Let's say I pick you up around eight o'clock."

So that was that.

Chloe fled McGuire's office before she found herself agreeing to dropping off his dry cleaning.

She and Bob were watching a clip on a monitor, one of her assignments due to air, when Rosie, clipboard in hand, bustled into the studio. "Listen, there's a protest meeting going on out at Ashfield parklands. Caller rang in. Usual thing, the greenies versus a developer. Rowlands, big shot. He wants to put in a shopping centre. Some of the locals are all for it but it would mean clearing a section of bushland where the koalas hang out."

"But surely the shire council is falling over itself trying to protect the wildlife?" Chloe lifted a brow.

"Up to a point. Hell, is it us or the koalas? They're

all over the place. Shift the little devils. All they need is a good feed of gum leaves,'' Rose muttered.

"The right gum leaves, Rosie. And they are being killed on the roads despite all the signs.''

"Want the job or not? We could send Pamela.''

"Pamela can't give an accurate account of anything. No, we'll be there.'' Chloe lost no time switching off the monitor. "If people are prepared to talk instead of shouting at one another they might be able to come up with a solution.''

"I know Rowlands,'' Bob, fortyish, almost as short as Chloe, said casually. "He's not much good at listening.''

"I don't suppose he'll be there. It'll be one of his people.''

They arrived at the Ashfield parklands in twenty minutes flat, Chloe jumping out almost before the BTQ8 van streaked up onto the footpath.

"Oh-oh, trouble,'' Bob chortled. "I wasn't expecting anywhere near as many people.''

"The more, the merrier,'' Chloe said briskly. "Get a move on, Bob. Let the camera roll.''

"People do wacky things when a camera's on them, Chloe,'' Bob called. "Take care. I don't want any more broken equipment.''

"Look at that! BTQ8,'' someone cried as Chloe made short work of crossing the parkland. "Chloe Cavanagh. That's a blessing. We might get heard.''

By the time Bob arrived with his camera, Chloe was right in the thick of it. She'd be on the side of the koalas, of course, but you couldn't please everyone. A lot of people seemed to want the shopping centre to go ahead, when as far as Bob could see there was a perfectly good one back down the road.

Chloe, one of those journalists who could really get people talking, worked the crowd briskly, taking opinions left and right. Most were concerned citizens, a few troublemakers, a couple from the lunatic fringe, their heads swaddled in red bandannas, with matching red waistcoats.

"They won't be satisfied until there are no koalas left." A very tall woman glowered.

The Rowlands' representative, an attractive, middle-aged woman, stylishly dressed, smiled and took Chloe's hand. "Mary Stanton, Miss Cavanagh, a pleasure. I'd like you to know no company is more environmentally conscious than we are at Rowlands, as I'm trying to tell these people."

This was howled down while Bob, busy videoing at Chloe's side, suddenly aimed the camera at a tree. Chloe looked up expecting to see a koala so dopey on gum leaves it hadn't noticed it was broad daylight and there was a rally in progress, only to find a boy about nine or ten waving at her when he should have been at school.

"You'd better come down," Chloe called, swinging 'round in surprise as a voice spoke softly in her ear. No one. That was odd. Disconcerted, she began again. "Come on down from there." The child was straddling a fairly high branch. None too substantial. Hadn't anyone noticed?

"I'm all right." He gave her a wide toothy grin, and slid further along the branch.

"The koalas have absolutely nothing to fear from us," the woman from Rowlands was saying very earnestly. "We try to get along with everybody. Not all of these trees are grey gums. The wildlife people will be only too pleased to rescue the very small koala population."

"Who does that boy belong to?" Chloe asked, trying to puzzle out where the voice had come from. A soft melodic voice, young, infectious, with a kind of bubbling happiness. She really didn't like the boy up there even if she knew she was being overly protective. It all had something to do with losing her little brother. Boys were always climbing trees. They had a lot of talent for it. But just looking up was giving her vertigo.

"All I want to ask is this," a stout woman in baggy jeans and a T-shirt two sizes too small, cried over the top of the male protester beside her. "Do we really need another shopping centre? There's a good one about a mile down the road."

"We don't all have cars, love," an elderly lady decorated in beads piped up. "The way I heard it they're going to sell out to a chain store. I feel terrible about the koalas but a new shopping centre right here would be exciting. I could walk over every day. Meet people."

"And you, sir?" Chloe asked, confronting an elderly man with military medals festooning his jacket.

"Why doesn't Rowlands pack up and go back to where he belongs," he barked.

"We can't give in to the greenies," a young mother with fuzzy blond curls, babe in arms, was exclaiming. "We all want the shopping centre. Everyone except *those* guys." She gestured towards the red bandannas.

"You couldn't put it somewhere else?" Chloe asked Mary Stanton doubtfully.

"Not a chance. We've done our homework. We have community backing."

At that there was an outcry, people on the fringes rushing in to protest, some with the light of battle in their eyes.

It should have made Chloe uneasy but for some reason she was focused on the boy in the tree. What was the big deal? It wasn't all that high. Yet...

When the branch suddenly snapped it was no real surprise to Chloe. People underneath panicked, running out of harm's way, but Chloe, the slender, the fragile, the petite, zeroed in. She wordlessly put up her arms, waiting for the boy to topple into them.

Incredibly he did.

People gaped in amazement, blinking like rabbits, honestly not believing their eyes. Chloe was spinning across the springy grass almost dancing, holding the boy aloft before they both suddenly fell, full stretch, side by side, to peals of merriment.

The crowd, a moment before in full roar, fell silent, then broke into a delighted round of applause and some giggles, as first Chloe then the boy leapt lightly to their feet. "How the heck did she do that?" one of the red bandannas asked in wonderment.

"She must be pumping iron," his companion replied.

"Look, isn't that sweet?" the old lady cried.

The boy had leaned up to kiss Chloe's cheek, fumbling in his pocket for a piece of paper for her autograph. How could a skinny, five-three maybe five-four girl with a mop of wild red hair have the strength to catch him? He figured she had to have had some help from her guardian angel. His had disappeared the same day his dad had left home and never returned.

Everyone wanted to shake Chloe's hand.

"It was nothing," she felt compelled to say, still trying to grasp how the boy had seemed to weigh little more than Samantha, her baby goddaughter.

"Adrenaline," an elderly man, an ex-professor explained. "One becomes absolutely superhuman in a crisis. Wonderful, my dear, and your cameraman got it."

"What a turn-up that was!" a protester in scruffy running shoes cried.

The crowd was delighted, for the first time turning to one another, wondering, smiling, ready for a friendly chat.

"You know there's another possible site we passed on the way," Chloe addressed Mary Stanton, who was giving her wide-eyed attention. "Huge corner block near a nursery. A For Sale sign on it.'' Had she really noticed all that?

"Old Waverley's farm,'' Military Medals supplied. "He won't sell to any developer,'' he added sternly.

"You tried him, did you?'' Chloe prompted the still confused Mary.

"We certainly did, but he was very hostile,'' Mary managed ruefully.

"Try him again,'' Chloe suggested. "He's sitting in the blue Holden over there.'' She waved a hand.

Mary took a deep breath. "You know him, do you?'' As she had just witnessed, anything was possible.

"Never met him in my life, but I'm sure that's he.'' My goodness, *why?* Chloe thought. If she was psychic, she wanted to be the first to know.

"I can't bowl up to a stranger.'' Mary turned to Chloe, flustered. "You could be mistaken.''

"All right, anyone know Mr. Waverley?'' Chloe's voice echoed like a silver bell.

Sure enough, Running Shoes answered. "Old Jack? He's sitting over in his car. Probably hoping to bump up the price of his farm. That's where the shopping centre should be, if you ask me. We could all agree to that.''

"Well, I never!'' Mary Stanton thrust her shoulder bag under her arm. "Normally I don't revel in these contentious occasions but this has been really *amazing.* I just might be able to get Mr. Waverley to listen.'' She touched Chloe's arm. "Thank you, dear. I've never seen a young woman so vibrant with life. Or so *strong.*''

"Keep me posted,'' Chloe called, shooting a hand behind her to grasp a bony wrist. "Just a minute, Archie.''

The boy's mouth fell open in astonishment. This Chloe was a female to be reckoned with. "How did you know my name?'' He grinned.

"You told me, didn't you?'' Chloe looked down brightly.

"No, I didn't." Archie blew out his breath. She didn't look at all different from the people around her but she certainly had powers. "I'm called after me grandfather, Mum and I are going to live with him."

"You can tell me all about it when we give you a lift home," Chloe said, "but first things first, Archie. Why aren't you at school?"

"They won't miss me," Archie whispered. "The koalas are my friends. I don't want to see them go."

Around them the protest meeting was breaking up, the crowd faintly dazed, collectively beginning to lose all memory of that extraordinary incident. If old Waverley would sell out, things could work out. That Chloe Cavanagh was a magical girl.

"I can't understand it," Bob said as they stood watching the film run through the monitor. "I've got everything bar the moment when you caught the kid and started your astonishing dance."

"The crowd surging around didn't help, Bob. Sure you had the camera trained on me?"

"Are you crazy?" Bob gave her an injured glance. "Of course I'm sure. Hell, Chloe, you should be ashamed of yourself for asking. I'm one of the best in the business."

"Well, you're never going to live down this one, Bobby." Chloe patted him kindly on the shoulder. "All we have is this shot of Archie and me in deep conversation."

"It was a miracle," Bob suddenly announced. "I know it. How am I supposed to video a miracle? It just doesn't happen."

"If you say so, Bobby." Chloe laughed. "I've got to tell you, I've never felt like that in my entire life. It was like some other being got hold of Archie. I suppose it's not all that unusual. I had a friend who lifted a car off a neighbour's child. The mother backed out the garage not realising her little girl was there. Ian jumped the fence when the mother screamed and lifted the rear of the car right off the toddler. Do you know, she wasn't even hurt.''

"I'd say the kid had a darn good guardian angel.'' Bob scratched his head in some perplexity. "Let's run the tape through again. I want to check if something's wrong.''

They were still talking about it in the corridor when McGuire happened along.

"Okay you two? You look like you're back from a space flight.'' He paused for a moment to study them.

"There are some things in life, Chief, that just don't add up,'' Bob said. "Chloe and I were at a protest meeting a couple of hours ago—''

"Cavanagh never outlives her enthusiasm for protests.'' McGuire's black eyes were mocking.

"Don't I know it. But she's so helpful. People love talking to her. Anyway, this most amazing thing happened.''

"Tell me,'' McGuire urged, his deep voice a purr.

"It's nothing,'' Chloe murmured briefly, feeling embarrassed.

"Nuthin' don't say it.'' Bob tilted his head to address his tall Chief. "There was this kid up a tree. About ten, stopped home from school so he could join the protest. Course the mother didn't know. This big branch snapped under him. You had to hear the noise. Everyone scattered but not Chloe. While we all thought the kid could break a leg, Chloe, wait for it, positions herself like Arnie Schwarzenegger while the kid takes a nosedive.''

"No. So what did he break?'' McGuire asked laconically.

"What I'm trying to tell you, Chief, is Chloe *caught* him.''

McGuire said nothing for a moment, not taking his eyes off Chloe's flushed face, then he patted Bob's arm. "Sounds like you two stopped off for lunch. Cracked a bottle of wine."

"Never on the job," Chloe said. "I'm still not sure how I did it. I've had this funny voice in my ear all day."

"A visit to your doctor might help. You wouldn't have it on camera, I suppose, Bob?" McGuire asked.

"Now this is the really *amazing* part. I got everything else but some outside force seemed to put the camera into freeze."

McGuire set his fine white teeth. "You'll have to excuse me, folks. Ordinarily, I love to hear the mad stories you two make up."

"It wasn't a story, truly. I did catch him," Chloe said.

McGuire wasn't convinced. "You? Listen, you look like you'd have trouble emptying your shopping trolley. Heck, what do you weigh?" He took a step towards her, eyeing her slight figure, then before Chloe could move he swept her off her feet in one lightning-fast movement. "I'd say about fifty-four kilos." He actually bounced her like a baby. "Am I right?"

She was utterly devastated. Her heart did a mad somersault and the blood whooshed in her ears. *"Put me down."*

"Soon." McGuire saw the rush of feeling flash through her eyes. Probably saw herself as Jessica Lange borne aloft by King Kong. "It's a joke, right?" he asked with elaborate casualness.

"There were plenty of witnesses." Bob was fascinated by the sight of Chloe looking like a porcelain doll in the Chief's arms. He had to be dreaming all of it. "I can find you someone to speak to," he offered.

McGuire laughed. "So there's magic in you, Cavanagh." Just holding her made him feel bedazzled.

"Magic to move people. Catch them if you have to. That has to be the reason. It's also quite possible you two screwballs dreamed the whole thing up."

Bob looked shocked. "We've got too much respect for you, Chief, to waste your time."

McGuire looked down at Chloe, noting every nuance of her expression. The scent of her was in his nostrils; honeysuckle, golden wattle, the fragrance of Spring.

"Chief," she said, exasperated. She knew he could hear her unsteady breathing. Those smouldering black eyes zooming in on the telltale rise and fall of her breast.

"This is where it all falls apart, Bob. Cavanagh couldn't possibly break the fall of a ten-year-old boy. You know it. I know it."

"What happened was a miracle," Bob proclaimed like a convert.

"Nope. You're just mad." McGuire lowered Chloe to her feet, keeping his hand on her shoulder for a moment as though recognising she was very fluttery. "Sorry, you two. Got to run. You might like to be there when the jury returns a verdict on the Chandler case. I've just had a tip-off it could be late this afternoon."

"Does this mean you still trust us?" Chloe challenged.

McGuire looked back over his shoulder, gave a twisted grin. "Sure, Cavanagh. What you obviously need is a good night's sleep."

"I guess you could call it mass hysteria," Bob said later.

Chloe looked away from him. She could still feel McGuire's strong muscular arms wrapping her body. She could still feel the shock waves, the chemistry as old as time, the brush of heat. It shamed her. "Let's put it out of our minds," she advised. We have to concentrate on the Chandler job. It has to be guilty."

''There's always a shock verdict, Chloe.'' Bob sighed. ''I've discovered that. Hang on a minute and I'll get another tape. There must have been something wrong with the other one.''

CHAPTER TWO

BEFORE she left Friday, Chloe popped her head around the door of McGuire's office. He was on the phone and he gave her a quick warning look: Don't interrupt.

"Right, what is it?" he gritted when he finished what was clearly an aggravating call.

Unbelievable! Why had she accepted his offer to drive her to the party?

"I wasn't sure if you knew where I lived."

"Piece of cake, I've run past the house several times."

"Whatever for?"

He looked back at her, a tight smile at the corner of his mouth. "Why not? I like to know all I can about the staff. Bit big for you, isn't it?" It was a beautiful old Colonial, the family home, he had since been told, but it had to be a drain on her resources, physical and financial.

"I wouldn't want to be anywhere else," she said simply.

He was sympathetic to that. "So see you, then."

"Fine. Wonderful." She backed out quickly, muttering under her breath. Maybe he would be in a better mood tomorrow. If not she would simply call a cab.

Saturday morning found her shopping for the week's supplies. Nothing much. She lived on fresh fruit and salads. She bought ham and cheese from the delicatessen, a roast chicken, a couple of loaves of bread she could pop into the freezer. There was no time to cook.

35

Mostly she didn't have the inclination. Not after long hours on the job. Occasionally she and her friends went out to dinner when she made up for the slight deprivations. Early afternoon was spent in the garden trying to bring some semblance of order to the large grounds she was gradually turning to low-maintenance native plants. Her mother had adored her garden. So had her father when he had the time. Now they were both gone from this place.

A sense of loss beat down on Chloe but she tried to fight it back. In the early days after the double tragedy, she had experienced an overwhelming debilitating grief, a sense of futility and emptiness. How could she live without her father *and* mother? But when her mother had come out of the coma and into a waking dream state Chloe had started to fight back. She wanted to be around when her mother was returned to *full* life, even when the doctors told her day after day that was never going to happen.

Her skin glistening with tears, Chloe dug in a flowerbed overflowing with daisies, petunias, pink and white impatiens, double pelargoniums with a thick border of lobelia. A magnificent Iceberg rose climbed all over the brick wall that separated the house from their neighbour's, spilling its radiance all over the garden. Her mother loved white in the garden, the snow white of azaleas, candytuft, the masses and masses of windflowers she used to plant. The azaleas continued to bloom prolifically in Spring but she couldn't afford the time for all the rest. Eventually she supposed she would have to sell the house. McGuire was right. It was too big. Once they had been very comfortably placed. Not rich, but her father had been a well-established specialist physician. Now money was going out at a frightening rate. It worried her dreadfully she might have to shift her mother from her nursing home. "Jacaranda Hill" was one of the very best, a large converted mansion with beautiful grounds and a reputation for excellent care. Chloe couldn't fault the way her mother was being looked after, but it was very expensive.

Mid-afternoon found her pushing her mother's wheelchair across the nursing home's lawn, finding a lovely shady spot under one of the many magnificent blossoming jacarandas that gave the nursing home its name. A man-made lake had been constructed some years back in a low-lying area of the garden, now its undulating edge was totally obscured by the lush planting of water iris, lilies, ferns and ornamental aquatic grasses. A small section of the large pool was taken up with beautiful cream waterlilies but the important thing for the patients was the sparkle and reflection of the water, the way the breeze rippled over its surface, marking the green with molten silver.

Chloe in jeans and a simple T-shirt sat on the grass beside her mother's chair, holding lovingly to her mother's quiet unresponsive hand. Strangely, despite all evidence to the contrary, Chloe never had the feeling her mother didn't recognise her, though the blue eyes so like her own seemed to be looking into the next world already. Totally without fear, but inturned. Maybe she was seeing visions, Chloe thought. Maybe she was in spirit with her husband and son, or there could be dozens of responses trapped inside her head. Chloe never saw her intense dedication to her mother as a duty. Being there was simply a measure of her love. As always on her visits, Chloe told her mother what was happening in her life. She spoke as though her mother was fully present and as interested in what Chloe had to say as she had been in the old days when life was full of sparkle and neither had questioned the happiness and stability of their family life. She spoke about her ongoing dealings with McGuire, what she was doing around the house and garden, her various assignments and, of course, the extraordinary incident of the day before. The really *odd* thing was, Chloe's own memory of it was beginning to blur. She had to really concentrate before it all faded.

"I don't believe I was holding him at all," she confided to her mother in remembered amazement. "I could feel the warmth of this solid little boy's body. I could see the sheen of perspiration on his skin. The crowd was speechless. There I was waltzing around with Archie quite calmly. It just doesn't make sense. It was like I was transformed. McGuire thought we were having him on. He told me to go home and get a good night's sleep. But it *did* happen. That's the mystery. What do you think?"

Then came the shock.

"What?" Chloe, who had been looking out toward the lake whilst she was speaking, shot a startled upward glance at her mother. Her warm voice had clearly sounded in Chloe's mind.

But Delia Cavanagh's expression was unchanged. A frisson of something that was almost awe rippled through Chloe's body from brain to heart to the tip of her toes. Was she going mad? In some way she couldn't possibly fathom, she was convinced her mother had spoken to her at some level. Some subtle communication.

"Mumma!" She clutched her mother's hand more tightly, finding what was happening difficult to grasp, but there was no response on her mother's tranquil face nor did a muscle move.

"Oh, God!" Chloe tried desperately to collect herself before she burst into tears. She wasn't entirely right in the head. That was it. Psychological damage from severe trauma was a reality of life. Yet she *had* caught that whisper as it rippled past her ear. She had. She had. What else did she have to cling to but hope? Her faith in God had lessened over this terrible time.

Chloe struggled to her feet, upset and without direction, only, she realised with a rush of sensation, someone was giving her a helping hand. On her feet she stopped abruptly as though she could very easily bump into them. She even rubbed her hands together waiting for the electric little tingle to subside.

"This is insane," she said out loud, causing a passing nurse to stare at her. Yet there was comfort, an easing of her grief.

Chloe dusted off her jeans and began to push her mother's wheelchair in the direction of the pretty little summerhouse at the far end of the lake. A beautiful pink rose clambered over the white lattice walls, and the pair of stone deer donated by a patient's grateful family, flanked the entrance. It was their usual route. What was unusual was her extraordinary notion this third person, this *invisible* person, accompanied them on their journey. The person who had taken her by the hand.

Spirit power, Chloe thought, giving her mother's shoulder a gentle squeeze. She was going to have to start saying her prayers again. Renew the communication she so abruptly had broken off with a great and loving God.

Chloe had never taken as much trouble over a party; never spent so much time trying on different dresses, or regarding herself so long and critically in the mirror. She was down to two dresses now. The lime green silk, long with a halter neck, or the floral-print chiffon, sleeveless with a ruffle around the crossover V-neck and a sort of handkerchief skirt. Each conveyed a certain look. Cool and classic, or that delicate ethereal look she couldn't seem to escape. Neither dress was new. She didn't feel she had the right to spend the money anymore, but they were still in fashion. Maybe the flowered chiffon had the edge. The very feminine look was in and the fabric was beautiful, rose pink peonies with a tracery of jade leaves on a turquoise ground. The chiffon would have to do. She could be the Spring fairy.

A very strange feeling ran through her all the time she dressed. Pleasurable anticipation, normal enough in the circumstances, but she was haunted by the element of sexual awareness. Since when did she find McGuire sexy? Since when was she all atremble at the thought of being close to him? She disliked the man, was highly wary of him and had said so at length. Nevertheless she was excited and it sparkled in her looks.

Chloe opened the front door to McGuire as the grandfather clock in the living room was chiming eight. She'd known it was to be a black tie occasion but she hadn't expected to see him look so—gosh, she couldn't avoid the word *splendid,* in evening dress. She almost had to look away.

"Hi," he offered with dark, gleaming eyes. "You look enchanting." A rare enough quality, but it was true. Tonight she wore her marvellous hair—red, amber, gold, a combination of all three—in an unfamiliar style. Pulled back off her face and arranged in a thick upturning roll but molten little tendrils sprang out around her face and nape. Her deep blue eyes, large and liquid, had picked up the colour of her dress, her skin was blushed porcelain, her mouth surprisingly full, tender, even a little pouty. He wondered as he always did what it would be like to kiss it, to open soft lips with the tip of his tongue.

She was always immaculately turned out in her little blouses and skirts, the snappy little suits, but he had never seen her in an evening dress before. The frothy shimmering ruffle of the bodice plunged low to reveal the shadowed cleft between her delicate breasts. He had to fight down the irresistible urge to reach for her. He knew she would only recoil in dismay.

"Why, thank you." She dropped a graceful little bob, some note in his voice had got to her. This was McGuire, remember? Her old combatant and sparring partner. "Would you like to come in for a moment?" Keeping him on the doorstep was impossibly rude.

"Yes, I would." He stepped across the threshold, looking like someone who could very easily mix it with the mega-rich. "This is a wonderful old house," he said almost wistfully, glancing down the wide hallway with its glowing parqueted floor and rosy Chinese rug. A circular rosewood library table holding a jade horse on a carved stand and a large crystal bowl massed with white roses stood midway between the graceful arches that led to the formal rooms.

"I love it." Chloe smiled, standing at his shoulder. "Let me show you through, that's if we have time."

"I'd like that." Amazingly his whole expression had softened. "The house was built by your great-grandfather, I understand." It had heritage listing he knew.

Chloe paused, lifting her chin. She so hated people talking about her. "Who told you that?"

He gave an easy shrug of his powerful shoulders, breaking the slight tension. "I do a lot of checking."

"I suppose it goes with the territory," she answered wryly.

"You should know, Chloe."

At the use of her Christian name, so honeyed and intimate, a mild giddiness overtook her.

"If one could really chart the course of one's life, this is just the sort of house I'd have liked to live in," he said.

"Really? I thought you'd like something very modern, very strong, with sweeping clear places." And terrible pictures that looked like cubic puzzles on the walls.

Once again his black eyes roved over her, checking out her too innocent expression. "I won't say I don't like to integrate old and new, but in terms of architecture

I love these old Queensland Colonials with their sweeping verandah and white iron lace. They're perfect for the subtropical climate. I particularly like the high ceilings and large rooms.''

''A big man would.'' She was surprised by how sweetly that came out. They walked side by side, Chloe in her exquisite flowered chiffon, McGuire in his beautifully cut evening clothes. It was all so extraordinarily civilised.

''Someone had a very graceful hand with the decorating,'' he commented.

Chloe felt her throat tighten. ''My mother.'' She couldn't say a word more.

He admired the classic elegance of the living room, the mix of fine antique pieces with overstuffed chintz-covered sofas and armchairs in shades of ivory, peach and rose. A huge gilt-framed antique mirror hung over the fireplace with its beautiful white marble surround, and he walked towards it, studying the detail. ''It must comfort you to have the stamp of her personality all around you.''

''Sometimes,'' Chloe said softly, surprised by his perceptiveness. ''Other times it hurts dreadfully.'' She gestured towards an adjoining room. ''Come through to the library. It's my favourite room.''

The instant before she turned on the lights, Chloe came close to believing someone was sitting in her father's wing-back chair beside the fireplace. She even drew in her breath.

''Everything okay?'' McGuire stood very close, tall, powerful, protective.

''Of course.'' It had to be an optical illusion. Particularly when she had the sense of someone *small*. Her father had been almost as tall as McGuire, but a completely different build, very spare with long, elegant limbs. She didn't feel ready to deal with the odd things that were happening to her. She couldn't dismiss them, either.

"You've gone a little pale."

"I'm fine," she said huskily.

"Do you ever feel nervous by yourself?"

"I've got my guardian angel on call." Her eyes mirrored the sudden comfort that wrapped her soul.

"I'm glad." His finger touched the tip of her nose, gentle as a feather, then he turned to inspect the large, graceful room.

He looked around keenly, showing considerable interest in everything, Chloe thought, the plaster work, the cedar panelling, the inbuilt floor-to-ceiling bookcase, the leatherbound gold-foiled volumes. Even the 19th-century French gilt chandelier. If she gave him enough time he might make an offer for house and contents. "You must have enjoyed growing up here," he murmured, the slight moodiness of his expression lending him the disturbing charm of Jane Eyre's Rochester.

She couldn't speak for a moment until her voice was under control. Though he was far from *her* ideal, he was, she began to realise, a ruggedly handsome man who carried himself superbly. "Where *did* you grow up?" she asked gently. The graciousness of her own surroundings were definitely having their effect on her, but he smiled his familiar taut smile.

"A small town outside Sydney, but I guess what you'd call the wrong side of the tracks."

For once a sharp retort was easy to resist. "But you've come a long way."

"That was the intention, Chloe. As far away as I could get." The intonation was harsh. He shot back a cuff and glanced down at his gold watch. "Thank you for showing me your beautiful home. I'd like to see more, but I think we should be on our way."

"Of course." She flushed a little and as he passed

her, he very gently stroked her cheek. "Now I know why you're such a princess," he said in a deep, low voice.

They were gliding away from the house before she could contribute another word. "I didn't know you drove a Jaguar?" It was, in fact, a late model.

"I've been promising myself one since I was a kid."

"It's my kind of car." She smiled.

"Of course. You didn't think I was going to pick you up in what I drive to work?"

"I didn't think at all."

"Why's that, Cavanagh?" He shot her a challenging glance.

"Hey, you've been calling me Chloe," she protested for a second, strangely hurt.

"And you've been calling me nothing at all. To my face. I know what you call me behind my back."

"Oh, please, don't believe it all." Chloe was embarrassed. "We're going to a party, remember?" She realised with a sense of shock she wanted to maintain the unusual harmony that flowed between them.

"So, *say* it, then," he prompted gruffly.

"Say what?" Inside the soft enfolding darkness of the beautiful car with its smell of fine leather mingled with her own perfume, the atmosphere was oddly intimate.

"My name," he answered, shooting a glance at her. "Gabe, Gabriel, whatever you like."

Chloe sucked in her breath. "Gabriel, the Messenger of God. You must admit it's a shade incongruous with your powerful physique and dark colouring."

"You'd relate better to Lucifer?"

She could see his eyes, dark and shimmery like the night. "Even for you that's too scary. What do you say to a truce? I'll call you Gabriel for the night, if you continue to call me Chloe. We can revert to our normal selves Monday morning."

"Suits me." He nodded. "I mean, can you imagine us being friends?" He sounded openly mocking and he had good reason.

"You know what they say, anything's possible," Chloe replied jauntily.

"I don't think you could handle it, Cavanagh." He glanced at her briefly. God, she was exquisite.

"You gather correctly."

"I'm just your normal guy."

She laughed, a sound of pure rejection. "No, you're *not*."

"I'd still like to get this whole thing cleared up. What *exactly* about me bothers you so much?"

Everything. Your looks, your force of character. "Gabriel I have no problem with you at all," she said sweetly.

"Oh, but you *do*. Don't smile about it."

"Well…" She considered. "You really like to stir me up."

He made a deprecating sound. "I have to admit I do."

"And you have your own reasons for it."

"True. But I seek to help you, Chloe, before you run yourself ragged. I might be a bit abrasive at times but I believe my intentions are good. You did what you liked under your old boss."

Chloe admitted that inwardly. "Clive went a lot earlier than he should have."

His smile was faintly crooked. "You're just prejudiced. We're on the same side, you know, even if our relationship hasn't been all that smooth."

"Clive didn't bark at me." She smiled.

"And what do you think the answer to that may be? You can't twist me around your little finger, neither can you march in and out of my office uninvited."

The colour in Chloe's cheeks deepened. "That's not true. I always knock."

"When you remember to. Anyway that's all camouflage. I think the problem is *physical*."

She was glad of the darkness to cover her shock. This was unchartered country. "Well, you do have a lot of *presence*," she managed. In fact it was particularly powerful.

"Really? You make me feel like Conan the Barbarian." His glance mocked them both. "All those haughty little high-born expressions."

"I can't see what *I* think should bother you at all."

"Hey! I'm asking the questions," he drawled.

"All right. Fire away. I'll have to rack my brains for a soothing answer. If it's any comfort to you, I know at least a dozen women in the building who find you extremely attractive."

"Fourteen at the last count," he said laconically.

"What I can't figure out is why you're not married." She *didn't* say that, did she? Someone had cast a spell on her.

He shot her a sardonic glance. "If I asked *you*, would you accept?"

For a split second her heart quaked in her breast. She was no match for McGuire. "You've got to be joking!"

"No," he said in a practical voice. "You have a lot going for you. You're beautiful, you're brainy, a bit on the volatile side but certainly not dull. You know the industry, so you wouldn't be wondering all the time where I was."

Chloe shook her head, glancing at him in slight alarm. "Not a good idea at all. You and I as marriage partners doesn't fit my wildest scenario."

"Okay, Chloe. I'm just having fun. You don't trust *anyone* with your heart?" The question was so smooth and gentle she was taken aback.

She answered sadly as if to herself. "No."

One wouldn't have to look too closely at the reasons.

At the pain and despair which had to be in her heart. "I believe in love, Chloe," he said with great dignity. "I've no good reason to, but I do. I had a very bleak childhood." He could have said terrifying with a violent father and a mother trapped by fear. "All I could ever think was, run, run, run, but I stayed for my mother's sake."

Chloe was stunned by the revelation. "Gabriel, I'm so sorry." A tremendous sympathy flowered from her body.

"Gracious lady." His voice sounded both tender and a little scathing. He glanced at her. How beautiful...how beautiful. He had craved beauty all his life, yet something about her made his heart throb painfully. It had from that very first day when she walked into his office and he could only stare. "No need to be, Chloe." He spoke dismissively. "It might have been a struggle but it made me tough." His rugged face was dark and shadowed. "I know the toughness bothers you."

Chloe couldn't answer. There was no way to deny it, but tender-hearted, she sensed she had wounded him. This vigorous, confident man who held his head so proudly. She would never have suspected it.

A hush fell over the interior of the car. It was far from relaxed; strong emotion had touched them and a force was at work.

Sir Llew Williams, owner and chairman of BTQ8 along with other profitable enterprises, lived in a very large Mediterranean-style villa on what was commonly known as Riverside, Millionaire's Row. Cars lined both sides of the wide street which at the height of summer became a brilliant avenue of scarlet as the giant poincianas burst into hectic flower. McGuire didn't even attempt to find a parking spot but drove straight up to the tall, decorative wrought-iron gates, where he was admitted by a security guard who checked his name against a list.

"Who's a favourite, then?" Chloe gently crowed.

"Don't knock it." He spoke dryly. "You wouldn't have been able to do much walking in those shoes." He glanced down at her narrow high-arched feet criss-crossed with a few flimsy turquoise straps.

"Listen, you know you don't have to bother about me," she said as he came around to the passenger side to help her out.

"Chloe, I'd be glad to."

Once out of the Jaguar she let go of his hand quickly. She was getting these intense tingles all the time. "That's very kind of you, Gabriel, but I don't want you to think you must look out for me. I'm used to fending for myself."

He hunched his powerful shoulders slightly. "Sure, but I'm here if you need me."

She gave him a faintly puzzled little smile. "Why the concern, sweet though it is?"

"It won't take Freeman long to notice you," he said bluntly, taking her arm and leading her along the flood-lighted garden path.

"Goodness, a man who's had *three* wives already." Chloe sounded shocked.

"It's fairly obvious he's looking for number four."

"I daresay that's possible, but you have nothing to fear. All those tabloid stories! He's a dreadful man in some respects."

He smiled grimly. "Chloe, it might be an idea if you kept your voice down. It has the peal of a silver bell."

"Sorry." The warning wasn't lost on her. "None of us is perfect."

"That has to be right, but some are worse than others. I'm just begging you to be very, very careful. Two of his wives had flaming red hair."

Chloe laughed quietly. "Keeping it flaming must have cost a good deal of money. I appreciate your concern, Gabriel, but really, I can take care of myself."

"Just don't listen to his pitch." As they neared the door, his words were just barely audible. "I feel sure he's going to make it."

Which was exactly what happened.

The instant they moved into the marble foyer, Tara Williams detached herself from a laughing group, charging towards McGuire. She grasped his hand and reached up on tiptoe to kiss his cheek.

"Gabe, you gorgeous man! How wonderful to see you. Daddy said to take you to him the moment you arrive. And…" She paused, looking wide-eyed and guileless. "Chloe, isn't it?"

Of course she knew. Chloe was a familiar sight on television. "Chloe Cavanagh, Miss Williams." Chloe smiled. "I'm so pleased to be invited to your lovely party."

"Daddy likes to have a few of the staff in from time to time," Tara answered ungraciously, though she attempted to conceal it with a smile. Cushioned by so much wealth she obviously felt she could say and do as she pleased, Chloe thought. She watched as Tara looped two hands around McGuire's arm, staring mesmerically into his face with eyes that were a startling ice blue. Her rich brown hair fell thick and straight just clear of her shoulders; her dress was very glamorous, long, slinky, red silk-jersey, with a rather daring keyhole cutout. In Chloe's opinion she was showing too much bosom, but it seemed to be the fashion and no doubt the men didn't mind.

Chloe went on smiling prettily even when it was evident Tara was about to carry McGuire off, leaving Chloe to her own devices. It might have been particularly appalling had she been shy, but Chloe was no shrinking violet. "Excuse us, won't you?" Tara tossed Chloe another of her big courtesy smiles. "I'll send a friend of mine over. Pru Gregory. You'll like her. We went to school together. I simply must hear what Gabe's been up to."

McGuire in fact was regarding Tara rather sardonically. Which was odd. Surely with all the rumours they got on better than that? It even appeared to Chloe he was about to ask her to join them and thus spoil Tara's evening, when Sir Llew strode towards them. Tall, heavily built, with the ice cube eyes he had passed on to his daughter, he had a mane of silver hair so thick it looked like it had been professionally blow-dried, which for all Chloe knew it could have been, and jet-black bushy eyebrows, which some thought dashing and others ridiculous. There was no Lady Williams. Tara's mother had literally given up the ghost when Tara was an incredibly spoiled fourteen and the number one person in her father's life. Which probably explained why Sir Llew had thought it best never to remarry.

"Gabe, my dear fellow." Sir Llew put out his hand as if he had never felt more fond of anyone in his life. "I'm so glad you've arrived. I want you to meet Christopher."

McGuire looked amused. "I did meet him once in Washington when I did a stint there, Sir Llew. He would have forgotten."

"Actually, no," Sir Llew chortled roguishly. "You weren't exactly writing nice things about him at the time. Ah, Chloe." He turned to include Chloe in his expansive smile. "How lovely you look, my dear. You must come, as well. Chris adores a pretty face."

"You're a hell of a lot more than a pretty face," McGuire muttered beneath his breath to Chloe as Sir Llew led them all full steam across the glittering foyer to one of the most over-decorated living rooms Chloe had ever seen. Though she was far from being a minimalist, she thought the room could do with a few things less. Everyone appeared engrossed in conversation, yet they fell apart spontaneously as Sir Llew proceeded on his way like a modern day Moses.

In a cosy corner sat the multimillionaire entrepreneur, Christopher Freeman, with a captive audience all around him. Late forties, not tall, almost slight, but dapper in his expensive evening clothes. Freeman was extremely attractive in a dissipated kind of way, with thick fair hair and razor-sharp grey-blue eyes.

A woman of uncertain age was sitting beside him on the brocade-covered sofa, intimidatingly glamorous, regarding Chloe with an odd flicker of hostility. Chloe didn't quite know why.

She was to find out.

From the very beginning Christopher Freeman had been a cradle snatcher. Introductions were exchanged. McGuire said something quite witty about their earlier encounter, which Freeman, too rich to care about what anyone thought, appreciated. Both Chloe and McGuire were invited to join the charmed circle.

"Just try to look intelligent, my dear." The ruthless woman smiled more tolerantly at Chloe, obviously thinking she and McGuire were a couple and Chloe probably wouldn't get the point of anything that was said.

It wasn't the case. Though Chloe didn't put herself forward, she was well able to take part in a discussion which included world politics, a few jokes and a lot of gossip. It lasted almost half an hour before McGuire, smooth as you please, just as he would close a staff meeting, extricated them from the great man's side.

"God, he hasn't changed a bit," McGuire said disgustedly. "The perfect promoter. Floater of deals."

"He was being very nice to you," Chloe ventured.

"And to you." McGuire's words were light, laconic, but a faint anger registered in his eyes.

"At least he liked the enlivening conversation. Most people must sit back open-mouthed and let him talk. It must come as a diversion to have someone like you around." McGuire had had no hesitation levelling a few criticisms at Freeman's views. Criticisms, Chloe had to admit, she agreed with. Christopher Freeman's world was money. Exclusively. He had lost all touch with the man in the street.

At different stages of the evening, Chloe found Freeman at her shoulder, obviously keen to enjoy her company. Although it was flattering in a way, Chloe was beginning to feel uncomfortable with the way his eyes continually rested on her mouth. Was he one of those people who liked to lip read or had he something else on his mind?

McGuire apparently thought so because he wasted no time drawing Chloe aside. "It might be a good idea if you stick with me for the rest of the evening, Chloe," he suggested. They were alone on the terrace, which was cool and quiet.

"Wouldn't that cramp Tara's style?" she asked rather mischievously, only McGuire continued to gaze at her in exasperation.

"With a man like that, you don't need to give an inch."

Play it cool, Chloe thought. He is your boss even if you don't heed the lecture. "Gabriel, if you think I'm interested in Christopher Freeman you're completely out of your mind," she said sweetly.

He waved that away. "But he's interested in *you*. He likes nothing better than the chase, then the takeover."

Chloe's voice carried a trace of the redhead's volatile temper. "Listen, I appreciate your concern, Gabriel, but let's get one thing straight. I can look after myself."

"Not so I've noticed," McGuire replied unforgivably. "Freeman has an ego the size of Centre Point tower. You might well find he'll refuse to believe you're not equally attracted."

Chloe's deep blue eyes sparkled. "Despite the fact he's old enough to be my father?" She looked up into McGuire's face, which to her surprise suddenly appeared strikingly handsome. It certainly fared much better than Freeman's in every regard.

"Chloe." He sighed heavily. "That's no comfort to me. Men as rich as Freeman generally get what they want. He makes no secret of the fact, the younger the better."

Clearly he was sincere, so Chloe spoke more gently. "Gabriel, please allow me to take my own chances. You're overreacting, which is very unlike you."

"Well, I'm going to pray that you're right." He looked down at her, saw the same thing Freeman was seeing, a ravishingly pretty, highly desirable young woman, only in his case he knew when to hold back. He didn't believe Freeman did. "I've had this little voice in my ear all night," he confided. "Very, very odd. Like a counsellor. I know Freeman from way back. He's a lot trickier than a young woman of your limited experience can imagine." The instant he said it he felt a sharp little twinge, like someone had pinched him. He even winced.

"Limited experience?" Chloe tilted her chin. Was he telling her he knew she had never had a passionate love affair in her life?

"I think you know what I mean," he said, watching the colour roll over her beautiful skin.

"No, I don't. Tell me about it," she invited, stepping a little closer to his very much taller and heavier figure.

"Chloe, we're not going to have an argument here, surely?" He had to smile at the light of battle in her eyes.

"Too right. You came as my boss, not my minder. I don't need you to watch me like a hawk."

But she does.

It was that voice again, thoroughly unsettling him. A sweet pure voice. Like the voice of a boy soprano. McGuire hit his head none too lightly with his hand. He'd been working very hard lately. Long hours. Too little sleep. Maybe he was going ga-ga.

"What is it, what's the matter?" Chloe was bewildered. "You're all right, aren't you?"

He stopped abruptly. "What do you call that ringing in the ears?"

Chloe stared at him in consternation. "Tinni… tinni…" She searched her brain. "Tinnitus. Ringing in the ears. Is that what you've got?"

"Must be," he said laconically. "I don't think it's as serious as schizophrenia."

"Gabriel." She found herself troubled. She reached out and clasped his hand.

The sweetness of the gesture entranced him, gave balm to his genuinely unsettled feelings. His smile was very white. "I'm okay, of course I am. Let's go inside, shall we? I can see supper is being served and I have absolutely no intention of handing you over to Freeman."

That should have been the end of it, only Tara shamelessly suggested to Christopher he had made a conquest which Freeman the egotist complacently accepted. He was, however, a mite surprised. Chloe Cavanagh was a beautiful and interesting young woman but he hadn't detected any of the usual signs. Moreover she had the big fellow McGuire constantly at her side. A man to be reckoned with, Freeman knew intuitively. As a journalist McGuire had been first rate, maybe too straight to go down well; too unrelenting in the quest of the truth. He didn't put a great deal of faith in what Tara Williams had to say, either. It was abundantly clear she had the hots for McGuire.

The instant Tara succeeded in detaching McGuire from Chloe's side, Freeman walked towards her, this time his manner a touch more courteous, impersonal. He knew a class act when he saw one.

She lapped it up, he thought, visibly relaxing. They got to chatting about—of all things—his life. How he had adored his mother, hated his father, how he had done very badly at school because he was sick of listening to stupid teachers' ramblings, his first big break, his first million at twenty-four, his first marriage, a jolly girl but she couldn't take the pace, his love affair with the United States. He didn't really notice it, but he was being interviewed. Chloe talked little, inserting key questions from time to time. He was charmed.

Across the room, Tara was rapturous at having Gabe to herself. She found him intensely sexy, so big and powerful, wonderful to talk to, a touch spiky, with a rather formidable aloof core that nevertheless made him more interesting. She had wanted him from their very first meeting when her father had invited him home to dinner, though it had become abundantly clear she would have to work hard to land him, which was her quest. Most of her friends were already married, or at least engaged. She wasn't going to allow Gabe McGuire to get away. She *couldn't*.

For his part, Gabe realised with increasing irritation he wasn't enjoying this party at all. Every time he turned his head he could see Chloe's lovely profile etched against the light from a nearby lamp. Opposite her, knees almost touching, was Freeman talking non-stop, smiling, animated, confident, immensely comfortable with this slip of a girl. Chloe was wonderful as an interviewer, McGuire thought ironically. Maybe she was after a story? Freeman so far as he was concerned had had an entirely different agenda.

Why don't you take her home? someone whispered in his ear.

"I don't know that she'll want to come," Gabe replied in amazement.

"What was that, old chap?" one of the guests turned around smilingly to ask.

Goodness, had he spoken out loud? "Sorry. Just talking to myself."

"I do it all the time." The man smiled indulgently.

Nevertheless Gabe was rattled. Who *exactly* was it who was talking to him? Not that it wasn't good advice and he should act on it. Gabe glanced at his watch. Well after midnight. No doubt the party would see the light of day, but he felt it wasn't an unreasonable time to leave.

Both Freeman and Chloe looked up at his approach.

McGuire was so physically impressive, Freeman at five foot eight, he always said five-ten, felt an almost unbearable stab of envy. "Dare I break up this little chat?" McGuire sounded light-hearted, amused, when his black, black eyes said something entirely different to Chloe. "I'm about to say my goodbyes, Chloe, if you're coming with me."

Chloe, knowing McGuire, knew she didn't have a lot of choice. She looked across at Freeman with a gentle, charming smile. "Gabriel has been kind enough to offer me a lift home."

"Couldn't you stay?" Freeman asked, looking vastly put out. "I mean, I'd be delighted to drive you home. I have a limousine on call."

Chloe was aware of McGuire's brilliant dark gaze on her. "I've had a lovely time," she said, when she really hadn't, "but finally I must go. It was wonderful talking to you." Chloe stood up and Freeman did too. "Well, good night." She gave him her hand.

"But I must see you again." He looked his consternation.

"We keep her pretty busy at BTQ8," McGuire came back.

"You've been so kind, I can't tell you," Chloe murmured, conscious of McGuire's towering figure.

"Well, I could come on your station," Freeman drawled enticingly.

"We haven't got that kind of money," McGuire said with one of his biting smiles.

"I'll do it for free if only Chloe interviews me," Freeman said. "And I have proper control, of course, not that I don't trust Miss Cavanagh."

"I'm sure it would lift the ratings," Chloe couldn't resist saying. These days Christopher Freeman was almost impossible to get to.

"So it's a deal?" Freeman gave Gabe a cool smile.

"I'm more than happy with it," Gabe lied. "I'll phone you Monday, if that's okay?"

"I insist on taking you and Chloe to lunch." Freeman could see he wasn't going to get rid of McGuire so easily. It was on his face.

"Fine."

"Interviewing Christopher Freeman on 'Lateline.' I can't believe it!" Chloe said as they left the Williams' mansion well over twenty minutes later. Tara had kissed McGuire goodbye quite blatantly on the mouth, ignoring Chloe totally.

"No need to go wild." There was a slight edginess in McGuire's deep attractive voice.

"Heck," Chloe said. "You don't mind, do you? It's quite a coup."

"I agree, but is it *worth* it?"

"Anyone would think I was about to fall in love with him."

McGuire's expression was mocking. "Most women would be very happy to marry a billionaire."

"I'm afraid you're right, but I don't happen to be one of them. The only person I'd get into bed with is the man I love."

"Have you met him or are you still looking?"

Chloe moved back in the plush leather seat. "There must be *some* lovely men out there. Most I meet are totally unsuitable."

"I expect that includes me." He glanced at her with open challenge.

"Actually, no. Isn't that strange? In many ways you impress me very much."

"I think you're lovely, too." He looked over at her and gave a sardonic smile.

As the car pulled up outside Chloe's house, she found herself flooded by sensations so unfamiliar she actually started to stammer. "Th-thank, thank you, so much, Gabriel, for going out of your way."

He looked at her with a mixture of amusement and indulgence. "I've loved every minute we managed to be together."

"Honestly, you're dreadfully sarcastic." She was quick to open the door.

"I generally mean what I say, Chloe. Hang on, I'll come around. I have every intention of seeing you to your door, maybe waiting while you check out the house. One can't be too careful these days."

"Gabriel, don't be ridiculous." She was feeling more and more shaken by the minute.

He took her hand. "Do me the kindness of easing my mind."

"But I'm in and out of the house all the time." The last thing she needed was for Gabriel McGuire to turn his intense energies on her, let alone look at her with any kind of raw emotion. Talking to Christopher Freeman had been a piece of cake, dealing with McGuire was and always had been acutely disturbing. Even this one evening had accelerated their odd relationship.

At the door he took the key from her, let them into the house while he waited for her to do a quick inspection of all the rooms. He even walked around himself, peering behind doors, lifting out curtains, turning on the switches to floodlight the rear garden.

"Why don't you get a dog? A German shepherd?" His gaze scrolled the backyard.

"And what does the poor thing do all day and half the night when I'm away?"

He sighed, looking broodingly handsome. "No, that wouldn't work." He turned off the exterior lights. "It's getting late. I'd better go."

"Yes." She had thought about offering him coffee and rejected it on the basis there was too much prickly excitement. "Thank you again."

"What are you doing tomorrow?" he asked unexpectedly, walking towards her.

Chloe took a very deep breath. "I have lots of household chores to catch up on. Then I visit my mother."

He nodded, looking down at her with quiet approval. "You must love her very much?"

"I do." For a second her eyes glistened.

At the front door he turned. "Let me handle Freeman, Chloe."

"It's *me* he wants to talk to," she said impishly.

"Lord, yes. His interest was very apparent to us all. Well, good night then."

"Good night, Gabriel." She looked up at him, feeling a tremendous rush of the underlying attraction she sought so valiantly to hide. She acknowledged it for a single moment in her eyes.

"It's so rare of you to smile at me like that." He turned her face up to his, scanning the small classic features, the alluring full mouth, reading the blue eyes that flickered her myriad thoughts. Then he bent his dark head and kissed her.

It was brief, so brief, yet she felt the throb of it right through her body. On her mouth, in her throat, in her breasts, deep in the pit of her stomach, tingling down the length of her legs.

When it was over she looked up at him speechlessly, for once in her life deprived of words.

"Sleep well, Chloe," he said. "May your guardian angel watch over you."

Then he was gone, loping down the short flight of steps, along the ungravelled drive, out onto the quiet tree-lined street without once looking back.

That was a kiss women would die for, Chloe marvelled as she fumbled several times to lock the front door. And from a man she had long viewed with a mixture of hostility and awe. She had always known at some point McGuire would shock her. From now on she would have to keep a very careful eye on that dangerously complicated and complex man.

CHAPTER THREE

SUNDAY morning Chloe awoke with a tremendous start. The doorbell was ringing. A glance at her bedside clock told her it was almost nine-thirty. She had slept in, a rare luxury. She staggered out of bed, threw on a robe and padded to the front door, holding her riotously curling hair out of her eyes.

A young man stood on the verandah holding the biggest floral arrangement Chloe had ever seen outside society weddings, gala dinners and the like. There were masses of flowers, roses, carnations, lilies, orchids, clouds of baby's breath, exquisite foliage all wondrously put together in a large white wicker basket.

"Miss Chloe Cavanagh?" Who could mistake her or that fabulous red hair?

Chloe stared in amazement. "Somebody has made a mistake." These were flowers for a hospital; flowers to make a patient's day.

"I don't think so." The young man smiled, moving the arrangement fractionally so she could now see the logo of a well-known nursery that also specialised in the cut flower trade, on his pocket. "One-twenty-one Sunderland Avenue."

"I didn't think anyone delivered on a Sunday." She wobbled a little as she took the full weight of the arrangement.

"We do if it's worth our while. That's some arrangement you've got there." He grinned.

Inside the house Chloe pondered what to do with it. The library table was the obvious place but she rather liked her own bowl of roses. The basket was too heavy to hold, so temporarily, she set it down on the floor, reaching for the card that went with it.

"Thank you for a delightful evening. Christopher." Lord! She hoped he didn't expect her to ring around to find out where he was staying then put through a gushing thank-you call. Beautiful as they were, she simply didn't need this floral offering. It was too excessive, too expensive, and it imparted a message she didn't want to hear. In some things McGuire really did know best.

In the office Monday morning McGuire called her in, his manner very much back to business. The kiss they'd exchanged might very well have been something she dreamed up.

"I've lined up that luncheon with Freeman for Wednesday," he told her, waving her into a chair. "Keep the afternoon free, 1:00 p.m. at Michaels." He named the swishest restaurant in town. "I've also spoken to Sir Llew who's delighted Freeman will do it for us. Not out of the kindness of his heart as he at first volunteered. Top dollar. I've spoken to Gray, as well." Graham Hewett was the name of the top journalist who hosted the show. "It won't come as any surprise to you that a few people will have their noses put out of joint."

"I'm prepared for it," Chloe said.

He looked across the width of his desk at her, at her beauty which gave her such an advantage, unfair a lot of people thought, but it was allied to a keen intelligence and a very professional on-camera manner.

"You've come a long way in a short time," he said musingly.

"I hope you're happy for me?"

"As a matter of fact, I'm about to offer you a raise."

"Really?" Chloe was both surprised and delighted. "This might be the start of a good news week. Dare I ask how much?"

"I don't think you'll be disappointed." He named a figure that she found slightly staggering. It would ease some of her anxieties about keeping her mother on at the nursing home.

"That's very generous of you, Chief." She was back to the familiar form of address.

"I'm glad you feel that way, Cavanagh," he lightly mocked. "Anyway you're worth it to the station, providing someone doesn't break your pretty little neck," he finished more soberly.

Chloe didn't laugh. "We all take that chance."

"I know. The only trouble is there are more and more unhappy hurting people out there, ready to lash out at government, at the media. And always the ratbag to stir them up. I want your promise you'll show extra caution in all your assignments. I've already spoken to Bob." He considered for a moment, frowning. "Come to think of it, I might give you another cameraman."

That sounded an alarm. "Oh, no, Chief, Bob and I are a team."

"A team of short guys," he said bluntly. "Neither of you would clear five-four. Bob, quite frankly, is out of condition, as well. I'll swap him over with Giles Stockwell."

Chloe was dismayed. "Please, Chief, don't do anything like that. I promise I'll take all the necessary precautions. A bodyguard is not the answer. The couple of scrapes I've got into have been my fault. I admit it. I was hot on the story. Bob urged caution all along."

McGuire sighed. "All right. I'll go along with it for now, but I want to make it perfectly clear to you, back off from any situation that looks dicey. Times have changed, I'm afraid."

Chloe nodded. Indeed they had.

"By the way, the De Havilands are giving Freeman a little shindig up at their mountain eyrie this Sunday," he said without enthusiasm. "Quite a lot of people will be going. Freeman himself requested you come along, unless you've something better to do."

Chloe didn't answer for a minute. She looked up to find McGuire examining her intently. "You're not going to believe this but he sent me a basket of flowers yesterday so wide it was all I could do to get it through the front door."

"Why *wouldn't* I believe it?" he asked in a deep rumble.

"Well, I didn't think you credited him with being so romantic."

"Surely you're not entertaining the joyful hope he is?" he retorted quite sharply.

"If you *must* know, I took them out to the nursing home," Chloe relented.

"Didn't you resist the impulse to keep a single rose for yourself?"

"Chief, the whole purpose of my talking to Christopher Freeman was to get a story," Chloe said in a serious voice. "I accomplished that. I seem to recall he deeply resented *your* line of questioning when you were on the job."

"Resent Away is my motto."

"My only reason for following any of this up is *professional*," Chloe stressed, aware of his antagonism.

"Was I implying anything else?"

"I think so. Anyway, I visit my mother every Sunday without fail. What time are you talking?"

"It's open house." He shrugged. "The buffet will be open all day."

"Are *you* going?" she asked, thinking he was bound to be. Along with Sir Llew and the bold Tara.

"I've got to tell you, Cavanagh, I am," he drawled. "Does that make a difference?"

"Indeed it does," she said breezily. "I need the benefit of your presence to keep Freeman in line."

He gave a crooked smile. "Thank you for your honesty, Chloe. It's not that you want to spend the day with me?"

"No way," she said sweetly, tucking back a stray curl. "From what I saw of Tara Williams, you're taken."

"Don't talk rot," he said, looking broodingly handsome.

"I always let my instincts roll."

"What my Irish grandmother used to call a woman's intuition." He laughed.

"Exactly. I understand perfectly if you want to get going fairly early."

"No. I'd prefer the excuse to wait for you. What time could you leave?"

"About midday, something like that. I could stay with Mum for a few hours."

"Midday would be perfect. It'll take us a good hour to get up the mountain."

"I've heard it's a fabulous house."

"It is, but the view of the Glass House Mountains is even better." He hesitated, looking uncharacteristically uncertain. "I don't want to sound intrusive, but I'd welcome the opportunity to meet your mother."

"Gabriel!" She spoke his name, sounding very surprised and forlorn.

"I could pick you up around ten, take you to the nursing home. We could go on to the De Havilands' after that. It's on the way," he pointed out persuasively.

"You *do* know that my mother is in a waking dream state?" Chloe asked, pain in her dark blue eyes.

"Yes, Chloe, I do," he said gently. "I'm sure she won't object to a friend."

Chloe bent her head. "No," she said in a low voice.

She had no idea how he had come to be a friend, but he was. "She knows about you, anyway."

"Maybe I'm not so happy about that," he said with sardonic amusement. There had been plenty of times she had stalked out of the office maddened.

"I sit with her and hold her hand," Chloe said by way of explanation. "Push her wheelchair around the grounds. They're lovely. Especially at this time of the year when the jacarandas are about to burst into flower."

"Well, at least I can help you there," he said, his cynical heart melting at the still-blue light of tears that stood in her lovely eyes. She was breathing deeply to maintain her control, the pearly nacre of her teeth just visible between her parted lips. He remembered with anger how Freeman's rapt gaze had focused on Chloe's cushiony mouth the other evening. Not that he could blame him. Sometimes he had called her into his office for the sheer pleasure of looking at it. She would be wonderful to make love to. Wonderful to bring to full sensuous life. The child of a violent dysfunctional family, McGuire knew instinctively Chloe in an entirely different way had suffered damage.

The rest of the time they discussed assignments. The ones he knew Chloe could handle well, the ones he preferred to leave to other journalists. That afternoon she was to interview the novelist, Jake Wylie, with a view to a segment on "Lateline." Tomorrow there was Professor Sophie Gordan, the outspoken academic and defender of women's rights; one of the recipients of the recent Young Achievers awards, a brilliant young aboriginal artist, and Piers Edmiston, the visiting concert pianist and expatriate Australian.

McGuire looked up from his pad. "I almost forgot. I've had a call from the Turf Club. They particularly want you to present the Fashions on the Field awards at the Spring Carnival. 'You're so beautiful and friendly,'

I quote. Daniel Shepherd has offered to dress you. Does that appeal?"

"Absolutely!" Chloe gave him her heart-stopping smile. "I *love* his designs! I even bought one for a friend's wedding but not anymore. Too expensive."

"All free, Cavanagh. And free publicity for them. You should look ravishing. You might like to confirm things yourself." He handed her a slip of paper with names and telephone numbers on it. "We're upping your dress allowance, as well."

Chloe clutched at her heart. "You can't expect me to take this in all at once."

"You pay for dressing, Cavanagh," he told her. "The okay has come from the top. Sir Llew is impressed with you and he's notoriously hard to please."

"I bet you had something to do with it all the same," she said shrewdly.

He laughed briefly, mocking, self-derisive. "I'm a super guy, Chloe. Maybe you'll find that out."

At the last minute, because of work pressure, McGuire had to pull out of the midweek luncheon appointment with Christopher Freeman.

"Explain the circumstances, would you?" There was a faint, almost undetectable look of edginess on his face. He contemplated Chloe on the other side of his desk. She was beautifully turned out in a sugar pink suit that did wonderful things for her hair and her complexion. She even had a touch of the celestial, he thought, with her luminous aura and that pearly pink lipstick on her soft luscious mouth.

"Of course. I'm really sorry you're not coming," Chloe said. And she was.

"You sound like you actually mean that." His tone registered a sardonic surprise.

"I do."

He smiled at her, his expression half pleased, half ironic. "Are you sure you can put up with him on your own?"

"I think so. For someone so incredibly successful, I don't find him at all imposing." Not like you.

"You've never seen him doing business, Chloe," McGuire answered a little grimly. "He has a deserved reputation for being absolutely ruthless."

"He can be charming," Chloe offered mischievously, McGuire was looking so openly Big Brotherly.

"Just remember, he knows how to flatter women, he knows how to get them into his bed, what he doesn't know is how to *appreciate* them."

"Do you mean you do?" Chloe asked lightly, widening her blue eyes.

"Put it this way, Chloe," he rasped. "I feel strongly about the institution of marriage. When I do get married it will be for the long haul. Freeman tends to chop and change, if you've noticed."

"You're really a very intense person, aren't you," Chloe said, thinking that was true.

He gave her a sharp look of acknowledgment. "If the definition is 'feel deeply,' yes. I have expectations for the future, Cavanagh. They don't all relate to career possibilities as you seem to think. I want a wife and family. I want the role of husband and father. A wholeness in life."

"Then you'd better turn your attention to it," she retorted sweetly.

"Maybe I already have," he drawled. "As regards Freeman, all I'm doing is urging you to a certain wariness. Unfortunately Freeman has the capacity to cause harm. You'd be foolish if you didn't face it."

Chloe shook her radiant head. "I understand, Chief. You've no cause for concern. This luncheon is strictly on the job."

Freeman, of course, had a concealed agenda. To lure Chloe into his web.

"I'm sorry Gabe couldn't make it," he said when they met at the restaurant, his expression totally belying his words. "What a character he is!"

"He is that," Chloe agreed, feeling Freeman's hand at her elbow as the maître d' escorted them to their table.

The beautifully appointed riverside room was almost filled with people, many of whom looked up in recognition of the high-profile Freeman with the popular young TV personality Chloe Cavanagh in tow.

"I don't think it will take Gabe long to reach the very top," Freeman continued when they were seated beside the plate-glass window that overlooked the lovely tropical gardens and the esplanade. "Maybe even stealing Llew's job."

There was a certain malice to it, even a kind of envy. "I don't think McGuire's into *stealing*."

Freeman's smile was faintly rueful. "All right. All right. I understand loyalty to the boss."

"The loyalty is deserved." The words were sincere but Chloe kept her tone light. "McGuire works harder than anyone I've ever known. Not to mention putting the rest of us through our paces. I used to have quite a soft spot for my old boss but I've been forced to admit we were going nowhere until McGuire arrived."

"You call him McGuire, then?" Freeman sounded pleased.

"McGuire. Chief. He doesn't mind either."

"I thought you were calling him Gabriel the other night?"

Chloe smiled. "We agreed Christian names would sound better for the night."

"So there's no romance there?"

"Whatever made you think that?" Chloe asked, trying to puzzle out why he should think it.

"For the very good reason he exuded protectiveness. I wouldn't care to get on the wrong side of your charismatic friend."

"Isn't that a wee bit melodramatic?" Chloe asked lightly.

"Not at all. I've had a great deal of experience, Chloe. Gabe McGuire would make a dangerous enemy."

"It's a good thing, then, we're all on the same side."

The waiter arrived sometime later and took their order. Fresh-from-the-bay, steamed-in-the-shell scallops with ginger and spring onions for Freeman, tiny bay lobsters in a lime sauce for her, followed by the truly superb tropical fish, the barramundi cooked in the Asian way for her, with roast lamb with eggplant and zucchini ratatouille on couscous for him. Chloe declined dessert. Freeman thought he might well have that "wicked-looking chocolate torte on the trolley." Afterwards they fell into pleasant and easy conversation, with Freeman on his very best behaviour. This wasn't a rush job, he had seriously decided.

Consequently Chloe was back to the office much later than she intended, running into Jennifer Bourne, the station's senior woman journalist as she returned from a political rally; the Prime Minister in the hot seat.

Chloe didn't expect a friendly greeting. Jennifer had become increasingly hostile as Chloe climbed the network ladder.

"Hi, Jen!" Chloe called in a relaxed voice, walking faster to catch up. She hated all this bitterness in the air.

Jennifer, a tall, attractive brunette in her early thirties, turned around. "Ah, our little Chloe as immaculate as ever. Where have you been? Not on the job in that get-up?"

"Actually I've been out to lunch." Chloe didn't dare say with whom.

"That's amazing," Jennifer said acidly, glancing at

her watch; nearly four. "How do you manage to get around Gabe?"

"Boy, how many times *haven't I?*" Chloe retorted with feeling.

Jennifer brushed her response aside. "You had no one else to blame but yourself. You should have let someone else track down that criminal Ed Cleaver. I know Sir Llew wasn't happy about it. I wouldn't brave such a nasty piece of goods."

"All he did was threaten, Jen. He didn't do anything."

"Go on." Jennifer held up a hand. "He broke Bob's camera. An inch closer to you and he would have broken your pretty little nose."

"Jennifer, what's the matter?" Chloe asked gently. "We used to be friends."

Jennifer was silent for a moment, looking of a sudden faintly shamed. "Maybe you're having too much fun playing Gabe's little pet."

Chloe had to laugh. "How can you *say* that? You've been in on plenty of our spats."

"Just a smokescreen," Jennifer broke in. "Was I ever wrong about you. I realise now that you're all about tactics. The fiery little redhead who looks as fragile as a figurine. I saw you two together the other night at Sir Llew's party."

"You never spoke to me," Chloe said, still hurt. "Never came near me in fact."

"You were too busy latching on to Freeman."

"It was nothing like that, Jen," Chloe protested. "Freeman came after me."

"Why wouldn't he?" Jennifer cast a withering eye over Chloe's chic, petite figure. "Of course, I've got it. You're after an interview."

Chloe touched the older woman's arm. "Jen, there's

no use denying it. I'm a journalist just like you. Getting interviews with famous people is what it's all about.''

"Infamous, don't you mean?'' Jennifer flashed back. "He might be a billionaire but a lot of people hate him.''

"That goes with the territory. Can you think of any-one in that category who doesn't have lots of enemies?''

"Oh, let's keep walking,'' Jennifer said in an angry, frustrated voice. "Gabe doesn't do any pampering of me.''

Chloe chose her words carefully. "You really like him, don't you?''

"I have great faith in him,'' Jennifer answered sharply. "He's brilliant. He's in this cutthroat business but he's got integrity. He has to take a lot from the top.''

"I mean on a *personal* level,'' Chloe said.

Jennifer looked over Chloe's glowing head for a few seconds. "He'd never look at *me*. Sir Llew is doing his level best to throw Gabe and that nasty bitch of a daugh-ter of his together.''

Chloe shrugged. "Well, I've heard the gossip but he didn't seem too interested to me.''

"You know as well as I do there are many ways to the top,'' Jennifer said harshly.

Chloe couldn't help it, she snorted. "I don't think you have to worry, Jen, Gabriel McGuire is going to make it on his own.''

Chloe hadn't been at her desk more than fifteen minutes when she got a buzz from the man himself. McGuire's voice crackled with pent-up energy. "Do you think you'd better tell me why the hell you've been gone so long?''

"I'd love to, Chief,'' Chloe said with infuriating sweetness.

"Would two minutes in my office do?''

"Gotcha.''

She was on her way out as her friend Mike Cole was

coming back in from covering a golf final. He held the outer door for her. "Hiya, Chloe. You look wonderful. Like a strawberry ice cream. Where have you been?"

She paused for a moment, winked. "Lunch with Christopher Freeman."

"No kidding?" Mike looked thrilled for her and vaguely alarmed. "I bet you had a time fending him off."

"He was a perfect gentleman, Mike. Besides, it's all on the job, an interview's been arranged. I'm off to report to the boss."

Mike laughed. "Is there a problem?"

"There's always a problem with McGuire."

"Only when you push him too far," Mike called after her. "Your goddaughter has been missing you. So has Teri."

"What about I call in early next week. I expect to be free."

"Make it tea."

"Great." Chloe waved back happily. She would confirm that with Teri, not that she had ever known a time however unannounced when Teri hadn't welcomed her with open arms.

"So how did it go?" McGuire wasted no time getting down to business.

"Did you know that Freeman is an insomniac?" Chloe said, dropping gracefully into a chair facing him.

McGuire's rugged dark face took on a saturnine cast.

"No, I know what you're thinking." Chloe laughed. "Aside from his love life, he rarely closes his eyes until around 4:00 a.m."

"Perhaps he's exaggerating a little, though I'm not much of a sleeper myself," McGuire said.

"Too many problems in life?"

"*You're* a problem, Cavanagh." His black eyes moved over her. "Anything else you found out or would you rather save it all up for the interview? Sorry to cramp your style but I'll vet your questions before you put them to him.''

"I don't propose to insult him,'' Chloe said brightly.

"What about the little barbs, Cavanagh?'' he said with rich sarcasm. "You have been known to get them in.''

"I'll get on the wrong side of Sir Llew if I offend his friend.''

"Lord, yes.'' McGuire laughed a little bitterly. "It's been rather a long time since I did that. He hasn't forgotten.''

Chloe thought she had found the perfect point. "Sir Llew never held it against you,'' she inserted deftly.

"My track record might be one of the reasons,'' he drawled. "Initially he opposed me.''

That came as a surprise. Chloe shifted tack. "But you had the Big Guns onside?''

He nodded, cynically. "Unlike you, Sir Llew doesn't mix business with sentiment.''

"That's a tilt at me, of course.''

"You got it!'' he jeered. "You were the one who liked to say I'd never fit into Clive's shoes.''

Chloe's cheeks tinted a hot pink. "Well, I'm sorry. I was mistaken and that's that.''

"No apology?'' He kept his eyes pinned on her.

"I thought that's what *I'm sorry* meant.''

"No way. Sorry doesn't begin to cover it. Anyway—'' he shrugged the issue off "—what did you *eat?*''

Chloe heard the famished note in his voice. She even felt pressure on her shoulder, like her good fairy was giving her a nudge. "Gabriel, you've missed lunch.'' She sighed.

"What's new around here?'' He flashed her a wry smile.

"Why don't I slip down the road and get Spiro's Deli to make you up some sandwiches?" she offered. "Some good coffee, too. I have a flask."

"Cavanagh, you'd do that for me?" His mouth curved up slightly.

"Unless we send Rosie," she joked. "No, I'm feeling quite the Good Samaritan. I'll go immediately. What do you want?"

"Listen," McGuire started, "I don't—"

"Allow me to do it for you. I bet you haven't had anything since breakfast."

"If you call breakfast an apple and a banana on the run," he said with a light mocking tone. "I don't have to send *you*, Chloe."

Chloe stood up. "I'm on my way."

At least she tried, but the moment she entered the foyer a powerful thuggish-looking man about forty with deep-set eyes and a sawn-off hairdo, hustled in the door.

"Hi, there, girlie," he bellowed.

The effect was electric. Amanda on reception shot up like her chair was on fire. "You want someone?" she croaked.

The thug ignored her, concentrating his attention to Chloe. "Ah, the little lady reporter." He patted himself on the chest for being so clever. "It's got nuthin' to do with you. Aren't *you* lucky."

"Who is it you're wanting? I might be able to help you." Chloe did a good job of covering her own alarm. This was one scary individual. She put her hand behind her back, trying to give Amanda a signal she hoped the normally bubbly receptionist would act on. There was a panic button situated just under Amanda's desk.

"Sure." The man sneered. "You want me to get tossed out of here, right? I understand that a reporter mate of yours, Bart Taylor, has been making a *lot* of people uncomfortable."

Chloe kept her expression calm. Bart had been investigating the drug scene and he was a very good reporter. "And what's *your* name?" Chloe asked. Something like Crusher, no doubt.

"That's you lot all over," the man said nastily. "Pokin' your noses into things that don't concern you."

"We're the media, aren't we?" Chloe challenged. "If you'll sit down I'll get someone to listen to your complaint. You're here to complain?"

"That's correct, girlie. Why not to you, now you're here. You're never off the television."

"I don't have the authority to speak for management." Where was security? Any other time you'd have to struggle to get past them. "Wait there and I'll get someone."

Chloe made to move off, only the man reached out and grabbed her arm.

"Hold it right there, girlie."

Chloe's whole body tensed. Was there ever a time she wasn't going to be called "girlie," she thought briefly. Amanda, who had never been confronted by such a situation, still stood immobilised but when the man pulled Chloe in front of him like a shield, Amanda let out peal after peal of shrieks from some inner reservoir.

Crusher was instantly outraged. "Shut up," he exploded as though he was the only one entitled to do any yelling. But Amanda, once started, was impossible to stop. She kept up a continuous shrill, keening like an attack-trained fox terrier, her pretty young face flushed a hot pink. There was a commotion in the corridor. A female voice began to shout incomprehensibly, then McGuire was pushing through, a towering presence with an expression of absolute disgust on his dark glowering face. Why was Cavanagh always in the thick of things? And why was Amanda shrieking like a bat out of hell?

"What the hell goes on here?" he demanded.

"Amanda shut up. *You*—" he addressed Crusher "—would you like to let go of my staff member." His voice vibrated with such anger even Chloe felt a cold chill. "Chloe, get over here."

Crusher who had lived all his life in a tough environment, knew when to give way. He let go of Chloe, abruptly giving her a little push towards McGuire who fielded her like a football, then sent her on a surging pass down the corridor where she was caught by a staff member who found the whole thing incredible. Someone else, Bob, was crawling on his hands and knees to get to the panic button behind Amanda's desk.

"Hold it, buster," Crusher yelled.

"Do what he says, Bob. Everything's fine."

"Where's Taylor?" Crusher demanded of McGuire, losing interest in Bob.

"I take it you've got some kind of beef," McGuire answered in a very tough voice indeed. "Just what *is* your problem," he barked.

Crusher all but crossed his eyes. "You don't know what's goin' to happen if Roberts keeps asking questions," he muttered with a kind of anguish. "They'll take it out on me." His gaze shifted to Bob, who was showing signs of heroism. "I told you to hold it. I gotta gun."

No! God, no! McGuire thought. This nut could turn out to be a walking time bomb. "Why would you be such a fool?" he rasped. "There are security guards on the premises and a patrol car on the way." Want to hear a joke, he thought bitterly. The security guards were probably enjoying a long, leisurely afternoon tea.

"I've got nothin' to lose," Crusher said pitifully. "That investigation has turned me into a fugitive."

It's clear I have to tackle him, McGuire thought. Security wasn't coming to the rescue. The fellow was big, hard, powerful-looking and obviously mixed up in the drug scene, but he'd faced worse. For some reason McGuire didn't see him as a killer. He didn't believe, either, he was armed, but maybe he was high on drugs. The man's body was starting to tremble violently. McGuire decided to change tack, instinctively listening to the little voice that started up in his head. "I wish I could help you," he said more kindly. "Investigations can be painful to a lot of people. On the other hand, I'm not going to do anything until you hand over your weapon."

"My life's been hell, man," Crusher responded to a hint of kindness.

"Why don't you go to the police? Ask for protection."

"They'd find me." Crusher's voice broke with emotion.

"You've spent time in jail?"

"Plenty." Incredibly he presented a proud grin.

"What state was this? Where? Queensland? New South Wales?"

All the time McGuire was talking he waited for the moment when he could safely take this man down, only a small figure in pink came hurling through the door like a guided missile, slamming into Crusher's back with the force of a runaway truck. Crusher grunted in pain, turning his head in utter confusion to see that pipsqueak girl. How could she possibly pummel so hard? She must have spent time in bad company.

It was all McGuire needed. While Crusher was so diverted, McGuire took him down in a first-class rugby tackle. Crusher hit his head on the tiled floor and passed out like a light.

At this point Bob reared up, ran to the panic button and pushed it.

"That's *my* job," Amanda snapped amazingly.

"For God's sake, Chloe." McGuire looked up at her,

his rugged face almost blank with disbelief. "I've never asked before, but are you doing weights?"

"The element of surprise, Chief." Chloe was trying to act casual. She had no idea what was happening to her. She wasn't on steroids. It was just like that other time. She assumed *powers*.

In the corridor quite a crowd had gathered, each with a different account, parting for the two security guards who now decided to push through into the reception area, looking mightily alert.

"What took you so long?" McGuire rasped.

"Sorry, sir. Sorry, Mr. McGuire," the two men blurted in unison. They sprang towards the groaning man on the floor.

"You'd better check him for a weapon," McGuire advised. "He said he was armed. I don't believe it myself."

"He isn't," Chloe said.

"And how would *you* know?" McGuire was grimly amused.

"I'm pretty sure, Chief. Poor devil's a basket case."

"And not only *him*."

"He's clean, Mr. McGuire," one of the guards confirmed, finishing his search and handcuffing the man's hands behind his back. Outside the building, the sound of a police siren rent the clear air.

"You okay, Chief?" Chloe asked.

McGuire momentarily lowered his dark head into his hands. "Sure. I just like sitting on the floor."

"Need a hand up?"

"I'm almost sure you could do it, which is ridiculous." He looked up into her lovely delicate face.

"A job worth doing is worth doing well." Chloe put out her hand and McGuire took it, fixing her with a mocking look.

She couldn't budge him. No way. There wasn't even

a suggestion of her former power. Instead he pulled her down into his arms.

"You're weird, Cavanagh. Do you know that?"

"I can't help it," Chloe said, with not the slightest desire to pull away.

By now the reception area was filled with people and Bob was happily videoing away for all he was worth. McGuire looked like a man who could handle any situation, but Chloe, locked in his arms, didn't look like she could be a threat to anyone past their tenth birthday.

How very deceptive appearances could be.

Amanda, almost fully recovered, had an admiring little group around her when two burly-looking policemen bustled in the front door.

"Right. Who's in charge here?" One of the policemen called in a loud voice.

"Why you are, Cavanagh, who could doubt it?" McGuire murmured, lifting Chloe and himself to their feet. "Gabe McGuire," he identified himself to the older police officer. "I'm the station manager."

"Can we clear this lobby? There are too many people milling 'round if you ask me."

The younger policeman took hold of the prisoner's grubby shirt and hauled him to his feet. "Gee, Blocker, can't you ever keep out of trouble?"

Crusher, properly identified as Blocker, glared balefully. "I didn't do nuthin', I only came here to talk."

"Well, you can talk at the police station, it's only a couple of streets away."

"Take him out into the car," his senior ordered. "I'll get a statement from McGuire here."

"Right, back to work." McGuire raised his voice only marginally, but it had its effect. "Do you want to come through to my office?" he invited the burly policeman.

"No, that's okay. You can tell me here." He placed his booted foot on top of a chair. "Miss Chloe

Cavanagh, right?'' Lord, she was cute. He couldn't wait to tell the wife. She always watched Chloe Cavanagh on the telly.

"Yes." Chloe smiled. "I was actually first on the scene."

"Mind telling me everything that happened?"

"Not at all," Chloe said in her professional voice, then launched into a full account of the afternoon's events from the moment Blocker came through the door, how McGuire intervened, how he rescued her, how she tore through the back part of the building after McGuire pushed her out of harm's way, how she took up a position outside the front door within hearing but out of sight, waiting for the precise moment when she could bound in and divert Blocker for a few moments while McGuire did the rest. "I saw us as a team," she said, moving her head so she could read the policeman's notes better.

"Really?" His steely gaze had softened miraculously. "I guess she's a lot stronger than she looks."

"I studied ballet for about eight years," Chloe said modestly.

"Of course she did!" McGuire seconded staunchly.

If I start to open up about my powers, someone might recommend me to a psychiatrist, Chloe thought.

About ten minutes later the police were ready to leave. "What's going to happen to him?" Chloe asked her newfound friend.

"If he's smart he'll start cooperating with us and we can get to the root of why he came to the station," Senior Constable Drummond said. "Neither of you seemed too perturbed he just *might* have had a gun?"

Chloe didn't trust herself to answer.

"He just didn't sound at all convincing," McGuire said. "He was distraught, not violent. I took comfort from that."

"Well, that should cover it, I guess." Constable Drummond slapped his notebook shut. "We'll let you know what happens next. Personally, I wouldn't want to cross you two."

"Like what happened to my sandwiches?" McGuire asked the moment the police had gone, his expression deadpan.

"I had a choice!" Chloe smiled. "Save you or take up a more strategic position at Spiro's Deli."

"You're crazy," he said for maybe the third time.

"Not really. You only need cheering up."

His dark eyes brightened. "I keep thinking I need to get something to eat. I could, of course, hang on if dinner wouldn't ruin your figure."

For a minute Chloe couldn't take it in. "You're asking *me* to dinner?"

"Something like that." He shrugged. "Just the two of us. No witnesses. I know I'm taking my chances just being with you."

"You mean you might be in danger?" This feeling of excitement was becoming increasingly familiar.

"It seems to be a regular part of your day."

"We survived."

"Sometimes I think it's because you're getting a bit of help." He gave her a wry smile.

"Where would we go?" Chloe asked, suddenly feeling marvellous.

"Let that be my surprise. Go home now. I'll pick you up around eight. I won't be able to get away before then."

Her eyebrows rose. "I thought I had to do the responsible thing and finish my day like everyone else."

"I'm sending Amanda home, too," he pointed out reasonably. "I'm sorry I barked at her but that shrieking wasn't something you'd like to hear every day."

"Poor Amanda!" Chloe sighed. "She'll jump at everyone who comes through the door now."

"Given that it has never happened before, she might settle down. On the other hand, she appeared to enjoy her fifteen minutes of fame. Now do what I tell you for once and take yourself off."

Chloe stared up at him, a little frown between her delicate brows. "I don't know why I *ever* thought I didn't like you," she said.

His brilliant eyes were deliberately sheened with challenge. "Let's see if *liking* is as good as it gets."

It was a taunt, she knew, and it brought a soft flush of colour back to her cheeks.

CHAPTER FOUR

THE restaurant McGuire chose was on the beautiful island-enclosed bay some thirty kilometres from the city. The great expanse of water was all ashimmer, filled with the reflected dazzle of the moon and the stars. Midweek the place wasn't crowded so they sat out on the wide, cool verandah enjoying the music of the palms that swayed along the foreshore and the fresh clean tang of the salt air as it blew in from the sea.

McGuire had ordered a lovely wine as soon as they arrived, now they sat sipping it from voluptuous long-stemmed glasses. He must have found time to nip back to his apartment, Chloe thought, watching the golden play of candlelight over his deeply indented chin. His was the kind of dark olive skin that quickly showed a swashbuckling beard, but he had obviously shaved, showered and changed his city clothes for smart casual with a whole lot of dash. In all fairness she had always admired his dress sense even as she wondered from whence it had come. Now it made her feel like a terrible snob. She herself had spent time choosing her short slip dress in a dusky shade of lilac crepe. It was beautifully cool. Perfect for such a glorious summer night. Had she known they were going to go bayside she would have worn a hibiscus behind her ear. Something about McGuire brought out an earthy streak in her. One could even call it sensual.

At any rate they both ordered oysters.

Chloe for her part scarcely knew what she was doing. It seemed impossible to believe she was here enjoying herself with Gabriel McGuire. She had always been so wary of him, fearful in a way, yet she had begun to relax the minute he had picked her up in the car. Maybe it was the wonderful cocoon effect of the Jaguar. She hadn't realised he was so witty, either. She knew he was remarkably well informed as she had to be herself. That was their job. Keeping abreast of what was happening all around the world, but frequently she found herself bursting out laughing at something he said while he looked back at her with black mocking eyes. She who had done so little to make him feel wanted let alone appreciated.

Of course they had to order seafood in an area celebrated for its marine bounty. Mountains of indulgence; tiger prawns, mouth-watering crab, scallops, baby lobster, calamari, perfect little fillets of catch of the day, all served on a large, colourful platter with a crisp and crunchy salad and tiny freshly baked rolls with a generous sprinkle of poppy or sesame seeds. McGuire with his much greater height and body size was still eating long after Chloe had stopped.

"Believe it or not," he said, "I'm going to have dessert."

"Go right ahead," Chloe encouraged him. "That was absolutely delicious but I couldn't manage another morsel. The food is wonderful here."

"We'll come again," he commented casually.

"You're going to ask me?"

"I was always going to ask you," he drawled, "I've just been waiting for the tiniest hint of a thaw."

Chloe cupped her hands around her flushed cheeks. "What really came between us?" she asked.

He gave her a hooded look. "I told you before, Chloe. Part of you doesn't want anyone getting too close."

"Maybe," she acknowledged, her blue eyes darkening. "And what about you, McGuire? You don't open up to anyone, either."

"I might to you."

There was such a depth to his voice she drew in her breath. "Then tell me about yourself *now*."

"What is it you want to know?" Suddenly his dark face assumed its brooding expression.

"We've had such a lovely evening, are you sure you want to be too serious?"

He reached out and briefly caught her hand. "Little one, I'm always serious," he said.

Whenever he touched her he made her heart pound. "Was your childhood really as bad as you intimated?" she asked, trying to keep her voice steady.

"Is this the start of an interview, Chloe?"

"No, Gabriel." She shook her head very seriously. "I'd really like to know."

"I don't know now that I ought to tell you." He was suddenly angry with himself. Why lay it on this innocent?

"It might help you." Chloe had the oddest sensation someone was at her shoulder. In fact she half turned to see who it was. No one, of course.

"Are you going to introduce a clinical note?" McGuire asked in a wry, sardonic tone.

"Don't be like that, Gabriel. I've acknowledged a few of my little hang-ups."

"Mine nearly crippled me," he said bluntly. "Growing up as you did in a beautiful environment with a loving mother and father, you could scarcely relate to *my* kind of background."

"Try me."

"I usually keep most of myself invisible," he said, then shrugged. "All right—my father was a Vietnam veteran. A helicopter pilot. He came home an entirely different person from the one who went away, my mother always said. All the pain that was locked inside him disrupted his whole life. And ours. My mother and me. Dad couldn't control natural aggressiveness that over the years grew into outright violence.''

"Oh, Gabriel, I'm sorry.'' Chloe leaned her head heavily on her hand.

"It happens, Chloe, over and over. Males are aggressive creatures right from the beginning. Most learn how to channel it, turn the drive into productive avenues.''

"*You* have,'' she said gently.

"Thanks, Chloe.'' His voice was dry. "But *you* have trouble with my image.''

She flushed a little. "Maybe the fault lies in me. I'm frightened of powerful emotions.'' Powerful men. "Can you understand that?''

He didn't answer for a moment, his eyes fixed on her, as beautiful as a dream. "Indeed I can. Actually I think you're very brave.''

"Goodness no!'' She remembered too well the awful times when she couldn't face the day.

"Your losses might have swamped anyone else.''

"Well, as you observed, Gabriel, I haven't got off scot-free.''

"Nor me.''

"You used the past tense when you were talking about your father.'' She picked up his story.

"He died, Chloe, prematurely. The only way he could live with himself was to drink.''

"And your mother?''

"She's okay.'' He shrugged. "Not good, but okay. She lives with her sister in Tasmania. I see her at least a couple of times a year. She always tries to tell me how sorry she is she wasn't stronger.''

"For you?'' Chloe could see how it might have been.

He nodded. "I was six foot at fourteen. It took two more years before my father discovered he was going to have to treat us in an entirely different way.''

"So your goals and your hopes are for a stable home life," she said sympathetically.

His expression was very deep. "I have a clear picture of peace and contentment, Chloe. Love and understanding within the family."

"I hope you find it, Gabriel," she said softly. "In fact I'm going to start praying for you this very night."

"I may need it." He sat forward, his powerful shoulders hunched a little.

"If you decide on Tara Williams," she responded a little more tartly than she had intended.

He laughed. "I like you when you're bitchy, Cavanagh."

"I'm not being bitchy." She didn't like to think she was. "Why are you looking at me like that?"

"All right, *jealous,*" he jeered softly.

She groaned. "You fairly *amaze* me, McGuire."

"What have you got against Tara?" he asked, still amused.

It nettled her. "Heck, Gabriel, where have you been? She's terribly rude. She looks down her nose at everyone. She doesn't actually *do* anything, does she?"

"I've been told she does some social work occasionally."

"She's Sir Llew in a woman's body," Chloe said.

He considered that. "Maybe she is. A touch. But there's no doubt it's a marvellous body."

"You'd know, would you?" Chloe felt a sudden sense of heat.

"I believe I have *eyes,* Miss Cavanagh."

"I just want the best for you, Gabriel," she said simply.

"Well, at least that's cleared that up. Ready for coffee?"

"Why not."

It was when coffee was being served Tara Williams

and an escort, a big, overweight middle-aged man, flashily but expensively dressed, entered the restaurant. Tara was laughing merrily, drawing attention.

Chloe, facing the lobby, nearly fell off her seat.

"Lordy, Lordy, when was the last time you saw Tara?" she demanded.

McGuire didn't turn, unlike most people in the restaurant. "As in *Gone With the Wind?*"

"Second pick," Chloe said sharply.

"Tara Williams?" he guessed. "At the party."

"Well, don't look now but she's on her way over."

"Really? She has someone with her?" he asked mildly.

"Let me reassure you he couldn't compete with you in any way. Dark, balding, and decidedly overweight."

"That would be Al Jacobsen," McGuire said in a casual tone. "The real estate developer. He's in town."

"I hope you're all excited about meeting him," Chloe said. "They're being shown onto the verandah. I'd say directly past this table."

McGuire's expression was unconcerned. "I had a feeling they might be. Would you like to finish up that coffee?"

"Are you suggesting I gulp it down?" Chloe looked away. "I can make us coffee at home."

"Is that a promise?" One black eyebrow shot up.

"Nothing like that. Just a suggestion."

"Not very satisfying, Chloe." His black eyes glowed. "All right then, a *promise.*"

A moment later Tara, looking startled, pointed her right arm dramatically. "Gabe, it can't be! Now here's a surprise." She turned back to her escort. "You've met Gabe McGuire haven't you, Al?"

"No," Al confessed, "I haven't." He smiled, displaying big strong white teeth.

Within minutes waiters were running in all directions

wondering if this was going to be a table for *four*. Even the soft clack of conversation inside the restaurant had stopped. Most people knew Chloe from the television, Tara Williams's face was equally familiar from the social pages, the two men were vaguely familiar, both exuding a languid, big-man authority.

Tara gave Chloe a cold, brilliant smile. A kind of I've-only-got-to-speak-to-Daddy-and-you're-fired smile. "I didn't know you and Gabe were friends?"

Chloe looked up, her tone gentle. "Now and again we call a truce. It doesn't last long."

The two men, as was men's wont, were shaking hands in a friendly fashion. McGuire, looking very tall and urbane, introduced Chloe.

"Maybe we can all have a drink together," Al Jacobsen suggested happily, while a waiter rocked back and forth on his heels waiting for a signal.

"Unfortunately, Al, Chloe and I have to drive back to the city," McGuire said smoothly.

Al considered that. "I know. It's easy to go over the limit. I've got a limo waiting outside."

"Well, its been nice meeting you, Al," McGuire said, shepherding Chloe into the aisle. "We'll leave you both to enjoy dinner. The seafood is wonderful here."

"So I understand," Al Jacobsen said, his deep-set dark eyes sparkling greedily. "Tara only discovered the place about a month ago."

"Didn't *we* come here, Gabe?" Tara asked with a neat blend of memory lapse and possessiveness.

"I can't take the credit, Tara," McGuire's expression was smooth and pleasant.

"I'm only in town for a week or two, Miss Cavanagh, but you can be sure I'll watch your show." Al stared down at Chloe with pleasure.

"She hasn't got a show." Tara wrapped her arms

around Al's sleeve. "Little segments, save the koalas, that sort of thing."

"'Little segments, save the koalas, that sort of thing,'" Chloe quietly fumed when they were safely inside the Jaguar and purring back to town. "I suppose, if Tara decided, I could get the bullet."

"Tara has *no* say," McGuire pointed out crisply.

"Are you sure of that?"

"They don't keep *you* on, Cavanagh, they don't keep *me* on."

Chloe turned to stare at his rugged profile. "You're joking, surely?" she asked cautiously.

"Chloe, you're what is known in the trade as a valuable piece of property."

"Ho!" Chloe sat back inhaling the rich leather. "That being so, I should be paid more for my services."

"You got a raise, didn't you," he countered.

"And I'm very appreciative of it, but Jana Wendt has asked for six million in compensation." Chloe named the most glamorous and powerful female presenter in the country currently at war with her station.

"Six million we cannot do," McGuire told her bluntly. "But you never know. You've got distinct possibilities. Possibilities you don't realise. What I want most of all, I've decided, is to get you in front of the camera."

"Hosting a show?" Chloe's smile bloomed.

"You're quite accomplished for one so young."

It was dreamlike, their harmony. Where is all this largesse coming from? she wondered. It was delightful and frightening all at the same time.

Back home Chloe sat McGuire down in the living room and went off to make coffee. A promise, was a promise, after all.

She was just about to carry it in when McGuire walked into the kitchen, instantly lessening the scale of the room.

"I got lonely out there," he complained.

"I could scramble you some eggs if you're hungry," she joked.

"I really enjoyed this evening, Chloe." His black gaze was locked on her. "I hope you did, too."

"There's a lot to be said for being friends," she pointed out lightly when all her pulses were aflutter.

"I'll have my coffee now, if you don't mind."

"Help yourself." She pushed his cup and saucer gently towards him. "Sugar, cream?"

"No, just black and strong. More than anything else I need a clear head."

She looked at him a little shocked. "We only shared a bottle, Gabriel."

"It's *you* I find intoxicating, Chloe," he said with more concern than ardour. "Are you going to sit down or are you going to hover like an angel?"

She not only felt like standing up. She felt like running. For McGuire to find her intoxicating? That was *stunning.* She could feel his magnetism, his male power all around her.

"I can give you an after-dinner mint with that," she managed.

"Sit down, Chloe, *please,*" he begged. "I'm not about to grab you and press you to my manly chest. I've got a lot to think about."

"Like what?" Chloe asked faintly, slipping into a chair.

"We'll leave all that for a later date." He wasn't ready to explain. "This is good coffee."

"Supreme. I get it from Aromas."

"I love that dress, the colour. It sheens your eyes with lavender. You look beautiful."

"McGuire, I think you mean that," she said gently.

"Is there somebody floating around this kitchen?" he asked abruptly, looking up and around the ceiling.

Little ripples of sensation feathered around her skin. "As you said to *me* once, it's high time you got a good night's sleep."

"You don't feel some tender, solicitous presence?" he persisted, giving her the full battery of his black wonderful eyes.

She stared at him. "I didn't know you were religious, Gabriel."

"I haven't been, particularly up to date. Not that I don't *think* a lot." He sighed. "Bear with me for a while, Chloe."

"The truly odd thing is, I believe you. A few strange things have been happening to me, as you know."

"You're not lifting weights?" He attempted a joke. She was so feminine, so fragile, she took his breath away.

"No. You've put exactly how I've been feeling into words. A tender, solicitous presence."

"Every woman living alone needs that." McGuire looked across at her in her lovely lilac dress. From the moment he had laid eyes on her she had reminded him of something magical. A princess in a fable, sitting on a white unicorn, her long silky mane of red-gold hair flowing from under a high-peaked hat; those blue eyes and the slender graceful limbs. He supposed he was crazy about her but she needed nothing more than friendship and protection. She was far too precious for him. She had never known ugliness and fury.

"I suppose I'd better go," he said, rising instantly to his feet. "There's always an early morning start."

"I'll come with you to the door." Chloe sprang up like a deer, conscious of the powerful tide of feeling that swirled in him at some subterranean level.

He had a way of stalking ahead, of suddenly becoming preoccupied, so that Chloe, at his shoulder, bumped into him when he halted.

"God, I'm sorry." He gave her a hawklike scrutiny as though his tall, powerful body could have done her an injury.

"Really, I have to dance to keep up with you." She smiled.

Her smile was so soft, so sweet, he was entranced. "Good night, Chloe." His hand, large but beautifully shaped, grasped her gently beneath the chin. All would have been well, he only meant to kiss her briefly, a chaste salute, but Chloe at the last minute looked intently into his eyes. Into his *soul*.

He groaned. On a deeper level he moaned, his desire for her flaming out of bounds. He caught her to him, in his passion half lifting her off the floor, lowering his head in blind hunger, bringing his mouth down heavily over hers.

The effect was galvanic. The tender brutality of his kiss robbed Chloe of all breath. His physical strength was overwhelming, the fire that was in him. She had never been kissed so deeply, so voluptuously, in her whole life. Her whole body was quivering, quickening, clamouring. She was losing herself. Losing her shields and with them her defences. When his hand moved hungrily, tormentedly, over her breast she cried out as if in a mad ecstasy of panic, the blood glittering in her tight-stretched veins, silver shafts of pleasure piercing her very core.

He released her immediately, like an eagle shot to earth.

"I'm sorry, Chloe." His deep voice was startlingly harsh. He steadied her because she was swaying, nodded abruptly and strode to the front door.

Chloe hurried after him not at all sure what was happening. That *couldn't* have been a kind of self-disgust in his eyes? "I'm just fine. I was a little afraid for a moment."

"That's what I have to think about, Chloe." He turned back to her, his dark face taut. "You are indeed afraid of me."

"In a different way from what you think, Gabriel," she protested. For all his cleverness, his sardonic wit, she had hurt him. "You don't have to rush off like this."

"Oh, yes, I do. You bring me pain, Chloe, in some way. I suppose there's such radiance all around you."

She reached out, clasped his hand, bracing herself for his rejection. "I don't understand what's happening here."

"Oh, yes, you do, Chloe." He rejected her claim flatly.

"*Tell* me."

"You're not simple. You may be a virgin, don't ask me how I know, but I believe you recognise desire when you see it. I want you. I want you very badly. You've known it from the beginning. That's what makes you as nervous as hell."

"Gabriel, I'm a grown-up woman."

"That cry for help was genuine." His expression was grim.

Her face flamed. She dropped her startling blue eyes. "Maybe it was," she said in a subdued voice. "I've always done my best to stay clear of the rapids." She knew allowing Gabriel to make love to her would take her completely under.

"Maybe that's wise, Chloe." He gave her an odd smile. "Never mind, we can put the wall back up in the morning. See you." He sketched a brief military-type salute.

"You're still coming with me to visit my mother on Sunday?" she called as he opened the door to his car.

"If you want me to, Chloe."

"Of course I do."

Wave to him, a voice said. Wave him off.

She could *hear* the voice. It wasn't a voice in her head.

"All right," she said aloud. There was a lot of this sort of thing going about.

McGuire preparing to reverse out of the drive took one last look at Chloe, standing in her lilac dress, the exterior lights of the verandah making a glowing halo of her red-gold hair. She was waving so sweetly it all but eased the ferment that was in his heart. He waved back before he could prevent himself, distracted for a moment by a luminous patch of light that suddenly moved into his line of vision. It struck him it had an outline of maybe a small boy with some sort of white appendages he couldn't name. A trick of the light of course. Chloe obviously saw nothing by her side.

Even as McGuire continued to peer intently through the windscreen, sheened with salt, he now saw, the light changed, lost its extraordinary glow. He remembered all of a sudden what his mother used to say to him as a child.

"Gabriel, you have too much imagination."

Yet imagination was the key to wondrous new realms.

They saw little of one another for the rest of the week, though Chloe made a scoop, patched in live from the light aircraft terminal where an air traffic control officer was talking down a single engine Cessna. The pilot, a sixty-year-old grazier had suffered what his wife considered to be a heart attack and it was she who, with no actual experience save half a lifetime of flying with her husband, had to land the plane. It was a harrowing experience for all, Chloe feeding information to her channel, while everyone prayed for a miracle.

In the end the woman who had responded with the utmost courage managed to bring the plane down safely, after many terrifying kangaroo hops, to the resounding cheers of everyone at the airport.

Sunday morning Chloe was up early, dressed and waiting out on the verandah for McGuire when he arrived.

"Hi." She walked to the car, the morning sunlight firing her hair.

"How are you, Chloe?" He stood out on the driveway, looking, she realised, ruggedly handsome and devastatingly sexy, something she had always striven to ignore. But the time for all that was over, she thought fatalistically.

She smiled up at him, aware of a certain aloofness in his manner. "I'm fine. We stole Channel Nine's thunder with the airport piece."

"We did indeed." He held the door for her. "I heard late last night the husband is expected to pull through."

"Yes, I know. I called the hospital myself."

"You care, Chloe, don't you?" he said. "You don't walk away."

"I could never be so unfeeling." Chloe turned her head, saw the first time the large sheaf of pink roses on the back seat.

"For your mother," he said, slipping behind the wheel.

"That's very kind of you, Gabriel. They're lovely. Mum always loved flowers so much. I believe she still does."

"I'm sure." His expression softened.

"No phone call from Tara?" Chloe asked when he seemed predisposed to silence.

He eyed her somewhat coolly.

"I would have thought she'd be furious with you,"

Chloe found herself saying. Better a reaction, than no reaction.

"No use being furious with me." He shrugged, smoothly overtaking a slow-moving vehicle. "I don't take to it."

"But she *did* ring?"

"Heck, yes." He suddenly gave a quick, dashing grin. "I could do very well for myself there."

"Are you ambitious enough?" Something flashed in Chloe's blue eyes.

"I have to admit, Sir Llew is applying a little pressure."

"Is he? Isn't that disgusting?"

"You don't think I'd make a good match?" He flicked her a mocking glance.

"*You* were the one who spoke so eloquently about love."

"And you don't consider Tara lovable."

Chloe clicked her tongue and shook her head. "I don't know why I started this conversation."

"No, that's all right, Cavanagh," he said kindly. "Let there be no secrets between us. I can scarcely want you *and* Tara."

"Why me?" she asked, for some reason feeling like crying.

"Maybe the fact that you rejected me so completely made you that much more desirable."

"Is this true?" If so, it wasn't what she wanted to hear.

"No, it's nonsense. You took my breath the very first moment. I looked up and you were there. An angel come down to earth."

Chloe was moved. "Gabriel, that's the nicest compliment I've ever had in my life. I don't deserve it."

"No, you don't, you horrible little creature. You never show me any kindness or respect. It wasn't long before

I found out you were calling me a megalomaniac behind my back.''

"But a splendid megalomaniac, Gabriel. I always knew you were very clever.''

"Too late, Cavanagh. I'll pay you back one of these days. Remind me.''

They arrived at the nursing home a full ten minutes before time, taking the opportunity to walk around the extensive grounds. The magnificent shade trees, the jacarandas, had almost overnight burst into exquisite lavender blossom, all of them soaring to forty feet and more, colouring the tropical air mauve. Other lovely trees grew in the grounds, the purple and white orchid trees, the bauhinias that lined the perimeter and went so beautifully with the jacarandas. As the jacarandas turned back to dense feathery foliage the brilliant poincianas and the very old magnolias grandiflora would come into flower. Chloe had seen all the flowering in her time of visiting her mother.

McGuire was impressed. They were standing by the lake watching the play of sunshine over the dark green water. Numerous radiant insects were hovering over the lovely cream waterlilies cupped by large leaves and birds sang their delight in so beautiful a morning.

"Impossible to believe there's a lot of traffic out there.'' McGuire looked off towards the distant street. "It's so peaceful here.''

Chloe nodded. "It takes a lot of upkeep. There are quite a few groundsmen.''

"And I imagine it's expensive?''

"I may have to sell the house in time,'' she confided. "If Mum doesn't recover. But I feel if I did anything…'' She broke off unable to go on.

"I know what you mean, Chloe,'' he said simply.

Delia Cavanagh was sitting in her wheelchair, her back to them when they arrived. The light in the room was extraordinary, more silver than golden, clinging to her beautiful curly hair, shades lighter than Chloe's, more a bright copper, and to her soft blue robe.

"Good morning, Mumma," Chloe said, going to her mother and kissing her cheek. She turned the wheelchair. "I've brought someone to meet you. You've heard about him often. Gabriel McGuire."

Gabriel moved forward, holding the pink roses in one hand and taking Delia's fragile blue-veined hand with the other.

"Hello, Delia, I'm Gabe."

You have to get better, he thought, feeling a deep lunge of sympathy within him. Delia looked so completely peaceful yet she had slipped away from life. Understandable in a way. Chloe had told him her mother had adored her husband. Maybe this tremendous *hush* was Delia's choice.

Chloe, upset, took the flowers and set them down on the bedside table while her mother looked dreamily on, not registering Gabriel's presence by so much as the blink of an eyelid. Only while she was sitting there, her wheelchair bathed in a rainbow of sunlight, aquamarine, citrine, amethyst and garnet, like jewel colours seen through a prism, a change came over Delia Cavanagh; a spontaneous mental lift when for the space of a heartbeat she rediscovered happiness.

She *smiled*. A smile that lifted the corners of her mouth and showed in her eyes.

Chloe, the victim of countless crushed hopes, turned an anguished face to Gabriel. "She smiled, didn't she, Gabriel?" she begged of him.

Gabriel, stroking Delia's hand as if calling in healing power, couldn't bear her pain. "There's not the slightest doubt, Chloe." He felt he had witnessed not only Chloe's profound heartache but a moment of promise.

A minute but momentous *shift*.

"Come here to me." He put out his arm to Chloe, relieved beyond words when she came to him without hesitation, desperate for comfort. She was trembling, blue eyes glittering with standing tears.

"Mum has never smiled. Never once."

"She did then, Chloe." He couldn't bring himself to get her hopes up any further. But in his heart he felt there was a very slight possibility Delia Cavanagh could be coming back to wakefulness.

"Her doctors think she'll never recover."

But Gabriel had drawn reassurance from that smile. It was magical. "Doctors are sometimes wrong," he said carefully, even when the little flare of life, of intelligence, had died down in Delia as though she, too, conceded defeat.

"Maybe it's the drugs she's on. Maybe they are preventing her from—" Chloe broke off, a minute away from weeping. "Oh, God, I don't know."

It was cruel. Another hope dashed.

Yet there were vibrations in the room, vibrations far too subtle for the most powerful scanning device to measure. Vibrations that had entered Delia Cavanagh's body, beginning the work of lifting layer upon layer of miasmata.

By the time they were out in the beautiful grounds again, Chloe had stopped trembling. Gabriel was telling her mother a story about a trip he had made to Tibet, the Roof of the World. How he had been privileged to visit the Potala, the castle-like structure that was the private monastery of the Dalai Lama, where he and a few others had been granted an audience. He spoke of the Tibetan people, of the political situation, the religious rites, the prayer wheels and the awesome presence of the mighty snow-covered Himalayas. What was more extraordinary, Delia appeared to listen, her head cocked to one side like bird.

Two hours passed during which time Delia seemed to focus on things around her, more specifically, her eyes were brighter, the gaze more concentrated.

Chloe did not trust what was happening. Life was cruel. She had good reason to know that. Maybe this was even an intimation her mother was about to leave her. That her father would come for her. Perhaps he was standing beside her at this moment. Someone certainly was. *Not* Gabriel. No one could miss Gabriel, so tall, so strong, so solidly *visible*. This was someone *unseen*. Someone who nevertheless breathed gently beside her. Hadn't she held her own breath many times trying to check where that other sound was coming from? When she was a child she had loved the idea of having her own guardian angel. A guardian angel to look after her. Where had he gone? And *who* had come back in his place?

Watching Gabriel so at ease with her mother, Chloe was overwhelmed by these moments of order. Moments of supreme clarity in the chaos of life.

The trip to the mountains refreshed Chloe's spirit. This was some of the finest scenery in the land. They drove past orchards and farming land, finally entering the fantasy landscape of the Glass House Mountains sighted by Captain Cook from the deck of the *Endeavour*. At that time a storm had passed over the rainforest and the steep volcanic tors had glittered like glass. As always the sight of Tibrogargan crouched above the mountain road made Chloe's heart leap into her throat. One came on it so suddenly; around a steep curve and it was there! Utterly *unreal,* like some prehistoric monster rising out of the thick scrub. Then as they followed the highway, climbing ever upwards, Tunbubalda, Beerburrum, Beerwah, and Coonowrin, soaring above the lush greenery. In these rich, red volcanic soils grew pineapples, avocados, papaws, bananas and all kinds of citrus fruit with fresh produce selling from roadside stalls at the entrance to the farms. This was lyrical country and Gabriel stopped the car on a hill high above one of the beautiful beaches with its white sand and rolling turquoise surf, to get the best view of the fantastic Dreamtime pinnacles, ranged side by side.

The De Haviland mountain sanctuary sat on a promontory overlooking the distant blue ocean with the rich hinterland in between.

"Isn't this exciting!" Chloe cried when the main house came into view.

"It has an Indonesian feel, don't you think?" McGuire, too, was impressed. "It blends so beautifully with the landscape. We've got the towering volcanoes, mercifully extinct, but where are the rice fields?"

Chloe laughed. "He's a brilliant architect. I read he and his wife spent a lot of time in Java."

"Actually she's Balinese. A beautiful, graceful creature. One up on you, Cavanagh."

"Really?" Chloe hadn't known.

The property was on luxuriant acreage with a profusion of tropical trees, plants and shrubs in flower, the combined scents pervading the blue and gold air. Cars were parked all over the grounds but McGuire managed to find a spot sandwiched between a Bentley and a very dusty four-wheel drive.

Their hostess appeared almost as soon as they arrived at the entranceway to what was really a complex of pavilions built on three levels. Dressed in a fuchsia silk shirt combined with royal-blue silk trousers and a vibrant pink sash, her long, gleaming black hair flowing down her back, Luna De Haviland was indeed beautiful with skin like a golden peach, and a wonderful welcoming smile.

"Please come in and meet everybody. Our guest of

honour hasn't as yet arrived,'' she told them with a twinkle.

The De Havilands had amassed the most wonderful things, Chloe thought as they followed their hostess through the main pavilion with its carved Javanese ceiling beams and ornate panels they learned later had been rescued from old buildings.

There were a lot of people scattered all over the rear of the main pavilion with its wonderful projecting deck that overlooked the breathtaking views. For a Sunday luncheon everyone was very glamorously dressed in expensive designer gear with lots of 18-carat gold; the women in a profusion of silk shirts of brilliant colours and patterns worn with toning skirts or trousers. Chloe herself wore pristine white, the fine lawn of her sleeveless shirt appliquéd down the front with seashells picked out in black and gold, a wide white and gold belt cinching her tiny waist, her linen trousers narrowly cut. Chloe knew exactly how to dress her petite figure, the resultant simplicity stealing a lot of the more spectacularly dressed's thunder. She was in fact earning herself something of a reputation as a trendsetter. Hence the invitation to cover the Fashions on the Field.

Their host, a very distinguished-looking man with prematurely grey hair, came towards them linking his arm with his wife's, introducing them both to the people they didn't know, the low-profile seriously rich. They waved and called hello to the rest, the high-profile society crowd. Since she had become a ''media figure'' Chloe had been invited to lots of places so she knew a lot of people. It was part of the job.

Almost immediately they were claimed by a smart young group, getting caught up in light-hearted conversation, until Tara Williams arrived in a skin-tight sleeveless black stretch top with caramel-coloured linen trousers and some kind of elaborate gold choker around her neck.

"Hello, everybody," she cried, blowing kisses to right and left. "Daddy and Chris will be a little bit late. Very big do last night." She rolled her eyes.

Most smiled politely except one young man near Chloe who muttered something very waspish but funny. Though Tara obviously considered herself a young leader of society she wasn't terribly well liked. Something she was oblivious to. Now she made a bee-line for Gabriel, finding an empty space beside him when really there was none.

"Darling, how lovely to see you," she cooed, grasping his arm and kissing his cheek.

Chloe, who wanted no fuss, moved off.

Sir Llew and Christopher Freeman arrived about thirty minutes later and a short time after that their hostess carolled very sweetly, "Luncheon everybody."

"You'll sit with me, won't you?" Christopher, who had all but bolted himself to Chloe's side, now begged. "Come on, pick up a plate," he urged. "There's a simply marvellous vast buffet. Tara's well and truly appropriated your friend, McGuire, if that's who you're looking for."

Which was the case, Chloe was forced to admit, chagrined. She had in fact begun to wonder if they were going to settle themselves perpetually on the upholstered bench of the decking looking out over the view. Tara chatting one hundred to the dozen.

A lot of guests were quaffing champagne and Chardonnay at the rate of knots and Chloe wondered, too, just how they were going to get home. Maybe there were fleets of buses waiting she hadn't seen.

The buffet was indeed marvellous, served on large Indonesian platters filled with whole salmon, smoked salmon, lobsters and prawns, ham, crisp spiced chicken, with great bowls of salad, pork and beef dishes, cold and hot, the latter cooked in the Thai fashion and served with high fluffy piles of rice and stir-fried vegetables.

Although Freeman had wanted Chloe all to himself, others joined in, filling up the tables, including McGuire who had managed to lose Tara for a few minutes.

"Where have *you* been?" Chloe asked him a little coolly when he drew up a chair beside her.

"Surely you haven't missed me?" His black gaze was mocking.

"This is a party, isn't it?" She turned her face a little away from him so he couldn't see her expression.

"So why are you down in the doldrums?"

"I am *not!*" Chloe swung her head back, looking at him closely. His skin had picked up sun. It was glowing golden. "You're teasing, aren't you?"

"Yes, isn't it too awful? What about you and Freeman? I've told you not to hurl yourself at him."

"You know perfectly well that's not what I'm doing," Chloe said, responding to his bantering tone.

"Pay no attention to me."

"I won't."

"Ah, there you are, Gabe." Tara returned from the buffet, her plate piled precariously high. "Chloe, move over, there's a good girl. I want to sit beside Gabe."

"I was here first." Chloe looked up brightly.

"I guess she was." Gabe fetched up a sigh. "I never thought I'd see the day when beautiful women would fight over me."

"Who said anything about fighting? I only want to stay out of the sun." Chloe adjusted her chair fractionally so she was under one of the white sail awnings.

Tara laughed in annoyance and sat down abruptly, her expression changing as Christopher Freeman came charging back to Chloe carrying another bottle of Moët.

"No more for me, thank you, Christopher," Chloe said when he set down a flute in front of her.

"Goodness me, another one won't hurt you," he said in an amused but somewhat impatient tone.

"Another one and someone will have to wake me up. No, two's the limit. Especially in the middle of the day."

"I'd like another, Chris," Tara said, clutching the glass and holding it up to him.

"What about you, Gabe?" Freeman asked after he had satisfied Tara.

"No, thanks. I have to make it down the mountain."

"What a couple of spoilsports you are," Freeman drawled.

"We try to be," McGuire said.

"I've already asked my hostess if I can stay the night." A male guest seated near them flashed a white smile. "This is wonderful food. I don't know what to start on first."

It was much later when Chloe was repairing her makeup in the powder room, Tara dashed in and locked the door.

"Listen, just give it to me straight," she said breathlessly. "Are you after Gabe?"

Chloe scrunched a few of her loose curls before she answered. "Maybe he needs a woman like me in his life."

"*Tell* me." Tara had an odd expression on her face, half pleading, half frenzy.

"If it makes you feel any better, Tara, I'm not after anyone," Chloe said kindly. "I'm not ready to settle down."

"I think you are." Tara clicked her tongue. "This is the *third* time I've seen you with Gabe."

"Do you think I ought to apologise?" Chloe glanced at her watch. She really wanted to go home. The day had been hot and brilliantly fine but they could be in for one of Summer's late afternoon thunderstorms.

"Gabe and I have been getting on just fine," Tara was saying. "We're a lot more than *friends*."

"Oh, yes?" Was it possible?

"I had to take this opportunity to talk to you for a few minutes, Chloe. You mightn't have realised the situation."

"I had heard the gossip."

"Exactly!" Tara burst out triumphantly. "If you know the score you won't try to steal him off me, will you?"

"It's a free country," Chloe joked.

"I'd advise you to listen." Tara's voice slid down to sullen. "I could take measures."

"That's not a very pleasant prospect to contemplate," Chloe said. "Are you going to open the door? I bet there's a long queue out there."

Tara moved backwards, stretching out an arm blindly, trying to unlock the door.

"Just remember, your career is in your own hands," she warned.

CHAPTER FIVE

THEY had a slight argument in the car, Chloe brooding about her run-in with Tara. She didn't know what exactly drove her. It couldn't possibly be defined as *jealousy,* could it?

"Everyone seems to know the true story about you and Tara but me," she said, regarding McGuire's rugged dark face. It looked irritated.

"I don't know if I know it myself, Chloe," he said.

"You keep telling me no romance, but she seemed sincere."

"Where does the girl get it from?" McGuire mocked.

"Why would she warn me off?"

He shrugged. "Well she obviously thinks she could be the woman in my life, lucky girl."

"No *could be* about it. She told me you were much more than friends."

"God, that's an old line," he said in disgust. "Anyway what does it have to do with you, Cavanagh. You're not ready for any big romance."

"Certainly not with *you,* McGuire." Not very complimentary. Not even strictly true.

"Why should I believe you?" he countered. "I've only kissed you twice yet you made every other kiss I've shared pale into insignificance."

Chloe bit her lip. "It was hard *not* to respond," she said, especially when she was driven by unfamiliar passion.

"So there *is* a possibility," he asked, sounding more satirical than serious, "I could approach you on bended knee?"

"We were talking about *Tara*. How's she going to put paid to my career?"

He sobered. "I *told* you, Chloe. She can't do it."

"I don't want to labour this, but I've got one word for her and it's Trouble. You said yourself Sir Llew is trying to promote a match."

"Understandable. Sir Llew wants a strong man to take Tara off his hands. He's worked hard all his life giving her everything she wants."

"And a bit of a handful, is she?" Chloe asked with some point.

"I wouldn't know. What *is* this incredible attack upon me, Cavanagh? My little dalliance with Tara adds up to a big fat nothing. While Freeman is well into the chase?"

Chloe thought for a moment, remembering back. "I did my best to give him no encouragement. At least I hope I did. If you want to know, on closer scrutiny, I really don't like him."

"But you'd rather die than show it?"

"That would have been very bad manners, Gabriel. The party was in his honour."

"And all in all, we enjoyed it. Freeman was very put out when you decided to leave."

"So what? Tara didn't look so happy, either."

"True. Now can we get off these people. It's silly to argue. The house was magnificent, our hosts were delightful, the food was splendid. Now I realise we should have left twenty minutes earlier. I think we're in for a thunderstorm."

Chloe raised her head to peer through the windscreen. "It should be short and sweet. I just hope we make it further down the mountain."

"You're not seriously worried are you?" He glanced at her in concern.

"No, a little on edge. I don't like it when people go out of their way to be unpleasant."

"I don't like it, either, but put it out of your head. There's nothing between Tara and me. I took her out a few times…"

"Kissed her a few times?"

"Fair enough, but I didn't sleep with her, Chloe. Why don't you ask right out?"

"Far better I mind my own business," she said. Otherwise she would confirm his crazy suspicions that she was jealous.

Halfway down the mountain a station wagon suddenly emerged from a hidden driveway a couple of hundred yards in front of them, causing McGuire to brake abruptly while the other vehicle, very slow to move off, picked up speed. A woman was driving. There didn't seem to be anyone else in the car but there was a Baby on Board sticker affixed to the rear window.

"Wouldn't you know it," McGuire grumbled. "An overcautious driver and not a lot of places to overtake her. Surely she'd have done better to wait until we went past?"

"Maybe she didn't even see you, or she's got something against Jaguar drivers."

"We're running the risk of driving into the storm," McGuire said. "It seems to be over the mountain, wouldn't you say?"

Chloe looked out at the darkening sky. The billowing clouds were shaped rather like galleons, the sails pierced with blinding rays of sunlight that soon went out. The rain came down. At first lightly, then in a crashing torrent. McGuire turned his lights on, as did the vehicle ahead.

"At least we're nearly there," he said quietly. "We'll stop at the bottom and take shelter until the worst of it is over. Tropical storms are always short-lived affairs."

"I don't like it, Gabriel," Chloe suddenly said, and relaxed a pent-up breath.

"You're perfectly safe." He didn't turn his head, but spoke reassuringly.

"Not *us*." She shook her head.

"What's the matter, Chloe?" he asked.

"I don't know."

"Tell me what you're thinking. Share it." He could feel an answering energy building up inside himself.

"Someone could have an accident," she said.

"Well, Chloe, God willing, it's not going to be us. I'm a good driver and this is a very safe car."

"I know, Gabriel. I'm just going on instinct." She was, she realised, keeping her eyes trained on the vehicle that had now disappeared around the bend.

"You think it might be the station wagon?" he asked in surprise. "She's driving too cautiously to come to much harm. She's a nervous driver in fact." It was just as he said it, McGuire felt his first frisson of alarm.

As they rounded the steep curve both of them expecting to see the station wagon ahead, they were confounded by an empty road. There was no station wagon. No other vehicle.

"Where did she go?" Chloe was feeling so alarmed she was finding it difficult to swallow.

There were no farm houses, no dwellings on this stretch of the road. Nothing. Only as they drove slowly further on, they could see through a break in the tropical shrubbery a dry creek bed that was rapidly filling with water. About thirty feet along the creek bed was the station wagon lying on its hood.

"My God!" McGuire responded immediately, finding a safe place to stop. "She's gone over the side. We couldn't see any skid marks for the rain."

"And just look at the water!" Chloe cried. "I can't

see her moving about. Gabriel, we've got to get down there.''

"Get on the car phone. Get help,'' he said, opening out his door. "Leave this to me, Chloe. It could be dangerous.''

The sound of the rain was deafening. No wonder they hadn't heard anything. While McGuire picked his way down the ragged slope to the creek bed, Chloe dialled the 000 emergency number, proceeding to give all the relevant information; the exact location of the accident, the make of the vehicle, and the fact there appeared to be only one occupant, a woman driver. How marvellous these mobile phones were in an emergency, she thought. One shouldn't be without one. She threw open the passenger door and stepped out onto the slippery verge. It was still pouring and she saw to her horror the creek bed all but dry thirty minutes before, was now a raging torrent with debris in the form of fallen branches and twigs, being carried down from further upstream. Chloe had seen a flash flood before today. She knew exactly how bad things could get. She had to get to Gabriel. Lend him her assistance. She wasn't afraid of the water, though she realised she could be swept off her feet. She was an excellent swimmer.

Gabriel, meanwhile, was working his legs hard against the force of the water. Beside the car he now saw there was a baby in the rear car seat flailing and wriggling, its small face red with fright and rage, but mercifully held by the car seat's restraint. The mother appeared to be unconscious, slumped upside down but still strapped in. The next thing he knew, Chloe was sliding down the slope and into the water, working furiously to get to him. He had never seen anyone move so fast.

"There's a baby in here, Chloe,'' he yelled. "If you can get to her, I'll try to get the mother out.''

Help might be coming, but it could be too late.

By now both of them were soaked, a fine spray of rainwater sheening their faces. Gabriel got the rear door open. Chloe fought to reach in, got a hold on the baby with one arm and struggled to release the restraint. She didn't have time to look about for Gabriel who was now on the other side of the car trying his hardest to figure out the best way to release the woman who was noticeably pregnant. He was pretty sure he could grab her, but unconscious, she would be a dead weight. It was at times like this he was thankful he was a big man in his prime, blessed with splendid health and strength. He was going to need it.

"Chloe, get out of here," he shouted as he saw her with the screaming baby cradled in her arms. The mother was bleeding slightly and had a fair bit of swelling on one side of her head.

Chloe tried to oblige. She stood perfectly still for a moment and stared at the rushing water. It would be terrible if she lost her footing. She could even lose her hold on the baby.

"Come on, we're almost there," a voice said in her ear.

I'm some sort of case, Chloe thought. I'll just have to get used to it.

"To the right," the voice urged gently.

Chloe didn't hesitate though she was nearly up to her waist in swirling water. The rain was still coming down but the storm was losing its violence. Chloe proceeded with caution, planting one foot after the other, weighing down her body in between. At one stage it crossed Chloe's mind someone was leading her. Once she staggered as her foot hit a hidden rock, only to have herself righted.

"Don't be so hasty," the voice gently admonished.

"No," she replied, instantly obedient.

Finally she waded out and sat down hard on the bank,

realising the baby had stopped its wailing and was staring with great interest at a point past her shoulder, but she didn't turn to look.

"Gabriel, are you still there?" she shouted in a desperate panic. The station wagon had shifted position in the surging waters, the rear end swinging towards her. "Gabriel!" she cried, her voice full of anxiety.

"He's safe," the voice said.

"Who *are* you?" Chloe whispered, feeling a wonderful rush of comfort. No one answered. How could they?

A moment more and Gabriel loomed into sight, a colossus to Chloe's eyes, carrying the woman in his strong arms. At one point he stumbled and Chloe's stomach gave a sick somersault, but then he jerked upright as though someone had helped him find his balance.

"My hero," Chloe cried emotionally when he was almost at the bank. "How are you?"

"Hurting a bit." He was huffed.

"Stay with it," she urged him with great intensity. "You deserve a citation." And a great big kiss, as well.

The rain stopped abruptly, turned off like a tap. To mark the storm's passing a beautiful rainbow, "the bride of the rain," spread its magic arc across the sky, rose, violet, yellow and green.

Chloe began to jiggle the baby, filled with such tremendous relief she was alight. "Don't be afraid, darling," she crooned. Mummy was safe lying on the bank, dazed but conscious. Chloe snuggled the little creature close, immensely grateful it was summer, for although they were both wet, neither of them was cold. In fact, their clothing was drying remarkably quickly.

Gabriel turned away from his patient for one fraught moment to catch Chloe's face to him. He wanted to kiss her madly, triumphantly. And he did, putting his heart and soul into it, taking her sweet mouth with passionate urgency.

They heard the siren before an ambulance came into sight, followed by a police car. Both vehicles parked up on the verge and in another few minutes people were surging down the slope.

"Thank God," Chloe murmured, and the breeze whispered, Amen.

They waited until the ambulance left with mother and child, and the police said they could go home. A tow truck had already arrived and preparations were under way to right the vehicle before winching it out of the creek. The bed of the creek had been baked so hard the water was still rushing freely, holding its level, unable to soak into the soil. It was hampering operations but Chloe and Gabriel were happy to leave it to the experts. The police weren't happy about the "balding" condition of the station wagon's front tyres, the probable cause of the accident.

The woman had a concussion, her blood pressure was up, but she was quite coherent and anxious to thank Gabriel and Chloe for coming to their rescue and almost certainly averting a tragedy. Other motorists coming down the mountain afterward might have responded to their plight but by then mother and child could have drowned.

"We intend to call attention to this fine piece of rescue work," the policeman in charge told them.

"We don't want any publicity." Chloe shook her head. "We just did what anyone else would do."

"Perhaps, but I assure you not so well." There was an undertone of amazement in the policeman's voice. "I can understand your friend here performing such a feat, big strong bloke, but for you to ford a flash flood and rescue the baby gets to be a bit mind-boggling. You want to take out a lottery ticket."

The ambulance officer who had draped them both in blankets, seemed genuinely amazed when they returned them because their clothes were almost dry.

"Even with the heat of the sun, I would have thought it would take a lot longer than that," he said.

Chloe fingertipped her lawn shirt. The texture was as smooth as if it had been steam pressed, with no trace of the dirt and grit that muddied the swollen creek. Gabriel's clothes were the same.

They were very quiet on the journey back to Chloe's house, both shaken and trying to get the events of the afternoon straight in their minds.

"How did you do it, Chloe?" McGuire finally asked.

"Don't ask," she murmured helplessly. "I don't think we're supposed to ask."

"What does *that* mean?" He shot a glance at her. Her hair had dried into a glorious mass of waves and ringlets haloing her face. He adored it.

"Don't you get the feeling it was some kind of mystical experience, dear, strong Gabriel?"

McGuire watched a flight of brilliantly coloured lorikeets swoop above the car. "It's been ages since I had a mystical experience, Chloe, but you could be right."

"Have you *ever* had one?" Chloe asked, intensely interested in the answer. Gabriel, she had learned, was a very deep and unusual person.

"Once when I was a child." The dark cloud settled down over his face again.

"You don't want to tell me," she said gently, aware of the pain in him.

"It wasn't a good experience, Chloe, but if I tell you, I can't play it down."

Chloe leaned over, put out her hand and softly touched his cheek. "Was it about your father?"

"I'd done something," he began quietly, reflectively. "I'm not saying I wasn't a wild kid. I was. It was the price of growing up in a violent home. Dad took a belt to me and couldn't seem to stop. I was only about ten and I thought maybe I was going to die. Anyway, in my helplessness, hopelessness, I called out to my guardian angel to help me. I remember it very clearly. I said. 'If you're there, now's the time to help me.' I don't know what happened next. *I* saw nothing but Dad sure did. He dropped the belt and bolted up the cellar stairs as though the devil himself was after him. Fortunately for me, it wasn't the devil. I still have the unshakeable belief my guardian angel manifested himself in some way. My father didn't touch me for a long time after and never again so badly. Whatever he saw, it really shook him up.''

''And you've had to live with the pain of it all.''

''There were odd moments of happiness. In the right mood when things came together, Dad became the person my mother married. No ugliness, no menace. He was an entirely different human being.''

''Did he never have counselling?'' Chloe asked.

''No, he never sought help. He thought he was *beyond* help. It's the end, really, when we give in to despair.''

Chloe was beginning to see what it must have been like for the young Gabriel to pull himself out of such a tragic environment. Like today, he had shown great courage.

When they arrived home a BTQ8 van was parked outside the house.

''Oh, no!'' Chloe said in dismay. ''They've got the story.''

''See what it's like when the spotlight's turned on you?'' McGuire said laconically.

''I don't want to do this, Gabriel.''

''And you think I do? I hate to have my picture taken let alone being presented as some sort of hero. Come on, let's face it. It's news. People like to see this sort of thing.''

As they drove in the gates, the van followed them, everyone alighting at pretty well the same time.

"Hi, there!" Jennifer Bourne walked towards them, an attractive figure in a smart red suit with gold buttons. "Had a nice time up the mountain?"

"We enjoyed ourselves. You've got the story, right?" McGuire said wryly.

"Sure we have, Gabe. At least half a dozen people phoned us. After we finish here, we're off to the hospital to have a few words with mother and babe.''

"The baby won't be giving much away," Gabe said dryly. "He's all of eight months old.''

"You know what I mean, Boss.'' Jennifer shrugged. "Why so shy? I would have thought you'd love to get your picture in the paper. They'll turn up, of course. Maggie in publicity wants it, plus a spot on the news.''

"Let's get it over," was all McGuire said.

"Aren't you going to invite us in, Chloe?" Jennifer tried to smile at her limelight-stealing colleague, but didn't quite succeed.

"Sure," Chloe said, realising they didn't stand a chance.

"So when did you get to change your clothes?" Jennifer asked, her eyes raking Chloe's petite figure.

Chloe, poised at the top of the steps, turned back. "We haven't.''

"I find that very hard to believe," Jennifer drawled.

"Do you want to keep it a little secret?"

"No secret," McGuire said in a no-nonsense voice. "These are the same clothes we wore to the party. They've dried off in the heat.''

Jennifer, faced with their immaculate appearances, couldn't help herself. "Did you find a motel?"

"I beg your pardon," McGuire turned on her, frowning.

"Just joking, Gabe." Jennifer backed off hastily. "The two of you look like you've just stepped out of a fashion magazine. Weren't you supposed to be waist-deep in water?"

"What the hell do you think? That's why you're here."

Jennifer didn't look any too convinced but she had trouble fitting her scenario to the time frame.

It took roughly forty minutes before it was all over and afterwards McGuire stood up to take his leave.

"I'll leave you in peace, Chloe."

It was way too early for him to go. Chloe didn't think she could accept being on her own, although Christopher Freeman had at one point during the lunch suggested that they might like to go out to see "The Phantom of the Opera" with supper afterwards. As a suggestion it had had no appeal whatsoever and she had turned him down. Chloe wasn't attracted to Freeman in any capacity and she didn't fancy being anyone's Number Four wife, if indeed such was the intention. McGuire, with whom she had shared a somewhat jangled relationship and always on the work level, was now causing her heartache. For one thing, she had been too quick to judge him. *Prejudge* him really. And she'd been mistaken. He certainly was abrasive at times, very demanding as the station boss, but he was by no means the diamond in the rough she had sought to label him. He had many, many facets and considerable brilliance. She confessed to herself now her strong resistance to him had been emotional. It was as he said. She really did fear a close bond. Love was everything in life. The loss of it was appalling, involving lots of grief and pain. She should know.

"Chloe?" McGuire looked down at her slumped a little forlornly in an armchair.

"Oh, I'm sorry, Gabriel." Quickly she raised her head. "I'm feeling the reaction, I suppose."

"Is there anything at all I can get you?" he asked, concern in his dark eyes.

"No, I'm fine." She stood up, fixing a bright smile on her face. "Do you suppose we'll make the six o'clock news?"

"That's what they're aiming for."

She was about to say, "Do you want to stay to watch it?" but he seemed anxious to go. Perhaps he'd had enough of her and the misadventures that seemed to follow her.

It was Freeman, in fact, who rang later in the evening, sounding a little hung over and clearly surprised to find her at home.

"I thought I'd ring on the off chance you were still there," he explained. It was eight o'clock. "I thought you said you had a previous engagement."

"Which I had to cry off, Christopher," Chloe lied. She was facing the mirror above the console in the hallway, now she made a face at herself. "I've developed a splitting headache."

"No wonder, darling," he said with superficial sympathy. "You've been on television, do you know that? You and Gabe."

"I did see it." Chloe made a real effort not to sound so formal. On the one hand she didn't want to offend Christopher Freeman and put him off the interview, on the other she didn't want to give him the slightest encouragement to pursue her. Whether for some transient pleasure or a more serious involvement. Obviously he took their big age difference lightly. He kept on chatting at great length so Chloe had to pull up a chair, but finally he rang off, telling her she was wonderful and he couldn't wait for their interview and afterwards take her out to dinner.

Once off the phone Chloe looked around the silent house. Loneliness was almost tangible. Why hadn't Gabriel rung? It really was terribly laid back of him or maybe he was too busy dressing to go out again. She wasn't sure of anything he did. There could very well be an assortment of women in his life. All the women who worked with her found him outrageously sexy. She had even accepted his heart-thudding excitement. And he was a wonderful kisser. She might be a traumatised virgin but she had had plenty of kisses in her time. All of them totally eclipsed by McGuire's expertise and sexual intensity.

She could get into terrible trouble falling in love with someone like Gabriel McGuire. She wasn't prepared, either, for the fact his not ringing hurt her so much. Chloe walked nearer the hall mirror. Stared at herself. What she saw was a wistful young woman with good creamy skin, a mop of wild red-gold hair, she had washed it, rather unhappy blue eyes, the colour intensified by the colour of the satin flower-and-bird embroidered kimono she had bought while on a short assignment in Japan. It was such a lovely thing. It had immediately caught her eye. These days the catwalks were full of models wearing underwear in the guise of evening wear. She could go anywhere in this if she had to, only there wasn't anywhere to go. She could ring one of her friends, of course. Sally was always good for a laugh. Beth was a lovely person, hopelessly shy, but good for comfort.

No, something was ailing her. Something she didn't want to give a name.

Chloe found herself a book, a new paperback, and settled down on the sofa. A compelling psychological thriller, she read on the jacket. She had to read the first few pages a couple of times over to make sense of it. Too many characters, she decided. It needed too much of her concentration. As usual when she was very much alone, Chloe's thoughts turned with great melancholy to her mother. In the early days she had pleaded to bring her mother home; to look after her. She could pay for a carer when she was at work. She could work her legs off. Which she had, but the doctors had convinced her her mother was much better off in the nursing home where she could receive around-the-clock professional care.

Chloe let her head fall back against the sofa, the tears coming into her eyes. Now and again she indulged herself in the luxury of grief, when mostly she had to keep over the top of it to survive. But never to talk to her mother again? Never to hear her voice? Never to laugh together, as they had in the halcyon days. They'd had such fun. Never to exchange little presents. They had done that all the time, delighting in surprising one another with small gifts. The tears flowed down Chloe's cheeks, as deadly misery flowed over her.

"Don't give in to despair, Chloe," the unseen voice said. "Don't give up on prayer." Little multicoloured lights like tiny stars shone before Chloe's eyes. Some extraordinary refraction of light through her tears. Chloe sat up abruptly and went to find tissues to dry her eyes. All she ever got from these sessions was a blinding headache.

It was when she was in her bedroom the front doorbell rang. For an instant she stood transfixed then moved to the curtains, peering out.

Gabriel.

Propelled by a force totally out of her control, she ran, throwing open the door and staring up into his increasingly familiar face.

"Chloe, I was worried about you." His dark, brooding gaze moved intensely over her, seeing the unhappiness and the tears that still beaded her long eyelashes, making them stick together.

"Why didn't you ring?" she accused him. "Didn't you want to talk to me?"

"Why?" He gave a jangled laugh. "Chloe, I'm desperate to find the right words."

"You didn't want to share it with me? To say it was a moving little segment?"

"Chloe." He moved his hands a little helplessly.

"I'm glad you came back," she said in a breathless, out-of-control voice. "I want you to stay."

"Dear God!" He took the door from her nerveless hands, shut it behind them, grasping a handful of her hair and pulling her into his arms. "What is it? What's wrong?"

"I'm aching." Her voice was muffled up against his chest. "Sometimes I think I can't take it."

"I'm here now." It was wonderful to enfold her in his arms, to feel her slight beautiful body curving into his. Wonderful to give comfort. Only she started to stir, to move against him. He could feel the heat grow in him, the molten rush of blood through his veins. Was it just an aching child he held? A young person who had virtually lost both her parents in tragic circumstances? It was a woman's body she possessed. He could feel the softness of her breasts crushed against him, the shape of her beneath the too thin covering of her robe. One part of him, the excited male, wanted to tear it off her, but she was totally vulnerable and deep inside him he abhorred violence in any form.

"You're so beautiful," he said. "So very, very beautiful."

She lifted her head, startling him with the expression in her eyes. It couldn't be naked hunger, a hunger to match his own?

Then he was kissing her, not as tenderly as he intended but desperately, passionately, scarcely letting her breathe.

Stop, he thought. Don't frighten her. He wrenched his mouth way, cradling her, kissing her hair and her cheeks and her small, perfect chin. Not alarming her seemed very important, yet no man could be expected to endure such temptation. He forced himself to some kind of calm though his whole body was racked with the most exquisite pain.

"Gabriel, make love to me," she whispered. A plea, no doubt at all, and it tugged at his heart.

"Chloe, I *can't*." How in God's name had he said that?

"I need loving so badly."

Not *his* loving.

"Chloe, I can't do this." He held her firmly by the shoulders, half pressure, half bringing her back to control.

Her lovely face was tragic. "When you said you *wanted* me? You didn't even mean it."

"It's more than my life's worth to hurt you," he replied simply.

"Gabriel, I'm not a doll. I won't break."

"You're not sure of what you're doing, either. You don't love me."

She flushed with something approaching shame, pain, regret.

"Gabriel, I can't. Don't ask me. When I'm stronger, if Mum ever gets better, I'll make a huge effort, I promise. But for now I want you to love me physically. I don't know *why* when you're the most emotional man I've ever met. But you're good and kind. I just never knew it."

"Shut up," he said with dark, burning eyes. "I'm trying to think what I can come up with. You *are* a virgin, aren't you, Chloe?"

She felt horribly near to tears again. "Does it matter?"

"It matters a great deal," he said with a deep sigh.

"I know there aren't an awful lot of virgins my age about, but yes, I am." Chloe spoke with a false flippancy.

"You must have had a tough time fending off your admirers." He, too, tried unsuccessfully to lighten the tension. But it was quite, quite impossible. "Suppose I just start off kissing you?"

Chloe looked around wildly. "This isn't a joke, McGuire."

"No." There was a rather grim smile on his face. "The truth of it is, Chloe, I don't trust myself to make love to you. You've always seemed so incredibly delicate to me. Hell, the very first day I met you you made me feel overpowering. And hideous."

She was shocked. "When all I thought was you were rather tall and imposing with very beautiful dark brown eyes. I know my behaviour was hurtful, Gabriel, and I'm sorry."

"How sorry?" he asked, those dark eyes probing her face.

"Why should you be *sensitive?*" she asked helplessly.

"Only to you. You could fall in love with me, Chloe, if only you let yourself."

"When you're making such a fuss about making love to me?" she retorted.

"That's hardly surprising. I've made love to lots of pretty girls in my time but you're something else again."

"You mean, a virgin?" she said sadly.

"No, it's not that. Not entirely. In other ways you're pretty sophisticated. You're far from shy. You're very good at what you do, but I don't want to alienate you with my rough male desires. I have a feeling it's too new to you."

Chloe's eyes began to blaze. "Is it possible, I suppose it's just possible, you're trying to get square with me?

You want to teach me a lesson? Given the things I've said, it's understandable.''

He felt crammed up to the neck with talk. It wasn't talk he wanted. Neither did she. He lifted her in his arms with great ease, carrying her into the living room and settling her across his knees on the nearest sofa.

"The minute you say *stop,* God help me, I promise I will, even if I can't bear the pain."

"You're really weird, McGuire," she said with a wobbling little laugh.

"How weird?"

"Tara, for instance, wouldn't put up with this. She'd demand to be satisfied."

"I can't pretend she wouldn't," he said dryly.

"Then you have...." She never got any further. He twined his hand through her long thick hair so she couldn't turn her head away, then began kissing her, his mouth very gentle at first, the tip of his tongue curling around hers.

Such a soft beginning yet the build-up of excitement was so extreme it soared.

"Well, Chloe?" He lifted his mouth fractionally when she moaned.

"No... I mean yes." She was seething with need and filled with a wild impatience for him to kiss her again. She feared, really feared, he would stop, so she raised her body, letting her finger trace the deep indentation in his chin.

"Chloe," he muttered, the depth of his desire glittering out of his eyes.

"Let *me* kiss *you.*" She pushed his head back, climbing a little on him so she could cover his mouth.

He couldn't seem to stand it. Groaning softly, almost in anguish. The thought made her kiss him again. There was so much tension in his powerfully built body. She could feel the muscles of his face tightening under her hands.

"What are you trying to do to me, Chloe?" His voice was low and deep.

"I'm thanking you for saving that woman's life." She wanted to curl herself around him like a cat.

He took her light, fine-boned hands in his. "I've had quite enough thanks for that." He knew she wasn't aware of the powerful unconscious seductiveness in her, this vivid, fiercely hurting creature.

"I'm sorry, Gabriel." Chloe didn't meet his eyes.

"What for?" he asked gently.

"It must seem mad to you the way I'm acting."

"You're desperate for comfort, Chloe." He stroked her hair. "I only wish there was something more attached to it."

"My problems aren't your problems, either."

"I want you to share them, Chloe. You've had to live with too high a level of anxiety and grief. There's nothing more in this world I want than to make love to you." Dear God, how much. "Only something—someone—seems to be telling me I'd be taking advantage of you past a certain point."

"So what is this point, Gabriel?" she asked in a strange little voice.

"Well, I'm allowed to kiss you," he said, and began again. From wounded, Chloe became soothed. From over-excited she found absolute delight, as she discovered just how miraculous kissing could be. There was some kind of magic in him that gave her strength. His kisses deepened then lightened at just the right moment so she was able to surface from the tumult of emotions. His touch was tender but elusive on her body, constantly skimming but not stopping as though the consequences would be fatal in some way. Yet every part of her he touched, he changed. The lightest caress penetrated not only her body but her soul. It was a stunning piece of lovemaking, an exercise in healing, so that after a while Chloe began to feel she was flying. There were even wings attached to her shoulderblades. He would *have* to know she couldn't resist him.

I've got to have her, Gabriel thought. I've got to have and hold this beautiful creature. But his iron determination to give her time, to give her space, was rapidly leaving him, vanishing like a morning mist. He longed to cup her small naked breasts. He had never seen anything so pretty in his life as the sight of them through the drooping neckline of her feather-light nightgown. He was holding her high up against his heart but he longed to pick her up and carry her through to her bedroom, make love to her at will, make her his whether she loved him or not. His own emotions were bubbling out of control. He'd had to summon all his strength to keep at this level but he was becoming madly elated, wild for more. God help him, he wasn't made of stone. He bent over Chloe very carefully, her eyes were shut but her face was so radiant it brought a lump to his throat. He hadn't truly recognised his feelings for her until that moment. Oh, he had always known how much he *wanted* her. What he hadn't properly realised was, he loved her with all his heart. She was the object of his greatest hopes and desires.

"Chloe!"

If she opened her eyes and smiled at him with her lovely sweet smile he would carry her away, lay her back on her bed, peel the clothes from her. He could feel the trembling right through his body. The white heat of desire....

It was the rush of wind through the house that did it. The long filmy curtains began to dance and the lustres on the chandeliers began to sway and tinkle, playing a stream of silver music. A little ornament went over but didn't break.

"What was that?" Chloe sat up, literally snapping out of her dream state.

Gabriel laughed wryly. "I told you someone else was calling the shots."

"What do you mean?" Chloe sprang to her feet, going to the French doors where the curtains were billowing and swinging from side to side as though in the grip of a stiff breeze. "That's funny," she said, staring out into the night. "There doesn't seem to be any wind out there. The palm trees are quite still."

Gabriel stood up, righting the piece of Meissen depicting two winged cherubs holding a cradle in the shape of a swan. It was a lovely piece, mercifully quite intact. He nursed it for a moment—no expert—but realising it was valuable. "What about a cup of coffee?" he suggested as though he was only too willing to cooperate with the unexplainable. "Personally I'm thinking of joining a paranormal society."

Chloe, busy clamping the flying curtains, dropped them as she became aware they simply weren't blowing anymore. Like Gabriel, she had the decidedly odd feeling they were in the hands of some irresistible force.

"What a good idea," she agreed a little shakily, struck by the dazzle of the twin chandeliers. She looked towards Gabriel, wondering at his transformation from adversary and sparring partner to lover. The speed with which it had happened took her breath away. She stared at him for quite a while, giving each one of his features her startled attention. She felt as though she had never truly seen him before. She felt exquisitely shy of him, as well, yet deeply *connected*. She felt she would most likely die if he suddenly went away and left her.

"Chloe?" he prompted gently, thinking he would always hold the sight of her at that moment in his heart. He held out his hand to her.

There was a huge difference in the way they were saying each other's names, Chloe thought. Formerly it had seemed like throwaway banter, cheeky, cheerful, sardonic, outright taunting. Now there was a beautiful unusual *significance* that became more apparent each time they spoke one another's name.

"I'll always remember this night, Gabriel," she said, walking towards him as though drawn by a powerful, shining magnet.

Another severe test of my resolution, Gabe thought, his heart thudding, but he didn't want to push his luck. The moment when he could make his beautiful Chloe his own was close by but not yet. Still he allowed his eyes to reveal the depths of his feelings. "Walk me to the door, my little Chloe," he said. "I wish I could stay forever but I think I've been told to go."

CHAPTER SIX

IT WASN'T yet dawn. The nursing home was quiet, yet outside Delia's window a bird sang as though enchanted, the sweetness and purity of its tone causing sparkling tears like dewdrops to spring into her eyes.

Tears? She somehow felt she hadn't wept for a long time.

Delia lay absolutely still in the dark room, trying to concentrate on where she was. She was concentrating with all of her being, aware some extraordinary energy was oscillating around her body, scanning her heart, her muscles, her skin, exploring the control systems of the body that for so long had been under attack. She didn't want to draw a breath unless this mysterious source of energy ceased its operations. Now she felt it was scanning her brain, locking into the complex network of nerve connections that sent down instructions for her body to act on.

Regaining mental clarity, Delia was still only half aware of what was happening to her. But she knew to keep perfectly *still*. Being still was part of it, allowing the mysterious force to continue its work.

Time passed. Perhaps an hour. She didn't know. It was still dark, but she felt totally at peace, able to comprehend that something monumental was happening to her, that her flawed brain and body were communing with a great power. An infinite power. A power for good.

Delia closed her eyes tightly so she could pay closer attention to what was happening inside her. Aware the whole time the night-bird was continuing to pour out its heart in rapture.

Delia's brain was beginning to fire in a normal pattern. Lying there with her eyes closed she realised she wasn't in her own home. She was in some sort of hospital. She wondered where Chloe was. Chloe, her beloved girl. She couldn't trust herself to think of Peter, her husband. Had Peter gone? And Timothy, her baby boy. The child who had died. So cruel, so cruel. She had adored him from the moment they had put him into her arms.

Timothy Michael Cavanagh. Michael after her father. Both of her children had inherited her colouring, the distinctive red-gold hair and bright blue eyes.

Tim!

Very warily, Delia opened her eyes.

"Timmy, what in the world are you doing there?" she cried in the greatest amazement.

Although it was still dark outside, there was a shaft of light in the room. Such a vision! Like being locked inside a lovely great crystal.

Only Tim, who now approached the bed to stand beside her, wasn't eighteen months old. He was, she thought dazedly, more like eight.

"Darling boy, have I been asleep all this time?" she asked, full of wonder.

Tim bent, breathed gently on her, kissed her cheek.

It was perfect. A kiss straight from Heaven filling her heart with light.

Her window was in direct view. A ray of light was beaming through it with the beauty and radiance of distilled moonlight.

When Delia looked again for Tim he wasn't there.

"Timmy?" He couldn't go away. She had missed him so terribly all these years.

Where had he gone? She had heard no door opening. Where had the time gone? The years? She was certain it was Tim. Now it seemed impossible. Delia lifted her hands as her brain gave the message to her motor system to her muscles. There was still the soft glow in the room so she could see her hands clearly. They were very thin but still pretty. Peter had always said she had the prettiest hands in the world.

Peter.

The name struck like a knife in her heart, only when she turned her head Peter and Timothy were standing by the bed, hand in hand, their eyes shining with love for her, their bodies illumined as if starlight was glowing through them. How could she doubt it when they were smiling at her so lovingly? Her weak body was feeling so much stronger. *Stronger.* She felt like she could get up out of bed. Go to them. They held out their hands.

At six o'clock that morning when the nursing home was abustle with the start of a new day, Marge Harding, Delia's most devoted nurse, came into her room, wearing her usual bright smile. No matter Mrs. Cavanagh never responded. She was a lovely lady. It was Marge's earnest prayer one day she might be rid of her tragic disorder, or taken quietly in her sleep. Only Delia wasn't in the bed. To Marge's horror, her patient was lying curled up on the floor. Marge bent over her in alarm. Her first thought was Delia had died, only as she reached for Delia's wrist she found a pulse.

"Mrs. Cavanagh, Mrs. Cavanagh," she cried out in distress. She knew well enough the pulse rate was within normal limits, something very strange was happening here.

Another nurse, Marge's friend, Nora, hurried in, alerted by Marge's loud, anxious cry. She swooped on them and as she did so, Delia opened her blue eyes.

"Good morning, Nurse." Delia smiled as though she hadn't been "away" for a single minute. "Good morning to both of you. I had the most extraordinary dream last night." Unassisted she sat up, staring into their rapt faces. "I dreamed my beloved family came back to me. They *touched* me. My heart, and my soul. They made me strong again for Chloe. My Chloe needs me. I must speak to her."

Both nurses were too stunned to reply, although they were destined to relate the first moments of Mrs. Cavanagh's extraordinary recovery over and over.

There had to be hope to life, Marge thought. Miracles, too.

With God all things are possible.

Chloe received the news within ten minutes of her mother's "awakening," summoned to the nursing home by the matron in charge. Matron sounded thrilled beyond words yet Chloe detected a faint undertone of caution as though this caring professional doubted the evidence of her own eyes.

Chloe who had been sleeping soundly, jumped out of bed as though someone had set fire to it, racing into the bathroom calling aloud, "Oh, my God, Oh, my God!" This was a miracle beyond her imaginings. An answer to her endless prayers. Yet there was an element of terror in it, in case something went wrong. Maybe her mother had only responded for a short time.

"No, I can't think that!" she cried to the bathroom mirror, brushing her teeth and washing her face, splashing water everywhere in her haste.

In her bedroom, she threw herself into the first thing that came to hand, a mulberry T-shirt and jeans. She was so excited she had developed palpitations. Since the day her mother had smiled, over a week before, Chloe hadn't allowed herself to get up her hopes. She had until that day almost been emptied out of hope, but then a candle had flared in her heart, pooling into light and never going out.

She *had* to tell Gabriel. She had to share her consummate joy, Gabriel had become so close to her. He had seen her mother's smile. He had held her mother's hand and told her stories much the same as Chloe did herself. Her tyrannical McGuire was really a man of great strength and kindness.

It was early. Not yet 6:30 but she was certain Gabriel wouldn't mind an early morning call. He was probably used to them. Chloe dialled the number, so filled with bubbling emotion her hand was shaking. The phone rang a few times. Perhaps Gabriel was already up making breakfast. Then the receiver was lifted and a young woman's lilting voice said very brightly, "Hi, can I help you?"

For a minute Chloe was flooded with shock. Wrong number? No, she'd keyed in the correct number.

"Hello," the attractive voice repeated with an upward inflection.

Chloe, the brilliant young interviewer and outgoing TV personality, stood trapped, her heart cleft in two. Mixed in with the shock was a terrible sense of dishonourment, she would have to deal with at some other time. Not now. Now was for her mother.

She was about to hang up when Gabriel came on, sounding very brisk and businesslike.

"Who is this?" he demanded.

Chloe tried unsuccessfully to speak.

Gabriel lived alone. His mother lived in Tasmania. He had no sister. His only female cousin was married and living in the South Island of New Zealand.

For some reason, no doubt guilt, he suddenly queried harshly, "Chloe?"

Chloe dropped the phone like a hot coal. Another time she would have told him what she thought. That there was absolutely no meaning to the strong bond that was being forged between them. That she was violently and deeply shocked. But her mother was waiting for her. Her mother was her entire life. What was a little heartbreak compared to having her mother back again? She'd had plenty of hard knocks in life. She could take another one. But beneath the courage she was *stupefied,* heart and brain swelling with tremendous emotion, gratitude, wonder, alongside pain and confusion. Which showed how deeply Gabriel McGuire had penetrated her life.

The phone rang almost immediately after but Chloe ignored it.

Her hands clenched on the wheel to hide their trembling, she drove to the nursing home, stopping momentarily at reception to check it was all right, then racing down the corridors until she came to her mother's room.

She had to pause to catch her breath.

Her mother was sitting in the armchair Chloe normally sat in, dressed in a pretty pink tracksuit someone must have found her, because it was unfamiliar to Chloe. But the glorious smile her mother gave her wasn't.

Her mother was truly back. She was cured. Chloe had no doubts at all. She flew across the room arms outstretched and her mother stood so they came together, of a height, their arms wrapped around one another, each trying to rain the most kisses on the other's face.

"My darling, my darling!" Delia's voice was so filled with love it rang out like a happy bell.

"You've come back." Chloe stared into her mother's sweet face, saw the light in her eyes, the harmony, the serenity, the fire of intelligence. Her soul.

"For you, my little love." Delia clasped her daughter's hand in an ecstasy of togetherness.

Neither was aware of it but the tears of joy were pouring down their faces, spilling like beads of crystal from the fanned edges of their long eyelashes.

Delia pulled Chloe down into an armchair, took the chair opposite, eager to tell her daughter what she could tell no other. "Tim's been here. And your father," she said. "I saw them as plainly as I'm seeing you."

The shared confidence and the look in her mother's eyes had a galvanising effect on Chloe. For a moment her ears buzzed with a cadenza of sound and her heart momentarily shook. Was her mother's miraculous recovery a *total* reality or in some way had she been altered forever?

"No, don't be frightened, my Chloe," Delia begged, seeing the flash of sorry rue and astonishment in her daughter's face. "It is as I'm telling you. I *saw* them. It was no hallucination, so dry your tears, my darling. There's a lot more in store for both of us. Much happiness. It's been given to me to know."

Listening to her mother, Chloe was both enchanted and frightened. Heaven *had* smiled on them surely? So why did she have such difficulty accepting her mother's dream? For *dream* it had to be. Dream so vivid it lived.

While the two women sat in their closeness, Matron, her face rosy with pride and satisfaction in their patient's victory over a very great trauma, showed in Doctor William Gough, a leading neurologist, and the nursing home's senior resident psychiatrist, Doctor Simon Blakely. The great news had gone out. Now the testing would begin. The medical profession found it difficult to accept miracles.

Chloe remained while all the happy preliminaries went on, then as the questions grew more comprehensive, more searching, both men intimated they would like to speak to Delia alone. Both of them had attended her mother for months now. Both of them highly dedicated, kind men.

Chloe left the room, walking some distance along the corridor and taking a seat in an empty waiting room. One of the young nurses brought tea and biscuits to her and she sipped at the tea gratefully. Her head was awhirl.

She feared what her mother might say under questioning. The doctors might look askance on mystical experiences.

There was a slight commotion at the end of the corridor near reception. Curious, Chloe walked to the door of the waiting room and looked out.

Gabriel, dressed as casually as she was, was hurrying down the passageway, heading right for her. A nurse was coming after him, gasping.

"Sir, sir!"

"It's all right," Chloe called to the same nurse who had admitted her, a nurse she knew well. "I know this person."

She couldn't say, "He's a friend." She didn't know *what* to say.

"Chloe." Gabriel closed on her, so tall, so dark, so powerfully built she reverted to feeling overwhelmed. "I rang the house. You didn't answer. I felt desperately worried, then it occurred to me you might be with your mother." Really, it hadn't just occurred to him the idea had been planted like a seed. "Is she all right?"

Chloe tried to respond calmly. "She's regained consciousness. She's talking. She's told me so much. Some of it with the radiance of a vision. Her doctors are with her now." Probably deciding she's a little crazy, Chloe thought, turning her face away abruptly.

"Was it you who rang me this morning?" Gabriel put his hand beneath her chin and turned her face back to him, shaken by the deep withdrawal he sensed in her.

"No."

"I think it was, Chloe," he insisted, his rugged face a little grim.

"A mistake. For both of us."

"Chloe, what are you talking about?" His fine dark eyes were fixed unwaveringly on hers.

"It's all right, you know, Gabriel," she said evasively.

"Sweetheart. Was it because a woman answered the phone?"

She couldn't risk showing her heart, yet she wanted to fling herself at him so their bodies could do the talking. "Well I thought it a bit peculiar as you're supposed to live alone."

"So you immediately sprang to conclusions. Just like a child."

"I know. I can't be as adult as *you* are about this. Anyway what's it to me if some of your girlfriends sleep over?" She shrugged delicately, amazed she was retaining her poise.

"I can't deny it hasn't happened in the past, Chloe, but it hasn't happened for quite a while. I don't go in for polygamy. It's one woman at a time. The young woman on the phone was my neighbour, Sue Ashton. She and her flatmate, Patrica, had an early morning flight to Sydney. It will connect with a flight to Thailand. They won the trip as a prize but they had to get to Sydney first. I offered to help them carry their luggage down to the car park. I'm always up at that time. Sue and I were coming back up in the lift when you rang. Pat answered the phone, trying to be helpful."

"That's why they've gone to Thailand so they can't confirm it," Chloe said, covering her pain with ice.

"Do you *need* it confirmed? You can't simply believe what I say. You can't trust me?"

"Believing in what men say takes a lot of faith." My God, she thought, on this day of days, I sound awful. Jealousy *was* a sin.

"You mean, believing in *me,* don't you?"

Chloe covered her face with her hands. "I can't think, Gabriel. Too much is happening."

He relented abruptly, putting his own feelings aside. "I can understand that, Chloe. Sit down. The news is wonderful but it must have been quite a shock."

"We did see her smile, Gabriel."

"I think there's some heavenly intervention involved here, Chloe," he said with a gentle wry smile.

She leaned towards him but didn't dare touch him.

"I guess I blundered," she said contritely.

"You did."

"And I apologise." Her breath seemed to be shaking in her throat. She was sure she had lost him. Equally sure she couldn't live with the loss.

"The truth, Chloe, is I have my disappointments, too. I thought our lives had taken a different turn. I thought we were drawing close."

"Of course we were."

"No, not were, *are*. To make a commitment implies trust. You're going to have to decide if you trust me because I desperately want to keep this…friendship, the privilege of knowing you."

In the final analysis, he was the gracious one. "My life is very delicately balanced, Gabriel. It brings its own torments. Hearing a woman's voice at that hour of the morning gave me quite a jolt."

"I expect hearing a man's voice on your phone would do the same for me but I'd have asked to speak to you all the same. Now, let's forget it," he said briskly. Let's ignore the tremendous depth of feeling that has built up between us, he thought. He couldn't deny he was deeply hurt, but he was sorry he had introduced a jarring note. This was Delia's and Chloe's day. A day for joy not for recriminations.

"I'd love to be able to say hello to your mother if I'm able," Gabriel said, his eyes so dark the irises were almost the colour of the pupils.

"I'm sure no one could possibly object." Chloe spoke in a soft, conciliatory tone. "I expect they'll want to run a few tests. Brain scans for sure."

"Your mother is quite coherent?" Gabriel asked. He

realised this was a crucial time; that there might be a relapse.

"She's *herself,* Gabriel. As she used to be, but she is speaking a little strangely."

"How? In what way?" Gabriel said. For the first time he frowned, feeling a lurch of dismay.

"I don't think she wants me to tell another soul."

"I see."

She was acutely conscious she had hurt him.

"No, you *don't* see, Gabriel. I don't want to exclude you. Don't punish me, Gabriel, for a moment's aberration. Total trust doesn't come all that easily. It's just that Mum is talking like she's seen visions."

Gabriel surprised her. "I'm sure she has," he said in a matter-of-fact voice. "Is it a problem, Chloe?"

"Not everyone believes in visions," Chloe said dryly. "Doctors tend to talk more in terms of hallucinatory phenomena. They're a bit negative on things like angels."

"Maybe they haven't got it just right. I know plenty of doctors with strong religious beliefs. Stop worrying now, Chloe. I'm absolutely positive your mother will know how to answer every question that is asked of her."

Which was exactly what happened.

The three of them sat in the summerhouse for an hour after, such a radiance clinging to mother and daughter, Gabriel felt his worldly heart melt. The most beautiful pink rose grew all over the latticed walls of the summerhouse, the essence of its sweet perfume suspended in the golden air. Someone had plucked a single perfect rose and laid it on the table. Delia had gone to it, immediately picked it up, inhaled its scent, as if it had been meant for her, her blue eyes filmed with a quick wash of tears that left them quite brilliant.

She had greeted Gabriel as a welcome stranger, smiling and holding on to his hand. It wasn't until it was time for Chloe and Gabriel to leave that Delia told Gabriel very quietly. "But of course I knew you, Gabriel. You must have been there when my poor old brain let in a chink of light."

It had been decided Delia would be moved to one of the big private hospitals for a few days, taking things quietly, while she underwent a battery of neurological and physical tests, all connected with her total mental, physical and emotional wellbeing.

"I'm going to take you home, Mumma, very soon," Chloe promised. "You'll come through these tests with flying colours."

"I know that, darling," Delia said with sweet composure. "I'll be fine."

When they were in Gabriel's Jaguar about to drive away—Gabriel had decided to have Chloe's car picked up—Delia leaned in the passenger window. "Why don't you say hello to your little brother?"

A *perfect* miracle was too much to hope for. "Because I can't see him, Mumma," Chloe replied, not sure if she was about to sob.

"Turn your head a little to the right, dear. There in the jacaranda. You have to understand Timothy sometimes takes different forms."

"Yes, Mumma." Chloe, seeking to humour her mother, leaned forward and looked out. The jacaranda in full magnificent flower was only a few feet away from the drive. The white gravel was scattered with spent flowers. There was absolutely no one there. No one. Only as Chloe lifted her eyes she saw a pure white dove alight on one of the branches. Its feathers were so *luminous!*

"Look, Gabriel," Chloe said very softly, pointing upwards.

The beautiful dove had disappeared in the twinkling of an eye.

"What's happening?" Chloe asked as they drove away.

"I think we have to accept there's a force at work here, Chloe. A force for the good. It's helping your mother. It's helping you and me. The mother and child we rescued who might have been drowned. I'm not as sceptical as most, I've had my own extreme experience. It changes one's life. I don't reject other people's experiences out of hand. I guess you could say I'm a believer."

"But are the health professionals going to be believers, too?" she asked anxiously. "They might think Mum is still traumatised."

"She's certainly in a state of euphoria," Gabriel had to agree. "She could be hallucinating, Chloe. It could all be an illusion but it's not hurting her or us."

Don't be afraid to trust, Chloe. Don't be afraid to hope.

"Gabriel, did *you* say that?" Chloe asked in a startled voice. Ridiculous question. Gabriel McGuire had long since lost his boy soprano.

"What?" Gabriel shot a glance at Chloe's face. It was full of wonder, but slightly fearful.

"'Don't be afraid to trust, Chloe. Don't be afraid to hope?'" she repeated what she had clearly heard.

"I didn't." He shook his dark head. "But it's very good advice. Take the rest of the day off. It's all been overwhelming. I'll drop you off home, then be on my way."

CHAPTER SEVEN

THE interview with Christopher Freeman was pre-taped on the Tuesday and shown on "Lateline" the following evening. Chloe had declined his dinner invitation as sweetly as she could, but Freeman wasn't about to be put off, claiming it as his due.

"We'll dine at my hotel," he said, naming a very expensive one on the waterfront. The boutique variety. A luxurious home away from home with a very swanky, world-class restaurant.

It shouldn't be any great hardship, Chloe thought.

McGuire thought differently.

"Surely you could have found some excuse to put him off?" His dark, rugged face looked daunting.

Chloe's cheeks tinted slightly. "Look at it this way, Gabriel," Chloe explained patiently. "Something lost, something gained."

"I hope to hell we're not talking about innocence here," he shot back.

"You're being terribly difficult, aren't you?"

"Actually it's like a weight pressing on my heart. I don't like the man, Chloe."

"He came over as absolutely charming on the TV."

"You made him that."

"It's a sort of payback, Gabriel. He did the interview."

"Collected the money."

"He could very well be about to donate it to a shelter for homeless people."

Gabriel shrugged a powerful shoulder. "If he does we'll read about it in the newspapers. No, Chloe,

Freeman, like me, started on the wrong side of the tracks. He knows a great deal more than you and I do about the underbelly of life.''

''You're talking 'underworld'?''

''Not entirely.'' Gabriel looked glum.

''Gabriel, you said it yourself. I'm street smart. We're having dinner in a very posh restaurant in plain public view.''

''The Waverley, where he's staying?'' Gabriel's upward glance was sharp.

''The very same one.''

''What are you wearing?''

Chloe's eyes lit up with amusement, very nearly turquoise like her blouse. ''Gabriel, I wasn't aware you were interested in women's fashions.''

''Not very complimentary,'' he said dryly. ''Of course I'm interested. I always notice what *you* wear.''

''All right, then. I thought black. I have a little short number. Sleeveless, V-neck. A wrap-over dress they call it in the trade. One sensational faux diamond button to fasten it.''

''So you're not going to make it difficult for him?''

''I'll overlook that, McGuire. I'm proud of the way I handle men. At arm's length. He's sending a limo for me. The limo will take me home.''

Gabriel stopped his doodling abruptly. ''Would you like me to ring you? To check you arrive home safely.''

''I don't think that will be necessary. But it's very kind of you,'' she said sweetly.

''Okay, Cavanagh, have your fun. Just don't let that…''

''Steady,'' she warned.

''Get you on a couch.'' His deep vibrant voice had steel in it.

''I think you've forgotten I have a little dynamo packed into this woman's body.''

"I have seen flashes of it." Suddenly he smiled, softening his expression into devastatingly attractive. "Take care, Chloe."

"No *enjoy yourself?*"

"You need *me* with you to do that," he replied provocatively.

Chloe walked to the door, turned back and blew a kiss to him. "I just love you, McGuire."

She looked and sounded radiant as she had done since Delia's miraculous recovery. Gabriel looked after her as she went out of the door and gave a little mocking wave as she passed his windowed wall.

If only it were true.

Chloe looked around the lobby of the Waverley with the greatest of pleasure. The quiet opulence of the decor had enormous appeal for her. Big, beautiful, original oil paintings were placed strategically on the walls. Flower paintings in a marvellous impressionist burst of colour. Chloe had once interviewed the artist in the days when he was up-and-coming. Now he had arrived with an enormous change in his lifestyle. From a flat with no furniture to a lovely old Colonial on the river.

"Miss Cavanagh?" A tall, elegant man came towards her smiling, introducing himself as Dominic Collins, the hotel manager. "Mr. Freeman has asked me to escort you to his suite the moment you arrive."

Suite? Chloe's heart did a back flip. "We're dining in the Victoria Room, is that correct?"

The manager looked surprised. "Mr. Freeman has asked for dinner to be set up in his suite. I've checked everything myself. You won't be disappointed, Miss Cavanagh, I promise you."

There *was* a way out, Chloe knew. Turn around and leave. Only Dominic Collins was gesturing towards the lift that took the most affluent guests to the top floor and one of four luxurious suites.

Christopher Freeman came to the door at the very first tap, his eyes moving over Chloe with extreme admiration.

She was wearing black. He just loved redheads in black. It did marvellous things for her luminous skin. Skin he was dying to stroke. And she looked a little older. More sophisticated than he had yet seen her. He didn't want to be reminded at every turn he was old enough to be her father. Obviously she had worn the little black dress especially to please him.

"Chloe, how perfectly beautiful you look. Do come in. I thought we'd be happier dining in my suite than the main dining room. I like to be out of the public eye at least part of the time. I hope you don't mind." His eyes went momentarily beyond Chloe to the manager. "Many thanks, Collins, for escorting Miss Cavanagh up."

The manager bowed slightly. Not too much. "Everything in order, Mr. Freeman?"

"Everything is splendid!" Freeman enthused. "I'll ring through when we're ready. I think a sip of champagne first."

Chloe had to clear her throat quickly. She moved into the lovely large suite, gazing around with care. The only exit was the balcony and a jolly old drop from there. Gabriel must have made her nervous. Freeman was a man of the world certainly. She didn't suppose he was a rapist.

"Come and sit down, Chloe," he coaxed with his most winning smile. "I want to tell you how pleased I am with our interview. I've had so many phone calls. Everyone seems to think it went over terribly well. I don't always sound so charming, I have to tell you."

"Neither do I." Chloe smiled, as well. She crossed

the large open room, taking her time. The view of the
city at night was breathtaking, all the skyscrapers, the
tall buildings and towers a dazzle of light. The decor in
this particular suite had Art Deco elements, the design
of the armchairs and ottomans, the handsome display
case filled with pieces of genuine Lalique, the magnificent carpet with its broad bands of cream, deep blue and
tan bordered in black. Tiffany lamps stood on the tables
and mid-centre of the room a circular dining table had
been set up, covered in a white linen-and-lace cloth, and
set with the finest crystal, tableware and china. A small
arrangement of white orchids was set in the middle,
flanked by two silver candlesticks with tall slim tapers.
A basket containing a wonderful arrangement of mixed
lilies and orchids with tall spiky reeds, dominated a side-
board, in the Art Deco style.

"I expect your friend, McGuire, is worried at your
dining alone with me?" Freeman said facetiously.

Chloe smiled. "He can't seem to get through his head
you're the perfect gentleman, Christopher."

"Pretty much." He shrugged a dapper shoulder.
"Most of the time. I absolutely *love* you in that dress.
The hairdo, too. You have a marvellous mane of hair,
but the upsweep is very fetching. It shows off your neck
and your lovely bone structure." He poured a small
amount of champagne into two crystal flutes and offered
one to her, taking the other. "Cheers, Chloe. It matters
a great deal to me you decided to come. Now what's
this about your mother? I want to hear all about it."

At first everything went surprisingly well. Splendid food
was wheeled in and out of the suite; food Freeman at-
tacked with gusto and Chloe more sparingly. She was
responsible for keeping her petite figure. But what she
had was delicious; crab in creamy saffron sauce with a
decorative border of golden brown mashed potato, a

truly superb honeyed-ginger duck and a fruit mould served with brandied cream. Just a taste.

"Let's have coffee out on the balcony," Christopher suggested. "It's a beautiful night." Indeed it was. The city spread out in a glitter of light. Above them, the velvet black sky shimmered with a trillion stars. Chloe wondered what Gabriel was doing. Night-time was always so romantic. She would never cease to be amazed at how rapidly their relationship had changed. He had only to kiss her to strip away her defences. Only to kiss her for her to open her eyes and her heart.

"Chloe?" Freeman came up behind her as she leaned against the railing. "What are you thinking about?" he asked seductively, pretty well used to instant success.

How could she say, "Gabriel"? Only Gabriel had ever sent that all-powerful surge of longing through her veins. "Just admiring the view, Christopher," she said lightly. "The city skyline has changed so much of recent years."

"It has indeed," he responded kindly, when his New York penthouse overlooked the incredible drama of Manhattan. "I don't think you realise, Chloe…" He paused to slip his arm around her tiny waist. He wasn't a big man so he preferred his women small and light-limbed. "But I'm falling a little in love with you."

How ghastly. And I did this to myself, Chloe thought.

"I suppose you say that to all the girls, Christopher?" She confronted him with a gentle ironic smile.

Keep cool now. Keep your head. It's important at this point.

Was that the voice again or just her head buzzing?

"Sure I do." He laughed. "Only this time I mean it."

It won't help. "I was hoping you'd tell me about how you brought off the Avalon/Mercer merger," she said in a bright, intensely interested tone.

"You want to talk business on a night like this?" he scoffed.

"Christopher, I wouldn't hurt you for the world. I very much appreciate your giving me an exclusive interview. It was a considerable coup but I'm not into…dalliance, if that's what this is."

For the first time he looked taken aback, staring at her in unfeigned surprise.

"Chloe, you little devil, are you talking marriage?" As a suggestion, it wasn't half bad. She was young. She was beautiful. Highly intelligent, but not the genius he was. She was, in short, a little sweetheart.

Now it was Chloe's turn to be surprised. "The thought never entered my mind."

Christopher smiled at her, taking pleasure in their little game. "Confess you've considered it. I'm what's known as a marvellous catch."

"I'm sure of it, Christopher. *Every time.*"

"You don't like the idea I've been married before?" he asked anxiously.

"I know a lot of people do it. All the time."

Freeman grinned. "Like Liz and me. We're always looking for that perfect partner."

Keep looking, Chloe thought, but spoke sweetly. "I don't want to risk damaging our pleasant acquaintance, Christopher. I've so enjoyed meeting you but I'm not thinking of marriage for a very long time."

She went to turn away, but he reacted quickly, pulling her into his arms. "Maybe you need a little something to convince you," he said, and then laughed impishly.

Chloe fought an irresistible urge to hit him. Wipe the silly smile off his face. Did he *really* think she was playing games?

"Everything will be fine if you'd only relax," he said in a cajoling voice.

"Christopher, please stop." Chloe could feel the heat

of anger in her face but he laughed again, his early warning system hopelessly awry.

Freeman genuinely thought Chloe was teasing him. It had been a very long time, perhaps twenty years since a woman had rejected him. Why, he had read in countless women's magazines he was terribly attractive. His mirror told him the same.

"Well, I don't mind a little tussle if you don't." He smiled.

"I think not!" Chloe felt like a total idiot. "I really should be going." Just to prove the point she wrenched herself out his arms, preparing herself for a very quick getaway. She knew exactly where she had left her evening purse.

Something wasn't right, Freeman thought. He made a grab for her, intending to start all over again, more slowly this time, only he heard the sudden pop of a button, saw its sparkle against the black border of the carpet. It couldn't have been him. He couldn't have torn her dress. Why, that button was barely sewn on.

Three things happened at once.

Freeman, as near to shocked as he could be, endeavoured to pull Chloe back into his arms, anxious to placate her, perhaps scoop her up. She was a featherweight. He should be able to do it, besides he had a little present for her, a diamond tennis bracelet. Chloe, however, turned on him like a tiny fury, pushing him back, and then there was a very loud rap on the door.

"Who the devil is that?" Freeman cursed savagely, hopping about nursing the knee he had struck against the timber frame of the Art Deco armchair. He thought he was fresh out of surprises, but that little girl could very likely beat him, if it ever came to a fight.

"It shouldn't have been like this," Chloe was saying, trying to gather her open wrap dress together while she dashed to the door at high speed.

She threw it open, just knowing it had to be Gabriel.

"I *knew* it was you!" she cried, staring up at his tall, powerful figure. His eyes were glittering like jet, his cleft chin very pronounced.

"How very touching!" He took in her disarray with one furious glance. The milky slope of her small breasts, the low cut of a black lace bra, the bare midriff and glimpses of very small black lacy briefs and the sheerest stockings. He couldn't look any more. Enough that he was here. He'd been almost asleep watching an old Humphrey Bogart movie when a voice had jerked him back to wakefulness.

Chloe needs you.

A great anger overtook him, now flooding him with rage. Just this once Freeman was going to get what he deserved.

He put Chloe aside like a rag doll and started towards Freeman.

With the swiftness of sheer desperation, Christopher got behind the dining table ready to overturn it if he had to. He knew if McGuire landed just one punch on him he would surely lay him out, McGuire looked that bad. Like an avenging angel, eyes blazing, power radiating from his imposing body.

"Gabriel, Gabriel, he didn't do anything," Chloe blurted out, switching from high relief to panic.

"Did he not?" Gabriel slowed for an instant to allow his eyes to whip over her again. She looked so incredibly desirable it was like a blade to his heart.

"Wake up, McGuire." The plea was thick in Freeman's voice. "Let her speak."

Not for the first time Chloe blessed her miraculous turn of speed. She was somehow between them, half pummelling, half pushing Gabriel back. Her beautiful red-gold hair had escaped its roll, flying freely around her white face. "I lost the button on my dress, Gabriel.

That's all. Embarrassing, I know. It couldn't have been sewn on properly.''

''Do you think I'm stupid?'' Gabriel frowned ferociously on her.

''Well, I can tell you it would be pretty stupid to assault me,'' Freeman croaked.

McGuire laughed scornfully. ''Maybe you wouldn't like the story to get out, either.'' He endeavoured to get past Chloe but Chloe checked him with a single hand.

''Stop that, Chloe,'' Gabriel snapped, resigned to her miraculous feats of strength.

''We should talk. Just let me sew the button on.''

''I'm absolutely certain I saw a little sewing kit in a drawer,'' Freeman piped up helpfully. ''I can understand your jumping to the wrong conclusion, McGuire. What I can't understand is why you're here.''

''I had a call,'' Gabriel stated bluntly.

''Oh, really?'' Freeman's voice was flat with disbelief. He pressed his hands down on the white tablecloth, tremendously grateful the table was there between them. ''Why so emotional anyway? Why this excess of aggression? You're not married to Chloe, are you? Not engaged?''

''Looking after her is getting to be a big part of my job,'' Gabriel said, quite literally stuck to the spot.

''It's all a mistake, Gabriel.'' Chloe gave him a sweet little kitten's smile. She pushed needle and cotton through the button and finished off beautifully.

''I'm shocked that you'd think otherwise,'' Freeman added virtuously. ''I have the greatest regard for Chloe.'' He took a deep breath. ''Why I even asked her to become my wife,'' he lied.

A mad, ironic laugh burbled out of McGuire. ''Is this true, Chloe?''

''I think I could have managed it had I pushed.'' Chloe was fixing her hair as fast as she could.

"Christopher, thank you for dinner, but I think we should be on our way."

"If you must," Christopher all but whimpered with relief. Back in New York he had minders but no one seemed to think much of them here.

Only then did Gabriel seem able to move. "I don't think you've got anything left to say to Chloe?" He flashed Freeman a black challenge.

"Only that it's been a great pleasure meeting her. I don't think I can say the same for you, McGuire. As it happens I have to be back in New York by the end of the week."

"Well, bon voyage," Gabriel said.

Outside in the corridor, McGuire got back his strength. He put a hand beneath Chloe's elbow and all but lifted her to the elevator. On the ground floor he trotted her to his car, parked where it shouldn't have been in the circular drive, but no one appeared to have noticed or had any objection. He opened the passenger door, tucked her in, all the while burning with frustration.

Inside the comforting cocoon of the Jaguar, Chloe shook her head from side to side trying to absorb it all. Apparently she had flashes of superhuman strength. It could make a great story, only she didn't want the publicity. Even allowing for this strength, how come she had held Gabriel off so easily? It was odd. Very odd.

Gabriel slid behind the wheel, the expression on his rugged face as puzzled as hers. "Do you want to tell me the *real* story?"

"I thought I did."

"Oh, come off it, Chloe. I don't think I'll ever get over the fact you're so strong."

"For very short bursts of time," she pointed out fairly hastily.

"I don't know." Gabriel shook his head. "Maybe it's

a spell.'' He laughed at himself. ''Maybe it's a kind of hypnosis. What the hell's your secret?''

''I don't know,'' Chloe answered in a quiet, worried voice. ''I'm not on medication. I'm not even convinced it's *me*.''

Gabriel laughed again. ''You're getting a little help on the side.''

''It's the only explanation I can come up with. Anyway you're not telling why *you* drove out into the night. And what was that about a call? I didn't call.''

''What difference does it make?'' He shrugged. ''I arrived. You looked pretty damned upset when I did. I should have flattened that creep.''

''Then we could all get our pictures in the papers. No, Gabriel. I *had* to stop you.''

''God, I must be the biggest chump that ever lived,'' he groaned. ''Stopped by a redhead who doesn't come up to my shoulder. It wasn't very smart of you, either, wearing that dress.''

''I wanted to look a bit more sophisticated.''

''I mean, under the dress you couldn't have worn *less*,'' he said in a shocked tone.

''Oh, go to hell, McGuire.'' Chloe's voice rose a little. ''Why were you *looking* anyway?''

''Chloe, Chloe, the temptation was too great. You looked straight out of a male fantasy. Black lace bra, tiny little briefs, sheer black stockings. I thought nice girls wore petticoats?''

''Well, you're mistaken,'' she said tartly. ''As if it's any of your business. This dress is fully lined. It makes the wearing of a slip unnecessary. Besides, a slip would show when I sat down.''

''But why stir Freeman up?'' Gabriel persisted. ''Wasn't he already stirred up enough?''

''Sure, and *you* aren't?''

"That's because you know all the buttons to push," he said with a remote kind of mocking.

"Don't let's talk any more." Chloe looked out the window. "I don't remember asking you to come rescue me but thanks for the lift home."

Neither said a word from there on in. McGuire insisted on seeing her into the house, circling around, lifting the curtains.

"I don't know what I'd do without you," Chloe taunted. "What would you actually do if someone fell out of the drapes?"

"Me?" His handsome face twisted. "I'd do nothing. I'd leave it all up to you."

"So would you like a cup of coffee?" she relented.

"If you can't think of anything else?"

"What is that supposed to mean?" She swung back, her heart giving a hot little leap. He was wearing a black T-shirt with beige trousers. The tightness of the T-shirt showed off his splendid torso and the strength of his arms. He was wearing his hair longer, too. She supposed she had started it by saying what great hair he had so why did he get it cut so short? The result was a magnificent head of crisp jet-black waves. Mediterranean hair. Mediterranean appearance. Except he was very much taller than the norm. There had to be Greek or Italian in his background.

"So why are you staring at me?" he asked in a defensive voice.

"Well, why not?" she retorted. "You're a very handsome man."

"You mean it's taken you all this time to find out." His black gaze was ironic.

"No, but I used to think very dark powerful-looking men weren't to my taste."

"Tell me something I don't know," he softly jeered. "May I ask the type you *do* admire?"

"You're looking at him," Chloe said simply.

That stopped McGuire.

"That photograph of my father on the piano," she indicated. There were in fact a dozen photographs in silver frames on the closed lid of an ebony grand. Gabriel moved towards the piano and picked up a photograph of a handsome man in his early forties. Fine distinguished features. Ash-blond hair, grey eyes, a very attractive mouth of generous proportions. Chloe's mouth. Otherwise she closely resembled her mother.

"Your father was a patrician," Gabriel said with genuine feeling.

Chloe went to him and stood by his shoulder. "His name was Peter. A better man would be hard to find. I loved him with all my heart. Loved and admired him. He was so clever. Destined for great things. Then he was killed."

"That's the way the cards are dealt, Chloe," Gabriel sighed. As he went to put the photograph down, a standard 8x10, Gabriel fancied he saw another face superimposed on Peter Cavanagh's. His whole body went still as he stared. Red-gold hair, big blue eyes, a sprinkling of freckles across a cute nose. A boy of around eight. A boy who looked very much like Chloe. A second passed and the illusion, more like a trick of the light, disappeared.

"So when are they going to allow your mother to come home?" Gabriel asked as he followed Chloe into the kitchen.

"We're looking at the weekend. Even the doctors are talking a miracle."

"I must think of seeing my mother," Gabriel said. "Life is so short."

"Can't you treat her to a holiday? Her and your aunt?" Chloe asked.

"Of course I can," he said in frustration. "I *want* to.

The difficulty is getting my mum to agree. Don't let's say any more about it, Chloe. It hurts me.''

"I'm so sorry, Gabriel. I just want you to know I understand how you feel.''

"Do you?'' He looked at her with a kind of fierce tenderness.

"I know the pain in you.'' She reached out without thought, tracing the outline of his disturbing mouth. Such a yearning was in her, a yearning that had been smouldering since the first time he had kissed her. All she had to do was touch him for excitement to flare like a spark in dry grass.

"Chloe?'' he said.

"Gabriel,'' she answered him, watching hypnotically while he put his arm around her waist, drew her to him. "If I don't go home now,'' he said very tightly, "I'm taking you to bed.''

Chloe stared into the taut dark face looming over her, the features not sculpted but hewn. She could sense the frustrated passion in him, the protectiveness that plagued him. In a moment she was certain he could put her violently away from him. It couldn't happen. Not when she wanted him so desperately. She had lived with loneliness too long. Now she wanted the shelter of this man's arms around her. His passionate love. Obeying her instincts, Chloe allowed her body to settle into his. It was a rapturous feeling, enormously soothing yet blissfully sensual. Her eyelids closed even as her mouth opened to his wild, heart-shaking kiss.

Could she live up to such passion? This magnificent tide of desire that left her enmeshed in a pleasure beyond all imagining.

"Chloe, I want you so badly.'' His hard-muscled body was shaking with the force of it. Was she simply falling in love with love? Wanting love so desperately to make up for the years of deprivation. He felt like pouring out his soul to her but if he didn't keep something back he knew he could be very badly hurt.

She was so light. Like a drift of apple blossom. The radiance that was in her streamed from her mouth. She was *Woman*. He lifted her, not sure what he was doing, not wanting to shock her. Maybe they were hopelessly unsuited? Mismatched? Beauty and the Beast, he thought wryly even as a kind of anger prowled in him. He knew under his granite exterior he was an emotional being. Why didn't he stick to his usual women, women who knew their way around the world? Gabriel didn't realise he was rocking her, standing in the kitchen rocking her like a baby, her curly head burrowed against his chest.

Any minute now that mystery wind would blow up, blustering headlong through the house, sending curtains flying and ornaments toppling over.

After a few minutes of waiting, Gabriel realised it wasn't going to be one of those nights. There was no one and nothing to break the spell.

"Chloe?" He looked down at her snuggled in his arms.

"Don't go away. Don't leave me," she said in a trembly voice.

"I don't think I can." His tone was half tender, half despairing.

"Do I have to lead you to my bedroom?" She reached up and clasped her arms tightly behind his neck.

He cut her short. "Chloe, this is for *real*. You *do* see that? I want you more than I've ever wanted anything in this world. If I start to make love to you there's no *going back*."

She got a good firm hold on him. "You don't have to treat me as though I'm crushable, Gabriel. I want you, too. I want to identify with you, body and soul. You're not luring me. I'm luring you." She had to make an effort to overcome his scruples. He had to be among the last men in the world to have them.

''So be it!'' Gabriel said while the front door quietly opened and shut as if someone had gone out.

In the quiet of her lovely bedroom, Gabriel undressed her with exquisite delicacy. She was so absolutely the opposite of him, so small, so soft, so full of grace with her fragile bones and the incredibly silky quality of her skin; skin that had the freshness of spring flowers. He had expected to find a certain tenseness, perhaps apprehension, from her altered breathing, but she was responding with a glorious eagerness and ardency, a trust in him as her lover. Her *first* lover. Nothing could change that. He wanted it to be a beautiful, unforgettable experience, one that she would remember every time she closed her eyes.

A late moon had risen, riding high in the sky, flooding the bedroom with a silvery light.

If I live to be a hundred, these moments would always remain with me, Chloe thought. She was totally disarmed by the tenderness of Gabriel's lovemaking. It had such *meaning* to it, yet she felt the force of his sexuality right down to her marrow. His marvellous hands shaped her body, keenly exploring its delicate construction, so different yet so complementary to his own. She had to arch her back in ecstasy. Her bedroom was a temple. The moon was at the window transmitting its luminous beams. Such rapture was pouring into her like a torrent and all from Gabriel's worshipful mouth and hands.

Once he bent his head to question her and she answered shyly, giving him the liberty to bring her tremulous yearning body to full readiness. Every nerve in her body was a string of some wondrous instrument played with harmony and power by a master hand. Innocent that she was, Chloe didn't know she was giving the depth of her own feelings their fullest expression.

At a certain moment she cried out, disturbed by a sudden spear of pain, then the wonderful ripples began, the scarcely-to-be-borne glorious stream of excitement that rolled in, in fuller and fuller waves, gathering her up in its mighty motion until it left her on the sublime shore of Heaven, locked in Gabriel's embrace.

CHAPTER EIGHT

IT WAS a wonderful day when Chloe brought her mother home. Gabriel was going to visit later but he hadn't wanted to intrude on this very special time when Delia returned to the peace and the privacy of her own house.

Surprisingly, though it was very emotional, there was no sense of grief, just the silent acknowledgment that Delia's husband and Chloe's father had gone, never to live with them again. Both women felt very much as though Peter accompanied them in spirit. They stood in the brilliant sunlight admiring the garden which somehow had sprung overnight into full glorious bloom. Great masses of white and blue agapanthus tightly furled the day before, showed magnificent full heads. The white Iceberg rose was flowering more profusely than ever, but what was most extraordinary, the garden beds that flanked the front step and ran the full length of the house to either side, were thick with tall, gleaming white lilies; the lilies her mother loved and Chloe had never seen flower all the time her mother had been in the nursing home.

"Oh, darling, I've missed it all so!" Delia exclaimed, her arm wrapped around her daughter's waist. "You've kept everything so beautifully. How did you do it when you've had to work so hard?"

Chloe was very much at a loss to say how. Although she had kept everything as neat as she possibly could, turning the garden to native low maintenance, here it was looking absolutely spectacular with a massed display of perennials. That at least was explainable, but she was certain she had pulled out all the annuals because she simply didn't have the time to replace them. Yet there they were in wonderful combinations of colour.

"Shall we go into the house, darling." Delia drew a deep breath of satisfaction. "I'd love a cup of tea."

Over the next few days, Chloe was immensely grateful her mother had settled in so well. Delia had several devoted friends who had kept up with her progress through thick and thin, visiting her in the nursing home, bringing little gifts and flowers, no matter their old Delia didn't know them, now their telephone calls came through to Delia herself. They were overjoyed for her, told her repeatedly what a wonderful daughter she had and begged to visit when Delia was properly settled in.

In the old days Delia with her distinguished physician husband had been invited everywhere. They had very many friends. Now Delia knew who were the true friends.

For Chloe it was a hectic time getting her outfit together for the Turf Racing Carnival on the following Saturday. As a judge and TV presenter she had to look good. Money was no option. The channel was paying for her to be outfitted from head to toe. Gabriel had given her carte blanche.

In the end it came down to two designer suits. One, white in a summer-weight wool and silk mix, the jacket, the hem of the short skirt and the collar of the button-fronted little vest piped in black. Her shoes were white with a black trim; a wonderful wide-brimmed black hat that really made a statement. Or, a bright pink suit with a longer split at the front skirt, a beautifully fitting collarless jacket with gold buttons over a rose-printed pink silk camisole and again a lovely big hat adorned with a crush of roses, very chic pink sandals colour-matched to her suit. Both of the outfits looked so good, everyone including the young designer had difficulty making a final choice.

"I'll bring my boss in," Chloe offered, holding out the pink jacket to an assistant. "He has excellent taste and the station *is* paying for it."

But Chloe couldn't get Gabriel that day. He was closeted with two "Big Shot Americans" definitely in the industry, who appeared to have known Gabriel when he was stationed in Washington.

"He was a star in the making," Jennifer, standing by Chloe's desk, told her. "Gabe told me he loved his time in the United States. He claimed he learned everything he knows there."

"He still wanted to come home," Chloe said, knowing a moment of sheer fright.

"You know perfectly well Gabe's on a different level from the rest of us," Jennifer answered scornfully. "He's not running to his full potential."

"I agree." Chloe spoke in a subdued voice that wasn't lost on Jennifer. "I think his stint here is only a stepping stone. A kind of springboard to higher things."

"Personally," said Jennifer with some relish. "I believe he could be off to greener pastures. He's not the boardroom type, is he? He's an out there and at 'em kind of guy. A dynamo. I shouldn't be surprised if we get a shock announcement. He's going back to the States. He even managed to get a bit of an accent when he was there."

"It's a cosmopolitan voice," Chloe said.

"True. He's a big man with a big role to fill, so don't get too fond of him, Cavanagh." Jennifer gave Chloe a taut smile. "I'm really pleased to hear about your mother. You wouldn't want to leave her."

Impossible to leave her, Chloe thought, as Jennifer moved off. Delia was gaining strength and balance every day but Chloe couldn't deny her mother's trauma hadn't changed her. Not a lot of people carried on conversations with the little son they had lost. Now that she thought about it, Chloe realised she wasn't all that "normal" herself, hearing voices as she did from time to time.

Quite a few of her colleagues took time out to enquire about her mother and pass a remark about McGuire's visitors.

"I hope they're not trying to talk him into going back to the States," Bob said, looking quite downcast. "He's the best boss we've ever had. We need a strong guy running things. We might have been a bit anxious when he arrived. It took a while to get used to his style after poor old Clive, now we're all so supportive. Even *you,* Chloe."

Chloe nodded emphatically. She couldn't speak for the lump in her throat.

"I guess he's too damned young, too great-looking, to stay *behind* the camera," Bob mused. "There must have been a lot of excitement in his life working over there. I mean, we're talking about the most dynamic, the most powerful country in the world. Gabe's such a force himself."

"We'll know soon enough, Bob," Chloe cast a glance in the direction of Gabriel's office. "By the way, I've got a couple of outfits picked out for Saturday. You're still going to photograph the whole thing?"

"Chloe, love, could you get anyone better?" Bob asked. "So what *is* the look?"

"Smart, exclusive, definitely the outfit to wear to a big race meeting. One's pink, the other's white."

"You'll look great in both." Bob turned to walk away, then paused. "Poor old Jen has her nose out of joint. She used to do these Fashion on the Field events."

"I know." Chloe gave a heartfelt sigh. "I know she's

hurt but I didn't have anything to do with being asked, Bobby.''

''Well, love, you've got it all over Jen, haven't you? She's a good dresser and she *is* attractive, but not a patch on you. Sponsors want the best every time. I'm just sorry Jen's got so sharp-tongued. She shouldn't call attention to the fact she's so jealous.''

''It can't be easy being passed over.'' Chloe realised in time it would happen to her. ''All I can say is, I don't deliberately stand on other people's toes.''

''Course you don't, love. You're as sweet as you're beautiful. There's Gabe now.'' Bob looked down the corridor. ''He's showing his pals out. Or he could be going out to lunch with them. He's putting his jacket on.''

Lunch it was. Gabriel left the message with Amanda at reception.

It wasn't until late afternoon that Chloe got a call to see Gabriel in his office. She sat down in the chair opposite him waiting for him to speak. Gabriel on the job wasn't the same person who had made love to her, turning her whole life inside out. At the station, Gabriel was *McGuire,* very much her boss, the man who had single-handedly brought BTQ8 to the top of the ratings, a man much admired in the field of television news.

His dark head was downbent as he studied some printed page in front of him, something he found very interesting because his concentration was genuine and intense. He was wearing a blue-striped Oxford shirt with a red silk tie with a small pattern in white and navy, the colours accentuating his dark golden skin and, as he looked up, his very white attractive smile.

''So how's it going, Cavanagh?''

She decided to respond blithely, hiding her concerns. ''I managed to get a few moments with Elle Macpherson before she attended the sneak preview of her new movie, plus a quote from George Clooney. There had to be at least a hundred international television, radio and print journalists all fighting me to get to them. George is gorgeous and the fans were going wild. Everyone loves Elle, but I have to tell you pandemonium broke loose when Clooney arrived. Women were weeping and fainting.''

''You're kidding!''

''No way. You had to see it to believe it. Anyway our shoot will be on the news tonight. Elle was wearing a sensational pink Valentino. No wonder they call her The Body. Which reminds me. We're having difficulty picking which outfit I'll wear on Saturday. Both of them look good. I thought if you had a minute you could make the final choice.''

''Sure.'' He didn't even hesitate. ''I'd be delighted to. Brad Devine has pulled out of the judging at almost the last minute. Some gig he can't get out of so the organisers have asked me to take his place.''

Chloe felt an upthrust of pleasure. ''That's great. You can keep me company.''

''That's the intention.'' He smiled. ''How's Delia?''

''She's settling in better than I ever thought possible. Her old friends are ringing her, wanting to visit. For the moment though she's content to enjoy being home and wandering around the garden.''

''So?'' Gabriel studied her, seeing the wry light in her eyes.

''She's still talking to Tim,'' Chloe confided quietly.

Gabriel's shapely mouth curved. ''These days I'd have to say he's probably around. Don't worry about it, Chloe. If it helps your mother it's doing no harm.''

''No.'' She sounded unconvinced. ''I hope you don't mind if I ask this?''

''Ask away. I don't have to answer,'' Gabriel mocked.

''How did lunch go with your American friends?''

Gabriel speared a hand through his thick jet-black hair, so a crisp wave fell onto his broad forehead. It gave him a very attractive, rakish look. "One of them is the president of a top TV station," he explained. "The other is the New York reporter, Joe Costello. Joe's won all the big awards in his time, made the covers of all the magazines."

"So what did they want with you?" Chloe asked, aware it had come out much too abruptly.

He shrugged. "Believe it or not, Chloe, they want me for their news team. Joe in particular remembers me from my years in Washington."

"When were you going to tell me?" Chloe cursed herself as soon as she said it. Who did she think she was, his wife?

"Chloe, we've been both tied up all afternoon until now," he answered mildly.

"I'm sorry." Chloe was beginning to feel very unsure of herself, close to abandonment.

"There's no need to be sorry, Chloe. I'm telling as few people as possible. Of course that doesn't include you. What I want to know is how do *you* feel?"

"About the possibility of your going back to the States?"

"That, too."

Her lashes veiled her eyes. "I would never deny you your big chance, Gabriel. You deserve every success. A bigger career than you've got now."

He was silent for a moment. "Chloe, this is only the beginning. I always intended to put BTQ8 back on the map before I moved on. I love challenges. I thrive on them."

"You're really a reporter at heart, aren't you? An investigative reporter. Clever and dedicated enough to get to the bottom of the toughest story."

"I enjoyed that part of my life, Chloe," he replied.

"And it's not over." Chloe was feeling more and more alone.

"I need a chance to think. I can see from your expression you might miss me?" Gabriel asked.

"Maybe I would." Chloe sat perfectly straight.

"You couldn't think of coming with me?"

Chloe could feel her heart give a painful lurch. "No, Gabriel. I can't leave my mother. She's been given a second chance at life but I don't think she's truly over all the things that have happened to her. Probably never will be."

"You mean, because she says all these strange things?"

Chloe nodded, lowering her blue eyes. "It's beautiful but it's terrifying, too. I have to be on hand, Gabriel. You can understand that?"

"Of course I can," he answered a little harshly. "I know you'd deny your own chance at happiness to be there for your mother."

"My mother is part of my happiness," she insisted.

"Chloe, I understand perfectly." He never moved his dark eyes from her face. "We've come a long way, haven't we?"

It was impossible to deny. "I'm not sure that I haven't fallen a little in love with you," Chloe said. She had to turn her head away to say it. *A little?* When he'd taken her over in every way. Central to everything was her deep-seated fear of loss. Maybe she would *never* feel safe and secure. She had always known, too, her relationship with Gabriel McGuire carried an element of danger.

"But you still find it impossible to trust me?"

"Explain. In what way?"

"You've been too vulnerable for too long, Chloe," he said. "Falling in love can be shattering. It *is*. Do you really think I haven't formed a considerable emotional attachment to you?''

Chloe felt a surge of anger. ''I know you could break it, Gabriel, if you had to. On your own admission you're highly ambitious.''

''I've already suggested we needn't be parted.''

''Join you? On what basis, live-in lovers? Pay attention. I can't leave Mum on her own. For all the miracle of her recovery, I still wake up every morning wondering how long it's going to last.''

''You have to have *faith,* Chloe,'' he told her, his expression intense.

''I don't have *that* kind of faith, Gabriel. I know all the terrible things that can happen. Anyway, we haven't got to the point of making any deep commitment to one another.''

His own temper flashed. ''*Haven't* we?''

''Well, *I* haven't.'' Chloe lifted her chin, her eyes huge and vividly blue.

''I'm sorry, Chloe.'' He shook his head. ''I know you too well. You let me love you and it *was* love. Not sex.''

''It was fantastic.'' Even that was an inadequate word.

''And totally meaningful. I haven't made any decision, Chloe. I'm not threatening our relationship. I'm only letting you know what's happening in my life. I know you'll keep it private.''

Chloe, the redhead, shot up out of her chair. ''That was completely unnecessary, McGuire,'' she flared.

His look was wry. ''Well, I know it was. Actually I was just…''

''Filling in time?''

''Calm yourself, Chloe,'' he said acidly. ''You're going to have to do some mellowing before you get yourself a husband.''

''Well, one thing's certain, I couldn't stay married long to *you.*''

"I haven't asked you, for a start." There was an answering glint in his coal black eyes.

"What would be the point if you're heading straight for the States?" She spoke quite loudly, causing him to wince.

"Keep your voice down, Cavanagh. Is that all right with you?"

"I'm sorry." She apologised immediately.

"Why don't we have something to eat later?" he suggested in a more amiable tone. "Or we could take it home to be with Delia."

"Thanks for the kind offer but I've got all kinds of things to do," she snapped.

"Like what?"

Chloe flushed. "I'm going to make a great big casserole. A hearty Italian stew, Hunter's style. Something that will keep us going for a week."

He laughed. "I could help you slice the onions."

"I'm afraid, no. I'm someone who believes in only one cook to a kitchen. Is there anything else or may I go?"

Gabriel placed his hands in a steeple beneath his cleft chin, studying her. "Cavanagh, you're taking me right back to the early days when you were such an uppity little thing."

She raised her delicate winged brows. "Maybe we'll start to feel bad about one another again."

"Not *me*, Cavanagh," he confirmed bluntly. "You, I like. Now—" Gabriel consulted his desk calendar "—I can fit you in tomorrow about ten-twenty, ten-thirty."

"Fit me in for what?" she asked in haughty puzzlement.

"Let's start all over again. Aren't *you* the one who asked *me* to help you with your outfit?"

"Oh!" Chloe stood there looking angry and injured

and quite, quite beautiful. "You don't really have to bother."

"Do you mind?" he said with a laconic inflection. "The station is paying for this. I do have to bother. Ten-twenty in this office, and can you take this pile of blurb down to Ray Hope and tell him to put it through the shredder and start again."

"You don't have to be nasty," Chloe said, taking charge of Ray's news story.

"I can't see being kind is going to do it. I'm the boss, Cavanagh. It might pay you to remember it."

Gabriel took less than a minute the next day to make the final decision on her outfit. "The white and black," he said confidently. "I'm just crazy about that hat."

"So what's wrong with the pink?" Chloe asked.

"It's lovely but it's more like a garden party. The other is pure race glamour. Trust me on this one, Cavanagh."

When they arrived at the course the following Saturday, Chloe was delighted she had.

"You look perfect. Absolutely perfect," the Chairman of the Turf Club told her enthusiastically, a connoisseur of thoroughbreds. "You're going to have the devil of a day trying to pick winners, dear. I haven't seen so many good-looking, well-dressed contestants in a long while. Best of luck."

Chloe had already caught a glimpse of Tara Williams, resplendent in a fire-engine-red suit, the skirt of which was only one step away from a micromini, with a huge red-banded black hat adorned with a big red-and-black ribbon-bow centre front. Chloe as yet didn't know if Tara was going to be one of the contestants. Anything to get herself on TV, Chloe thought. There were plenty of white outfits, more of pink. Pink in all shades seemed to be the in-colour. A stunning lime green number with a lovely white hat bordered in the same green. A truly terrible polka dot outfit that seemed to faze the eye, and a very chic orange ensemble spoiled by the fact the white and orange hat was worn too far back on the head.

Gabriel was the big surprise, resplendent in tails and a pearl grey topper, with a beautiful blue-and-silver tie and a white carnation in his buttonhole.

"You're continually surprising me, Gabriel," Chloe said, staring up at him in open-mouthed admiration. He looked wonderful, the most dashing man there.

"You little snob." His brilliant black eyes gleamed.

"I don't mean to be, truly. That's awful to say that."

"You're exceptionally snobbish," he said, determined to take a rise out of her. "But you look just beautiful. I really know how to pick an outfit."

"At least let me share in it. Where's Bob?"

"He's circulating. That's his job. You can float around looking exquisite while you're waiting to chat up all the socialities pretending not to notice the camera." Gabriel, from his vantage point of six-three looked over the head of the large crowd. "Was that Tara I saw minus her skirt?"

Chloe laughed then. "It's terribly short, isn't it? Too short isn't elegant."

"It's not bad when you've got racehorse legs."

"Are you saying my legs are too short?" Chloe clutched at her large hat as the breeze threatened to get under it.

"Let's put it this way. They're not too short for your body."

"I get the feeling you're teasing."

"How well you know me."

In the end it was a lot of fun, the large crowd cheering and clapping when the winner was announced, Miss Katy Nugent, in the lime green outfit. Tara, who had been a contestant, stalked up to Chloe, her lips tightly pursed. How she had missed out on first prize when her outfit was far and away the most stunning and her father owned the station, was beyond her. Her whole attitude let everyone in the vicinity know she'd been wronged.

"I might have known, seeing you're involved," she hissed at Chloe.

"All fair and square, Tara?" Chloe shook her head. "You look striking, but Katy's outfit was the big crowd pleaser. Three out of the four judges picked it."

"I bet Gabe didn't." Tara tossed her head.

"I'd rather not say. That would spoil things. I'm sorry you're disappointed."

"I am pretty angry," Tara agreed grumpily. "Personally I thought the green outfit looked like she made it herself."

Chloe just smiled back, further enraging Tara. "Of course you must be feeling pretty damned disappointed yourself," she said, pulling a face.

"Actually, I feel on top of the world," Chloe countered, knowing something distasteful was coming.

"Well, yes, about your mother. That's great news," Tara had the grace to say, "but you must have heard Gabe looks like leaving us. Ah, that wiped the smile off your face."

Chloe's small frame stiffened. "How did you know?"

Tara didn't know. She had overheard her father speculating with someone on the phone. It was no secret Gabe had been visited by American media people. "Gabe told me, of course," Tara lied. "I guess he owed me that. After all, we were lovers at one time." She stared at Chloe through narrowed lids.

"That's news to me, Tara." She had to learn to *trust* some time.

"There are lots of things about Gabe you don't know." Tara's gaze slid across Chloe's face with a mixture of pity and triumph. "Bye, bye, now don't let me spoil your day."

Well she did try.

Chloe didn't confront Gabriel when he returned to her side. He was in excellent spirits, handing her a list he'd jotted down.

"What's this?" she asked as they walked up the steps to the stand.

"I'm no punter, but today I'm backing any horse whose name has even a remote connection with *Angel*. I've just won a thousand dollars on a rank outsider, Mysterious." He laughed.

"That's wonderful!" Chloe exclaimed, sitting down and beginning to read. "Hail to All, Little Angel, Proud Guardian and Heavenly Prince." She turned to him, trying hard to thrust every doubt from her mind. "We have to bet on something, I suppose. The only race I follow is the Melbourne Cup."

"Along with everyone else in the country. So what's it to be? I've got five minutes to put our money on Hail to All."

Every last horse on Gabriel's list ran a place.

Chloe was in the paddock watching the runners for the last race parading, when the beautiful bright chestnut gelding, Solar Gold, race ready and in peak condition, was suddenly spooked by a flying object. It turned out to be a woman's hat. The breeze was coming in stiff gusts now, dislodging the offending hat that all but landed at the gelding's feet. All might have been well, the young woman strapper who had been leading the horse was well experienced, but she just as suddenly sneezed violently from the flying dust, lost control of the reins and fell backwards. The magnificent animal, turned out to perfection and hyped up to race, reared. Power ripped through its muscles from shoulder to haunch. The strapper managed to roll away but before anyone could sort themselves out, Chloe who had belonged to a pony club for most of her childhood, was propelled into action. Instead of standing well back as everyone else around the ring was doing, she slipped through the opening, holding up her arms grasping for the reins, all the while talking to Solar Gold in a soothing secret language made up of little bitty clicks, a snatch of song, and some very odd vowels and consonants that all ran together.

As Bob, who managed to capture the whole thing, later said, it was like "some mystical language" only the horse could appreciate. From a spooked animal, Solar Gold became wonderfully self-possessed. All need to blow off steam was quite forgotten.

"Say, that was fantastic!" the girl strapper told Chloe, sounding amazed and embarrassed. She moved to resume Solar Gold's reins. "You obviously know a lot about horses."

Chloe permitted herself a smile though she was feeling a little strange. "I was the proud owner of a pony by the time I was six," she confessed.

"Go on." The strapper started to say something but changed her mind. It would take a lifetime to learn the line of patter Chloe Cavanagh had used. Whatever it *meant*.

"I'm going to make sure this makes the papers tomorrow," Bob crowed. "That's if I managed to get the shot at all." He grinned, harking back to the koala rally.

Gabriel, when he heard, all but ran to the ring. A colleague from one of the other stations had filled him in.

"I've never seen anything like it in my life, Gabe," his friend said with a silly grin. "Chloe hasn't changed much, has she? Always in the thick of it. Personally, I'd be a bit worried about her if I were you. She might want to take over your job. Next Sir Llew."

Gabriel, full of personal anxiety, couldn't agree more. Chloe's guardian angel was as impetuous as she was.

When Chloe saw Gabriel rushing towards her, a sweet grateful smile appeared on her face. "Oh, Gabriel," she said, and let him take her protectively in his arms in a wonderful hug.

"Chloe." His breath rasped. "I've decided it's time to take you home. I'm not even willing to turn my back on you for a moment."

"I'm fine, fine. Don't worry," Chloe murmured, and then came as close as she had ever done in her life to fainting.

The doctor made her lie quietly for a time. "Does she often do this sort of thing?" he asked Gabe.

"Only in emergencies," Chloe piped up, lifting her head from the small pillow.

"I told you to be quiet, young lady," Doctor Fraser admonished her. "I'm very interested to find out what exactly happened. Even run a few tests. Everything seems perfectly normal but she's acting as though she's been pushed hard. Too much excitement, I suppose. It has that effect."

"There's nothing wrong with me," Chloe said, and certainly looked it. "Gabriel insisted we stop to see you."

"I'm sure Gabe did the right thing," Doctor Fraser, who was Gabriel's own doctor, replied. "On your own admission, you almost fainted."

"Well, I feel terrific now," Chloe said, and she did. The peculiar languidness had left her, the tingly sensation in her body like an overload of electricity. She felt full of vitality. Her eyes were sapphire bright and there was a lovely natural pink in her cheeks.

"I'll keep a sharp watch on her," Gabriel promised.

"All right. You're welcome to see me again," Doctor

Fraser said as he walked them to the door. "Gabe, it must be time for your yearly check-up?"

"I'll be in touch," Gabe promised, desperate to get Chloe alone.

"Why don't we call in at my place first?" he suggested rather tautly as they pulled away from the surgery. The incident at the racecourse had brought home to him how essential Chloe was to his very existence. It was all part of the ecstasy and the terror of loving. "I want to talk to you and we're almost there."

Once in his apartment, Gabriel shut the door quickly, leading Chloe through to the living room. It emanated the sort of dynamic male elegance he had himself, Chloe thought. It was a very masculine apartment, the furnishings and the artworks making strong statements. Reflecting Gabriel's personality. She watched him strip off the formal jacket he had worn with so much dash, loosening his silk tie. Chloe took her own jacket off and hung it neatly over the back of a chair, adjusting the collar of her sleeveless vest. Then she turned and made herself as cosy as she could in the corner of one of the oversized burgundy leather sofas. She could sense Gabriel was off balance. She herself was unnerved by the tense current that glittered between them.

"What am I going to do about you?" Gabriel demanded without preamble.

"What do you *want* to do about me?" Her sweet smile flashed then faltered at something in his expression. Something that terrified her. A kind of wrenching pain. "You don't want to hurt me, Gabriel. Is that it? You can't bring yourself to tell me you're going away?"

"Lord, Chloe, you've decided that, have you?" He groaned, then sat down opposite her, enchanted by how she looked tucked into his large, clubby chair.

"Well, you did tell Tara." Chloe hadn't meant to say

that at all, only he was looking so handsome and arrogant.

"Did I, by Jove!" Gabriel's rugged face tautened, making him look very formidable.

Chloe bit her lip like a child. She picked up a rich brocade cushion and hugged it like it was protection. "All right, you didn't. I knew that in my bones. But no one is asking you to give up a wonderful opportunity, Gabriel, least of all me."

"Least of all you," he scoffed, throwing up his hands. "Don't talk like a little fool, Chloe. You're very important to me. You have needs that have to be met. Demands you can make on me. Let it out."

It would be wonderful if she could but, incredibly, she was fighting to keep it in.

All too aware of it, Gabriel abruptly stood up, moved across to her and took the cushion out of her arms. "What's this, another defence?" He let his fingers slide down her satiny cheek, feeling the consuming fire start up inside him. "You're hurting, aren't you, and you don't know what to do about it?"

Her whole body was responding to his touch. Little pulses flicking here, flicking there, drumming in time to the high beat of her heart.

"Try and understand me, Gabriel. I haven't had a good life."

"That's all changed, Chloe." He stroked her hair away from her face.

"Has it?" She let out a long, shuddering sigh. "Are you going?" she demanded.

"Its pretty clear you wouldn't come with me," he said.

"No, my mother needs care, Gabriel, you see."

"Chloe, your mother isn't sick anymore. I feel that very strongly. You've been there for her through thick and thin. Now she's home, gaining in strength every day.

I'm here for you in any capacity—friend, supporter, provider, protector, anything you want—but you have to take responsibility for your feelings.''

"What, pack my bags and come with you to New York?'' Chloe flared.

"I don't believe I said I was going anywhere,'' he drawled. "On the other hand, I can see you're quite willing to let me go.''

She hung her head, her breath strangely in her throat. "Gabriel, don't do this to me. If you went away, I'd be lonely all my life.''

"How lonely?'' he asked bluntly, as if doubting her declaration.

"I couldn't change back to what I was. You've been my teacher. You've filled my life even when I didn't want to give my heart away, when I didn't want to place my trust in you.''

"So what's changed?'' he asked laconically. "Oh, hell.'' He pulled her across his knees. "Why am I putting you through this? I guess wild horses wouldn't drag it out of you.''

For a heart-stopping moment she stared into his eyes. "You want me to tell you I love you, or what?''

"Don't you think it might be a good idea?'' he suggested dryly.

"All right, I love you, totally, completely,'' she said fiercely. "Does that satisfy you?''

"No.'' He shook his dark head. "Would you marry me tomorrow? No, don't take time off to think up a good excuse. Just answer from the heart.''

"Gabriel.'' She covered her face in shock, confusion and a frantic joy. "If you don't stop teasing you'll drive me really crazy.''

"That's the intention, now answer.''

She lay back in his arms, her dilemma in her eyes.

"I'd do anything. I adore you. But I can't hurt my mother."

He bent, kissing her hard. "As if I'd want you to."

"But I can't bind you to me in this way, Gabriel," she agonised. "I love you. I want the best of everything for you."

"Why would you think I wouldn't have the best of everything in *you?*" he responded. "One of the things that makes you so beautiful is your sense of loyalty. Your sense of family. I never had a family, Chloe. It was the tragedy of *my* life. *I'm certain* we can make a family together. However ambitious I might be, I can satisfy my goals right here."

"You do mean that?" she begged. "You're not just saying it because it's what I want to hear?"

"Chloe, I've already told my American friends I'm home to stay," he said easily. "*Home.* Doesn't that say it all? The most important thing in the world to me is how much I love you and how much you love me back. Power and possessions don't define what I want from life. I want to be successful, sure, but more than anything I want a wife I adore. I want children to love and enjoy."

"How many?" she tried to joke but it didn't quite come off. "It does have *something* to do with me."

"Two or three, okay?" He dropped another kiss on her mouth. "I want to love and protect them until they're ready to take on the world. Is it too much to want, Chloe?"

"It's the same thing I want," she said, an answering profound feeling in her eyes.

"So you're going to marry me, after all?"

"Oh, yes, darling." Her arms lifted, tightening around his neck. "I can't think of anything more wonderful."

"You're not going to make me wait long?" His black eyes burned with infinite desire.

"No, darling."

Chloe really didn't know why but as she slipped down into Gabriel's passionate embrace, she felt like wings were closing over their heads. Wings that enfolded them in a shining cocoon.

Why not? Love is a very special kind of magic.

HEAVEN

Mr. Bliss chose that same day to voice his concerns about young Titus with Lucas. Chloe's birth guardian angel was well and truly on the mend and looking much more like his ancient splendid self.

"It's not that Titus hasn't brought great joy into Chloe's life," Mr. Bliss said, "which is highly commendable. But like all youngsters he's impulsive. For instance, just today he directed far too much energy into Chloe's body. Not intentionally, of course. Simply doesn't know the strength of his own powers."

"Exactly, Mr. Bliss," Lucas sighed. "As they say, one can't put an old head on young shoulders."

"You do realise he was Chloe's little brother in the other life?"

"Well, I never!" Lucas flapped his wings in astonishment, then tucked them neatly back again. "Surely this sort of thing doesn't happen often?"

"Rarely, very rarely." Mr. Bliss made one of his beautiful prayful gestures. "But it has all turned out terribly well. As I say, Titus has been of great service to his mother and Chloe. In fact he's been working overtime. I'm thinking very seriously of awarding him his three-quarter wings."

Lucas responded with a smile full of loving kindness.

"He'll be thrilled. What it is to be so young and vigorous!"

Mr. Bliss laughed and nodded. "You, of course, will be returning to your given charge, Lucas." His brilliant dark eyes crinkled. "We're all so pleased you're back to your old self and the wing is functioning perfectly. It will be easier for you, too, now that Chloe has found her nice Gabriel."

"Even we angels can do with a little bit of help," Lucas said with great good cheer. "And Titus, have you anything in mind for him, Mr. Bliss?"

"Exactly the same question I've been asking myself." Mr. Bliss drew his fingertips together. "I see Titus as a guiding star," he said very pensively. "Really, I should be thinking of placing him with a baby."

EPILOGUE

CHLOE was always to remember her son's birth as a time of white light. The blazing white lights of the city, the lights from the other cars as Gabriel raced her to the hospital—she was early by two weeks. There were more lights at the hospital entrance, at reception, the brightest dazzle in the delivery room where she was taken, great radiant orbs. She remembered the tremendous sense of urgency. The hospital staff bustling around her. Gabriel's dark golden face almost as pale as hers with anxiety. She remembered his warm strong hand as it held on to hers for dear life. Finally a nursing sister had to prise them apart.

She remembered a nurses's voice telling her very earnestly to breathe deeply.

"That's it, dear, breathe in, hold it, relax."

How *could* she when the pain kept coming for her? Until finally, miraculously, she needed no one to tell her what to do.

Her son wanted to be born. She heard his first triumphant cry.

Here I am!

That was when the heavens opened, pouring forth their glory.

When they put him in her arms she thought her heart couldn't hold all the joy that was in her. Her marriage to Gabriel had brought such happiness. She had thought her cup had spilleth over. Now this. This adorable little bundle, perfect in every respect from the soft silky down on his head—dark like Gabriel's—to his wonderful little toes, with their tiny perfect pearl nails.

She kissed him. *Kissed* him, exulting in his entrancing baby's smell.

My son!

The sister who was with her bent over the bed beaming her delight at a safe, beautiful delivery. "You've got a little angel there, Mrs. McGuire, and no mistake!"

"Haven't I." She smiled radiantly, her face Madonna-like in its love and pride.

The following day the family returned; Gabriel, a new father, walking on air, Delia with a wonderful bloom on her, thrilled at being a grandmother, Janet, Gabriel's mother who had flown to the mainland especially for the birth and was staying with Delia with whom she had formed an instant rapport, all of them transported with joy and a great sense of hope for the future.

Gabriel took his baby son in his strong arms, an endearing sight, he being such a big man and the baby so tiny. "He's absolutely perfect, isn't he?" he breathed with reverence. "Our own miracle of love."

"He's that!" Both grandmothers came to stand at Gabriel's shoulder, their faces soft and beautiful with shared joy. "So what are you going to call him, my darlings?" Delia asked, entranced her little grandchild was actually clinging to her finger.

Gabriel's brilliant eyes rested lovingly on his wife, his treasure. "I thought maybe Michael?" He waited for her all-important approval, but his beloved Chloe was staring at some point over his shoulder. Her lovely face was filled with such wonderment she might have discovered the secret of the universe; her cheeks filled with the soft pink of a blossoming camellia as if she had absorbed the beauty of the flower. How he loved her. His wife, now the mother of this wonderful tiny bundle.

Behind the family tableau Chloe continued to focus on the shimmering image that was slowly beginning to materialise.

An angel! Michael's guardian angel. The knowledge penetrated like a shaft of heavenly light. The angel was bending close, looking down on the baby with a smile of such tender radiance Chloe felt her heart melt.

"Timmy?" she whispered, as full knowledge descended on her. "Is it really you?" It had to be. She had never seen anyone look so much like herself. Hair, eyes, features, but she could never attain such…such…*glory!*

The angel hung suspended a moment more, poised over the baby, such a small angel to have such *splendid* wings! They enclosed the family group.

So attuned to his wife, Gabriel moved back to the bedside, certain something important was happening to her.

"Darling?" he questioned, willing her back to him.

Smilingly, she reached up to take his hand, on her face an expression of such joy she was shining. "Michael! Of course. I love it already. After all, we do have a tradition of angels in the family."

A WEDDING WORTH WAITING FOR

by

Jessica Steele

CHAPTER ONE

THAT Tuesday started just like any other. Karrie was showered dressed and ready for work. She had debated whether or not to tie her blonde, gold-streaked shoulder-length hair back in some kind of knot, but had decided against it, and had brushed it into its normal straight, but just curving under at the ends style. Just because Darren Jackson had yesterday warmly remarked 'I'd love to walk barefoot through your delicately pale, ripening corn-coloured tresses' there was no need to get paranoid.

'Poetical—but I'm still not going out with you' she'd replied with a laugh. Darren, who worked in the same office, had been trying to date her ever since she'd started work at Irving and Small three weeks ago.

Karrie checked her appearance in her full-length bedroom mirror and felt she looked neat and ready for work in her smart burnt orange two-piece. She cast a glance at her—what were they?—'delicately pale ripening corn-coloured tresses', and, with a hint of a smile on her sweetly curving mouth at Darren's over the top description, she left her room and went downstairs.

Any hint of a smile, however, abruptly departed as she entered the breakfast room. The chill in the air was almost tangible—her parents weren't speaking. To each other, that was. What else was new? Karrie had grown up in a household where warring glances and icy silences alternating with storming rows were the norm.

'Good morning!' she offered generally, brightly, striving hard not to take sides.

Bernard Dalton, her father, ignored her—he still hadn't forgiven her for leaving his firm and for daring to go and

5

take a job elsewhere. Her mother did not reply to her greeting, but straight away launched into a bitter tirade. 'Your father was kind enough to telephone me at seven o'clock last night to say he was *too busy* to make the theatre, as *promised!*'

'Oh, dear,' Karrie murmured sympathetically. 'Er— perhaps you'll be able to go—um—another time.'

'The play finishes this week. Though I suppose I should be grateful that he rang me personally. The last time he got Yvonne to ring.'

Yvonne Redding was Bernard Dalton's hard-worked secretary. 'Um…' Karrie was still striving for something diplomatic with which to reply when her father, with never a moment to spare, finished his breakfast and, without a word, went from the room. Karrie had spotted his briefcase in the hall. It would take him but an instant to collect it on his way out.

'Furniture. Just part of the furniture, that's all we are,' her mother complained in the silence that followed the reverberating sound of the front door being slammed shut after him.

'Er—Jan was looking well.' Karrie sought to change the subject. Her cousin Jan was newly out of the hospital after an operation to remove her appendix, and, because Jan's flat was in an opposite direction from her own home, Karrie had driven straight from work last night to see her. Hence, she had not been around when her father had phoned. She and Jan were the best of friends, and it had been going on for ten when Karrie had eventually returned home. She had thought her parents were at the theatre, but her workaholic father had not been in from work yet and her mother—clearly not at her happiest— had gone to bed early.

Mrs Dalton it seemed, was too embittered that morning by this latest lack of consideration on the part of her husband to be very much interested in her niece's progress.

And Karrie eventually left her home to go to her office reflecting that never, ever was she going to marry a man of the workaholic variety.

The further she drove away from her home, however, the more her more natural sunny humour began to reassert itself. Chance would be a fine thing! Well, there was Travis Watson, of course—he was always asking her to marry him. But he knew that marry him she never would. It was true that she hadn't reached twenty-two without a few possible candidates moving into her orbit—but she had always moved out of theirs. It was a fact too, though, that since she intended to be two hundred per cent sure— and with her parents' example before her, why wouldn't she?—that the man she said yes to was going to have to be extremely special in more ways than one.

She drew up in the car park that belonged to the giant firm of Irving and Small with a hint of a smile back on her lips, glad to be part of the purchase and supply team. With new contracts being secured all the time, it meant her section was often at full stretch, but she enjoyed working there far more than she had ever enjoyed working for her father.

She had previously worked for her father at Dalton Manufacturing for a pittance. And, though money had never been a problem, she had started to resent that he expected her to put in similar hours to himself, something that had caused a great deal of friction at home—her mother loudly complaining that she was losing her daughter to the firm too. Which had led Karrie to suggest to her father that she wouldn't mind leaving work at six most evenings, only to be told by him to go and find another job elsewhere if she didn't like it.

So she had, and some stubbornness she hadn't known she possessed had refused to make her budge and retract her resignation when her father had exploded in fury at her nerve.

'You'd give up your chance to ultimately have a seat on the board!' he'd ranted.

Ultimately! She wasn't falling for that carrot being dangled in front of her. He'd promised her her own department in two years if she joined him from college and learned the business. She'd been there four years and it hadn't happened yet.

Leaving her car, she headed for Irving and Small's main building. 'Karrie!' She turned—where had Darren Jackson sprung from?

'Morning, Darren,' she smiled; she didn't want to go out with him, but she liked him.

'I still can't believe your flaxen hair is natural!'

Flaxen! Yesterday, according to him, it had been 'delicately pale ripening corn'. Her hair colour was natural, and had never seen a chemical dye, but she had no intention of discussing that with him.

'Looks like being a nice day,' she commented pleasantly as they entered the building.

'Every day since you joined the firm has been nice,' he replied.

She still wasn't going out with him. 'Concentrate on your computer,' she tossed at him, and as they entered the open-plan office they shared with a dozen or so others she parted from him and went to her own desk.

The work was interesting but not so complicated that it did not leave space for private thought, and in one such moment Karrie fell to thinking of her father, who loved his work more than his home. Countless were the meals that were cooked for him and which, because he didn't come home, were thrown away. And, thinking back to last night, countless were the times he and her mother had arranged to go out somewhere, only for his secretary to ring and say he would be delayed. Countless were the times Karrie had seen the excited light go from her mother's eyes.

Karrie knew that her mother had at one time adored her father. She probably still did—or he wouldn't have the power to hurt her. But, while it upset Karrie when she thought of her mother's hurt and unhappiness, she knew better now than to try to interfere. She had once tried to talk to her father about his neglect of her mother, and, aside from earning his deep displeasure, had done her mother no favours either when her husband had treated her even more badly than before, the end result being that her mother had become ever more bitter.

'Have you got...?' Celia, a colleague from across the aisle, interrupted Karrie just as she was mentally writing in indelible ink that, if she knew nothing else, there was no way *she* was going to have the kind of marriage her parents endured.

Breaking away from what she was doing, she felt no end of pleasure that, having worked in purchase and supply for so short a time, she was immediately able to answer Celia's in-depth query.

It was around mid-morning, when Karrie had just decided to visit the coffee machine—that Tuesday having been marked down as the same as any other, with nothing in any way noteworthy to change it—when something quite out of the ordinary did happen. She stood up, stepped into the aisle—and bumped into a tall, good-looking man who was making his way to a far end door that led to where the higher executives worked.

Something in the region of her heart actually lurched. She opened her mouth to apologise, but whether or not she did, she couldn't remember, because as her soft and wide brown eyes met the piercing blue ones of the man in his mid-thirties, so her voice seemed to die on her!

He nodded. Had she spoken? Or was that his way of acknowledging her presence? Feeling suddenly the desperate need to get herself together, as he took a side step Karrie turned and went smartly out from her office.

Lucy, a girl who sat immediately behind her, was already at the coffee machine. Which was perhaps just as well, because Karrie had forgotten completely to take any coins from her purse to feed the machine.

'I've enough change!' Lucy offered, to save her going back. And just then Heather, the young woman who worked behind Celia, came to join them.

'I'm not stopping!' she announced to the pair. 'Farne Maitland's just arrived to see Mr Lane, I don't want to miss seeing him when he comes out if this is only a flying visit.'

'Farne Maitland's here?' Lucy asked in hushed tones.

Heather nodded, hurriedly putting coins into the refreshment machine. 'And Karrie very nearly knocked him over!'

'You didn't!' Lucy exclaimed.

'Who is he?' Karrie asked, realising that Heather must have witnessed her bumping into him.

'You don't *know?*' Lucy cried. But it was Heather who answered her question.

'He's on the board of the Adams Corporation, our parent company. He likes to keep his finger on every pulse. Though…'

'Though he doesn't visit Irving and Small anywhere near often enough,' Lucy put in.

'You're obviously smitten,' Karrie teased.

'So are half the women who work here,' Lucy agreed. 'Such a waste—all that male, and no wife to go home to!'

'You're going to have to lower your sights, duckie,' Heather laughed. 'You know he's never likely to look at any of us.'

'A girl can dream!' Lucy retorted, but didn't have time to just then. 'I'd better get back. Jenny isn't in today.'

'Somebody's always away—no wonder we always

seem to be short-handed. Thank heaven you've joined us, Karrie.'

Karrie smiled. It was nice to be wanted as part of the team. Though because they were busy that day she didn't linger over her coffee break.

But back at her desk she found she couldn't help wondering if the man with the piercing blue eyes, Farne Maitland, was still in with Mr Lane, or had he left the building? He was, indisputably, extremely good-looking, and had a certain kind of air about him. He was a bachelor, apparently, and half the women at Irving and Small were smitten with him. But seemingly he didn't go in for dating any of them. He should be so lucky...

Karrie stopped her thoughts right there. Good heavens, what on earth was she thinking? Abruptly she channelled her thoughts away from the man and concentrated on the work in hand. But the present task she was engaged on was not that taxing to her brain, and she glanced up when a door up ahead opened. Two men came out, as if Mr Lane intended to escort his visitor through the banks of computers and out to his car.

But then Farne put a stop to that by extending his hand to Gordon Lane and making his adieus from there. Karrie, aware that the man from the Adams Corporation would walk by her desk at any moment, suddenly found her computer screen of the most compelling interest.

Indeed she was glued to it, staring at the screen as if rapt as she waited for Farne Maitland to go by. Her desk was about halfway down the long room—she'd be glad when he passed; what on earth was the matter with her?

He was close; she knew he was close. She lost track of what she was supposed to be doing, but tried to make out she was absorbed anyway. From the corner of her eye she saw the grey of his expensive, exquisitely tailored suit. Just concentrate, or pretend to for a few more seconds, then he'd be gone. But he drew level with her desk—and—halted.

Her insides turned to jelly. She stopped what she was doing—it was nonsense anyway—and looked up. Oh, my word, did he have it all! She stared into piercing blue eyes that seemed to be making a thorough scrutiny of her face. Vaguely it occurred to her that he had recognised that she was new, and that perhaps he had paused in passing to make her welcome.

He was still standing there at any rate when, his survey of her over, he looked into her velvety brown eyes. His voice, when she heard it, was the sort that could quite easily liquefy her bones—if she'd let it.

But he was amusing too, and she realised she was feeling at her most light-hearted when he asked solemnly, 'And whose little girl are you?'

Solemnly she eyed him back. 'Mr and Mrs Dalton's,' she replied prettily, wanting to laugh but managing to hold it in.

She saw his glance go from her merry eyes and down to the ringless fingers of her left hand. Then his eyes were steady on hers again, as, unhesitatingly, he enquired, 'So tell me, Miss Dalton, are you having dinner with me tonight?'

Karrie had all but forgotten her surroundings, forgotten that she was in a large office with a dozen or more other people. But as Farne waited for her answer, a hush seemed to descend over the office—and she could only be astonished at his supreme confidence that in front of everyone he was asking her out!

She supposed few had turned him down, so she smiled as she replied, 'Can't. I'm washing my hair!'

She could tell nothing from his expression as to how he had taken her refusal. Then she saw his glance go to her squeaky clean, washed-only-that-morning, shoulder-length gold-streaked luxuriant blonde hair, and suddenly he was laughing. She watched him, fascinated, and then the laugh that had started to bubble away inside her a few seconds earlier would no longer be suppressed. All at once her laughter mingled with his.

And that was all there was to it. A moment or two of shared laughter, then Farne Maitland was extending his right hand. She offered her right. They shook hands, and he went on his way—and she did not forget him.

Apart from anything else, how would she get the chance? No sooner had the double doors at the end of their office closed after him than three chairs wheeled over at speed to her desk.

'He asked you out!' Heather exclaimed.

'And you turned him *down!*' Lucy squealed—as if she just could not believe it.

'We hadn't been properly introduced,' Karrie laughed.

'What's that got to do with anything?' Celia wanted to know.

'He—er—was only being pleasant because I'm new here.' Karrie thought she'd better down play it a little.

'He's never asked any of us out!' Lucy stated.

Darren Jackson walked up to the group. 'None of you has hair the colour of cream and golden honey!' he explained.

'Shut up, Darren!' Karrie's three colleagues told him in unison.

The fact that she had turned down a date with Farne Maitland was still being talked about the next day, and Karrie did not like to confess that, in a way, she was sorry that she had said no. According to office gossip, his visits were few and far between. So Lord knew when she might see him again.

Not that he would ask her out a second time. Not after having been turned down in front of an office full of people. Not that her refusal had bothered him. He had laughed. She had liked his laugh. She had joined in.

Would she refuse a second time? She didn't know. Though since in all probability he had only asked her out on impulse, she felt sure the thought that he might not ask her out a second time was something she should put entirely from her mind.

She wished she could so easily forget him. Thoughts of him, pictures of him—tall, darkish-haired, sophisticated—seemed to spring into her head at the oddest of times. Darren again asked her for a date on Thursday—and she thought of Farne Maitland. He had laughed when she turned him down; Darren didn't.

She went to visit her cousin again that night. 'Anything new happening in your life?' Jan asked. Karrie thought of Farne Maitland—but couldn't tell her.

'I'm enjoying my job,' she smiled.

'You should have left Uncle Bernard's firm years ago!' Jan stated categorically. 'In fact, you should never have started there—you know that old saying, a cobbler's children are always the worst shod!'

From that Karrie gathered that her cousin must be meaning something along the lines that the boss's children always had the worst deal—and were always the worst paid and treated.

'It wasn't so bad,' she commented lightly, but saw that Jan didn't look anywhere near convinced.

'Now that you've made the break with Dalton Manufacturing, have you thought any more about leaving home?' Jan asked.

Because her cousin was family, and had first-hand experience from childhood overnight stays of the strife that went on in the Dalton household, Karrie had been able to confide at one particularly bad time that she wouldn't mind leaving home.

'I can't,' she answered simply, forbearing to mention that her parents still weren't speaking. 'It seems—sort of disloyal to my mother, somehow.'

'Aunt Margery's too sensitive. You'd have thought she'd have toughened up by now,' Jan mused, but kindly offered, 'You know you're always welcome to come and stay with me if things get too unbearable.'

Karrie thanked her, and later went home. But on Friday she felt sorely inclined to take her cousin up on her offer. The cold war was over. Her parents were speaking again. That was to say they were yelling at each other, rowing. Karrie did not stay downstairs to find out what the problem was this time—experience had shown hostilities could erupt over the merest trifle. She went upstairs to her room and stayed there.

Oh, how she wished it could be different—her parents could still be at it—neither of them prepared to yield an inch—a week from now. Where had it all gone wrong? Well, she knew the answer to that one: at the very beginning.

After one gigantic explosion, when her father had slammed out of the house, her mother, near to hysteria, had instructed a sixteen-year-old Karrie to 'Never give yourself to any man until you've got that wedding ring on your finger!' Her mother had then calmed down a little to go on and tearfully confide how all her rosy dreams had turned to ashes. She and Bernard Dalton had married after a very brief courtship, when Margery Dickson, as she was then, had discovered she was pregnant. They had been taking precautions, apparently, but she had conceived just the same.

A week after their wedding, however, she had suffered a miscarriage. Bernard Dalton had accused his wife of tricking him into marrying her, and the marriage that had never had time to get on any steady footing had gone steadily downhill from then on.

But Margery Dalton had adored her husband, and had hoped that, when she again found herself pregnant, matters between them would improve. But things had gone from bad to worse when, instead of presenting him with the son he had taken for granted he was entitled to, she had given birth to a daughter. She'd had an extremely difficult time having Karrie—and was unable to have another child.

And Karrie had known from a very early age that she would rather not get married at all than have the kind of relationship her parents had. And from the age of sixteen, when her mother had taken her into her confidence about her father believing he'd been tricked into marriage, she had known that she was never going to give herself to any man before their wedding—regardless of what sort of contraception might be around. No man was going to have the chance of accusing her of trapping him into marriage.

Not that she found any problem with either of her deep-dyed decisions. For one thing, while she was not lacking for men who wanted to take her out, she had never met one she would dream of getting engaged to, much less marrying. And as for sharing her body with any of them—while it was true she had enjoyed skirting on the perimeters of the kissing pitch, she had not felt the least inclination to go to bed with any of them.

Karrie was brought rudely out of her thoughts by the sound of doors slamming downstairs. It sounded as though it was going to be one of those weekends. She wondered, not for the first time, why her parents didn't just simply divorce and go their separate ways. But again came to the same conclusion she had come to before: the love they had once had for each other must still be a strand more strong than the hate that had grown up between them and weaved its way in between that love.

The phone rang—her parents, deep in battle, probably wouldn't hear it. Karrie took the call on the phone in her room and discovered some relief from the prospect of a bleak weekend in her friend Travis. Travis was a couple of years older than her, uncomplicated and nice, and was ringing to see if she wanted to meet up.

'I'm free tomorrow, actually,' she told him, adding quickly, 'Providing you aren't thinking of proposing again.'

'Wouldn't dream of it,' he lied, and they both laughed, because they both knew that he *was* lying.

'Quail and Pheasant?' she suggested as a meeting place, knowing Travis seized up in fright in her father's company. Her home was the smart, detached residence of a successful businessman—that it was more often than not an unhappy home was something Karrie could do little about.

'I'll call for you,' Travis answered bravely, and seemed inclined to stay on the line chatting.

When later Karrie ended the call, however, and went and got ready for bed, it was not Travis Watson who was in her head, but the man she had bumped into last Tuesday, the man who had asked her out and, unoffended at her 'hair-washing' put-off, had laughed and shaken her by the hand.

Farne Maitland could afford to laugh, of course. No doubt he had women queuing up to go out with him. Without question, he already had his Saturday evening planned.

Somehow, that notion did not sit well with her. For goodness' sake, she scoffed. As if she cared in the slightest that sophisticated Farne Maitland had a date tomorrow with some equally sophisticated female. Perish the thought!

It took her a long while to get off to sleep that night. But when previously she had known full well that the strife between her parents was the reason for her wakefulness—nightmares in childhood—she could not in all truthfulness say now that the hostility between her parents was the cause for her sleeplessness that night. Somehow, having conjured up a picture of Farne Maitland out wining and dining some ravishing sophisticate tomorrow, she did not seem able to budge the scene from her head!

Karrie was able to scorn such imaginings when she got up the next morning. Good gracious, as if she gave a button whom he dated that night. So why did she think of him so often? She pushed him out of her head, and continued to do so until just after ten that morning, when the phone rang. Expecting that the call might be for her father, who was out, as was her mother—though not together—she went to answer it—and got the shock of her life. The caller, staggeringly, was none other than the man who had occupied more than enough time in her head!

'Hello?' she said.

'Farne Maitland,' he announced himself, and, while her heart seemed to jerk straight out of her body, Karrie began to doubt her hearing—had he said 'Farne Maitland'? How on earth had he got her number? He was going on, confident apparently, from that one word 'hello' that he was speaking to the right person, 'I expect you've got a date tonight?'

Her mouth went dry. Was he asking her *out*? She swallowed. 'Been stood up?' she queried lightly.

She just knew he was smiling, fancied she could hear laughter in his voice, when he countered, 'Would I make you second best, Karrie?'

So, as well as finding out her phone number, he—having supposed she would instantly know who he was—had bothered to find out her first name as well! There was laughter in her voice too—she just could not suppress it. 'So you want me to break my date for tonight?' she asked.

'I'll call for you at seven,' he stated. And Karrie was left staring at the telephone in her hand.

For ageless seconds she stood staring at the telephone. She couldn't believe it! She had a date with Farne Maitland that night! Would you believe it? Would you believe not only did he know her first name and her telephone number, but, since he intended to call for her at seven, he had obviously found out where she lived too!

Suddenly a smile, a joyous smile, beamed across her face—hadn't she feared he would never again ask her out?

CHAPTER TWO

FEARED? Feared that Farne Maitland would never again ask her out? Karrie could not believe she had actually thought 'feared'! What rot! What utter rot!

Still, all the same, she owned she was quite looking forward to going out with him that night. Oh! What was she going to do about Travis? Normally she would never have broken a date with one man to go out with another. Oh, heavens, was her thinking going haywire or what?

Half an hour later she felt on a more even keel and did what she had to do rather than what she should have done. What she should have done was to somehow make contact with Farne Maitland and tell him she was not going out with him—though how she didn't know, when she had no idea of where he lived, much less his phone number. What she did do was go over to the phone and dial Travis Watson's number.

'Are you going to be very put out if I tell you I can't make tonight?' she asked.

'*Karrie!*' he wailed, and followed on swiftly. 'You're going out with somebody else?'

'Oh, Travis, don't make me feel guilty.'

'You should!'

'You're my friend, my very good friend, but not my boyfriend.'

'You're saying a good friend wouldn't mind being passed over for something better?'

'*Travis!*'

'Oh, all right. Come to tea tomorrow.'

'Without fail,' she promised.

'I love you,' he said.

'I love you too—as a brother.'

Karrie came away from the phone wishing Travis would meet someone really special and that they would fall mutually in love. He was nice, really nice. He deserved someone special. And with that thought—'someone special'—Farne Maitland was in her head again.

Her mother came home at lunchtime, but not her father. Karrie dared to ask where he was. 'He didn't say—but he'll be cooking up some business deal somewhere. I wonder why he doesn't take his bed to his office; he's always there!' Margery Dalton complained bitterly. 'Are you out tonight?'

'To dinner, I think.'

'You don't *know*?'

'He didn't say.'

'Travis?'

'I'm having tea with Travis Watson tomorrow,' Karrie said. 'I'm going out with a man called Farne Maitland tonight.'

'Farne Maitland?' Her mother weighed the name up. It meant nothing to her. 'Is he new or have I met him before?'

'I met him on Tuesday, at work,' Karrie replied. 'Though he doesn't work at Irving and Small,' she tacked on hastily. 'That is, he…' Suddenly she felt all shy and flustered just talking about him. 'He works for their parent company,' she added, and quickly changed the subject to enquire, 'Have you anything planned for tonight?'

'I've a good murder story to read—though I wouldn't mind planning one,' she volunteered, and even though Karrie knew that her mother meant her father, she had to laugh.

Karrie was no longer smiling when, that evening, dressed in a short-sleeved above the knee black dress that was a perfect foil for her delicate colouring, she waited for Farne Maitland to arrive. By then self-doubt had begun to creep in. Normally she was quite confident about herself. But she didn't normally go in for dating such men as Farne. Would he find her gauche, too unsophisticated?

Oh, she wished that she'd never said yes! Her sense of humour asserted itself when she realised she couldn't actually remember saying yes. Or, for that matter, agreeing she would go out with him at all. Her confidence started to return—it would serve him right if she wasn't in when he called.

From her bedroom window she saw a long black car purr smoothly into the drive and elegantly wind its way to the front of the house. Butterflies entered her tummy, her confidence flying as, taking up her small evening bag, she left her room and went down the stairs.

Once in the hall she stood composing herself as she waited for Farne Maitland to ring the bell—he'd think her more than eager if she had the door open before he'd got within yards of it.

The bell sounded. She swallowed and suddenly felt extraordinarily hot. She went forward and pulled back the stout front door, some kind of greeting hovering on her lips. But as she stared at the tall man, with that darkish hair and those piercing blue eyes, her voice died on her. He too seemed stuck for words, though she discounted that a moment later.

He surveyed her from where he stood, and then the most devastating smile winged its way from him to her and, his tone light, he said, 'I refuse to believe there is anything false about you, Mr and Mrs Dalton's daughter, but, tell me truly, did your hair become that fantastic colour completely unaided?'

Her insides went all marshmallowy, but from somewhere she found an equally light tone to reply, 'I would never lie to you, Mr and Mrs Maitland's son. It's never seen a chemical dye. My father's not in at the moment, but come in and meet my mother.'

Still feeling a little shaky, Karrie turned about and led the way into the graceful drawing room. Though Bernard Dalton was rarely, if ever, on the receiving end of it, her mother had charm. She conversed pleasantly with Farne who, with abundant charm of his own, chatted in return until, all courtesies dealt with, he commented, 'I've a table booked for eight.' And, her mother, acquainted with the fact that Karrie would not be ravenous for a sandwich when she got home, said goodbye.

That was when Karrie discovered that she had worried needlessly about being unsophisticated. For Farne Maitland seemed to enjoy her company as much as she enjoyed his, and from the start there was never a moment when he allowed her to feel gauche or awkward.

'Have you lived here long?' he enquired as he steered his car down the drive.

'All my life—I was born in this house,' she replied.

'You find it convenient for getting in and out of London daily?'

'Far from it,' she smiled, starting to feel more and more relaxed. 'But that's where my job is.'

'I'm glad,' he responded.

'Glad?' Why was he glad it took her an hour each way to get to and from her place of work?

'Glad you no longer work for your father.'

'Is there anything you *don't* know?' Honestly! His research into her background hadn't stopped at just finding out her first name, address and telephone number!

'What's the point of taking the responsibility of being on the corporation's board if I can't take advantage of the perks of the job?' he grinned.

Her heart flipped over. My word, was he something else again! 'I expect you're always checking the files of Irving and Small's personnel department?' she suggested.

Farne took his glance briefly off the road and gave her a warm look. 'You're the one and only—and I wouldn't lie to you,' he said softly, and something wondrous which she couldn't give a name to started happening inside her. His eyes were back on the road when he asked, 'Are you going to forgive me that—in complete confidence, in case it worries you—I had the director of Personnel fax me your application form and CV yesterday?'

Wow! Karrie took a steadying breath. 'Do I get to see *your* curriculum vitae?'

'Ask anything you want to know,' he offered, and she could not help but be impressed by his utter openness.

Her dinner with him went splendidly. Farne had a table reserved for them at a discreet, stylish—and, she suspected, very expensive—eating establishment in London. And, true to his word, he unhesitatingly answered every question she put to him. Although, since she didn't want him to gain the impression that she was over-eager to know everything about him, she made her questions as impersonal as she could.

'Do you live in London?' she asked.

'I've a house here,' he answered.

'You should have said. I could have—' She broke off, the *I could have met you here* left unsaid.

But she had to laugh when he stated, 'We didn't have much of a telephone conversation, did we?' And added, to her startlement, 'I was afraid if I stayed to say more you might find a reason not to come out with me.

Her eyes widened, she stared at him. 'I... You... You've never been turned down yet, have you?' she challenged. Forget her accusation that he'd been stood up. She didn't believe it for a moment.

'Oh, ye of short memory,' Farne reproached her. 'Have you forgotten how, only last Tuesday, you preferred to wash your most remarkable hair rather than go out with me?'

'Ah!' she said, and smiled, and looked at him as he, unsmiling, looked back at her.

'Devastating!' he murmured.

'I know,' she replied, trying to pretend that her back-bone hadn't just turned to so much water. 'But I do my best. So, you live in London, you work in London, where do you go for holidays?'

'Holidays? What are those?'

'It's tough at the top,' she offered.

'Heartless woman. Where do you go?' he wanted to know.

It was eleven o'clock before she knew it, and they hadn't had coffee yet! 'Can you believe that?' she gasped.

'May I hope you've enjoyed the evening as much as I?' he asked, as an attentive waiter appeared just then, bearing the coffee.

'It's been wonderful,' Karrie answered truthfully, and didn't want it to end.

'Would you like to go on to a club?' Farne suggested.

But Karrie, having been quite truthful about the evening being wonderful, suddenly started to feel a little concerned that it should be so. First dates were often stilted, difficult experiences. First dates. Would he ask her out again?—oh, she did hope so. She closed her mind to such thinking. 'I don't think so,' she refused nicely. It had gone eleven now. Farne had to drive her home yet, and then get back to his place. And while, okay, he might be able to cope effortlessly with arriving home with the morning milk delivery, if this evening got any more wonderful she was going to have one dickens of a job keeping her feet down on the ground.

Disappointingly, he did not press her, but accepted her decision without question. Without, she noted, looking in any way disappointed himself.

They drove to her parents' house in comparative silence—so different from the way they had been tonight—and Karrie started to wonder if maybe she was the only one who thought the whole evening so marvellous.

Farne had seemed to be enjoying himself, though, and, as he'd indicated, he hadn't hung back from answering anything she wanted to know. She had learned that he was an only child, like herself, and that his parents lived in Dorset. Also that from the age of seven he had been sent to boarding school.

That piece of information had shaken her a little at first. It had somehow seemed quite dreadful to her that anyone should think of packing any child as young as seven off to school and away from home. Although, on thinking about it, thinking about her own childhood, fraught by angry rows and arguments, those times she had put her fingers in her ears hoping not to hear them, she just had to pause to consider which of them had had the happier childhood. Still, all the same—boarding school at the tender age of seven!

'You're very quiet, Karrie?' Farne suddenly broke into her thoughts.

'You'd hate it if I sang.'

She sensed he was smiling, but because she was suddenly unsure about more or less absolutely everything— very unlike her; perhaps she was going down with something—Karrie said nothing more until Farne had driven up to her door. On detecting movement, the security lights of her home switched on, and as Farne left the driver's seat so Karrie got out of the car too.

'Thank you for a very pleasant evening,' she said sincerely, and, still feeling a mass of uncertainty, she offered her right hand.

Farne glanced down at it but, instead of shaking hands with her, he took hold of her right hand in his left one, and caught hold of her other hand too. 'It seems,' he said, holding both her hands in his, his eyes on her face, 'that I shall have to let you go.'

Karrie opened her mouth to make some kind of comment. But there were no words there, and she closed it again. Farne still had hold of her hands—she was going nowhere.

Then suddenly her heart started to drum, for his head was coming nearer. She stood there, unmoving, as gently Farne touched his lips to hers. It was an exquisite, tender kiss.

And over all too soon. As was the evening over. For a moment she felt his hold on her hands tighten, then he was stepping back and letting go of her. Having already said her thanks for the evening, there was nothing more for her to say. She turned from him, at a total loss to know if she or Farne had been the one to put her door key in the lock.

Without a word, she went in. She closed the door and when, an age later, or so it seemed, she heard his car start up and move off, she moved too. Silently, softly, her head in the clouds, the feel of Farne's hands still on hers, the feel of his marvellous mouth still on hers, she dreamily started to climb the stairs.

She got ready for bed, touching her fingertips to her mouth where his tender kiss had touched. She got into bed, and closed her eyes. Again, dreamily, she thought of him. Farne Maitland. She had been out for the evening many, many times, but that evening, she had to own, had ranked as extremely special.

Her dreamy mood seemed to extend over into Sunday. Farne Maitland was still in her head as she showered, threw on a pair of trousers and a tee shirt, and went down the stairs. She headed for the kitchen. Her mother had help with the domestic work three mornings a week, but not at the weekend.

'Good morning!' she greeted her mother brightly. 'Need any help?'

Her mother was busy cooking bacon and eggs for her husband, and, as always, she refused any offer of assistance. But her eyes left what she was doing and fastened on her daughter. 'How did your evening go?' she asked, and was unsmiling.

Somehow, and Karrie realised it was ridiculous, her evening suddenly seemed very private, and not to be shared with anyone. She gave herself a mental shake. For crying out loud—this was her mother!

'Fine!' she understated with a smile, and went on to babble on about where she and Farne had dined and what they had eaten. Her voice tailed off, however, when she became aware that her mother was looking just a mite concerned. 'What…?'

Margery Dalton began speaking at the same time. 'He, Farne Maitland, seems—different from your usual boyfriends,' she said carefully.

He was hardly a 'boyfriend', but Karrie had to agree he was certainly different from anyone else she had ever been out with. 'He is,' she answered quietly.

'Oh, Karrie, I fear so for you!' her mother suddenly cried, every bit as though she had lain awake all night worrying about her.

Karrie was quite taken aback, but attempted to rouse her mother's sense of humour anyway. 'That's your job,' she teased.

But Margery Dalton, the bacon she was cooking forgotten, seemed to have worked herself up into something of a state. 'He seems more—worldly than any of the…'

'Oh, Mum.' Karrie tried to quieten her mother's anxiety. 'If you're using Travis Watson as a yardstick—everybody's more worldly than Travis.'

'But Travis is safe—and you're as unworldly as he is. With this new man of yours, he won't be content to…'

'Mum, I probably will never see him again.' Karrie thought it politic to end the conversation.

'You will.' How could her parent sound so positive? Karrie wished she could be that confident herself! 'Promise me, Karrie, that you won't do anything silly,' her mother urged in a sudden rush.

'Silly?' Karrie had no idea what her mother meant for a moment. But it did not take long for conversations she'd had with Margery Dalton over the past six years to come back all at once and make her meaning exceedingly clear. Silly as in getting herself pregnant!

'Oh, you've no need to worry about...' Her voice faded—she could see that her mother was looking extremely upset. Karrie smiled. 'I promise,' she said, without further hesitation—her mother had enough to contend with without being caused further grief if Karrie didn't give her her word. At last she got a smile out of her mother.

They met up as a family when breakfast was ready—her father was in a grumpy mood as he complained, 'This bacon's frizzled!'

Margery Dalton charged straight into battle. 'Don't eat it, then!' she bit back.

Bernard Dalton gave his wife a venomous look and, not taking her orders, crunched his way through his breakfast and left the two women in his household to get on with their own thoughts.

Farne had kissed her, Karrie mused dreamily, kissed her and squeezed her hands. Prior to that he'd stood with her, holding both her hands. 'It seems that I shall have to let you go' he'd said. Did that mean anything—or nothing?

Nothing, of course, you chump! What did you think it meant? Well, precisely nothing, she supposed, but... Would he ring her next week, perhaps the week after? He'd left it four days before ringing her yesterday. Today was Sunday. Sunday, Monday, Tuesday, she counted. Would he ring her on Wednesday? Oh, she did hope so. But perhaps he wouldn't ring at all.

The fact that she must be looking as bleak as she felt

at that thought was borne out when her father, looking her way, asked sharply, 'What's the matter with you? Are you sickening for something?'

Karrie glanced at him, becoming at once aware that his questions had caused her mother to look at her too. With both parents studying her, Karrie knew a desperate need to be by herself.

'I've never felt better,' she answered brightly—and as soon as she could she went up to the solitude of her room.

Once there, she faced that her father had not been so very wide of the mark when he had questioned what was the matter with her, and asked, 'Are you sickening for something?' She was. Something wonderous was going on inside her which she hadn't been able to give a name to. She, was falling in love. Oh, my word!

With Farne Maitland in her head the whole of the time, it had gone eleven before Karrie realised it. Aware that she couldn't stay in her room for much longer if she didn't want her mother coming up to check if her father had been right and there was something the matter with her, Karrie knew she would have to go downstairs. The problem with that, though, was that her father was far too observant, and, should he glance her way and find her, in some unguarded moment, looking anxious or dreamy, then he wouldn't keep it to himself. Her mother would then be on to her. But, for Karrie, this fragile emotion that was gaining strength was, in its infancy, intensely private, and therefore not to be spoken of or shared.

It was a sunny summer's day, so she decided to risk the twice-a-week gardener's wrath and do some weeding. Changing her slip-on shoes for a pair of plimsolls that had seen better days, she pulled back her hair and secured it in rubber bands in two bunches, and reckoned she looked workmanlike enough for her task outside.

'It's a shame to stay indoors on such a lovely day!' she announced, popping her head round the drawing room

door, where her silent parents were absorbed by the
Sunday papers. 'I thought I'd tidy up the rose bed.'

The rose bed was tidy already, she saw. But she decided to tidy it anyway, and was soon on her knees totally
caught up—in thoughts of Farne Maitland.

Her concentration was briefly disturbed when, around
fifteen minutes later, her father steered his car round from
the rear of the house where the garages were. He wound
down a window as he passed and commented, 'Old Stan
will have your hide if you mess that up,'—Old Stan being
the gardener—and went on down the drive.

Karrie smiled and waved to her father, and tried to
concentrate once more on her weeding. Never had an evening sped by so quickly. They'd talked and talked, she
and Farne, and she hadn't felt gauche or unsophisticated
in his sophisticated company once. She supposed it said
a lot for the man himself that he'd made her feel so comfortable with him. Oh, she'd just die if he never phoned
again. Even while she knew there would be nothing in
the world she could do about it if he didn't ring her, she
fell to wondering—did he like her? Just a tiny bit? He
must do, mustn't he? Otherwise he wouldn't have phoned
her in the first place. Oh, she did so hope that nothing
she'd said or done had put him off. Had she…?

Her thoughts at that moment were suspended after the
sound of a car purring into the drive broke into them.
Thinking that it was her father, returning from wherever
he'd been, Karrie looked up—and got the shock of her
life!

It was not her father's car which made its elegant way
up to the top of the drive and which halted outside her
front door. But the long, sleek black car in which she had
been a passenger only last evening!

At first Karrie thought that she'd had Farne so much
on her mind that she was imagining that he was there.
But no, as the man in his mid-thirties extracted his long

length from the vehicle and, having spotted her, began to make his way over to her, she could see for herself that it was none other than Farne Maitland!

Hurriedly she scrambled to her feet. She wanted to call out a greeting, but her voice seemed to have died on her. Had she left something in his car? Her brain went dead too—she couldn't remember. Had he called on her to return whatever it was?

Suddenly she became aware of his faultlessly cut trousers, shirt and tie—and her own grubby appearance. Then Farne was there, standing looking at her, his glance going from the bunches she had made of her hair, over the fine bone structure of her face, and down to her dirt-fingered tee shirt, baggy kneed trousers, and ending at her worn and soiled plimsolls. Karrie, left blushing furiously, was absolutely certain that she couldn't have looked more scruffy if she'd tried!

'Caught me looking my best again!' she attempted, wanting the ground to open up and swallow her.

'I didn't think women did that any more,' he remarked teasingly about her blush, his blue eyes now holding her brown ones.

Trust him to notice! He smiled, and her knees felt as saggy as her trousers at his smile. 'I only do it when there's an "R" in the month,' she managed to trot out lightly—regardless that it was July.

His glance went down to her upward-curving mouth. 'I'm on my way to lunch at The Feathers,' he informed her, mentioning a smart hotel nearby. 'I was passing when I thought I'd stop and ask if you'd join me?'

Like a shot! Her heart went all fluttery. She wasn't going to have to wait to see him! She wasn't going to have to wait and hope he would phone! This was happening *now!* 'My mother will hate me!' Her prevarication was no prevarication at all. No way was she going to deny herself this opportunity of a few hours of his company. 'I'll let you be the one to tell her she's peeled too many potatoes while I go and get cleaned up.'

Taking Farne indoors, she left him talking with her mother while she went sedately up the stairs—and then positively flew around getting ready.

Fifteen minutes later, wearing a dress of a delicate nasturtium colour, Karrie—just as sedately—returned down the stairs and went into the drawing room. Farne got to his feet. 'Hope I didn't keep you too long,' she smiled, having completed the quickest scrub-up and change on record. He made no answer—but his glance was appreciative.

'I'll see you when I see you,' Margery Dalton said, knowing full well that her daughter had an appointment elsewhere for tea.

Karrie had been to The Feathers Hotel quite a few times before. But this time, lunching with Farne, everything seemed so much better, brighter—magical.

Again she enjoyed his company. He was amusing, charming, attentive—and gave every appearance of seeming to enjoy being with her as much as she enjoyed being with him. Oh, she did so hope it was true, that it wasn't all part and parcel of his natural charm—and that he wasn't like this with everybody. In short—she wanted to be special to him.

After lunch she excused herself and went to the ladies' room to freshen up and to give herself something of a talking to. For goodness' sake—special to him! They hadn't known each other a week! She had been out with him twice. *Twice*—that was all—and she wanted him to regard her as someone special in his life!

Grief—he was a man about town. He could have his pick of just about anybody. What was so special about her? Karrie just then had a blindingly clear—and unwanted—mental picture of standing in front of Farne, her hair pulled back in two rubber bands, dirt everywhere—

and also a picture of the polished and elegant women she was sure he more normally went out with. Special—get *real!*

Pinning a smile on her face, she left the ladies' room to join him. They went out to the hotel's car park and, striving hard not to think that the drive to her home would take only about twenty minutes—less than that if Farne happened to put his foot down on the accelerator—Karrie got into the passenger seat.

More joy was hers, however, when Farne forgot to turn left at a road junction. 'You've missed the turn,' she felt honour-bound to point out.

'I thought we might go and take a look at the river,' he replied. Her heart rejoiced. 'That is, unless you're desperate to get back?'

She was desperate to stay exactly where she was, with him. 'It's very pleasant down by the river,' she answered, desperate not to be pushy, but having a hard time not grabbing at every opportunity to be in his company.

In no time they were in open countryside. When Farne pulled over by a footbridge and asked, 'Fancy a stroll around?' she thought it a splendid idea.

They walked over the bridge, and, keeping by the water's edge, across a couple of fields. And it was in one particularly grassy area that Farne commented, 'If we'd had a car rug we could sit down.'

'You city boys are too sissy for words,' Karrie scorned, and was seated on the grass before it dawned on her that was exactly what Farne had intended she should do. 'You're too smart for me!' she accused, but he only grinned and joined her. For the next hour they seemed to amicably fall into a discussion on any subject that happened to crop up. Music, books, ski-ing. She didn't know how ski-ing had got in there, but it had; everything was just so relaxed and easy between them, somehow.

They both seemed to have gone from sitting to resting,

lying on their elbows as they watched a couple of swans majestically glide by, when suddenly Karrie became aware that Farne was not watching the birds. He had turned and was looking at her.

'You're very lovely,' he murmured quietly—and all at once her heart was rushing like an express train. There was something in his look, something in the very air that seemed to tell her that Farne wanted to kiss her. Well, that was all right by her; she wanted to kiss him too.

His head came nearer. He looked deep into her eyes, giving her every opportunity to back away. She smiled a gentle smile—and he needed no further encouragement.

Gently he took her into his arms, moving her unresisting form until they were lying together on the grass. Unhurriedly, his lips met hers in a lingering tender kiss, and it was the most wonderful experience she had ever known. Never had she known such tenderness, and, as her heart started to pound, Karrie knew that Farne Maitland was the love of her life. She was no longer falling in love with him. She *did* love him, was in love with him, and nothing was ever going to change that.

When their kiss ended Karrie was left struggling to make sense of what had happened to her. She moved a little way away from him, not how she wanted to move at all, but some instinct was taking over from the sudden confusion she found herself in. All she was clear about was that this would be the last she would see of Farne if he gained so much as a glimpse of her feelings for him.

She sat up, hugging her arms around her knees, as she tried with all she had to recover from his wonderful kiss—and the certain knowledge of what was in her heart.

'What's wrong, Karrie?' Oh, heavens—gauche, did she say? He was so quick, able to spot a mile off that something was bothering her. Yet she couldn't find an answer to give him. 'I've offended you?' he asked, his tone quiet, concerned.

She shook her head. 'I...' she said, but couldn't bear that he should think she found his kiss offensive. 'To be honest,' she began, 'that ranks as one of the nicest kisses I've known.'

She was aware that Farne was sitting up too. Then she felt his hand come to her face, and gently he turned her so he could see into her eyes. The concern in his voice was reflected in his eyes, though there was a twinkle there too as he asked politely, 'Perhaps you'd care for another?'

Laughter bubbled up inside her. 'Thank you very much all the same,' she answered prettily, 'but I shall be having my tea soon.' She saw his mouth start to tweak up at the corners, and stared for a moment or two in total fascination. Then suddenly that word 'tea' started to get through to her, and, 'Oh!' she exclaimed.

'Oh?' Farne queried.

'I've got to go home,' Karrie said quickly. 'Travis is expecting...'

'Who the hell's Travis?'

Karrie blinked. What had happened to his concern, that twinkling in Farne's eyes? All there was now was out-and-out aggression! But she loved him too much to be able to contemplate quarrelling with him.

'Our first row!' she mocked, feeling wretched and anxious, but determined to laugh him out of whatever was bugging him.

He did look a shade amused, she was glad to see, but, albeit with his aggressiveness under control, he still wanted to know, 'So who's Travis?'

Karrie stared at him. Farne knew she was an only child, and had no brother, so he must realise that Travis was either a cousin or man-friend. Surely he wasn't angry that she had a male friend! Her mouth went dry at the thought that Farne might be just the tiniest bit—jealous. Oh, for goodness' sake—as if! Still, all the same she wanted only ever to be as open and honest with Farne as he was with her.

'My date—last night. The one I broke to go out with you was with Travis.'

'You're seeing him this evening?'

Dearly did she want to explain that Travis was just a friend and nothing more than that. But this newly awakened love she felt for Farne made her sensitive to everything. To explain anything of the sort might make Farne think she saw her friendship with him as more important than just two dates should signify.

'I—promised,' she said.

'Did you tell him why you were breaking your date?' he questioned, his expression unsmiling.

Karrie wanted him happy again. She remembered Travis saying something when she'd phoned him yesterday about being passed over for something better, and smilingly asked Farne, 'You think I should have told him I'd had a better offer?'

Farne's glance went to her upward-curving mouth. 'You've charm enough for a man to forgive you anything,' he commented. And Karrie thought he was going to kiss her again.

She wanted him to kiss her again. But this newly found love was making a nonsense of her. Abruptly, she stood up. Farne followed suit, making no attempt to touch her, or to dissuade her from keeping her promise to Travis. She wished she hadn't got to her feet, because she knew now that this wonderful interlude with Farne was over. And it was.

Back at her home, he got out of the car and stood on the drive with her for a minute or so. Karrie wanted to invite him in, to prolong this wonderful time in his company. But she'd noted that his car keys were still in the ignition. Quite obviously he wanted to be away.

'Thank you for rescuing me from the weeding,' she

smiled, and without thinking went to shake hands with him. She saw his right eyebrow go aloft, and quickly put her hand behind her back—and could have groaned aloud. How was that for sophisticated?

But at least her action caused Farne's expression to soften. 'Charm, did I say?' he smiled, and, leaving her to guess whether he meant she had or had not charm, he placed his hands on her upper arms and bent down and kissed her lightly on her left cheek. 'Thanks for dropping everything to come out with me' he said, and went to his car. Without another glance or a wave, he drove off down the drive.

Karrie felt bereft. She was unsure whether Farne truly thought she had charm. But what she *was* sure about was that she'd been totally crass to think for so much as a moment that Farne felt even the smallest iota of jealousy about Travis.

For such an idea to have any substance it would have to mean that Farne Maitland cared sufficiently to be jealous in the first place. And he'd just shown how much he cared, hadn't he? He'd gone away without so much as a backward glance.

'Thanks for dropping everything to come out with me' he'd said. Karrie supposed that there were few women of his acquaintance who would not do likewise. Did he know that? She tried to get cross. Tried to make believe that in the unlikely event that he was passing next Sunday, and stopped by to ask if she'd like to join him, she would tell him that she couldn't possibly. Fate gave a cruel chuckle—on two counts.

Firstly, having fallen in love with Farne—and Karrie freely owned that this ranked as the most idiotic thing she had done to date—she could not see her denying herself any chance of spending some time with him, if chances there were.

Secondly, there would be no chance. She had been out

with him twice—today only because he was passing. Somehow, bearing in mind the way he had departed just now, she had a very strong feeling that there would not be a third time.

CHAPTER THREE

KARRIE dressed with care to go to work on Monday. Much good did it do her. She had not truly expected Farne to walk past her desk on one of his rare visits—so why should she feel such a dreadful ache of disappointment when five o'clock came and she had not so much as seen a glimpse of him?

She drove home, giving herself much the same pep talk that she had given herself yesterday after Farne had gone. She was not going to see him again, and that was the end of it. He might, possibly might, walk by her desk in three months or so's time—did that mean that her nerves were going to act up, as they had today, every time so much as a shadow, a footstep, was seen or heard near her desk?

Where was her pride? She was in love—she had none. She had tried, really tried, to convince herself that she could not be in love—why, she barely knew him! But it made no difference.

'Had a good day?' her mother asked when she arrived home.

'The work gets more and more interesting,' Karrie answered.

'Going out tonight?'

Had her mother expected that Farne Maitland would telephone her at her office? Get him off your mind, do. 'What, and miss whatever it is that smells so wonderful coming out of the kitchen?'

The phone rang; Karrie jumped. Her mother, nearest to it, went to answer it, and Karrie's palms grew moist as she waited to hear who was calling. It was her father's secretary.

40

'Looks as though we'll be having large helpings—your father is "unavoidably detained". Now doesn't that make a change!'

The telephone rang a couple of times that night, and each time Karrie suffered the same reaction. She took herself off to bed, knowing that she'd be a nervous wreck if she went on at this rate. Oh, why couldn't she have fallen in love with someone like Travis?

Karrie went to work the next day determined that that day was going to be different. But it wasn't. She drove home that evening feeling as wretched and fidgety, with such an aching restlessness inside her that she found it the hardest work to show her mother a smiling face.

She rang her cousin Jan that night for a chat, and wished that she could confide in her, but she couldn't confide in her mother either. The love, the ache, was much too private. Karrie had seen nothing of Farne that day—nor did he phone that night. Not that she had expected that he would ring her.

She awoke on Wednesday, striving to stir her lost pride into action. For goodness' sake—never before had she waited for any man's phone call! Bubbles to him; if Darren Jackson asked her to go out with him again today, she'd jolly well go.

'Fancy coming for a Chinese after work?' Darren asked as soon as he saw her.

'Sorry, Darren, I've got something on tonight,' Karrie replied—well, perhaps if he asked her again tomorrow, she excused the pathetic mess Farne Maitland had made of her. The truth was she just didn't want to go out with anyone but Farne.

She threw herself into her work, and in part succeeded, sometimes for seconds at a time, in wiping Farne from her thoughts. Then, at around half past ten—time never used to drag like this—a shadow fell across her desk. She looked up—and was hard put to it not to leap out of her seat with joy.

'How's my best girl?' Farne enquired with charm that sank her.

Her heart at once went into overdrive. 'You're only saying that 'cos it's true,' she replied, every bit as if she hadn't ate, dreamt and slept Farne Maitland since last Sunday.

He grinned and went on his way—and Karrie casually left her desk and headed for the ladies' room. Her hands were shaking so much she wasn't going to accomplish very much work anyway.

She washed her hands and dried them, and checked her appearance in the mirror, never more glad that, clad in a crisp linen two-piece, outwardly at least, she looked perfectly composed.

Karrie had been in the ladies' room getting herself together for about five minutes when the panicky notion dawned on her that Farne's visit to Mr Lane might only be a fleeting one!

Suddenly it seemed of vital importance that she saw him again. She needn't talk to him—what was there to say? She just wanted to see him one more time.

She went quickly, only just managing not to run. But she was right to hurry she saw as soon as she entered the over-large area where she worked. Because Farne, having already completed his business, had left Mr Lane's office and was even then walking in the aisle between the rows of desks.

Karrie continued walking towards him, though not so hurriedly now. Knowing they would pass, she had a pleasant 'Bye' ready, then found that it was not needed. For he halted in front of her and she had no thought to move out of his way. She stopped too. Her feet were taking her nowhere for the moment.

As he looked down, so she looked up, but had time

only to marvel that that oh, so superb mouth had actually
kissed hers, had given her that most wonderful tender kiss
on Sunday, before Farne, a smile somewhere deep in his
eyes, casually enquired, 'Coming out for a coffee?'

Yes, yes, yes. 'I'm working,' she answered. Sack me,
fire me. I don't care. I just want to go with him.

'Then it will have to be coffee tonight—after dinner,'
he stated.

He wanted to take her out! She felt sure her feet had
sprouted wings—she felt as if she was floating on air.
'You drive a hard bargain,' she accepted, but was suddenly aware that she couldn't hear the clatter of nearby
computer keyboards. They, she realised, had an audience.

Farne seemed suddenly aware too, for he made no attempt to delay her further when she side-stepped him and
continued on to her desk. Before she had taken her seat,
however, she was already starting to wonder—did she
really have a date with Farne that night, or had she mis-
construed his remark?

But apparently several of her work colleagues were of
the opinion that she and Farne were having dinner together that night, because no sooner had the door at the
far end closed than chairs were being scooted up to her
desk.

'You're dating *Farne Maitland!*' Lucy exclaimed in
awe.

Karrie had kept to herself the fact that she had seen
Farne last Saturday and Sunday. 'Am I?' she asked—still
not very sure about tonight.

'That was a definite date if ever I heard one!' Heather
opined.

Fortunately, at that point Mr Lane wandered into their
office, and, as quickly as a bomb-burst, four chairs—
Jenny was back at work—scooted away.

Karrie drove home at the end of her work day, striving
to caution herself that Farne could have just been teasing.

She would get ready—just in case he called for her—but she wouldn't be too upset if the doorbell stayed silent. Well, not desperately upset.

'It's just you and me tonight,' her mother said when she got in. 'Your workaholic father's too busy to come home!'

Her mother, Karrie felt, was starting to sound more and more bitter by the day. 'Actually, Mum, I'm not wanting a meal either tonight. I…'

'You're starting to get just like him!' Margery Dalton complained. 'Meals cooked and not wanted.'

'I'm sorry. I…'

'It never occurred to you to pick up a phone, I suppose?'

Karrie felt dreadful. 'I should have done. I'm sorry,' she apologised again. With her mother in sour mood, now did not seem the right time to explain that she hadn't phoned because she wasn't terribly certain that she would be eating out. It was only now, with her possible date with Farne looming closer, that she realised that she wasn't the least bit hungry, and that, in or out, she didn't think she could eat a morsel.

She went up to her room to shower and get ready for what might be a night in, and found that on top of her anxiety she was feeling all upset at having been taken to task by her mother, who had accused her of starting to get just like her father.

She didn't want to be like her thoughtless father. She loved him, of course she did, but sometimes she did not like him very much. Karrie didn't like the way he treated her mother, nor the fact that, because experience had shown that she only made matters worse, she could not do anything to put things right between her parents.

Karrie was out of the shower and blow drying her hair when it came to her that she didn't want to be like her mother either. Her mother was so embittered. Yet Karrie was positive she hadn't started out that way. Her marriage to Bernard Dalton had done that to her. And, while Karrie felt so sad about that, she felt she could not bear it if one day she woke up and found that she had grown into the same kind of person her mother had become.

But Karrie shrugged her sadness and fear away. Hang it all, there was no earthly reason why she should be embittered. She gave a hurried glance at her watch and, since she wanted to be ready by seven—just in case—realised she'd better get a move on. Besides, what had she got to be bitter about? With any luck, the man she was in love with would be calling for her soon.

Karrie was ready with five minutes to spare. She used those five minutes to watch for Farne's car turning into the drive. She felt so churned up inside she could barely stand still because of the high tension of her emotions.

He won't come, he won't, she told herself, striving for calm—and then she saw his car in the drive, and almost burst into tears from the strain of it. But she didn't, and flew down the stairs on winged feet.

Her mother was on the telephone, but broke off. To Karrie's relief she saw they were friends again when her mother smiled. 'Farne's here—I'm just off,' Karrie told her.

'Have a good time!' Margery Dalton bade her.

The doorbell sounded. Karrie managed to wait five seconds before she went to the door. 'My mother's on the phone,' she smiled, by way of explaining why she wasn't inviting him in, her heart fit to burst with her joy at seeing him again.

'Then we'll go, shall we?'

It did not require an answer, and Karrie thrilled to his touch as he placed a hand under her elbow and they went over to his car.

'Busy?' she enquired as they drove along, feeling suddenly tongue-tied.

He took his attention off his driving for a brief moment so he could look at her. 'Doing my stint,' he agreed pleasantly. 'How about you?'

'I manage to keep occupied,' she murmured of her extremely active section. But she didn't want to talk about her; she wanted to know more about Farne. 'I don't suppose you're at board meetings every day?' she enquired.

'You suppose correctly,' he answered. 'Though, prior to my attending a meeting in Milan on Friday, there's a board meeting tomorrow.'

He was going to Italy! Karrie pushed panic down. She'd never used to be like this. Until she had fallen in love she'd have said she didn't have a panicky bone in her body. Yet here she was fretting that because he was off to Italy—giving no mention of when he was coming back—it could be an age before she saw him again! Not, of course, that she had any guarantee that he would want to see her again after tonight.

Somehow or other she managed to keep up a light conversation with him until they reached the restaurant where they were to dine.

It was another splendid establishment, the menu looking most appetising. Although by then Karrie was so in love with Farne she would have been equally happy to eat eggs on toast in the humblest of eating-places. She had thought she couldn't eat a thing—but suddenly her appetite was back.

'So...' Farne began, in between the lobster bisque and the mouth-watering main course, 'tell me about Travis.'

'Travis!' She stared at him in astonishment. Travis was a dear, a love, but there was no place for him in her thoughts tonight. 'You want to know about Travis?'

'You had a date with him on Sunday,' Farne reminded her.

She was reminded of her idiocy in thinking for so much as the most fleeting of moments that he might be just the scrappiest bit jealous. He looked it! Smiling, easy, conversational. 'I went to his place for tea.' She saw no reason not to tell him.

'He lives alone?' Farne asked sharply. My word, what had happened to his being smiling, easy, conversational?

'He's quite good at it,' she flipped his way. 'Anyhow, I don't ask you about your women-friends!' she flared with hostility—and as Farne stared at her a gentle look all at once came to his blue eyes.

'Oh, Karrie,' he crooned softly. 'Our second row!'

She laughed; she couldn't help it. But she wished she could fathom this love business. No way did she want to quarrel with Farne yet, but a second or two ago she had been ready for pitched battle!

'Where were we?' she asked, calling a truce.

'You were *not* asking me about my women-friends.' He had instant recall—and frightened her half to death when, his look keen, direct, he queried, 'You care?'

Too close! Much too close! 'Of course, desperately,' she replied, and, to show him how seriously he could take that, she grinned. Farne's eyes stayed on her, but she was never more glad when, to prove he hadn't taken her seriously anyhow, his mouth started to pick up at the corners. Then the waiter was there to clear away their used dishes and to enquire what they would like for pudding.

Karrie had thought Farne had forgotten all about Travis. But she was just dipping into her chocolate and nut meringue when he questioned, 'He wants to marry you, naturally?'

'Naturally,' she replied, but, not at all on his wavelength, she then had to ask, 'Who?'

'The one who presides over the teapot.'

Laughter bubbled up in her again. She had been laughing inside for most of the evening. 'You know I can't tell you that!'

'Why not?' he wanted to know.

'It ain't done!' she replied, and loved him the more when he seemed to understand.

'Your manners are impeccable,' he commented.

'One tries,' she answered demurely, and as she looked at him across the table, so their eyes met.

She found it impossible to take her glance from his, but sensed a tension suddenly, and wondered if he felt it too. His expression was no longer smiling as his eyes flicked to her mouth and back to her eyes again.

But her heart started to crash away when, a moment later, his voice audible for all his tone was low, he stated quite clearly, 'You know, of course, that I want most desperately to kiss you.'

She swallowed. Even though she knew he was watching her every expression, her every movement, she couldn't help it. She wanted to say something ridiculous such as, I thought you preferred cheese and biscuits to a sweet, but the words wouldn't come.

'Oh…' she said, and suddenly words were there. 'And—er—do you often get these sudden urges?' she enquired.

'There's nothing sudden about it,' Farne replied. 'I've wanted to kiss you since first I saw you this evening.'

Oh! Her heart seemed to be leaping about like crazy! 'If—it was one of your—er—Sunday kisses, I might well have enjoyed it,' she replied quietly, the way, the wonderful way he had kissed her last Sunday forever remembered, forever magical.

At that juncture a waiter appeared, enquiring if they would like coffee. 'Karrie?' Farne queried. But she reckoned she'd got enough to keep her awake that night without the added stimulant of coffee.

'Thank you, no,' she said, observed that Farne had declined too and a short while later, when they went out to his car, she was starting to regret her decision. A cup of coffee would have allowed her another fifteen minutes of his company—if she had drunk it very, very slowly.

They were in his car and Farne was steering it away from the restaurant when she realised that the chance to spend more time in his company was still there—if she was prepared to take it—when he offered, 'My house isn't far away if you fancy finishing off the evening with a coffee there?'

Oh, how she wanted to say yes. Suddenly, though, she went hot all over. Farne had stated that he most desperately wanted to kiss her. And, although she gave him top marks that he hadn't made a grab for her in the car park just now, did his idea of coffee mean the same as her idea of coffee?

She began to feel wildly agitated all at once—starting with the clashing of the strident cymbals that always sounded when she thought of her upbringing. 'You've a board meeting tomorrow,' she reminded him, and, fearing he might counter that he could handle a late-night coffee and a board meeting next day without the slightest trouble, she added, 'And I have to leave home before eight if I'm to be at work on time.'

All was quiet in the car for a moment or two, but Karrie felt that she had never loved him more when, accepting her decision, respecting it, Farne reached for her hand and, with his eyes on the road up in front, brought it to his lips and gently kissed it.

Oh, she loved him, she loved him. The thought of not seeing him again was torture. Oh, to be more emancipated so that she could ask him out. But she wasn't, and she couldn't, and he was going away on Friday, and life was so unfair.

They spoke little on the journey to her home. She had a tremendous amount on her mind, all to do with him and how she could have prolonged the evening but hadn't. But too soon, it seemed, they were turning into the drive of her home.

Farne steered the car up the drive. The security lights came on but he stopped his car in a comparatively unlit area. Karrie went to get out—his hand stayed her. She turned to him, could see his face fairly clearly, and, words not needed, wanted his kiss then as desperately as he had said he wanted to kiss her.

He reached for her, his arms coming out for her. Like someone who knew she had been born to be in his arms, she went to him. 'Karrie,' he breathed her name, and then his lips met hers, and it was absolutely sublime.

She clung to him, hating that the car's controls prevented her from getting that bit closer. But it was a perfect joy to be in his arms, to feel his mouth against hers, searching and finding her every response.

His mouth left hers briefly, and he transferred his lips to her eyes and the side of her face. She felt his body heat as her hands clutched at him, and she found her hands were somehow beneath his jacket.

She went to pull back, but found she couldn't for the moment when, his mouth over hers once more, she felt the caress of his hands move over her back. Things were happening to her which were unexpected and starting to make a nonsense of her. Then she was left gasping when, in a tender but caressing movement, Farne's caressing right hand found its way to capture the full swollen globe of her left breast.

'Something wrong?' he asked throatily, her gasp having got through to him apparently.

Wrong? No! It had never felt more right. His touch to her breast was exquisite. Though if anything was wrong it was her. She was enthralled by his intimate touch—and had never expected to feel this way!

She pulled back, and he removed his hand from her breast. And she had to be glad that he had because with that wonderful sensitive touch gone, it allowed her some kind of capacity for thinking.

'I...I'd better—go in,' she said shakily.

And felt just then that she had made another wrong decision. Because, not trying for a moment to persuade her otherwise, Farne moved and placed a gentle kiss to the corner of her mouth and pulled back, remarking, 'You have to leave home tomorrow before eight.' Though whether he was reminding her or himself, Karrie was too bemused to know.

Leaving his car, Farne walked with her to her front door, taking her door key from her and inserting it in the lock. Karrie didn't want him to go. She didn't, she didn't. 'Happy landings on Friday,' she wished him for his Milan trip. She smiled up at him to show that it didn't hurt. 'Goodnight, Farne, and th—' She didn't get to finish, for Farne broke in suddenly.

'Come with me!'

Karrie stared at him, stunned. His words so unexpected she could barely take them in. He couldn't be meaning what she thought he was meaning. Could he? 'Come with you?' she just had to question.

'Come with me to Milan,' he urged.

'B-but...'

'My meeting will only take a couple of hours. We can spend the afternoon exploring the city, have dinner. Stay the weekend. What do you say?'

'I—er—I—I have to—er—I'm a working girl,' she stammered.

'I'll get you back for work on Monday.'

Help her, somebody! Farne seemed to have overlooked completely the fact that to go with him at all meant that she would have to take Friday off work. And yet—if she went with him she wouldn't have a heart-sore weekend, wondering when, if ever, she would see him again. No, she decided, turning her mind away from the greatest idea she'd heard in a long while. 'I…' she began, ready to tell him that she couldn't possibly go with him. Only just then it suddenly occurred to her that, starting with her refusal of coffee back at the restaurant, she had already made two wrong decisions that night, and she heard herself say, 'I think I'd like very much to come with you.'

He smiled that wonderful devastating smile of his. Then she was in his arms, and again it was bliss. But this time he did not kiss her, just held her close for a few moments before he let her go and opened the door to her home. 'I'll call for you at six on Friday morning,' he said, and pushed her inside.

She waited to hear the sound of his car start up. Then she went slowly, her head in the clouds, up to her room.

Karrie awakened the next morning and was instantly a mixture of joy, excitement and anxiety. She was going to spend more than just a few hours in Farne's company. She didn't expect him to love her, but to have invited her along must mean that he liked her quite well! Oh, the sheer joy of that! But she was anxious that somehow, sticking as near to the truth as she could, she was going to have to ask Pauline Shaw, the supervisor of her very busy section, if she could take tomorrow off.

A little earlier than was usual, Karrie left her room to go in search of her mother. She found Margery Dalton in the kitchen. Her mother was the first to speak, and Karrie felt warmed by her smile. 'Did you have a nice time last night?' she asked pleasantly.

'Oh, it was wonderful,' Karrie couldn't refrain from saying. *He* was wonderful. Yet, not wanting anyone to spoil anything, and even though she had always been able to tell her mother everything before, this new and private love she felt caused her to feel a shade chary when she went on to reveal, 'I'm going to Milan tomorrow, with Farne, for the weekend.'

Oh, don't spoil it, don't spoil it, Karrie silently begged

when she saw her mother's smile abruptly depart. She even thought her parent had gone a little pale. There was no mistaking the anguish in her voice. 'Oh, Karrie, Karrie, haven't you listened to a word I've been saying to you all these years?' Karrie stared unhappily at her, sensing she hadn't finished yet. 'Oh, love, you're so unworldly. You know nothing of contraception. Not that I've any faith in…'

'Oh, I'm not going to sleep with him!' Karrie felt shaken, but could confidently put her mother straight on that point.

Only to be shaken anew, and to be faced with a welter of fresh problems, when her mother asked sadly, 'Does *he* know that?'

Karrie drove to work that morning and could have done without being stuck in a traffic jam. It gave her too much space for thought. Did Farne think she was going to go to bed with him? Indeed, until her mother had brought her up short on the subject, Karrie realised that she just hadn't got round to thinking past the fact that she had to snatch at this most terrific chance of being able to spend *the whole weekend* with him.

She thought back to the previous evening, those fantastic kisses they had shared in his car. She hadn't backed away from those kisses, had she? But had more eagerly returned them, and his embrace. Indeed, not until Farne's caressing touch had intimately arrived at her breast had she demurred in the slightest. But did Farne think…? Again she remembered his hand on her breast—oh, grief! Had she accepted his invitation under false pretences?

There was only one way to find out—but she shied away from contacting him to ask. He'd think her mad! Or a fool! As her mother had said, she was unworldly. Any other twenty-two-year-old would *know* without needing to ask, she punished herself. She couldn't ring him; she just couldn't!

And yet, in all honesty, how could she not? She had awakened that morning anticipating a happy, joyous time just being with Farne. But what if Farne had awakened that morning anticipating a happy joyous something else? What sort of happy joyous time would it be if she left it until they were in Milan before she thought to mention that her idea of happy and joyous was extremely different from his. For heaven's sake, he was a man of the world. An experienced man of the...

A car behind her tooting furiously caused her to be abruptly aware that the traffic had started to move again. Karrie raised her left hand in apology and drove on, realising that there was no way she could go to Milan without first getting a few ground rules sorted.

For, while last night Farne's touch had aroused in her unexpected emotions, there could just be no way whatsoever that she would contemplate sharing a bed with him. Apart from anything else, didn't she know, chapter and verse, the unhappy consequences that could ensue if she turned her back on everything her mother had ever told her? Everything she had grown up knowing.

No, embarrassing though it would be, feel a fool though she would, Karrie faced that the first thing she must do when she got to the office was to put a phone call through to Farne. She had to make contact with him; she couldn't leave it until they got to Milan.

Her decision to call Farne first thing, however, had to wait a few minutes, because, before she had stowed her bag away, four of her colleagues crowded round her desk. 'Where did you go?' Lucy asked without preamble.

'When?'

'Last night!' Heather exclaimed impatiently.

'With Farne Maitland,' Celia added her share.

'Ah!' Karrie mumbled.

'What's he like to go out with?' Jenny wanted to know. Absolutely divine. 'Quite pleasant, actually.'

'Are you seeing him again?'

According to my mother, I'm sleeping with him tomorrow night. 'I wouldn't mind,' Karrie smiled.

'Neither would we,' they chorused in unison.

And Karrie laughed, stowed her bag, said she needed to see Pauline Shaw about a small matter, and went swinging in to their supervisor's office. 'May I see you for a moment?' Karrie asked, noticing that Pauline, never wasting a moment, was already hard at work.

'Of course,' Pauline smiled, though her expression quickly changed to solemn, as she exclaimed hurriedly, 'Please don't tell me you want to leave!'

'No, nothing like that,' Karrie speedily reassured her. 'Though I do need—er—may need tomorrow off.' She started to feel guilty—should feel guilty, she well knew—but her love for Farne was stronger. 'I—er—it's a domestic matter,' she felt forced to add, when Pauline was obviously waiting for her to state some reason for maybe—or maybe not—requiring the following day off. 'Er—I can work late tonight if it's any help?' guilt made her offer.

'Would you?' Pauline accepted gratefully. 'As you know, what with winning that huge contract and everything, we're very pushed.'

Having apparently got the next day off, by the look of it, it seemed a small thing to work late for two or three hours that night. Karrie had just one more request to make. 'Er—I need to make a private phone call…'

'Use my office—I need to see Mr Lane; I'll go now,' Pauline offered, and was smiling again.

No sooner had Pauline left her office, however, Karrie broke out into a cold sweat. Oh, she couldn't! Farne was a sophisticated man, for goodness' sake! How on earth could she say what had to be said?

Karrie found the number of the Adams Corporation, knowing that there was only one way to say it. She asked the switchboard for an outside line and dialled, only the honesty of wanting things out in the open preventing her from putting down the phone. That honesty insisted it was all settled before they left England.

'Adams Corporation?' answered an efficient-sounding voice before she was anywhere near ready for it.

'Mr Farne Maitland, please,' Karrie requested, and sorely felt the need to collapse on to Pauline's chair as she waited.

Though she was not kept waiting long before a superefficient-sounding female stated pleasantly, 'Mr Maitland's office.'

'Oh, good morning,' Karrie returned, equally pleasantly, realising she was going to have to get past Farne's PA before she could begin to have anything settled. 'I'd like to speak with Mr Maitland, please.'

'I'm afraid he's not available. Can anyone else help you?'

'Oh, no, thank you all the same. It's a personal matter,' Karrie explained. A second or two of silence followed, and she realised the PA wanted more than that. 'I know Farne has a board meeting today. I thought I might reach him before it started,' she went on, hoping the fact that she knew of the board meeting would confirm she and Farne were personal friends—though realising belatedly that the fact that there was a meeting that day was probably common knowledge. Karrie grew desperate. 'It really is most urgent that I make contact with him today,' she added.

'Would you like me to pass that message on to him?'

'I can't speak with him now?'

'I'm sorry. He truly isn't available. He isn't in the building but elsewhere, in talks which began an hour or more ago.' Good heavens—even her workaholic father didn't start work before eight-thirty! 'From there Mr Maitland is going straight to the board meeting, and will return to work late to complete his full to overflowing diary.' Karrie felt dreadful. Poor Farne. By the sound of it, he didn't have a minute to breathe that day. 'If you'll let me have your name, I'll inform him of the urgency of your message,' the PA ended, her tone as pleasant at the end of the conversation as it had been at the beginning.

'Karrie Dalton,' Karrie supplied. And because she loved him so much, and was only then realising the extent of the pressures he daily coped with in his work, felt compelled by her love to add, 'But perhaps it isn't so urgent after all that he makes contact.'

She went back to her desk, and even though she realised that she had left it more or less to the PA's discretion whether or not she passed on the message that she had called, Karrie jumped every time her phone rang during that morning. But, having no intention to have a conversation with Farne at her desk, her plan to have his call transferred to Pauline Shaw's office was not put into operation. Farne did not ring.

Karrie went to lunch, aware that, since he probably hadn't so much as set foot inside his office yet, if he was going to ring at all, it would be at some time during the afternoon.

She returned to her desk; there was still no call from Farne, but Travis rang. He had purchased a picture for his flat and was keen to have her opinion on it. 'But I don't know anything about art!' she protested.

'That doesn't matter!' he said enthusiastically, and Karrie, realising he was desperate for someone to come and see his latest acquisition, did what any true friend would—bearing in mind she wouldn't be able to call round at his flat Friday, Saturday or Sunday.

'I'm working late. All right if I come about eightish?' She'd be packing for Milan at midnight!

Travis was delighted and, after she'd said goodbye to him, thoughts of Farne were soon back in her head.

Indeed, with Farne so much on her mind it wasn't until later on that Karrie remembered to ring her mother to let her know she would be late home that night. She had already upset her parent once that day; she had no wish to do so a second time.

It had gone nine when Karrie at last arrived at her home. Travis had wanted her to stay to supper, but with her mind more on Farne she had wanted to get away. Farne had not rung her at the office, but as she let herself in through the front door she realised there might be a possibility, if his PA *had* mentioned her call, that he could well have telephoned her home!

'Farne didn't ring, did he?' she asked her mother after she had greeted her.

'The phone's been silent all day,' her mother answered, and seemed so distant with her somehow, so absent, that Karrie just knew that she was still very upset about her Milan trip with Farne.

'Nothing will happen, Mum, I promise,' Karrie said impulsively.

Her mother shrugged. 'It's your life!' And, as if not trusting her promise, added, 'Ruin it as you wish!' and walked towards the door.

'Moth-er!' But her mother wasn't listening.

Karrie got herself something to eat and had a horrendous time being torn in two by love and loyalty to her mother and the overwhelming love she felt for Farne. She didn't want her mother upset, but hadn't she just given her promise that she would not flout what had been drummed into her by her parent over the years?

Perhaps her mother was anticipating an intention that had never been in Farne's mind anyway. Before her mother had mentioned it Karrie owned that she hadn't put any interpretation on his invitation to Milan other than to just plain and simple enjoy each other's company.

Oh, how she wished her mother had just wished her a

happy time and left it at that! Karrie could feel herself growing all hot and bothered again, and started to wonder if she might ring Farne at his home. From his remark last night that his home wasn't far away from the restaurant she had an idea of the area where he lived.

She quickly found the telephone book, but straight away saw that Farne's number must be an unlisted one. By then Karrie was feeling so stewed up that had she known his address she would have got her car out and driven over to see him.

But she didn't have his address, and she didn't have his phone number. And, since his PA must obviously have thought better than to bother him with what had subsequently appeared to be a non-urgent message from someone the PA had plainly never heard of—there'd been so sign of recognition when Karrie had given her name, not that she had expected there to be—Karrie accepted that Farne would have no reason to ring her, but would call for her early tomorrow morning as arranged.

From being down in the depths, Karrie's spirits gradually started to lift. Then, at the thought of seeing Farne tomorrow, excitement gained a quick foothold. She loved him. She loved him, oh, so very much. Surely to go with him to Milan couldn't be so very wrong—could it?

Her eyes went dreamy at the thought of just being with him, and Karrie went upstairs to pack.

CHAPTER FOUR

BOTH her parents were still in bed the next morning when, suitcase in hand, Karrie left her room. She went silently down the stairs, knowing that she was going to Milan without her mother's approval, which had put a small blight on her anticipation.

She watched for Farne's car. The moment she saw it turn into the drive her heart went all fluttery. She loved him. She didn't intend to do anything she'd be ashamed to tell her mother about—so where was the harm?

So that Farne should not ring the bell, and disturb her parents, Karrie quickly gathered her case and bag, and went out to meet him. By the time she had quietly closed the door behind her Farne was out of his car and coming over to her.

She looked at him: tall, all male, immaculate and sophisticated in his business suit—and she was going to spend the weekend with him. Suddenly she felt inadequate, shy, her confidence torn asunder. She tried to form some sort of a greeting, but as Farne stared down at her it got stuck in her throat somewhere.

But he was intelligent and clever, and those piercing blue eyes missed not a thing. 'You look scared,' he observed evenly. 'Was it something I said?'

She felt better. He hadn't said a word—he was teasing. 'You aren't going to gobble me up?'

'Sugar and spice? Now there's an idea,' he smiled, but was suddenly serious, all sign of banter gone when 'Hell's teeth!' burst forth from him. 'You're not afraid of me, are you?' he questioned, looking truly appalled at the very idea.

60

'I don't scare *that* easily.' She rushed to try some teasing of her own, all at once having the most dreadful feeling that just the merest hint from her that she was in any way afraid or apprehensive about this weekend and the trip would be off. 'Good morning,' she added, and was heartily glad when, his eyes on her saucily smiling mouth, his appalled look vanished.

'You could, Miss Dalton, quite easily ruin a man's sanity,' he commented. And, bending, he lightly kissed her cheek. 'Good morning,' he answered her greeting and, relieving her of her case, they were away.

Karrie almost immediately recovered her equilibrium. In fact, by the time they reached the airport she was amazed that she had for a moment felt in any way shy or inadequate. By the time they had landed in Italy her confidence was back in full force. It was because of Farne, of course, she fully recognised, his charm, that something special about him that made everything right. She left the airport building with him, her heart full—he was so easy to be with. They conversed agreeably and Karrie found she was falling more and more under his spell.

A car and a driver were waiting for them, the driver clearly known to Farne, who, after a *'Buongiorno, Urbano,'* followed up with a fast flow of Italian incomprehensible to Karrie's ears, left Urbano putting their luggage in the boot while they got into the car.

Milan was bustling, busy—and the driving like none Karrie had ever seen. She wondered which hotel they were staying in. But it was only then, when she realised that she would soon know if Farne had booked them into two rooms—or just one—that she began to lose her feeling of well being and start to grow uptight. She didn't want a row with him, she truly didn't. But if it was room, singular, then Karrie knew that words would be exchanged.

She was still fretting on the subject, realising that this could be the end—it seemed incredible that less than two weeks ago she hadn't known of his existence, and here she was in Italy with him—when suddenly Farne broke into her thoughts.

'What's troubling you, Karrie?' he asked quietly.

Grief! Talk about observant. She would swear she had given away nothing of the fact she was having forty fits inside. 'Not a thing,' she replied, getting more tense by the second but knowing she was going to feel the biggest fool breathing if she mentioned a word about their accommodation, not to mention embarrassed to her back teeth should any such enquiry result in Farne saying, Of course you're having your own room. 'I was just—er—sort of wondering—um—whereabouts our hotel might…'

'We're not using a hotel.' She turned to stare at him. 'The company keeps an apartment here. We're staying there—' He broke off. 'That all right with you, Karrie?'

'Fine,' she said. 'Fine,' she repeated. An apartment suggested more than one bedroom, didn't it?

As was proved when the driver had dropped them and their luggage off and Farne, after exchanging a few words with a man on security duty, took Karrie up in a lift to the apartment. Once there he escorted her inside and showed her around. As well as a very pleasant sitting room, a dining room and a kitchen, there were, in fact, three *en suite* bedrooms.

'You're in here,' Farne said, showing her into one of the bedrooms. 'I think you'll be comfortable.'

'I'm sure I shall,' she smiled. Farne had dropped her case down but had hung on to his own, she saw.

He glanced at his watch. 'I'll just make us some coffee, then I'll be on my way.'

'I'll make it,' she offered, feeling good suddenly, not to say ecstatic. 'You go and do whatever it is that men do while women slave away in the kitchen.'

'I love your non-feminist streak,' he grinned. 'Men read the paper.'

He went to one of the other bedrooms and Karrie cheerfully went kitchenwards. She found fresh milk in the fridge, and various other supplies, and set about making coffee. When Farne came in, propped his briefcase on a chair and looked at her with a tender look in his eyes, she felt truly on top of the world.

'You'll be all right while I'm away?' he asked, when by unspoken mutual consent they sat at the kitchen table drinking coffee.

'Oh, yes,' she replied, uncertain if she would go out or stay in, not wanting to be out if his meeting was of the short variety. 'There's some fresh salad stuff. Shall I make a salad for when you come back?'

He looked as if he might say yes. But, after a moment's consideration, 'We'll eat out,' he decreed. Then he turned, his eyes fully on her. 'I found some sort of urgent-non-urgent message to contact you on my desk when I eventually reached my office yesterday,' he seemed suddenly to remember.

Her brain went dead. What could she tell him? He was obviously waiting for her to say why she'd wanted to contact him, urgently or not urgently. Now that she knew she was to have a room to herself, it all seemed so ridiculous somehow. Oh, she did so wish that her mother had not put such ideas into her head—but Farne was waiting.

'It was—er—nothing, really.' Karrie at last found her tongue. And, though she suspected that whether or not she could get Friday off had probably never so much as entered his head, the best she could come up with was the exceedingly lame, 'I just thought I'd let you know that I'd managed to get today off—so—um…' leave it there, do; you're making a hole to fall in '…there was nothing to worry about. I—um—sort of realised then, when I was speaking to your PA, that it, my call, wasn't so urgent after all.' Karrie could feel herself growing hot. 'She—er—has a very pleasant manner—your PA,' she attempted to change the subject.

'I almost came over to see you last night.' Farne refused to change the subject.

Good heavens! 'Oh, I wasn't in!' she exclaimed. 'I was working late.'

He smiled. 'So long as you weren't out seeing someone else.'

How possessive that sounded. How wonderfully possessive. That honesty in her, however, had to have its head. 'Well, to be truthful, I did see Travis when I'd fin—'

'The devil you did!' All sign of good humour abruptly went from Farne's expression. 'I hope he didn't keep you out too late.' Was he being funny? She didn't think so.

Having been on top of the world meant that Karrie had a very long way to fall, and she knew she could forget she had ever for an instant imagined that the look in Farne's eyes had been in any way tender. There was nothing but a kind of aloofness which she didn't much care for. She had, she owned, been through a whole gamut of emotions recently, and now she added confusion to the list. But, while she might not be a feminist, neither was she a doormat.

'Not too late that I didn't have time to do my packing when I got in,' she found herself erupting.

'Am I supposed to say thank you for that?' he rapped.

'Suit yourself!' she retorted. She hated it when he did just that. He was on his feet, briefcase in hand, and without another word was on his way to the door.

Karrie got up too. She watched from the kitchen the way he smartly crossed the sitting room and went to the outer door. But, just when she was feeling about the most wretched she had ever felt in her life, he stopped, and turned.

And, across that space, they looked at each other. And Karrie, her spurt of anger gone, just could not bear that they should part bad friends. 'D-don't be angry with me, Farne,' she said.

But, as softly spoken as her words were, across that distance Farne heard them, and, tossing down his brief-case, he came striding back. 'I'm a swine,' he said, every bit as if he had known some of the same confusion that she had felt. Gently, he gathered her into his arms. 'How could I ever be angry with you?' he murmured. 'You're my—' He broke off. Abruptly he broke off.

'I'm your?' she queried—it seemed important some-how.

'My—guest,' Farne answered. 'I should be making certain you're comfortable, not pushing you to anger. I should be...'

'Going,' she laughed, all well with her world once again, in heaven to be in his arms. 'You'll be late for your meeting.'

His look said, I don't care; his voice said, 'You're right. Are you going to be good while I'm gone?'

'Exemplary,' she laughed.

He kissed her, a brief kiss to her mouth, then he was gripping her arms tightly for a moment, before taking a step back. 'I've got work to do,' he growled, and, turning smartly about, he left her.

The apartment seemed very quiet when he had gone, and Karrie, still warmed by his brief kiss, went and un-packed her case in a dream world. A dream world that kept her indoors. She knew she should probably leave the apartment and go exploring a little, but the way she felt then she did not want outside intrusions. He had kissed her, only lightly, only briefly, but he wouldn't have done that if he didn't like her, would he? Silly sausage, Karrie—do you think he would have brought you to Milan with him had he not liked you?

So, okay, probably in the circles in which he mixed, going to Milan for the weekend was no more to him than say, her going to the seaside for a day. But still, all the same, he wouldn't have brought her with him unless he liked her.

At that thought her confidence seemed to stabilise at much the level where it had been before she had known him. She felt hungry suddenly, and looked at her watch to see with astonishment that it was lunchtime, and that she must have been sitting around just thinking about Farne for an absolute age.

She had just decided to have a quick freshen up and change—they were eating out when he got back—when the phone reposing on the bedside table rang.

She stared at it as if fascinated, certain that it must be a wrong number. It continued to ring. Oh, crumbs, perhaps it was Security downstairs. Now then, did she say *Prego* or was it *Pronto?*' She picked up the instrument. 'Hello?' she said.

'Missing me?' enquired a voice she would know anywhere.

Like crazy. 'You've only just left!' she replied sedately.

'And there was I, anxious in case time was hanging heavily,' Farne said in disgust, and, getting to the purpose of his call, 'It looks as though I'm going to be tied up here longer than I thought. Can you fix yourself that salad after all, and I'll get back as soon as I can?'

'What about *your* lunch?'

'Somebody's making up some food here. You're not unhappy?' What a dear darling he was. She was his guest; he didn't want her to be down.

'I'm fine. Enjoy your meeting.'

She was going to have to stop this, Karrie thought ten minutes later. All she'd done in that ten minutes was replace the phone, and stand there looking into space.

Making a conscious effort, she went and fixed herself something to eat, tidied up and afterwards lay on her bed, wondering at this love that had come and stood everything she knew on its head. She had never used to be indecisive. True, she had never felt this way before—it was one enormous kind of emotion, this love thing.

She yawned delicately, recalling she had been up and about extra early that morning, and closed her eyes as she relived every moment since Farne had called for her just before six. She'd enjoyed being with him so much, during the journey to the airport, sitting beside him on the plane, the drive to this apartment. She hadn't, though, much enjoyed the spurt of anger that had flared between them when she'd mentioned having seen Travis last night.

Perhaps she shouldn't have mentioned it. Perhaps Farne considered it bad manners for her to be with one man and mention a date with another. She felt embarrassed suddenly. Oh, heck, put like that, it was bad-mannered. But it hadn't been a date as such—she had merely called in on her way home from work. True, it had been arranged, but Travis came in the category of friend, not a date.

Karrie decided then and there that she would explain to Farne about Travis at the first opportunity. She'd tell him about the picture, and about how she'd known Travis for an age. For heaven's sake, Farne might be under the impression that she went out with a different man every night! She would tell him. She would tell him about Travis. She would... She fell asleep.

When Karrie opened her eyes she couldn't think where she was for a moment or two. Some sound attracted her glance to the doorway, to the door she had left open— and her heart suddenly started to thunder. There, standing watching her, was Farne.

Quickly she veiled her eyes—oh, how she loved him— and moved into a sitting position on the bed, tucking her long shapely legs to one side. 'I was up early,' she excused, and could have groaned—Farne must have been up much earlier in order to get to her home for six o'clock, and he'd done a day's work since. 'How long have you been home?' she asked, her brain seeming to still be half asleep. For goodness' sake—she was sounding like some chummy wife! Home?

Farne's expression seemed amused, as if he enjoyed observing her getting herself together. 'Not long,' he answered, and, as if her room was private to her, and he had no intention to trespass, he made no move to come any closer, but added, 'Though long enough to see that even in sleep you are, as ever, extremely beautiful.'

Oh, help! She was glad she wasn't standing—she reckoned her knees might have given way. Farne thought her extremely beautiful! She felt all soft and squashy inside—she needed an antidote.

'Just because you want me to make you a cup of tea!' she accused, and, swinging her legs off the bed, and finding that her legs would hold her, she got to her feet. She was glad to see that as she moved nearer Farne walked away from the doorway. 'How did your meeting go?' she asked, striving for some sense of normality.

'Quite good,' he replied, and did her normality cause no good whatsoever when he placed a hand to her hair and stroked it down. 'It was sticking up,' he explained, an amused kind of light in his eyes.

'I look a wreck.'

'With your hair all mussed up? You look terrific.'

'Put the kettle on. I'll be with you in a moment.'

She hadn't truly expected him to obey her orders, but she guessed it amused him to do something out of the ordinary. He went to the kitchen while she doubled back to run a comb through her gold-streaked blonde hair, which was all over the place. She was back with him before the kettle had boiled.

'Did you have something to eat?' Farne queried considerately.

'Yes. Did you?'

He nodded. 'Can you hold out till eight for dinner?'

She gathered he'd reserved a table somewhere. 'Of course,' she said, and they were back to conversing easily as she made a pot of tea and placed cups and saucers on a tray.

Farne it was, however, who carried the tray into the sitting room. 'Are you going to have a rest before we go out?' she asked as she poured a couple of cups of tea and handed one of them over to him.

To rest, however, seemed a totally new and novel idea to him. 'I don't normally,' he murmured.

'I refuse to feel a fool!' she told him. 'You must have been up with the birds this morning.'

He looked amused. 'I love your concern.'

I wish you loved me. 'Are you going to go all short-tempered on me if…? I know it's bad manners to talk about the men I've been out with,' she inserted, and saw any appearance of amusement fade from his expression, but plunged on regardless, 'But I thought I'd like to explain about—' She broke off. Farne did consider it bad manners; she could tell.

But instead of getting up and leaving her, which wouldn't have surprised her, Farne stayed, drank some of his tea and, putting his cup and saucer down, prompted, 'About?'

Karrie smiled at him. She wanted him back to good-humoured, but she was committed now. 'About—Travis.' She looked at Farne. So far so good. He was still sitting there anyhow. 'We *are* just friends,' she emphasised.

Farne considered her statement—it didn't take him long. 'He wants to marry you.' It was not a question.

Since it wasn't a question, and she didn't want to answer it, she ploughed on anyway. 'So when yesterday he rang, and, well, to be honest, quite desperately sounded as if he wanted someone to come and admire a picture he'd acquired that day, I went...'

'You went to his home—where he lives alone,' Farne finished for her.

She stared at him. 'Where he lives alone! You sound like my granny!' Karrie just had to tease. And had her reward. Farne, regarding her innocent-looking, wide velvety brown eyes, saw the funny side. She was sure the corners of his mouth tweaked up a little—even if he was determined not to smile.

'You may pour me another cup of tea,' he decreed. Oh, she did love him so.

After that everything went swimmingly. They went by taxi that night to a superb restaurant where in Farne's superb company Karrie ate a superb meal—and was so enraptured by him that she could never afterwards remember what she had eaten.

They returned to the apartment by taxi too, and Farne had behaved so impeccably, looked after her so well, that Karrie had not the slightest qualm. 'Would you like a nightcap of some kind?' he asked when they were alone together, the apartment door closed on the outside world.

She shook her head. 'I couldn't eat or drink another thing,' she said, standing with him in the sitting room. 'Thank you for a wonderful evening, Farne.' She wanted to go and kiss him, but because of the love she felt for him was afraid of giving herself away, and dared not.

'The pleasure was mine,' he replied. Just four simple words, and he had probably said them a dozen or more times, but to her ears they sounded special.

'I'll say goodnight, then,' she said, and hoped and half expected that he might come over and kiss her cheek, perhaps hold her in his arms for a few seconds.

But he did not. He stayed exactly where he was, his

tone easy, friendly. 'Goodnight, Karrie, sleep well,' he bade her.

Alone in her room she showered and got into a pair of cream satin pyjamas—a recent present from her mother, who had seen and liked them—and wondered at the mixed-up person she had become since falling in love with Farne.

She had been concerned that he might have plans for this weekend that didn't match up with hers. That he might well—thank you, Mother—have seduction in mind. But he had just shown that, far from panting to get her into his bedroom, he wasn't even minded enough to take those few steps needed to place a kiss on her cheek.

Karrie got into bed and lay awake, sleepless for an age, just thinking of Farne and wanting to feel once more his arms around her.

As a result of her sleeplessness, it was late when she awakened the next morning. And she realised she would not have come to when she did had someone not come tapping on her door. She opened her eyes, a smile instantly on her face.

'Come in!' she called.

The door opened. Farne, casually dressed, in polo shirt and trousers, stood there. He declined to come in, however, but studied her idly from the doorway, and required to know, 'Are you going to lie there all day?'

She laughed. She loved him. 'Is the sun shining?' She knew it was.

'The sun's shining,' he advised.

'Then I'll get up.'

Farne left her, and so began the best day of her life. Regardless that it was Saturday, Milan, that large city in Northern Italy, seemed as bustling as ever. They hailed taxis sometimes, at others seemed to walk miles around piazzas and pizzales, strolled fascinated about a market they came across. And, although Karrie was sure that

Farne was more inclined to the more sophisticated pursuits, he seemed, to her delight, to be as enchanted with everything as she was.

They walked; they had coffee. They talked; they laughed. They walked, rode in taxis, had lunch and hadn't yet done with talking, finding they shared a similar sense of humour. After lunch they walked some more until, nearing five, Farne hailed another taxi and they returned to the apartment.

'I've made you walk too much,' Farne regretted when in the sitting room of the apartment she collapsed, feet in front of her, on to the sofa.

'Not at all,' she denied, sitting up properly, but with an impish grin. 'Just fan my feet.'

Farne's glance went from her saucy eyes to her wickedly curving mouth. 'Oh, Karrie, Karrie,' he muttered, and she had no idea what that meant. 'Tea!' he said, and left her to go and make some.

They dined at a different establishment from the one they'd patronised the previous evening. But tonight was no less wonderful. This time she had a vague recollection of eating rice, with some pork and vegetables in it, which, if it wasn't purely influenced by her heightened senses, tasted absolutely divine.

Farne placed an arm about her shoulders as they left the restaurant, and her insides went all trembly at his touch. His arm fell away from her, however, as the taxi hailed for them drew up. 'That was super,' Karrie commented, and meant more than just the meal; she also meant the extra, extra super day she had just spent with the man who held her heart.

'I'm glad you enjoyed it,' he said softly, and caught hold of her hand and held it in his until they reached the apartment.

But when, in the apartment, Karrie again would have dearly loved to feel his wonderful arms about her, Farne did not seem to feel any such need. 'Thank you for a lovely evening, for a lovely day,' she smiled, as a prelude to parting from him and going to her room.

'It was—special,' he said. That it had been special for him too caused her heart to loop the loop. But he teased, 'Try not to be too late up in the morning,' and her heart abruptly ceased its giddy antics. That, in case she didn't know it—which she did—was Farne's way of adding, it wasn't *that* special.

'Goodnight,' she said.

'Sleep tight,' he replied.

Karrie awakened very early on Sunday morning and, try as she might, she could just not get back to sleep. She relived yesterday, the laughter she'd shared with Farne. From start to end the day had been good. From that first 'Are you going to lie there all day?' to the last 'Try not to be too late up in the morning.'

Impishness entered her soul. Try not to be too late up? The next second she was out of bed and heading on tiptoe for the kitchen. At first she intended to make a pot of tea and take a cup into his room to him with some suitable comment about 'these people who stay in bed'. But on thinking about it, as she waited for the kettle to boil, Karrie remembered the way when, apart from showing her into the bedroom she had used, Farne had thereafter seemed to treat beyond her bedroom threshold as strictly private.

While she did not doubt that the female of the species were no strangers to his bed, she would afford him the same courtesy. His bedroom would be as sacrosanct as hers. In any case, it suddenly seemed more amusing to take him a cup of tea but to leave it outside his door about a yard away, so he would see it the moment he opened his door. With luck it would be cold by the time he surfaced—he would know from that that she had been up hours. Let him say anything like that again!

As it happened, however, her plan didn't so much as get underway. Just as the kettle switched itself off, Karrie heard noises that told her that Farne was already stirring. Frozen into stillness for a moment, she listened, and the next she knew Farne, bare-footed, bare-legged, bare ev-erything bar the robe that he wore, if that scattering of dark hair in the vee of the collar was anything to go by, was stepping into the kitchen.

He hadn't known she was there. She saw his surprise break into pleasure. 'What have we here?' he asked, the corners of his mouth going up in that way she loved so much.

'Spoilsport,' she becalled him. 'I was going to leave a cup of tea outside your door.'

'Then I'd better—' He broke off, his glance going from her eyes, to her mouth and, as if magnetised, down to her breasts—and Karrie, following his glance, didn't know where to look thereafter. Because, pushing at the cream satin of her pyjama top, the tips of her breasts had hard-ened and were giving away, to anyone with eyes to see, their whole swollen geographical identity.

'I...' she choked, and went to rush past him.

But a table was in the way, and in any event Farne had recovered somewhat, and, as though to stifle her panic, he caught hold of her, murmuring softly, 'Don't be em-barrassed, little one.'

'I'm...' I'm not, she wanted to say. But it would be a lie.

'Shh,' Farne gentled her, and, as though she was a child in need of healing, he bent down and kissed her brow.

But she wasn't a child, and as he leaned forward their bodies touched—and suddenly the very air was electric! 'Farne,' she whispered, and felt his hands dig into her upper arms, and the next moment she heard the sound of a kind of a groan, and a moment after that Farne was pulling her into the manly circle of his strong arms.

And Karrie went willingly. She wanted to call his name again, but was unable to say anything because his mouth was over hers, and it was wonderful.

He held her close up against him and kissed her again, his lips travelling down her throat, kissing, tasting, and she arched her neck in utter pleasure. Somehow she found that her back was against a wall, and went into a spin of delight when Farne pressed against her.

He kissed her again, and she felt the warmth of his hands through the thinness of her pyjamas. Karrie raised her arms over his shoulders, holding on as the warmth of his hands at her back seemed to burn into her.

Her senses seemed to go a little out of control as those caressing hands found their way beneath her pyjama top and she felt his touch on the skin of her back. She held him to her as he held her to him. But didn't know quite where she was when, as if having seen and never forgotten the veiled but hardened peaks of her breasts, it seemed that Farne just had to know more of them.

Karrie swallowed hard, clinging to him when she felt his tender caressing touch come to the front of her, stray tantalisingly around her ribcage, before finally, exquisitely, he captured the rounded globes of her breasts. She had never, ever felt any sensation like the ones that bombarded her then. She loved him, and as he kissed her, so she returned his kisses.

Then suddenly she wasn't so sure. Because, while still caressing one of her breasts with one hand, Farne seemed to want to explore more of what was hidden from him, and his other hand came to the outside of her pyjama jacket, his fingers already busy with the top button.

'Farne!' she cried; shyness, that he would see her naked breasts, was a cruel mistress.

'What?' he asked, his fingers halting at the hint of alarm in her cry. 'What, my…?' He didn't finish, but laid the side of his face against hers, and it was just as if the feel of the delicate silky smoothness of her complexion against his own bristle-roughened skin seemed to awaken him to something. For with a kind of jerky movement he was tearing his hands from her, as though scalded, and saying gruffly, 'I—need a shave.' He turned away 'And…' he seemed to be striving for control '…and you, Karrie, I think you'd better go to your room and—do me a favour—don't come out again until you're fully clothed.'

And Karrie, owning to feeling more than a little bewildered by what had taken place, went without a word back to her room.

The next time she saw Farne he was clean-shaven and dressed. Karrie had left it until she thought she had herself back together again after his kisses—oh, those wonderful kisses. But as she went into the sitting room and he turned, so she was certain she'd gone scarlet.

His glance stayed on her; she knew he had observed her pinkened colour, and could only wonder at the mess he had made of her emotions. After those liberties she had not so very long ago allowed him—she suddenly felt bashful.

'I'll—get the breakfast,' she said, and went quickly through the sitting room and into the kitchen.

Farne joined her, but, like her, did not seem particularly hungry. Neither was he very communicative. And any stray idea she might have had that perhaps they might investigate a little more of Milan before they caught their plane back to England was a non-starter.

'We might as well get off now,' he commented evenly, once cereal had been disposed of and the kitchen tidied.

A dreadful feeling swamped Karrie, that she had been too eager in the kissing department and that Farne had gone off her, but, nothing if not proud, she smiled cheerfully. 'I've stripped my bed. What shall I do about the laundry?'

Quite clearly such domestic matters had never had space on his agenda. 'Just leave it—somebody will come and clean up,' he replied, and that was about the sum total of their conversation for the rest of the time they were in the apartment.

Mutiny, another unexpected emotion when she loved him so much, entered Karrie's saddened soul on the drive to the airport. He'd done as much kissing as she had! And, if she remembered rightly, he'd been the one to start it. Or had he? All at once it seemed a moot point. She hadn't been backward in coming forward, had she? And, if she was truly honest, she had been wanting him to kiss her all weekend.

Such honesty she did not want—it tempered her mutiny. Made her remember what a marvellous day yesterday had been. If, as seemed likely, Farne had gone off her, then she would have to take it—but she would always have yesterday to remember.

The thought of not seeing Farne again was a bleak one as they boarded the plane. She felt all emotional, close to tears, close to chatting brightly about anything impersonal she could think of just to show him that she didn't care a light that he had gone off her. But at the thought that this was it, her time with him over, she just wanted to hide away in some dark corner and lick her wounds.

That, or let him know that, eager for his kisses she might be, but that was a mile away from her being a too easy conquest. So, all right, Farne had awakened in her a response which she found staggering. But that was a very long way from her consenting to any other idea he might have briefly toyed with. So, she loved him quite desperately, but for goodness' sake, with her mother's example of getting pregnant for love of a man, Karrie felt certain—now that she wasn't in his arms—that she would have called a halt to their lovemaking had he not done so.

'You seem very deep in thought?' Farne remarked pleasantly by the side of her.

They were talking again! He had got over whatever had been eating at him back in that Milan apartment! Karrie wished she could blank him, look through him. But she loved him, and it eased her aching heart that by the look of it they were not going to part bad friends.

'I was just thinking that I'll be home early this afternoon,' she lied.

'You're having tea with Travis?'

My stars—he was sharp! 'I haven't any plans to see him,' she replied—and there was where the conversation ended.

By the time the plane had landed Karrie's spirits were down on the ground with it. So much for her thinking she and Farne were going to part in a friendly fashion. She felt defeated suddenly. Which was when pride jumped up and came to her aid. They had just come away from the airport building and were on their way to the car park when she halted.

'You must have umpteen things you need to do. I'll take a taxi home,' she smiled brightly, only just holding back from stretching out a hand to shake hands with him—they'd gone on a little way from that. 'Thank you for a—'

'There's nothing I want to do more than drive you to your home,' Farne cut her off—and Karrie was so taken up with wondering was he saying he wanted more of her company, or was he saying that he couldn't wait to be rid of her, that she let him.

At her home he got out of the car with her, placing her case down by her front door. 'Thank...' she began again.

'You enjoyed Milan?'

With you, it was marvellous! 'Very much,' she replied soberly. 'Are you coming in? My parents...'

'I'll see them tonight,' he replied.

'Tonight?' she queried, startled.

'When I call for you.'

'Call for me?'

'You *are* having dinner with me, aren't you?' he asked, such a winning way with him Karrie felt sure she would have said yes even had there been any doubt in her mind about her answer.

She glanced at her watch, 'Well, since it looks as though I've missed my lunch,' she replied primly.

And a kiss landed on the corner of her mouth. 'Bye, sweet Karrie,' he said, and such a feeling of joy spread through her she was grinning idiotically to herself as she went indoors.

'You look as though you've enjoyed yourself,' her mother, coming out into the hall, remarked when she saw her.

'Oh, I did,' Karrie replied, and even the question she felt was there in her mother's comment could not dim that inner joy. Though because she knew of her parent's concern, she consoled her, 'And Farne behaved like the perfect gentleman he is.' Though she stretched the truth a degree or so by adding, 'The whole of the time.'

'I'm glad to hear it! Are you seeing him again?'

'Like—I'm going out to dinner with him tonight,' Karrie revealed.

And at her obvious happiness Margery Dalton caught a hold of her daughter's hand. 'Oh, baby, you're in love with him, aren't you?' she cried worriedly. And Karrie couldn't tell her just how much she loved him. How much her day began and ended with Farne. How he could make her laugh like no other. Or how the love she bore him could make her so vulnerable she could feel close to tears should he be a little uncommunicative with her. And then she knew that she had no need to, because her mother knew, and understood. It was all there in that kiss she placed on her cheek, in that choked kind of, 'My darling girl, be careful. Oh, do be careful.'

Karrie took her case up to her room, knowing full well what lay behind her mother's entreaty to be careful. She meant be careful not to give herself to Farne. Well, there was no question of that. Even if she was willing, which she was not, and given that she and Farne had shared a very heady skirmish on the perimeters of lovemaking that morning, Farne had shown a most definite reluctance to take things any further. Oh, she had got to him, she knew that—he'd as good as admitted it when he'd sent her away saying not to come out again until she was fully clothed. But she hadn't got to him so much that he wasn't in control of himself or the situation.

But what was she bothering about that for now? She was seeing him again tonight. Didn't that tell her something? So, okay, it was a trillion miles away from him being in love with her, but it did mean that he liked her. They had shared their weekend together—and he still liked her. Still liked her sufficiently to want to see her again!

Karrie was ready and waiting when Farne called. She had lain in her bath and dreamed. Shampooed and dried her hair and dreamed. And now, dressed in a cool, short-sleeved dress of the palest bluey-green shade, she felt she was dreaming again.

'Come in,' she invited, striving to steady her wildly beating heart. It seemed incredible that this tall, good-looking man with those piercing blue eyes, with whom she had breakfasted in Italy only that morning, should like her so well he wanted to take her out again that same night. 'My father's not in, but my mother is.'

Farne obligingly went with her to the sitting room, where he and Margery Dalton exchanged a few pleasantries. Then Karrie went with him out to his car. And again the whole evening was wonderful. It was a night she never wanted to end. Just to be with him was a joy.

So much so that when, at the end of another superb meal, Farne escorted her out to his car and, stating that it was still early, enquired if she would care to go back to his place, she did not have to consider it for very long. Her mother had warned her to be careful. But what was there to be careful about? She loved him—wanted, greedy though it might be, to spend some more time with him. And truly, if Farne had any intention or inclination to attempt to seduce her, well, he'd had ample opportunity only that morning—and had declined any such attempt. Besides which, she had no way of knowing for just how long her friendship with him would last, but, at the end of it, she would still love him, and she wanted to see where he lived, to remember it, to be able to picture him there.

'You don't have to. It isn't a life and death decision,' Farne teased easily when she was a long time answering.

'I'm sorry,' she apologised quickly, suddenly terrified that he was going to withdraw his offer. 'As you said, it's still early. I think I would quite like to see your house.'

He made no comment, but she felt his hand on her arm as he guided her in the general direction of his car.

His house was in an exclusive area—and when they got there, when he opened the door and showed her in, she fell instantly in love with it. They went from the hall to the high-ceilinged drawing room, full of discreet but expensive furniture. Comfortable fat padded sofas were scattered about. It was a home, his home.

'It's lovely,' she murmured sincerely.

Farne looked into her eyes. 'I'm glad you like it,' he said simply. He seemed taken for the moment by her large wide velvety brown eyes then, collecting himself, 'I'm being a bad host. Coffee?'

'No, thanks.'

'Something else?' She shook her head, and he smiled. 'Then come and sit on this sofa with me, and tell me more about Karrie Dalton.'

She laughed lightly. 'There's nothing more to tell,' she protested, but didn't protest when he caught a hold of her hand and took her to the nearest sofa.

He still had a hold of her hand when they sat down. He half turned and looked at her. 'You're beautiful,' he said softly. 'And I'm getting an undeniable urge to kiss you again.'

Her heart started to play the giddy goat once more. 'You won't, of course,' she said.

'Of course,' he agreed. 'What sort of a man do you think I am?'

Pretty fantastic, actually. 'You—um—certainly know the best places to eat.' She was striving her hardest to change the subject, when Farne leaned forward and placed a most wonderful, most tender kiss on her mouth.

Her heart went into overdrive. She wanted to hold him, to kiss him back—but she had not forgotten the uncommunicative way he'd been that morning when, unreservedly, she had returned his kisses.

Farne pulled back, his expression serious, something, some concern there in his eyes which she couldn't quite fathom. 'I promise you that wasn't planned when I asked you back,' he stated quietly.

'I'm sure it wasn't,' Karrie said impulsively. 'It's—it's j-just that I don't think it's a very good idea.'

'You—don't?' he answered, and she just knew that there was no way he would attempt to persuade her differently. More, she began to fear he would get up and start looking for his car keys.

'I don't have to go home yet, do I?' she asked.

'You want to stay, even though…?'

'Oh, Farne,' she said softly. 'I know you didn't ask me back here for any purpose other than because—well, because we seem to enjoy each other's company. And, well, I w-want to kiss you too, only I was too f-forward this morning, and y—'

'Too forward?' Farne echoed, and even appeared staggered by the thought.

'Wasn't I?' she asked, lately it didn't seem to take very much to have her mixed up and confused—it was happening again.

'My dear.' Farne sent her heart dizzy again. 'There was a kind of shyness about you this morning that I found quite enchanting.'

Shyness? She'd thought she'd been all over him. *Enchanting!* 'Honestly?' she questioned, and just had to beam a smile at him. 'I know I'm not very experienced—er—that way. But…' Grief! Shut up, do! You'll be telling him you love him next! 'B…'

'But you do have some experience?' He had gone serious again, she noted.

'Lord, yes,' she answered stoutly—never let it be said that she let the side down.

Strangely she didn't get any plaudits for admitting to such a thing, his expression unsmiling, grim almost. 'Just how many lovers have you had?' he determined to know.

'Well, I've never actually counted,' she began, when all at once it dawned on her that her notion of lovers and his notion of lovers was something quite totally different! 'Oh!' she exclaimed, shocked. 'I haven't… I didn't… I've never actually been to bed with any of the men I've kissed. I didn't mean—' She broke off abruptly when she saw that Farne seemed suddenly to be far more shaken than she was!

'I don't…' He stared at her, his look incredulous. 'Just a minute…' He seemed to need time to recover. 'You're saying—' He broke off again, then seemed to get his second wind. 'You're saying—let me get this straight.' He seemed to need to recap. 'Are you saying that you have *never* shared yourself, most intimately, with any man?'

'Oh, no!' she agreed, or meant to agree, confusion starting to reign supreme once more. 'That is to say, yes, you're right, I haven't.'

Farne caught hold of her hands and gripped them tightly in his. Just as though she had him as thoroughly confused as she was confused herself. 'You're a virgin?' He needed absolute clarification.

Karrie felt a little pink about the ears, but, 'Yes,' she confirmed, adding hastily, lest he run away with the idea that she was some prim and proper goodie-goodie. 'But I do feel all the—er—normal—um—reactions, in the—hmm—appropriate circumstances.'

Farne's answer was to raise both of her hands to his lips. He kissed first one and then the other, then, his look gentle on her, 'I believe I do know that,' he teased softly, getting over his shock and obviously referring to her response of that morning.

Karrie smiled shyly back, and thought better than to confess that the 'normal reactions' had only ever happened when she had been in his arms. Farne still had a hold of both her hands, and to feel the skin of his hands against her skin was setting off all sorts of tingling sensations within her. She glanced to his mouth, and suddenly felt an overwhelming need to feel that mouth, that wonderful mouth against her own again.

'You know more about these things than me, but tell me, Farne, is it purely a male prerogative to get an undeniable urge to kiss—er—?' His most fascinating mouth starting to curve upwards caused her to break off.

'A few minutes ago you didn't seem to think it a very good idea,' he reminded her, his tone warmly teasing.

She laughed, a light, happy laugh. 'Don't you ever change your mind?'

'Seldom,' he replied, and unhurriedly gathered her into

his arms—and Karrie had her undeniable urge satisfied when, tenderly, Farne kissed her.

'Oh!' she sighed when he pulled back from her.

'Oh—good?' he enquired.

'Oh, good—fantastic,' she whispered, and was kissed again for her honesty. And again, and again.

It was such bliss to be this close to him, their lips meeting, their arms around each other, Karrie never wanted it to stop. Then, gradually, the tenor of those kisses began to change. She loved him; she clung to him. A fire started to kindle in her for him. She wanted to get closer to him—and was enraptured when Farne seemed to want the same, to get closer to her.

She had no memory of actually lying down on the sofa with him, and was unaware of any movement until he raised himself on one elbow and looked down at her.

'Everything—okay with you, Karrie?' he asked softly.

She wasn't sure what he meant, but since she just had to share more and more intimate moments with him, she nodded assent, 'Oh, yes,' she sighed, just in case he hadn't seen her answer—and those intimate moments were wonderfully there when Farne kissed her again.

When he pressed closer to her, she instinctively pressed closer back. She heard a small sound leave him, and the next she knew he was lying over her, pressing her down into the softness of the cushions. And she had never experienced anything like it.

He kissed her throat and moved so he could caress her. She gloried in his caresses and felt his hands at her breasts; she wanted to cry his name, but his lips had claimed hers again. His hands left her breasts—but this time when she felt his hands at the fastenings of her clothing she made not one single demur.

Farne kissed her long and passionately, drawing from her every response. She loved him, and knew she wanted him, and yet was startled suddenly to feel his tender caress on her naked breasts.

'Farne!' she gasped.

'Karrie—lovely Karrie, don't be alarmed,' he gentled her. And she loved him, and things were happening inside her which shouldn't be happening. She wanted to give in to the pleasure of his touch, to rejoice in the feel of his sensitive hands on her.

'I'm not,' she whispered. 'But…' She wanted to touch him too. She swallowed. 'But—fair's fair.' She raised a hand and touched a button on his shirt. And had never known such intimacy when, her meaning at once clear to him, Farne removed his shirt.

Karrie swallowed down a moment of panic when she saw the naked expanse of his broad, manly chest. Then wonder was taking her as she raised a hand and touched the dark hair, then transferred her finger to touch one of his nipples.

'Fair's fair,' Farne murmured, and as, wide-eyed, she stared at him, a rush of shyness swamped her when Farne pulled back a little way and feasted his warm gaze on her full breasts with their hardened pink tips. 'Oh, you're so beautiful,' he breathed. 'Exquisite,' he murmured, and, while her desire for him was helping Karrie to overcome her feeling of shyness to have him see her breasts so uncovered, Farne stretched out a forefinger and touched the dusky pink nub.

'Oh!' she cried softly, and as his thumb joined his forefinger, and he gently held that pink tip, so suddenly, everything started to go wild within her. Farne kissed her, kissed her breasts, and moved over her again. She felt the bare skin of his chest against the bare skin of her breasts, and it was all so rapturously thrilling, gloriously unknown, that she only just held down from telling him how much she loved him.

But, when she had thought she was oblivious to all and

everything but this moment, she felt his hand come beneath the skirt of her dress—the top half of it somewhere around her waist—and, while she desired him madly, suddenly great strident alarm bells were starting to go off. She ignored them; she did not want to take heed of them. She was here with Farne, where she wanted to be. He was making love to her—it was what she wanted. Wasn't it? And besides, as he had that morning in Milan, he would stop any moment now.

Not that she wanted him to stop; she didn't. She was on fire for him—she didn't. Or thought she didn't. Then she felt the imprint of his palm on the outside of her briefs—and those alarm bells started clamouring louder. Farne kissed her. She adored him; she kissed him in return—then felt his fingers inside the top of her briefs—exploring! And that was when perhaps a sudden shyness at such intimacy broke through her need for Farne—and allowed long-held beliefs a space to give voice.

'*No!*' The word broke from her without her known volition. Then she was panicking. She struggled free—sure she meant yes, and not no, but instinct was urgently pushing her to sit up.

'No?' Farne echoed, sounding stunned, shattered as he too sat up.

'Oh, Farne, Farne, I can't,' she gulped. 'I just—can't.'

'You—can't?' he repeated, astounded.

'I'm sorry. Oh, I'm so sorry,' she apologised, having managed to get into her bra but desperately trying to make sense of a dress that seemed to have no armholes. 'I know everything about me has been saying y-yes—' her voice was staccato, shaking '—but I can't—not until I'm married!'

Total and utter silence met her last remark—and Karrie wanted to die. It was all right remembering—at this late stage—her upbringing, the message that had been hammered into her for years, but in the sophisticated circles

Farne was used to moving in such notions were probably regarded as crass.

'Not until you're married,' Farne stated, it seeming not to be a question, but more as though he was letting that message sink in.

'I'm sorry,' she apologised again, feeling dreadful. 'I know you must be hating me, but it's—important t-to me,' she stammered. This was the end; she knew it. 'I'm sorry, but it—it's important to me,' she repeated lamely.

'Important?' He seemed to be having trouble taking it in. He was certainly weighing his words anyway. Then he cleared his throat. 'Er—how important?' he asked slowly.

As she had known—he wasn't trying to persuade her. 'Ex-extremely,' she answered. 'Essential. I…' Her voice tailed off—and silence followed. Which was preferable to the derision she felt she would have forgiven him for in the circumstances.

But when Farne did break that silence it was not derision she heard. But, astonishingly—and very nearly causing her to go into heart failure—she distinctly heard him state quietly, 'In that case, Karrie, we'd better get married.'

Struck dumb, disbelieving, she turned and stared witlessly at him. But Farne wasn't looking at her. He was fully occupied putting her arms into the sleeves of her dress and fastening it up. She had still not found her voice when, shrugging into his shirt and buttoning it, he stood up.

'I'll take you home,' he said.

And Karrie, on shaky legs, got to her feet, too. Farne looked totally serious but, having found her voice, she was too terrified to say a word—just in case he was joking.

CHAPTER FIVE

KARRIE got out of bed the next morning having slept little. Her head was still spinning from the multitude of questions that needed answering, but which, in fact, boiled down to only one—had Farne been joking when he'd asked her to marry him?

Not that he'd actually *asked* anything. Used to making decisions, there had been no asking about it, but more a statement of fact. 'We'd better get married' he'd said. Not that she was complaining. She wanted to marry Farne. More than anything she wanted to marry him. Even now just the thought of marrying him, of being Mrs Farne Maitland, made her feel all fluttery inside.

But had he meant what he said? Was she supposed to take what he said seriously? She had been so all over the place when he'd said what he had that her brain hadn't been able to come up with so much as one single solitary question. Farne had *looked* serious, though.

But he'd been quiet to the point of silence on that drive to her home. And she had been in such awe at what had taken place that she had been lost for words. Farne had got out of the car with her and gone to her front door with her. He'd opened it for her, and then, he'd said, 'Goodnight, my dear,' bent his head and given her what she was sure must be the briefest kiss on record, his lips barely brushing hers—and he'd turned smartly about, and gone. This morning, she didn't know whether she was engaged to be married or not. Or if she had, in fact, dreamed the whole of it.

Karrie showered, dressed and got ready to go to work, pondering at the very real possibility that she might not even see Farne again. She went downstairs and had never felt less like eating breakfast, but, seeing her mother's gaze on her, made an effort.

'You were late in last night,' Margery Dalton commented pleasantly.

Both her parents had been in bed, and Karrie, needing to be alone, had been glad about that. 'Was I?' she smiled, knowing full well that her mother wouldn't mind knowing where she had been in a little more detail, but didn't want to make her mother's hair curl.

Besides which, Karrie mused as she drove to work, what had taken place between her and Farne, their love-making, was intensely private. She could hardly say, Oh, by the way, I might be engaged, but I'm not very sure. Come to that, not at all sure.

'Good weekend?' Darren Jackson fell into step with her as she crossed the Irving and Small car park.

'Super,' she said automatically. In view of last night's developments the fact that she'd spent the weekend in Milan with Farne seemed light years away. 'You?' she queried before he had the chance to ask if she'd gone anywhere special.

'Average,' he replied. 'You didn't tell me you were having Friday off.'

About to give him a sharp, I didn't know I had to, Karrie swallowed it down. It wasn't his fault that her nerves were shot and that she didn't know where the dickens she was. 'I'm sorry,' she smiled, and added pleasantly, 'Did you miss me?'

'Like—are you coming out with me tonight?' He was quick—but predictable.

They reached the office they both worked in. 'Bye, Darren,' she said.

'Come the Revolution!' he threatened.

Karrie shared a few minutes' chat with her female colleagues, and fielded Lucy's eager question, 'Are you go-

ing to tell us who your Saturday night date was?' Clearly
Lucy was fishing to know if Karrie had seen Farne
Maitland again. Karrie got on with some work. Lucy's
eyes would shoot out of her head if she revealed that not
only had she seen the board member of the Adams
Corporation on Saturday, but she had spent the weekend
in Italy with him.

Karrie so wanted Farne to call her that she jumped
every time the phone on her desk rang. But it was never
him. Many were the times she prepared to keep her voice
level and even find a laugh should he ring through to say
something along the lines of, it had just occurred to him
that she might have taken his light-hearted remark seriously last night. Oh, good heavens, she would say. I'd
have run a mile had I thought for a moment that you were
in any way serious. But her rehearsed phrases were not
needed.

Farne did not phone, and at around four o'clock that
afternoon, when Karrie was just feeling her most nerve-
racked, tired and burdened down with her unhappiness,
wanting only to go home and to hide in her room, her
supervisor came looking for volunteers to work late that
night.

Oh, crumbs! Pauline Shaw had been pretty super about
letting her have last Friday off. 'Count me in,' she smiled,
and took time out to ring her mother and let her know
she would be late.

Karrie arrived home a little after eight, her heart in her
boots. She did not want to ask her mother if Farne had
phoned, but if her mother didn't volunteer that information Karrie knew, shaming though it might be, that she
was just going to have to ask if there had been any calls
for her.

She entered the house, saw the drawing room door was
ajar, but instead of the usual icy silence—that was when
they weren't yelling at each other—Karrie heard the

sound of her parents actually talking quietly together. Who had died?

She went in. Two pairs of eyes were watching the door—her mother smiling gently, her father looking almost benign! 'Wh…?' was as far as she got.

'I didn't know you knew Farne Maitland,' her father stated pleasantly.

At mention of Farne's name all kinds of emotions went on the rampage within Karrie. She shot a hasty glance at her mother, guessing that, for all it wasn't a secret to be kept from her father, her mother must have told her father she had gone to Milan with Farne at the weekend.

Was her father taking her to task? She glanced back to him. His still amiable expression suggested not, but she decided to play it safe. 'I didn't know that you knew Farne either,' she answered carefully.

'I didn't. Until today—when he came to see me.'

Karrie's eyes shot wide, her heart lurching into overdrive. 'Oh!' she exclaimed faintly.

'Oh, indeed,' her father replied. 'Apparently he's called here several times recently, but I've never been home. As he particularly wanted to speak to me today, he thought rather than take a chance on my being home the next time he came around—' Farne intended coming to her home again! She swallowed, her palms moist, as her father continued, 'he'd come to my office.'

'He—Farne, he—um—wanted to see you today, you said?' Karrie found her voice.

Her father nodded. 'Apparently, Farne Maitland last night asked you to marry him, and you said yes.' There was a roaring in her ears. 'In the time-honoured tradition, my future son-in-law came to ask my approval,' her father ended, and while untold joy suddenly broke loose in Karrie—Farne had meant it, he had, he hadn't been joking—her mother, who had been silent all this while, could suddenly contain herself no longer.

'Oh, darling, I'm so happy for you!' she cried, and was off her chair and over at Karrie's side, embracing her while lightly scolding her for having never said a word at breakfast-time about Farne's marriage proposal.

Then suddenly they heard the sound of a car on the drive, and when Karrie wondered—surely that wasn't Farne?—her father was announcing, 'I knew I had a late meeting, so I invited Farne to a late dinner—you'd better go and let your fiancé in, Karrie.'

Fiancé! She went—quickly she went. But at the front door she suddenly felt too stunned by all that had happened to move. She wasn't ready to see him again; she just wasn't. The bell sounded. It was all too much, too fast.

She got herself together. This was Farne, the man she loved. She opened the door, and as her heart received another surge of blood at the sight of the terrific-looking man standing there she began to wonder if it would ever beat normally again. She knew that her face had gone scarlet.

'Hello,' she managed, and stepped back from the door.

Farne stepped over the threshold, his eyes taking in her warm colour. 'Hello, you,' he smiled, and bent to place a light kiss on her mouth, then, standing back, he commented easily, 'I thought a celebratory glass might be in order,' and she noticed then that he was carrying a bottle of champagne.

'My p-parents are in the drawing room,' Karrie, her head feeling like cotton wool, found enough voice to state.

Her father was in the drawing room; her mother had hastened kitchenward. It was all too much. Mumbling something about being grubby, having only just got in from work, Karrie left Farne talking to her father and bolted upstairs to her room.

She couldn't believe it! It was too fantastic! It was what she wanted, oh, so very much. And yet—something just didn't seem quite right. She couldn't put her finger on quite what exactly, but... Her excitement, her love for Farne suddenly overrode all and everything, and she quickly freshened up and changed into one of her smarter dresses—it wasn't every day she became engaged—and went downstairs.

Her mother was a good cook, and, given that they were having a very special guest to dinner who had been dropped on her at short notice, the meal—salmon *en croûte* hurriedly defrosted from the freezer—was quite superb.

Karrie was proud of her mother too, who, when there were probably quite a few questions she might have felt like asking Farne, was a model hostess and made sure that he felt comfortable. Farne, Karrie saw, was a model guest in return, conversing easily when required to, but leaving the floor entirely to her father at others.

It was getting on for eleven by the time they adjourned to the drawing room. Half an hour later Bernard Dalton stated that since Farne was now family, he was sure Farne wouldn't mind if he left them, that he was usually in bed before this.

'I think I'll go up too,' Margery Dalton added pleasantly, and Karrie, thanks to her parents' tact, was left alone with the man she now knew had not been joking when he had last night said that they had better marry.

She felt shy and awkward suddenly, and knew that perhaps she should say something a little personal. They were standing together in the middle of the room. 'I—er—my parents like you,' was about the best she could come up with—having a fair idea that it probably wouldn't bother him too much if they didn't.

'And I them,' he answered politely, and, putting his hand in his pocket, he brought out a small box. 'I hope you'll like this,' he said. 'If not we can change it.' And, so saying, he opened the box to reveal a most superb diamond solitaire ring.

'Farne!' Karrie gasped, and just stood staring at it.

'We'd better see if it fits.' She was so all over the place by then that it was no surprise to her that she offered him her right hand. Farne caught a hold of it, and made her tingle all over when he raised it to his lips and kissed it before returning it to her side. 'The other one,' he requested softly, and her backbone threatened to melt.

Her heart was beating crazily when, taking a hold of her left hand, Farne slid the ring home on her engagement finger. It fitted perfectly. 'It's beautiful!' she breathed, for the first time beginning to feel betrothed.

She looked up, straight into Farne's piercing blue gaze, 'Like its wearer,' he murmured—and she just had to stretch up and kiss him.

She felt his hands come to her waist, and wanted to be nearer. She took a step closer, her hands going up to his shoulders, their bodies just touching as their kiss deepened. But then, just as she thought Farne was going to take her in his arms, he instead gripped her more firmly by the waist—then took a pace away.

Her hands fell from his shoulders. She felt tongue-tied, as though she had been too eager. Colour flooded her face and Farne, after a moment of staring at her, took a quick glance to his watch. 'I've a very early meeting in the morning,' he said. 'I'd better get off.'

'Of course,' Karrie murmured, feeling a touch bruised—a couple of kisses wouldn't have hurt; they were engaged, for goodness' sake, and with her parents in bed they weren't likely to be disturbed! She looked down to her beautiful engagement ring. 'Er—talking of work—' she held up her left hand '—do I wear this to the office tomorrow?'

'Unless you intend keeping it a secret,' he answered, a degree sharply, she felt—oh, very lover-like!

'That's no kind of an answer!' she retorted.

He laughed. 'Forgive me,' he apologised, and gave her the answer she was seeking. 'You're an engaged woman, Miss Dalton. Wear it at all times.'

'I'll see you out,' she stated.

'That's my reward for daring to think you might want to hide from the many men who want to date you, the evidence that they stand no chance?'

Good heavens—was that why he had been so sharp? Startled, she stared at him. 'Charmer!' she accused, and wanted to kiss him again—but, remembering the last time she'd kissed him, not minutes ago, didn't.

She had opened the front door, and Farne was just about to go through and out into the night when their lips met again. 'Goodnight, fair maid,' he bade her, and lightly brushed his mouth against her own. Then he was gone. Charmer, did she say? He was all that, and more—was it any wonder that she loved him?

Karrie did not have to show her mother her engagement ring the next morning; her mother spotted it. 'When did you get it?' she exclaimed, taking hold of her daughter's hand and bringing it closer for inspection.

'Last night.'

'You weren't long after us in coming to bed,' Margery Dalton stated, and Karrie did not miss the note of approval in her voice.

'Farne has an early meeting this morning,' Karrie smiled.

In fact she felt like smiling all the way to her place of work. Once there, however, and having parked in the car park and made her way indoors, she began to feel a mite self-conscious about the magnificent diamond adorning her finger.

Because a lot of her work was computer-based, there was no way she could operate with one hand hidden. She took her place at her desk and wondered if anyone would notice what, to her mind, was shouting out to be seen. Perhaps no one would observe the ring which hadn't been in place yesterday, she mused. But thirty seconds later, as Celia walked by her desk, she knew she could cease wondering.

'Where did you get *that?*' Celia shrieked—and seconds later Karrie was surrounded.

'Who?'

'When?'

'No wonder you wouldn't come out with me!' Darren complained.

'Shut up, Darren,' Lucy and Jenny said together.

'Who?' Lucy joined in. 'Is he anyone we kn—?' She broke off. 'It's *never* Farne Maitland!'

Such silence followed that the proverbial pin could have been heard dropping. 'Er—it is Farne, actually.' Karrie, feeling a little pink, took a deep breath and owned up.

A stunned silence followed. It lasted about three seconds. 'Stone the crows!' Lucy gasped. 'I'd heard he was a fast worker business-wise—pulling off the un-pull-off-able, but, crikey, your first date with him was only last Wednesday!'

Confession time. 'I'd—er—been out with him before that, as a matter of fact,' Karrie owned, and was grateful not to be quizzed further.

Though she could have done without Jenny sighing, 'It must have been love at first sight!'

Karrie dealt with the rest of their remarks, and, work calling to be done, one by one they trickled back to their own desks. She, while getting on with her tasks, was left with space in which to realise just what it was she hadn't been able to put her finger on last night. That something that hadn't seemed to be quite right. She had more or less fallen in love with Farne at first sight. But he—he had never told her he loved her!

She puzzled at it as she worked. Did he love her—did he not? She hardly expected him to love her with the same all-encompassing love she felt for him; that would be too much to hope for. But did he care for her a little? Surely he did. He wouldn't have asked her to marry him otherwise—well, told her they'd better get married, she qualified. But for goodness' sake, he could marry just about anybody, so he must care a little, surely?

Karrie glanced up to see a beaming Pauline Shaw making a beeline for her desk. 'Mr Lane would like to see you,' she smiled. And as Karrie got to her feet and Pauline walked with her, she stated sincerely, 'I'm delighted with your news.'

Help—news travelled fast! 'Thank you,' Karrie answered quietly. She tapped on Mr Lane's door and was beamed at by his secretary, who stood up and went with her into Mr Lane's office.

'Miss Dalton,' the secretary announced, and went back to her desk.

'Karrie!' Gordon Lane greeted her—everyone was smiling that day, it seemed. 'I've just taken a call from Farne. He wanted to tell me personally of your engagement just in case you were feeling shy in any way. I can't tell you how pleased we all are at Irving and Small to hear such good news.'

Karrie reeled out of Mr Lane's office ten minutes later, having been advised that if she had the smallest problem about absolutely anything she must go straight in to see Mr Lane.

Back at her desk, she sank down on to her seat, starting to feel especially good inside. Farne must have appreciated what hotbeds of gossip offices were, and realised that their engagement would be a talking point until something else happened to someone and took precedence. He had known too that there was little Gordon Lane didn't get to hear about. And so, aware that she might feel a little awkward should she be called upon to account for the rumour, he had phoned Gordon Lane to tell him personally of their engagement and request that Gordon smooth any problems in her path.

And that just *had* to mean that Farne cared for her. He just had to. As busy as he undoubtedly was, Farne had found time to make that phone call. Karrie tried not to burst into song as she worked. She still found it incredible that she was actually engaged to him, and glanced at her engagement ring countless times to confirm that fact.

So what if he hadn't told her he loved her? She'd make him the best wife in the world. The poor darling. He'd been sent away to school at the age of seven—what had he known of love? Perhaps it was all down to him being sent from home at such a tender age that he had an inability to speak words of love. Her expression went all soft and dreamy. She would love and look after him, she vowed. As he had looked after her that day by making that phone call.

Farne telephoned that night. 'I was hoping to be able to get away so we could have dinner somewhere tonight, but I'm a bit snowed under. Do you mind if we leave it until Thursday?' he asked.

They hadn't arranged to meet, but she had been hoping that they would, and was disappointed. 'Not at all,' she answered brightly. Was she really, truly engaged to him? She looked at the ring on her finger, and her heart rejoiced. 'Thanks for phoning Mr Lane today,' she said lightly.

'You didn't object?'

To Farne telling her boss she was engaged, or to his interference in doing so? She had no idea. 'Was I supposed to?'

'You're lovely,' he said, and rang off.

His 'You're lovely' stayed with her all that evening and the next day, Farne filling her head so completely that there was barely any space to think of anything else. That was until Wednesday evening, when Travis Watson rang asking her if she fancied meeting him at the Quail and Pheasant.

Oh, crumbs. Travis thought he loved her; she couldn't tell him she was engaged over the phone! 'I'll meet you there in half an hour,' she agreed, and, her father not home, she went to see her mother to tell her she was going out.

'Farne?'

Karrie shook her head. 'Travis—I'd forgotten him. I'll have to tell him.'

'You're a good girl,' her mother said warmly, and while Karrie didn't know about that, she was grateful for her parent's understanding.

Travis was shaken when she told him, and said it wasn't fair, then declared that he would love her always, and that if she broke off her engagement he wanted to be the first to know.

'Still friends?' she asked as they parted.

'For ever!' he vowed, and Karrie went home knowing that Travis was a little hurt, but also knowing that while he might love her, he did not feel deeply for her. She knew, because now she knew what being deeply in love felt like.

'There were two phone calls for you,' her mother said when she got in.

'Farne?'

'Farne,' her mother confirmed, adding—as Karrie tried to get over her disappointment at having missed him, 'I said you were out with a friend.'

'Did he leave any message?'

'He said it wasn't important, and that he'd be seeing you tomorrow. Then Jan rang.'

Karrie had phoned her cousin briefly the night before, but took a quick look at her watch now. 'Is Jan all right?'

'As good as new,' she said.

'I'll give her a ring,' Karrie decided. It had only just gone ten, and Jan had a phone by her bed if she was tucked up with a good book.

Karrie spent a good half-hour chatting to her cousin before promising to call and see her after work on Friday. 'Unless your fiancé has something else planned,' Jan qualified for her.

Karrie lay in bed that night, trying to get the hang of being an engaged person. She still marvelled that she was actually engaged to Farne, and felt like pinching herself to see if it was all real, but was she supposed to be available at all times in case he wanted them to go somewhere? He came first with her, naturally, and it was right that it was so; after all she had, by wearing his ring, his wonderful ring, accepted to spend the rest of her life with him. Oh, how astoundingly fantastic that sounded. But surely being engaged didn't mean she had to stay home nights on the off-chance that he would ring?

She discovered the next night that Farne didn't seem too thrilled that she'd been out with a friend when he'd phoned. Her heart gave its usual rush when he called for her, and they chatted amiably as usual about all and everything on the way to the restaurant. But they were halfway through their meal when, since Farne hadn't mentioned his phone call, her curiosity got the better of her.

'I'm sorry I was out when you rang last night,' she began. 'Was it anything important?'

Farne eyed her steadily across the table. 'You were out with a friend, your mother said.'

What sort of answer was that? To her mind it sounded more like a question! But she remembered how she had previously admired Farne's openness, and wanted nothing hidden between them. 'I was out with Travis. He—'

'The hell you were!' Farne snarled, and she stared at him in amazement—the change in him was startling.

'Have you forgotten that you're engaged to me?' he demanded.

'No, of course not!' she retorted hotly.

'Then you'll oblige me by not seeing him again!' Farne commanded, no two ways about it.

'Travis is my friend!' she protested.

And had the wind totally taken out of her sails when Farne rapped, 'And I'm your fiancé.'

How wonderful that sounded. Karrie almost capitulated without a murmur, but then thought, Hang on a minute! While it was true only last night she had wondered about the business of being an engaged person, it seemed to her that certain ground rules were being laid down about which she wasn't at all sure.

'Don't you have any women-friends who are just friends?' she asked.

His expression was unsmiling. 'Is that likely?' he asked.

Karrie took in the totally virile look of him, and her heart did a crazy cartwheel. She suddenly felt all shaky inside. 'Probably not,' she answered. But because there seemed quite a lot at issue here—not to mention that the green-eyed monster jealousy was stabbing her with spiteful barbs—she added, 'Do I take it you've given up all your female—er…?'

'All ties have been severed, never to be rejoined,' he stated categorically, and she knew she could believe him; there was something very straightforward in those piercing blue eyes that told her so.

She loved him, and didn't want him stern and unyielding with her. And, she all at once realised, she wasn't very sure how *she* would have felt had he said that there was some female he was just friends with—and with whom he intended to continue having that relationship.

'Travis rang and invited me for a drink.'

'Do I applaud now or later?'

'Don't be a pig!' she erupted on a flare of anger. 'Or I won't explain to you—not that I need to explain anything… Well, I suppose since I'm wearing your ring you're entitled.'

'So explain,' Farne invited—and seemed, she thought, just a touch more affable.

'So…' She glanced to him and went all weak—was she really engaged to be married to him? It still felt unreal at times. 'So, anyway,' she got herself together, 'as you rightly guessed, Travis has asked me to marry him… I wouldn't have told you that but you're—er—a special case.'

She saw his mouth start to curve, as though he wanted to laugh, but he suppressed any such urge. 'I'll try to remember that,' he answered solemnly.

He really had the most superb mouth. 'Anyhow,' she again collected herself to resume, 'when Travis phoned I realised, because we have been good friends—I've never been to bed with him or anything like that,' she inserted hurriedly. 'Well, you know that. You're the nearest I've ever come to going to bed with anybody.' A flare of colour surged to her face, and she wished she'd never got started on this.

Then Farne, having observed her warm colour, was stretching out a hand to her across the table. 'I know, sweetheart,' he said softly, and she went all wobbly inside, and oddly all emotional—just because he held her hand and called her sweetheart. 'Go on,' he urged, seeming to gather himself together too as he let go of her hand. That stern look he had previously favoured her with hadn't returned, she was glad to note.

Feeling enormously cheered, Karrie felt able to finish. 'Well, because of everything, it didn't seem to me to be quite right to tell Travis over the phone that I was engaged to marry someone else.'

'You saw him only to tell him of our engagement?'

'I thought I should,' she replied. 'And you should have left your phone number; I could have rung you back.'

'Don't you have it?'

She shook her head, and he dipped inside his jacket and extracted his card, which he handed to her. Karrie popped it inside her purse and asked, 'Did you ring for anything in particular, or for just a chat?' Somehow she couldn't see him ringing for just the latter.

'My parents are expecting us in Dorset this weekend. I—'

'I've missed something!' she exclaimed.

'Like—go back to the beginning?'

'Would you mind?'

'Not at all,' he said lightly, and somehow they were both grinning. 'I phoned my parents with our news and they're anxious to meet you. I said we'd spend the weekend with them. I thought I'd better ring and let you know.'

Heavens! She just hadn't got round to thinking about Farne's family. Karrie owned to feeling nervous about the proposed visit. She did so hope they liked her. 'We wouldn't be going until Saturday?' she queried.

'You're doing something Friday evening?'

He was as sharp as a tack! 'I've arranged to see—'

'Not Travis!' Farne cut her off before she could blink.

'Would I dare?' she erupted. Then she laughed; she wanted to be friends with him. 'I'm going to see my cousin, Jan, who has been poorly,' she informed him, but, bearing in mind that perhaps she should consult him more in the future—for all he had arranged a visit to Dorset without asking her first—added, 'You can come too, if you'd like to.'

'Did I say you had charm?' Farne enquired nicely— that was the end of her backbone, which turned totally to jelly.

'What time do you want to leave on Saturday?' she asked.

'I'll call around midday. We'll have lunch on the way—take the scenic route. All right with you?'

'Thank you for asking,' she answered impishly—and thought for a moment that Farne intended to get up from the table and come over and kiss her.

He didn't, of course. Nor, when he took her home, and the house was in darkness, indicating that her parents were in bed, did he care to come in. 'Another full day tomorrow,' he excused himself when invited in, and held her but briefly; his kiss was even briefer—and then he was gone.

Karrie was again feeling nervous at the prospect of meeting Farne's parents when Saturday came. Though the more she thought of the tender age he had been when he'd been sent away from home, the more she felt convinced that Farne had known little love in his growing years. Such thoughts bruised her, and made her determined to show him warmth and perhaps a little love this weekend.

Which was why she was out of the house before he was out of his car when he arrived to call for her. 'Hello, Farne,' she greeted him cheerfully as he extracted his length from his car. 'How goes it?' she asked, going up to him and giving him a kiss on the cheek.

'No complaints, that's for sure,' he smiled, and she caught hold of his arm to take him indoors.

'Would you like a coffee or anything before we go?' she asked, after he had greeted her mother.

'We'll get off, shall we?' he suggested.

Having dawdled over lunch, it was late afternoon when they arrived at The Rowans, a kind of manor house, where Farne had been brought up. It was impressive, and as Karrie stood with Farne on the gravelled drive the prospect of meeting her future parents-in-law for the first time caused her nerves to start acting up again.

She felt the need to say something. 'Nice house,' she observed.

'Yours isn't so bad, either,' Farne smiled, and she felt the comforting touch of his arm across her shoulders as, carrying her overnight bag in one hand, his own belongings still in the car, he guided her over the gravel and into the house.

Adele and Silas Maitland were very different from the way Karrie had imagined. She had thought Farne's parents might be cold and stand-offish. But not a bit of it. 'My dear,' his mother greeted her warmly, 'we were beginning to think Farne intended to stay a bachelor for the rest of his days.' Karrie took at once to the tall, dignified woman who seemed so pleased to welcome her son's fiancée—to the extent that Mrs Maitland was not above putting her arms around her and giving her a kiss on the cheek.

'And this is my father,' Farne said unnecessarily of the tall, upright handsome man who was clearly an older version of Farne.

'My son told his mother you were beautiful,' Silas Maitland stated, as he gave her a fatherly peck on the cheek. 'As ever, he didn't exaggerate.'

After that everything went effortlessly. A short while later Farne showed her upstairs to where she would lay her head that night. The high-ceilinged rooms of the downstairs were repeated upstairs. Farne took her to an airy and light room with superb antique furniture plus double bed.

'My room,' he said. 'I think you'll be comfortable here.' Her eyes shot to his, and at once Farne was in there to reassure, 'Sorry, my dear, slip of the tongue, no more.' And, coming close, he gently brushed a strand of blonde gold-streaked hair away from her face. 'What I should have said was that this used to be my room, but because it has its own bathroom my mother's turfed me out into the room next door for this weekend.' That hand gently cupped the side of her face. 'You're all right now?' he queried.

She smiled at him, remembered how she was going to show him warmth and perhaps a little love this week-end—even though, having met his parents, she'd found them much more affectionate than she had imagined—and, 'I could do with a hug,' she said simply, and saw the smile she so loved curve his splendid mouth.

'Your wish is my command,' he said softly, and gathered her in his arms. And it was such bliss, such heaven to be held against him, cradled to him, that she felt she could stay like that for ever.

But it was not to be, because all at once Farne seemed to be pulling her yet closer to him, and yet, before she could obey the instinct to melt against him, he was putting her away from him, and, saying something about bringing his own overnight bag in, he was gone!

She guessed then that he was always on the move. Without doubt he hadn't got where he was in the business world by standing still. She unpacked her bag and shook out the elegant midnight-blue jersey dress she intended to wear to dinner that night. How peaceful it was here, and how well Farne's parents seemed to get on. There seemed to be such an underlying gentleness passing invisibly between the two that she just knew—unlike her own strife-torn parents—that Farne's parents never bellowed at each other in anger.

Dinner that night was such a pleasant affair, Farne's parents making her feel so welcome, that Karrie had long forgotten that she'd had ever felt the smallest anxiety about meeting them. Conversation was wide and varied, and only became more personal when Farne spoke of having dined with Karrie and her parents last Monday.

Then all of a sudden Silas Maitland was commenting, 'If I know my son, Karrie, it won't be too long before he has you up that wedding aisle.'

Karrie hadn't got around to thinking of the actual wedding—if anything she had assumed that they would be engaged for a year or so, as was usual with some of her friends. And so had a difficult time hiding her astonishment when, before she could think up a reply, Farne was there, agreeing with his father.

'You're right, of course,' he answered easily, and with shock, Karrie actually heard him add, 'We'll be married before the month is out.'

Karrie was still pushing through the shock waves of his announcement—before the month was out! There were only *ten days* to go before the month was out! Then she felt all eyes were on her—almost as if waiting for her to confirm Farne's statement.

Since this was the first she'd heard that their intended wedding was to be this month, she was not certain what to reply. But suddenly she realised that part and parcel of loving Farne was that she would instinctively support him in front of other people.

But, 'Um—yes,' was about all she could think to say.

It was enough, it seemed, because Farne sent her a wonderful smile and his father went to his cellar for some more champagne, and the whole evening turned out to be rather marvellous.

They stayed up talking quite late, with Farne saying that first thing on Monday he would arrange a special marriage licence. Then Adele and Silas Maitland were tactfully leaving them downstairs and going to bed. But when they had gone, and when Karrie wouldn't have minded at all another hug, Farne didn't seem inclined to want to linger downstairs.

If she had started to feel a mite peeved when he declared they might as well go upstairs too, then, as she

walked to the drawing room door with him, Farne nulli-
fied any such feeling by stating, 'My parents have fallen
for you, of course. But then, I knew that they would.'

'I like them too,' she smiled, then received a passing
kiss to the top of her head as they started to climb the
stairs, and her world started to right itself.

'Goodnight, Karrie Dalton,' Farne said at her door.

'Night, Farne Maitland,' she replied. Their lips met,
then Farne was opening her bedroom door and prompting
her inside—and closing the door, staying on the other side
of it.

Karrie lay in bed that night, reliving the whole evening,
her heart fluttering when she realised that in less than ten
days' time she would be Farne's wife! She lay awake for
a long time and recalled how he had said that his parents
had fallen for her. She wished that he had…and brought
herself up short. She was not, not, not going to go over
that torment—did he care for her, did he not—again.
Farne wouldn't be marrying her if he didn't want to, and
she loved him enough for two anyway. So, all right,
maybe he wasn't all that demonstrative. But did she trust
demonstrativeness anyway? Her father, in company outside the family, was well-mannered enough, and showed
her mother every attention—but his manners were sadly
lacking once they were behind closed doors.

They would fare well together, she and Farne. They
shared the same sense of humour, a lot of the same likes
and dislikes, and were mentally in tune. Nor could she
complain on the physical side. For, while Farne was not
forever trying to get her into bed, there was nothing re-
motely wrong with the sexual chemistry that had ignited
between them a couple of times.

She fell asleep and slept dreamlessly, though was later
than usual in waking the next morning. She yawned and
stretched, and then, remembering that the bed she was
sleeping in was the bed which Farne had often slept in,

she rolled over and buried her face in the pillow. The pillow on which she was certain he had often lain his head.

And suddenly she wanted him. Suddenly she wished he was in that bed with her. She wanted to hold him. Wanted him to hold her—she shot out of bed, no longer wondering what had got into her. She loved him and wanted to be made love to by him, wanted Farne to make her his.

She found fresh underwear and went and showered, all at once remembering the fact that before the month was out she would be married to him, and she started to sing. Karrie was still singing softly to herself when, after towelling herself dry, she donned a lacy bra and briefs and pattered back into the bedroom where her clothes were.

But it was then, having wondered at this eager-for-his-kisses woman that Farne had stirred into life within her, that Karrie discovered she was not so immodest as she was beginning to believe she had grown to be. Because suddenly the outer door opened and Farne came striding in—and she nearly died of embarrassment.

He halted, rooted, by the bathroom door—and she went crimson. It made no sense to her that although Farne had once kissed and caressed her naked breasts, now he could see her—her long length of naked leg, white lacy briefs that left little to the imagination, and white lacy bra with the pink tips of her breasts showing through—she wanted to run and hide.

He seemed stunned too, as startled as she, and he was blocking the way to the bathroom. 'Farne!' she cried, needing his help.

She got it when, rapidly getting himself together, rather than turning abruptly about and leaving her to her distress, he did the only thing possible. He closed in, taking her in his arms, his body hiding hers from his view.

'Shh,' he gentled her, his eyes on her warm colour.

'You're shaking,' he murmured, his arms warm about her, holding her steady.

'It's—r-ridiculous,' she stuttered.

'I know,' he agreed.

'A ten-year-old has more *sang-froid*.'

Farne smiled, an encouraging smile. 'You don't look ten years old,' he teased. But, lest she should be too strung up to take his teasing kindly, he promised, 'I won't harm you, Karrie, I'll never harm you.'

She smiled up at him. What a darling he was. She started to feel better, and was suddenly comforted to feel his warm hands on the skin at the small of her back. 'And I'll look after you,' she promised.

But felt she was treading dangerous territory when he smiled at her promise and, his smile disappearing, he asked, 'Love me at all?'

She looked down to his shirt, her heart starting to pound, and all at once realised that as Farne had never said that he loved her, so she had never told him that she loved him. She leaned her head against his chest, shyness to tell him mingling with nerves that he must never know just how much she loved him. 'A bit,' she answered. And was suddenly desperate to know his feelings. 'Er—how about you?' she asked, trying to make her voice sound as if it wasn't the most vital thing in the world for her to know.

Time seemed to stand still then as she waited. Then, casually almost, 'Some,' Farne answered, and added matter-of-factly, 'You're not shaking so much now. I reckon if I do a quick about turn—with my eyes closed, naturally—I'll be able to leave without causing you further blushes.'

She laughed. She adored him. 'I'm sorry I was such a fool,' she apologised, still conscious that she was standing in his hold, clad only in her underwear, but, after all her panic, feeling very much calmer.

'Think nothing of it,' Farne answered lightly, and seemed as reluctant to go as she suddenly felt for him to leave.

'Why did you come in, by the way?' she delayed him to ask. 'Did you want something?'

He shook his head. 'I'd been out taking a walk around and came back to my room, my thoughts totally elsewhere. I simply forgot that my old room is your room this weekend.'

'You're fallible,' she laughed.

'Did you think I wasn't?'

'I think...' Oh, I do love you so '...I'd better get dressed.'

Farne grinned. 'Pity!' he sighed. 'Got a kiss for me?' A hundred. Karrie stretched up and kissed his cheek. 'I've known you do better,' he complained. She smiled at him. He looked back at her. Then his hold on her tightened, and he bent and laid his lips to the side of her throat in the most tantalising of kisses. The magic that only he could arouse started misbehaving again, and she put her arms around him. He kissed her shoulder, but as she melted against him he gripped her yet more tensely—then all too soon he had straightened. He looked briefly into her eyes—then swiftly he left her.

So much seemed to have happened that weekend. Karrie was still thinking about isolated parts of it when Farne drew his car up at her home in the early evening. Was she really to marry him within the next ten days?

'Are you coming in?' Karrie asked. 'My parents are out visiting my mother's sister, but I make a terrific toasted cheese sandwich if you're hungry.'

'Do you mind if I don't? I've some papers I need to get together for the morning,' he explained.

'Not at all,' Karrie answered lightly as she got out of the car, but she did mind. Even as she felt mean that she did mind, she didn't want him to go back to his rotten paperwork. Or, if he had to—and it seemed he must—why couldn't she go to his house with him? She could sit quiet, make him something to eat... 'I enjoyed the weekend,' she rose above a love that never wanted the weekend to end to tell Farne as he walked to her door with her.

'As did I,' he said, as he took the door key from her and inserted it in the lock.

She smiled up at him and tried to take her mind off his wonderful mouth. 'Work tomorrow,' she remarked, bringing them back down to earth after the wonderful two days off they had shared.

'You'd better tell Gordon Lane he's going to lose you,' Farne commented.

'He is?'

'You're getting married, remember?' Farne teased. 'And your husband is taking you away for a long, long honeymoon.' Her heart went into overdrive—husband! She'd better go in; she'd be swooning away at any second.

She strove to get herself into more of one piece; it seemed logical, she supposed, given that the department she worked in was invariably stretched, to leave and give them the chance to employ someone else, rather than ask them to cover for her during what was going to be a long time away.

'I'll see to it,' she agreed.

'You won't regret it,' he promised, and kissed her, and left her. Karrie went indoors, knowing that first thing tomorrow she had better ask Pauline Shaw if she could see her.

That she would be handing in her resignation the next morning was soon put in doubt, however, when Karrie's parents came home shortly after nine and she informed them that she and Farne intended to marry within the next ten days.

'No *way!*' her mother stated promptly, sharply and un-equivocally. Karrie, having imagined that her mother would be delighted, stared at her in amazement. 'There is no way you're having any hole-and-corner wedding!' Margery Dalton decreed firmly.

'Hole-and-corner?' Karrie gasped, having not seen her hurried wedding like that at all.

'*I* had that sort of a wedding—rushed, and over in half an hour with none of my family there to support me. *You,*' she assured her succinctly, 'are not.'

'But…'

'But nothing. You're having a white wedding. Jan will be your bridesmaid—she'd like that—and…'

'I can still do that, and Jan can still be my bridesmaid.'

'It will take three months for you to have any sort of a decent dress made, and that's without us finding a suit-able slot for the caterers, and all else there is to arrange.'

Karrie had never seen her mother so resolute—for once her father was keeping out of it. 'Can't we…?' Karrie tried to protest once more.

'No, definitely no. You're going to have a lovely wed-ding. A wedding you can look back on and know that, whatever the future holds for you and the man you love, you started out right. Even if it does take six months to organise.'

'Oh, Mum,' Karrie cried, seeing her rose-coloured dreams of being Farne's wife within the next ten days disappearing fast.

But, on thinking of the great unhappiness her mother had suffered, she didn't have the heart to argue. And in any event, was her mother, with her ideas of starting out right, correct? Would it be better to wait? To arrange it so that everything was as near perfection as could be ar-ranged?

But she didn't want to wait! Against that, though, wasn't she being extremely selfish? Her mother had loved, guided and cherished her. Would it hurt to wait a short while? She wished Farne was there to tell her what he… Farne! Oh, heck, he intended to see about getting a special licence first thing tomorrow!

'I'd—better go and ring Farne,' she told her mother. 'Er—I think I'll go to bed anyway,' she said, and went up the stairs with a heavy heart. Once in her room, she found the card Farne had given her and dialled his number.

'Maitland,' he said.

'Karrie,' she said, and was stumped to know how to go on. He was probably going to hate her, and she wanted him only to love her.

'What's wrong?' he asked when she hadn't added anything.

'I'm sorry to interrupt your work.'

'You have a problem?'

'Sort of. I—um—thought I'd better ring you tonight rather than leave it until tomorrow.' He waited; silently he waited. 'I wanted to stop you from getting that special licence tomorrow.'

A deathly kind of hush followed, and she just knew that Farne was not a man to take lightly to having his plans thwarted. And that made her nervous and on edge, and pulled her all ways.

'There's some reason why I shouldn't?' he enquired, his voice so quiet she felt sure there was an explosion pending.

'My m… I've told my mother about our p-plans, and she won't agree to…'

'You're twenty-two, Karrie,' he pointed out, meaning he knew that she was of an age when she no longer had to consult anyone. It in no way helped with her growing feeling of edginess.

'You've been looking at my personnel file again!' she flared, but calmed down enough to go on. 'My mother says she will not allow me to have some hole-and-corner kind of wedding, and that—'

'Hole-and-corner!' Farne butted in incredulously, much the way Karrie had herself.

'And that it will take six months to get everything arranged: my wedding dress, the caterers, the—'

'Six months!'

He didn't like it one little bit; she could tell that. 'Yes. Six months,' she confirmed, trying to get angry—that or burst into tears.

Anger won when, not too thrilled, apparently, to have his decisions questioned, Farne rapped curtly, 'I'll see if I can find a place in my diary six months hence!'

Don't bother! sprang to mind. But she loved the bossy swine, and love was making a nonsense of the person she had believed herself to be. 'Do that!' she snapped, and she slammed down the phone.

By the time she had showered and was in bed she had calmed down to feel utterly miserable. Did other engaged couples go through this?

CHAPTER SIX

KARRIE slept badly, and left her bed the next morning wondering how such a wonderful weekend could have ended so disastrously. She had been so happy—but had gone to bed close to tears.

'Farne was all right about your changing the date of your wedding?' her mother asked the moment she saw her, her expression unrelenting.

'He's—er—going to check his diary.'

Margery Dalton smiled and, the wedding date satisfactorily put back, was conciliatory. 'I'm sure you'll see I'm right, darling. I stayed up last night making lists—there's such a lot to do. Aside from finding a first-class catering firm that isn't booked up a year in advance, there's the vicar to see, photographers to arrange, dress fittings, invitations to be printed—I shall need Farne's guest list, with all their addresses, by the way. And we'll have to arrange a meeting with Farne's parents, and...'

When Karrie got out her car and drove to work her head was spinning. To marry within the next ten days, a simple ceremony with perhaps just a few of their family and friends at a wedding breakfast afterwards, was already, at that very early stage, starting to sound a much better idea.

Karrie did not hand in her resignation that day. By the look of it she would be working at Irving and Small for the next six months. Or so she thought, until she went home that night and Farne rang.

'Are you over your bad temper?' he enquired pleasantly.

'*My* bad temper!' she exclaimed, but her heart lifted.

117

It was so lovely just to hear him she found it impossible to stay cross with him.

Though she came near to being flabbergasted when Farne went on, charm personified, 'The Reverend Thompson had a cancellation eight weeks next Saturday, and I've—'

'Reverend Thompson?' Karrie stopped him right there. '*My* Reverend Thompson?'

'I don't know about that,' Farne answered, a smile there in his voice. 'He's the vicar of St James's, your local church.' And, while all sorts of thoughts and emotions were rioting within her, he went on, 'I thought your mother would raise no objection to you being married in St James's.'

'She'd insist on it,' Karrie said faintly.

'Good,' Farne commented. 'I thought I'd better book that slot while I had the chance.'

'We—we're—you've booked the ceremony for—eight weeks' time!' she gasped, her heart fluttering even though she felt sure that it was more a natural kind of efficiency on Farne's part rather than any particular urgency to marry her.

'That's right,' he confirmed. 'We've an appointment to see Thompson on Friday.'

'We—have?' she murmured faintly. But recovering, and knowing that her mother was going to have a lot to say about it when she told her, she started to demur. 'Th-there's an awful lot to arrange.' While marrying Farne in two months' time—rather than having to wait six—would be terrific, she could already sense the pressure from her mother. 'Caterers are booked up a year in advance, apparently, and...'

'Rachel Price, my PA, has sweet-talked Dawson's into agreeing to put on extra staff.'

Dawson's! Her mother had spoken of approaching Pearson's! Though Dawson's had an excellent reputation, though they were expensive into the bargain. 'You've booked Dawson's?' Karrie asked, keeping her voice down, for all she was upstairs and her mother couldn't hear her.

'They've taken the booking provided we limit the guest list to a hundred.'

'My mother's going to love you.'

'What did I do?' he asked innocently.

She wanted to laugh, but guessed she was in for a tough time the moment she started to relay this discussion to her parent. 'My mother has her own ideas.'

'I'd better come over and see her,' Farne said straight away—making Karrie feel instantly better that, by the look of it, Farne would be there with her when they told her mother what had been arranged.

Farne came over that night and somehow managed to counter every one of Margery Dalton's objections. 'Limiting the guest list to a hundred seems sensible,' she agreed. 'Especially since Dawson's are likely to cost the earth!'

'I engaged them; I intend to meet their account,' Farne answered.

'Certainly not!' Margery Dalton answered. 'I want everything done as it should be. Karrie's father wouldn't dream of letting anyone else settle the account for anything that is down to the bride's parents. We want everything perfect for our daughter.'

And on that Farne backed down. He looked at Karrie. 'Naturally,' he answered, and smiled, and Karrie's heart swelled. It was almost as if he was saying that he thought her perfect.

She was aware that she was not perfect, but in the month that followed—which turned out to be very fraught on occasions—Karrie resurrected that moment of Farne turning to her and saying 'Naturally' many times. For, while there were countless calls on her time, Farne was equally as busy. So much so that he seemed to quite frequently break dates with her because of pressure of work, and she seldom saw him.

He kept the appointment he'd made for them to see the Reverend Thompson. Afterwards they returned to her home, but although both her parents were out, and there was a chance for them to spend some time alone with each other, Farne had to dash off in connection with some work he had to complete.

'I'll see you, then.' She forced a smile.

'Be good,' he said—when did she get the chance to be anything else? He then touched his lips to hers and was gone.

An hour later and Karrie had recovered her spirits to know, with certainty, that it wasn't particularly that she wanted to be bad. It was still essential to her that she was chaste on her wedding day. It was just that she loved Farne so much, and quite honestly found his arms a haven.

She spent Saturday with her mother and her cousin Jan at the up-market dressmakers her mother sometimes used. But, having looked at design after design, Karrie, while having seen several extremely nice dresses, was unable to see 'the' one.

'You really will have to choose, Karrie,' her mother declared. 'We just don't have the time for you to spend weeks and weeks making a decision.'

So she chose a style more to please her mother than herself.

Farne's parents came to London the following weekend, and the two families—her father under protest—met up for dinner.

The meal went exceedingly well, with her father on his best behaviour. Though he was full of complaints the next day, when her mother let him into the little secret of how much his daughter's wedding was likely to cost him.

'We don't know a hundred people!' he complained vociferously when, having demanded a breakdown of the figures, her mother started with the caterers.

'We know fifty!' her mother countered.

'Well, let the Maitlands pay for their half!'

'*You* would!'

Karrie couldn't take it, and, although she hesitated to interfere in her parents' rows, she felt she was directly involved in this one. 'I'll pay!' she butted in. She had some money left to her by her grandfather.

'You'll do no such thing!' Her mother rounded on her crossly. 'He makes such a big thing of duty—it's his *duty* to see that you are married in a manner that won't shame us.'

It seemed to Karrie that seldom a day went by when there wasn't a scene similar to that one. Oh, how she needed Farne's arms around her, needed him to tell her that everything would be all right. And she didn't like her wedding dress any better.

But he never seemed to be there. In fact, she seemed to be seeing less of him than ever. When she did see him she found scant comfort in his arms because he always seemed to be about to leave and do something pressing. So what had happened to that 'undeniable urge to kiss her' that he'd spoken of on the night when he'd stated they'd better get married?

It was Saturday, and there were four weeks to go before their wedding day. Karrie, who hadn't seen Farne since the previous Saturday, was starting to feel just a shade miffed that he was always so busy. She had things to do herself! She'd been for a dress fitting that day, and had chased off to the woman who was making the wedding cake with yet more instructions from her mother, yet Karrie knew she would have found space to see Farne any time he asked her.

Which made her contrary in the extreme when—wanting with everything she had to see him—shortly after she arrived home he rang and suggested dinner that night and she told him that she couldn't see him.

'You've got something on?' he queried carefully.

Not a thing. 'I've just spend an extremely exhausting day,' she excused.

'Your energy is boundless,' he stated.

'True,' she answered and, because she loved him, found she was confessing, 'I'm just being difficult.'

'Bridal nerves?' he suspected.

'I don't want you making excuses for me.'

'All right, sweetheart,' he said gently. Just that one word 'sweetheart' and she was ready to capitulate. 'May I take you to dinner tomorrow?'

Her backbone had melted. 'I'd like that,' she answered softly.

She was back on an even keel when she saw him the next night, or rather thought she was. As before they were able to talk about all subjects during the meal, and her heart swelled with pride just to be out with him.

'Did you give your notice in last week?' he asked as they were finishing off with coffee.

'I leave three weeks next Thursday,' she answered.

'You prefer not to leave sooner?'

'My mother's doing a splendid job organising everything, but she's starting to get a little uptight, bless her, and…'

'And you feel you'd like to be out of the way during the day?'

How at one they were, she and Farne, Karrie mused dreamily—but knew she had mused far too soon when, back at her home, they crossed the drive to her front door and Farne asked some question in connection with the invitations that had recently been sent out. She answered, quite without thinking, 'Travis has accepted already!' and saw storm clouds hovering.

'I didn't know you'd invited him?' Farne commented, a degree of frost forming on the warm summer night air.

'Didn't you?' It wasn't a secret. She had been going to suggest that perhaps Travis might be an usher but— perhaps not.

'Have you invited many more of your ex-boyfriends?' Farne enquired icily.

'Unfortunately I'm restricted to only fifty guests!' she snapped. And, reading from his arctic expression that he had gone off her in a big way, she added, 'I take it you won't be coming in?'

Farne stared down at her, his expression stern. 'I've work to do!' he grated—and went back to his car.

Karrie went indoors silently fuming. Not so much as a kiss on the cheek did she get, the un-lover-like, worka- holic swine. *Workaholic!* The word made her gasp out loud.

As it happened her parents had gone to bed. And Karrie, experiencing a sense of shock—that dreadful word 'workaholic' spinning around in her head and refusing to leave—went slowly up the stairs to her room. Workaholic—like her father!

She found it difficult to get to sleep that night. She wished she hadn't parted from Farne the way she had. She wanted to marry him. More than anything she wanted to marry him. But doubts about the success of her mar- riage with Farne were scrabbling to get a foothold. She pushed them away. All prospective brides had doubts, didn't they?

She felt a desperate need to contact him the next day, and could hardly wait to get home from work before she went up to her room and rang his number. 'Farne, it's me,' she said when he answered.

'Problem?' he queried straight away.

It was true, she supposed, that she seldom if ever phoned him. Well, she had only phoned him once, she recalled. 'No—no problem,' she quickly assured him. 'It's just—well—I thought I'd save you the trouble of ringing me to apologise for upsetting me last night.'

'I upset you?'

Didn't he know her day began and ended with him? 'I think, as you suggested, I'm getting pre-wedding nerves,' she admitted openly.

'Oh, Karrie, my dear. You've nothing to be nervous about, I promise you.'

She felt better already. 'I know,' she answered.

'Everything will be fine,' he further promised.

'I know,' she repeated.

There was a second or two's silence. Then Farne was announcing, 'You're not getting out enough.' It was true, she wouldn't mind seeing more of him—just being with him was reassuring. But that the two of them should be alone together more was not what he was proposing, it seemed, when he began, 'I tell you what…' She waited. 'I think it's about time your bridesmaid and my best man became acquainted. Will your cousin be free next Saturday?'

'I'll ask.'

'Let me know tomorrow.'

She was seeing Farne tomorrow? She would rather it was tonight, but he was a busy man and she mustn't be greedy. 'Until tomorrow,' she murmured, and said good-bye, straight away to telephone her cousin.

Any notion that she might be able to spend some time alone with Farne proved erroneous the next evening when he called for her. They were meeting friends of his, he informed her. But Ian and Ursula Fields were a very pleasant couple, and Karrie spent a very enjoyable evening with Farne in their company.

When Farne took her home, he kissed her on both cheeks, and made her laugh when he said, 'The extra one's because I deprived myself on Sunday.'

She hadn't thought he would remember that he'd gone striding off without kissing her goodnight last Sunday. She stretched up on tiptoe. 'Don't do it again,' she scolded, and touched her lips to his, holding on to his waist tightly when his mouth stayed over hers and he seemed reluctant to break away.

But break away he did. And, to show he wasn't going to kiss her again, he took a step away from her as he thought to mention, 'Some friends of mine are flying in from Barbados to see family and to take in our wedding. I'd like to introduce them to you. Shall we say Thursday?'

'Thursday will be fine,' she smiled, and never again seemed to see Farne alone for long after that.

On Thursday she met his newly arrived friends, and again she liked them and again enjoyed the evening. On Saturday, she and Jan went for a fitting, but Karrie still wasn't over-thrilled with the style of her wedding dress. On Saturday evening she and her cousin had dinner with Farne and Farne's best man, Ned Haywood.

Ned was a divorcee, and he and Jan got on famously. Karrie liked Ned too, and when he suggested that the four of them took in a show and had a meal the following Tuesday she was happy to agree.

But it was after that Tuesday, the theatre show having been superb, the meal afterwards and the company all she could wish for, when the bridal nerves that had spiked her began to act up with a vengeance.

For one thing life at home seemed to be becoming more and more stressed, with her parents' shouting matches going on continuously. Fortunately—or unfortunately—her father was spending more and more time at work, but the rows started the moment he set foot inside the door.

Karrie knew above all else that she did not want, and was not going to have, a marriage like that. She had been going to see Farne on Thursday, but because of pressure of work he rang to cancel. And that word 'workaholic' returned again and again to haunt her.

She told herself she was being unreasonable. For goodness' sake, she would be seeing him again on Friday! He was having a dinner party at his home especially so she should meet some more of his friends. Ned and Jan had been invited too. And, hang it all, Farne would be taking quite some time off work for their honeymoon.

But that thought gave her fresh cause to worry. Just how would they fare on honeymoon? Farne had desired her a couple of times; she knew that. But he hadn't desired her so much that he'd been prepared to lose his head over her, had he? She longed to be in his arms, but Farne obviously felt no such longing.

Karrie started to grow confused when she recalled that that Sunday night in his apartment, when he had decided that they would marry, it had been she who had called a halt to their love-making. Against that, though, Farne had had the whole of that weekend in Milan to attempt to seduce her had he been so minded. So, yes, things had got a touch heated between them that Sunday morning, but not so heated that Farne hadn't been able to easily put an end to the amorous interlude.

She went to work on Friday, telling herself over and over that everything was going to be all right, and rushed home that evening to shower and change. She had told Farne she would drive herself over to his home, but he'd insisted he would send a car for her. He hadn't cared for the idea of her driving home on her own afterwards when, depending how the dinner party went, it could be gone midnight when it ended.

Carrying a matching jacket to her dress, Karrie arrived at Farne's home and rang the doorbell at a little after half past seven—his guests were due at eight. 'Stunning!' he declared, on opening the door to her, his glance travelling appreciatively over her narrow strapped dress in a warm red shade.

'You look all right too,' she understated—he was just quite devastating in his dinner jacket.

His smile became a grin. He kissed her cheek. 'Come and say hello to the caterers.'

He escorted her to the kitchen, where several people were busy at work, and, having said a quick 'hello' to them, rather than disturb them, they went to the dining room where the table, laid for a dozen people, looked quite superb.

The awful thought hit her that Farne didn't really need a wife. He was able to—and did—hire only the very best people. 'Something wrong?' he asked, and Karrie blinked.

'Should there be?' she answered.

'You looked—sad, for a moment.'

'Nothing a quick hug wouldn't cure,' she laughed, finding it impossible to voice the question that had just come to her, the question she wanted to ask—Why, Farne, do you want to marry me?

'Come here,' he ordered, and she had her moment of bliss when he held her close to him. It will be all right, it will be, she told herself, and made herself pull out of his arms.

'May I just check my hair's all right before your guests arrive?'

He let her go, but caught a hold of her hand and took her upstairs to one of his spare bedrooms which was being used as a cloakroom that evening. 'Your hair looks fine,' he assured her, glancing at her shining blonde gold-streaked locks. 'Quite fascinating,' he murmured. But quickly added, 'I'll leave you to it.'

Left to it, Karrie tidied her hair, checked her lipstick, and, leaving her jacket on the bed, went downstairs to Farne's drawing room. He had just poured her a gin and tonic when the doorbell went.

'Our first guests,' he murmured, and suddenly, those three words sounding very intimate somehow, Karrie started to feel better about everything.

Everything went well from then on. Karrie liked his friends, and, realising she was the hostess for the evening, made sure to chat with those she sat next to during the meal, and to spend some time talking with each guest once they were back in the drawing room.

She was always pleased to see her cousin, and managed to get a few minutes with her to discuss the shopping trip they had planned for the next day—Saturdays just lately had seemed to be taken up with shopping and fittings.

The caterers had cleared up and departed about an hour since, when Karrie's glance was drawn, not for the first time in the last five minutes, to the sensational brunette to whom Farne was *still* talking. And suddenly, for her, things weren't going well at all.

Karrie turned her attention back to the man—Vaughan Green, she thought his name was—who was enthusiastically telling her about a recent trip he'd made to Peru. 'And you actually flew over the Nazca lines?' she queried, her expression smiling, interested. She had heard of the centuries-old mysterious line drawings on the desert floor.

'It's the only way to see them,' he opined, and was a wealth of information on the subject—she would not look over to where Farne was standing, she would not. 'And, of course, from there we just had to go to Cuzco.'

'The old Inca capital,' Karrie drew out of an unknown somewhere, and felt she might well take root if Vaughan Green gave forth on yet more of his favourite trip.

Her attention was slipping, but she somehow managed to hold a 'riveted' look and even smile and ask questions to show her interest. Then two of the guests said they had to get home to their babysitter, and it was a sign for a

general exodus, with Ned and Jan, having arrived together, being the last to leave.

'If I don't see you before, I'll see you in church,' Ned
quipped.

'And I'll see you tomorrow, Karrie,' Jan said. 'Don't
forget our shopping spree. Nine-thirty in the car park.'

'I won't forget,' Karrie smiled, and, having said goodbye to them, she stepped back. Farne closed the front door
and, while she owned she was not feeling very friendly
towards him, she was more than a little startled to see
from his grim expression that he was looking positively
hostile! She opened her mouth to ask what he was looking
so uptight about, then found she didn't have the chance.

'You *have* remembered that you and I are engaged!'
he barked furiously.

Very civil of him to wait until all his guests had gone
before he went for her jugular! But, having waited for an
age to be alone with him, it dawned on her that, presum-
ably, he considered she had chatted over-long with the
good-looking Vaughan Green—and Karrie wasn't about
to mildly take his rebuke.

'I'm surprised you remembered yourself!' she hurled
back at him, and, having gone completely off any notion
of spending some private time with him, just her and
Farne together, she headed for the stairs and went to the
spare bedroom to collect her jacket.

Who in the blue blazes did he think he was? He
couldn't have stayed longer at the brunette's side—
Eleanor, she thought she was called—if he'd been glued
to her. Damn the expense—she'd take a taxi. If Farne
I've-just-remembered-I'm-your-fiancé Maitland thought
he was going to drive her home, he could think again!

What right did he have to be furious? she fumed furiously—but, grabbing up her jacket from the bed, she
turned and found she had company. 'Explain!' Farne
rapped.

'Take a running jump!' she retorted, and went to charge past him and out through the door. Only she didn't get that far, because Farne put out a hand to stop her, and she spun round to give him a furious push—only he was firmer footed than she was, and it was she who fell backwards, off balance, and landed on the bed.

She struggled furiously to sit up, but was prevented from doing so when Farne came to sit on the side of the bed and, by the simple expedient of stretching out a hand to her left shoulder, held her down. She, Karrie realised, fuming, wasn't going anywhere until he said so. With sparks flashing in her eyes, she stared mutinously at him, but then to her astonishment she saw a hint of a smile come to the corners of his mouth.

But he was still holding her there when he drawled, 'You, Miss Dalton, are certainly one hell of a handful!'

So he had a sense of humour—she was not interested. 'I object to being wrongly accused!' she snapped.

'As do I!'

Huh! If he thought she was going to trot out how green-eyed she'd been because of his *'tête-à-tête'* with the limpet Eleanor, he could think again. Karrie opted to make believe that her remark implying he had forgotten they were engaged had nothing to do with any other woman, and sniped instead, 'You're a cold fish, Maitland.'

'I'm a—' He broke off, getting her meaning. 'You ch...' he began again. 'Have you no—?' Again he broke off, something entering his eyes that she wasn't too sure about as he threatened, 'Hell's teeth, Dalton, are you asking for trouble?'

She was made of sterner stuff than to give in to threats. 'From you?' she scoffed—and straight away wondered at the wisdom of her attitude when a look came over his face that hinted he had never been one to duck a challenge.

'Oh, you shouldn't have said that, Karrie mine,' he

murmured, and, while she was suddenly too stunned to move or do anything but watch, Farne deliberately removed his shoes, and then his jacket and then his tie, and, while saucer-eyed she stared, the next she knew he was on the bed with her, his body next to hers.

Her heart set up a tumultuous clamour, but when Farne reached for her and, his head coming nearer, placed his lips on hers—not briefly, as was usual, not just brushing and leaving, which was what she had become accustomed to this past six weeks, but lingering, with intent—her anger totally disappeared, delight taking its place. Punish me, punish me, she wanted to cry. I love it!

Then she guessed that Farne must have realised that, instead of backing away, she was responding, because, taking his mouth away from hers, he pulled back and looked down at her. 'Um—perhaps this wasn't such a very good idea,' he grunted.

Who was she to argue? 'Perhaps you're right,' she answered softly, and couldn't resist touching a finger to the corner of his mouth. She raised her eyes to look into his and, feeling starved for his kisses, wanted to plead with him to kiss her again.

What he read in her eyes she neither knew nor cared, for suddenly he gave a groan and, as if he just could not stop himself, his head came down again. It was all so wonderful—this was no fleeting kiss. His arms came around her; he held her to him. And when he broke that kiss it was only so he could trail more kisses down her throat. He pushed the narrow shoulder straps of her dress aside and kissed her shoulders, her silken skin, her cleavage.

His arms tightened about her and Karrie pressed closer against him, loving the feel of the length of his body against hers. She wanted to cry his name but was afraid to break the spell. She kissed his throat, found his lips on hers again, and, as Farne held her ever closer to him, and a fire started to flame out of control within her, she knew only that she wanted him, this man she loved.

She raised her arms over his shoulders, holding him close and revelling in that closeness. 'My dear!' he cried, and she had an idea that his control was pretty well shot too.

She was fairly certain of it when his fingers came to the fastening of her dress and he unzipped it. She held on to him, and kissed him, her mouth lingering with his as he removed her dress.

Gently, tenderly, he stroked and caressed her body, his hands caressing their way to her breasts, cupping them. She gave a gasp of delight, and he kissed her again. She wanted him to remove her bra, and was enraptured when not only did he remove it but he saluted each breast in turn with kisses. And then, while caressing the hardened tip of one of her breasts with one hand, he lowered his head to the other and took possession of it with his mouth, his tongue making a nonsense of the tip.

'Oh, Farne!' she cried, and just had to see his chest. She raised trembling seeking fingers, and they kissed while more of their clothing disappeared until they were both clad in just one item of underwear each.

Karrie was lost to everything save this need which he had created in her; her love for him saw it wasn't wrong that it should be so. She wanted to tell him of her love for him, but instead pressed closer to him, her naked breasts against his hair-roughened naked chest.

She heard a groan of wanting leave him, and gloried in that sound that echoed her own need. His hands came to her behind, caressed inside her briefs and clasped the pert and firm mounds. He pulled her to him, and she thought she would die from the pure joy of it. She wanted to tell him of her most urgent desire to stay the night with him. To lie with him throughout the night. In his arms, naked, just him and her love.

She pushed against him, heard an uncontrolled sound leave him, and thrilled anew when, giving passion its head, Farne pulled back to take in the length of her body, her swollen, throbbing, hard beckoning-tipped breasts, her naked thighs, and with a sound of wanting he bent to her breasts and trailed kisses down her body, to her waist, to taste her navel with his tongue and to kiss the silken skin at the top of her briefs.

He nudged the flimsy material aside with his mouth, and it was only then that Karrie felt in any way unsure. She gripped on to him hard as she fought to overcome an anxious moment that had absolutely no place in what was happening between them.

But, as though alerted that there was something alien in their lovemaking because of the way she jerkily gripped him, Farne stilled suddenly. Karrie, those anxious unsure few seconds behind her, had the most dreadful feeling that she had ruined everything. She wanted to beg, to plead— Let me stay, oh, please, please, let me stay. But as Farne took his mouth from her satiny skin and came to lie beside her, so the pride which she had thought lost all at once struggled to surface.

He did not kiss her again, but still lay close. While Karrie still desired him like crazy, yet sensed he was striving for calm, calm to overcome his desires—though why he should when she was more than willing—her pride all at once broke loose.

She turned from him, lay on her back and stared up at the ceiling. 'Promise me something, Maitland,' she managed, trying to ignore that her voice was anything but not husky.

'Of course,' Farne replied, taking his arms from her, his tone sounding a little strained—or was her hearing affected too?'

'Promise me that, if we have any arguments in the future, we'll always end them this way.'

Farne laughed, and Karrie was much relieved about that. 'Do I take it you might grow to like—um—a little of the—unknown?'

She laughed. 'A little of the unknown'—what a lovely name for it. 'Unless you intend to keep me here until morning—' please, oh, please '—I think you'd better take me home.'

Farne sat up, his back to her as he began pulling on his trousers. 'Mustn't have you late for your shopping expedition,' he said. And, grabbing up his shirt and the rest of his clothes, but not turning round to look to where she lay, as near naked as made no difference, he said 'I'll go and bring the car round while you get dressed,' and, almost casually, he strolled from the room.

CHAPTER SEVEN

HAD that been *her* last night? Karrie wondered many many times between waking on Saturday morning and driving to meet her cousin. Alone, and in the cold light of day, she was little short of stupefied that she had been so abandoned with Farne last night. She had actually wanted to stay the night with him! she recalled. How she would have felt this morning if she had, she had no idea.

What had happened to her belief, previously set in concrete, that she was not going to give herself to any man before marriage? Her preconceived notion that no man would ever have the opportunity of accusing her of trapping him into marriage? Where had those firm convictions disappeared to? Her unshakable opinion that 'nothing like that' would happen before marriage? Where had all those confident opinions etched ever more deeper in her mind over the years gone? Flying out of the window, that was where.

The truth of the matter was that she'd had not the smallest problem in sticking to her resolution before, because she had never been in love. So she had never been tempted. But in love, and tempted, she had—she had to face it—been as weak, as frail, as the next woman. Only Farne had saved her from herself.

And that, in itself, was a very sobering thought. For while she had been totally lost to everything—even that last-minute anxious moment could easily have been overcome had Farne wanted to overcome it—he had been nowhere near as lost. But for that small modicum of pride that had been her salvation, she had been ready to beg him to let her spend the night with him. But he, quite

135

obviously, she now saw, had been in no way so affected. 'I'll go and bring the car round while you get dressed,' he'd said, and while she had still felt like an emotional volcano he had sauntered from the room.

Karrie did not like the way she was feeling as she drove to meet Jan. Farne had said he loved her 'some', but was 'some' enough? On her part, Karrie knew that she loved him so much that he could very easily hurt her. Sometimes, she owned, when with barely a peck to her cheek he parted from her, seeming just a tinge aloof somehow, she went indoors feeling a trifle bruised because he seemed that bit uncaring. Was she leaving herself wide open to more hurt by marrying him?

Suddenly appalled by the way her thoughts were going, Karrie pulled into the car park, ''Lo, Jan,' she greeted her cousin, who pulled in just behind her and salved her guilty conscience for having such thoughts by going 'wedding' shopping with a will.

They shopped all morning, with a break for coffee, stopped for lunch and shopped some more. But it was around four that afternoon when, with paper and plastic carriers between them, they were passing one bridal display window and Karrie stopped dead. There, taking centre space in the window, was a white wedding dress that put all others in the shade. It was an entirely romantic concoction with a fitted bodice, embroidered throughout with pearls, round-necked and short-sleeved, the embroidery finishing just before the hips and the skirt of the dress falling from there in chiffon folds. With it went a pearl-embroidered coronet and chiffon veil.

'Oh, Jan!' she gasped.

'It's beautiful,' Jan breathed.

Karrie swallowed, knowing she was just going to have to have it. 'My mother will murder me,' she said.

Jan was right on her wavelength. 'Oh, she will,' she agreed. 'And if she doesn't, your father will.'

'It probably won't fit.'

'There's only one way to find out.'

There was no thought in Karrie's head as she stepped into the exquisite creation about what she would do with the other dress that was already being made and which she was due to collect the following Saturday.

'It's lovely!' she sighed and she looked in the mirror— the fit as though made for her.

'Oh, Karrie, you look fantastic!' exclaimed her partner in crime, and even looked a little tearful.

Karrie felt the prick of emotional tears herself. She swallowed. 'How much is it?' she actually heard herself ask—and swallowed again when she heard the price. It's only once, tempted a friendly inner voice—why shouldn't you look your absolute best? But you've already got a dress, another sane voice she wanted nothing to do with tried to tell her. Add the cost of the two dresses together and it was a staggering amount to pay for something she would only wear once. Quite ridiculous, said her head. 'You look fantastic', Jan had said. Karrie could see for herself how much this dress became her, much more so than the one being made. Besides which, she wanted to look fantastic for Farne. 'I'll take it,' she said—and didn't regret her decision for a moment.

Nor did she regret it when, refusing to leave it in the store to be collected later, and having purchased the coronet and veil to go with it, the assistant boxed the dress up for her and she and Jan, with their various bags, struggled to the car park.

She still wasn't regretting it when, leaving her car on the drive, she carried the box into her home. Her mother met her in the hall. 'What on earth have you got there?' she asked.

'Don't be cross. I intend to pay for it.'

'Your father never will—whatever it is. He says he's not paying for anything else, and that if I'd had the decency to present him with a son rather than a daughter he'd never have had this expense in the first place.'

'In a good humour, was he?'

Her mother laughed. 'Come on—out with it. What have you done?'

It was a great relief that her mother, once she was over the shock, fell as in love with the dress as Karrie had. 'It's gorgeous, darling,' she crooned. 'Come on, let me see you in it. Then you can hang it on the outside of the wardrobe in one of the spare bedrooms.'

'What do you think?' Karrie asked when for the second time that day she tried on the dress. But she could see the answer in her mother's tear-filled eyes.

'Oh, darling, you look sensational!' she whispered.

Karrie, feeling like crying too, returned to her room once she had hung up her wonderful dress, and gave herself something of a talking to. Perhaps it was natural for a bride to be a bit emotional—but her emotions had seemed to be up one minute and down the next for quite some weeks now.

Then the phone in her room rang. Her heart leapt. She picked up the receiver. 'Hello?' she said.

'How did the shopping go?' Farne's voice was matter-of-fact, not the smallest sign from his tone to reveal how, near naked and passionate, they had been in each other's arms last night. Her heart sank—if Farne had intended they should see each other that night, she had an idea he would have saved his small talk and questions about her shopping trip until then.

'Very well, actually,' she replied, hoping against hope that she had got it wrong and that they would see each other. It was Saturday night, for goodness' sake!

'You found what you were looking for?'

The more the conversation went on, the more convinced she grew that Farne was just observing a few pleasantries before he hit her with his reason why they would not be seeing each other that night.

'You can give me your opinion in two weeks' time.' If I turn up! Had she *really* just thought that? Aghast, astounded, disbelieving, Karrie knew her emotions were getting the better of her when, as if to forestall the words he was likely to say at any moment, she heard herself ask, 'Do you mind if I don't see you tonight?' Why did it feel like war, as if she had to get in with that question before he did? Wasn't that how her parents went on? Oh, no!

'You're exhausted from shopping?' Farne enquired pleasantly. But, just when she was thinking she might have got it all wrong, and that perhaps Farne was just phoning to arrange what time he would call for her, his voice had sharpened, and he was aggressively demanding, 'You're not two-timing me, Karrie?'

'Don't be such a distrusting rat!' she erupted hotly. But calmed down to reveal, 'I've walked my feet off today—and found a wedding dress at almost the last min—'

'I thought you were having your wedding dress made?'

'Logic and wedding dresses don't mix!' she told him loftily, certain he'd think her a fool if she told him that the dress she was having made just wasn't right and never had been. 'Anyhow, I suppose I could see you—if you don't mind seeing me with my steaming feet soaking in a bowl of water.' She had no such intention, of course, but was starting to feel very much better. By the look of it, she was seeing Farne that night. 'What time shall I meet you?' she asked.

And fell from a great height of expectation when he answered, 'Actually, Karrie, I have to go away.'

Her disappointment was crippling. But, having faced that her emotions were all over the place just lately, she strove to look on the bright side. So, okay, she wouldn't be able to see him tonight, but there was always tomorrow—and if not then, Monday.

'You have—a meeting?' On a Saturday night!

'I'm just on my way to the airport.'

Good of you to ring. 'Airport?' She'd hate it if he was going to Milan again. He had taken her with him the last time.

'Business calls, I'm afraid. I have to go to Australia unexpectedly.'

Australia! 'You'll be staying longer than overnight, I take it?'

'I'll be away about two weeks,' Farne replied evenly.

Two weeks! 'I see,' she commented quietly.

'Just under,' he qualified. 'My plane lands on the Friday evening before our wedding on Saturday.'

That was barely twelve hours before they were due to be married! 'Perhaps you'll let me know if your flight's been delayed!' There was I, waiting at the church!

'You're unhappy?'

You're bothered? Unhappy—she wouldn't see him for nearly *two whole weeks!* She wasn't merely unhappy, she felt destroyed—and at that moment her pride kicked in. 'I'm sorry,' she apologised, realising she'd been a touch waspish—must have been for Farne to ask the question he had. 'I didn't mean to be unreasonable. It's just that— well—you're always so level-headed, and I just thought— if panic starts to break out here—you know, the caterers going down *en masse* with flu or something…'

'Any problem, anything at all, ring my PA. Rachel is invaluable in an emergency,' he assured her, though there was a smile in his voice as he added, 'But I'm sure you'll cope famously.'

'Of course I will,' Karrie answered brightly, and, as tears rushed to her eyes, 'Have a good flight,' she bade him, and quickly put down the phone, tears running down her cheeks. She'd just about die if Farne had the smallest inkling that her heart ached so much she was actually reduced to tears.

Sunday passed dully, as did Monday and Tuesday. Karrie tried to keep cheerful by going along to the spare room every now and again to look at her dream of a wedding dress. She also kept herself buoyant with the belief that, for all he hadn't said he would, Farne would phone.

But he didn't call, and on Wednesday she started to grow well and truly despondent. On Thursday she stopped going into the spare room to look at her dress. On Friday evening the sultry silence that had been going on between her parents over the last few days ended in one almighty and horrendous row, when her mother for the first time ever, spoke of divorcing her husband.

'You've dominated me for the last time, Bernard-Bloody-Dalton!' she yelled. 'I'm seeing a lawyer the minute this wedding's over. I should have divorced you years ago. In fact, I should never have married you in the first place!'

Karrie left them to it, their raised voices reaching her in her room. She felt unutterably saddened. Her mother seldom if ever swore. And not only to swear, but to talk of divorce at this stage—after enduring years of strife—spoke of how truly dreadful things had become.

Karrie stared unhappily, unseeing, out of her bedroom window. She wanted only to think of happy things. To think of Farne coming home. To think of their wedding. She wanted, she realised, reassurance that her marriage would be all right. But Farne was in Australia and couldn't even be bothered to pick up the phone to ring her.

Nor did he ring over the weekend. Having driven to collect her unwanted wedding dress—having shown all the enthusiasm required—she raced home and dialled the callback number as soon as she got in. No one had telephoned since her aunt last night. Surely Farne couldn't be working *all* of the time!

By Tuesday, with her wedding just four days away—and still no phone call—that word 'workaholic' started to go around again in her head. 'Business calls', Farne had said. And, she sadly realised, it always would. Suddenly she had a ghastly vision of a life in front of her where Farne was always busy with his work—with never any time for her.

Now who did that remind her of? But she was not going to have a marriage like her parents' marriage. She was not—she was *not*. She would rather stay unmarried all her life.

When Karrie went to bed on Tuesday evening, she owned to be having serious doubts about marrying Farne. She loved him, was still as desperately in love with him as ever. But was she going to be made to pay for loving him so much?

She hardly saw him now—would she see any more of him when she was his wife? If her workaholic father was anything to go by, it seemed unlikely. Would Farne try to dominate her, the way her mother spoke of her father dominating her? Was she, Karrie wondered, to have the same battleground of a marriage as her parents had—the type of relationship she had long since decided she was most definitely not going to have?

She didn't want a marriage like that, nor the hurt that went with it. Had Farne loved her half as much as she loved him, there might have been a chance of them making a go of it. But loving her 'some' was not enough.

Karrie lay awake for most of that night with her mind in a turmoil. Had he loved her... But he didn't. He had desired her—the last time she had been with him had shown her that—but look how easily, casually, he had been able to overcome that desire.

Anyhow, there was more to marriage than the sexual

side. A man didn't have to be in love with a woman to desire her, she knew that much, sad though that fact was for her to face up to.

Karrie awoke hollow-eyed from a troubled sleep on Wednesday morning and knew that decision time had arrived. Any hope that everything would look better in the morning proved wrong. Nothing looked any better—and she just couldn't take any more. If Farne had loved her, it might have been different. But he didn't. It was just that he had obviously reached a time in his life when he'd made a logical decision that it was time to give up his bachelor freedom and take a wife. Well, tough—she wasn't playing. No way was she going to sit at home with her two-point-four children waiting for her workaholic husband to remember he had a wife at home. No way was she going to have her mother's life!

Her father had already left for his office when Karrie went downstairs. 'What's the matter with you?' her mother asked the moment she saw her. 'You don't look as though you've had a wink of sleep.'

There was no way to dress it up. 'I can't marry Farne,' Karrie told her parent tonelessly. And only then realised what a wonderfully supportive mother she had, because when she could have been forgiven if she'd thrown a fit, her mother didn't scream, or shout, or have hysterics or say, as well she might have, that Bernard Dalton was going to create blue murder when he had to pay the bills and lost deposits.

'Why, love?' she asked gently.

It was all too shaming to Karrie, and she just couldn't tell her mother the basic truth—that Farne did not love her. The rest, her fears for any future they might have had together, stemmed from there. Unable to lie to her parent, 'I just can't,' Karrie answered.

'You've obviously thought this through,' Margery

Dalton stated, taking in the dark shadows under her daughter's eyes.

'I have.'

'Right. Come and have some breakfast.'

Karrie couldn't eat a thing, but she went with her mother to the breakfast room and had a cup of tea. 'I'd better take the morning off and ring round and tell everybody the wedding is cancelled,' she told her parent shakily.

'You don't think perhaps you should tell Farne first? Or have you already?'

Karrie shook her head. Chance would be a fine thing. 'I don't know the name of his hotel, and—' forestalling her mother's question '—I don't want to ring his PA to find out.' It was that pride which had kept her from telling her mother that Farne didn't love her that rose up to prevent Karrie from letting his PA know that, when he had been away a good ten days, his fiancée hadn't a clue where he was staying.

'You've rather dropped this on me, Karrie.' Margery Dalton started to get herself together. 'If it's your decision not to marry Farne, then nobody's going to make you. But can you give me a few hours to get my thoughts in order before you do anything?'

'There's nothing to think...'

'Please, darling,' her mother requested. 'I won't pressure you in any way. But there's plenty of time for you to cancel everything tonight, when you come home from work.'

Karrie wasn't sure. Today was Wednesday, and the wedding was supposed to be on Saturday. That didn't sound to her to be 'plenty of time'. But in view of all the phoning and behind the scenes planning her mother had done for what had been going to be a very, very special day, Karrie felt she owed it to her to agree.

'All right,' she said, and added, 'I'm so sorry, Mum.'

'Don't give it another thought,' her mother said bracingly. 'Now, I suggest you get off to work...'

'You think I should go to work?'

'Weren't you saying only yesterday how with both Celia and Lucy gone off sick you, Jenny and Heather were having to cope with their work as well as your own?'

'I'm being feeble,' Karrie owned.

'You're a very upset young woman, that's what you are—but it will do you good to keep busy.'

'Busy' was an understatement for work at Irving and Small that day. And, as Farne, Farne, Farne buzzed round and around in her brain, Karrie was never more glad to have little time to think.

But she was in despair on the drive home as thoughts of Farne again took precedence. She should, she realised, have contacted him, or tried to, to discuss... But what was there to discuss? Oh, he had to be told, she knew that—and tried to get angry. It wasn't her fault if he couldn't be bothered to pick up the phone to give her a call.

She bit her lip; she wouldn't cry. She loved him so much but, like her father, Farne was never going to change his workaholic ways, and any marriage between them would founder, and she would end up embittered— and cause any sensitive child of the marriage nightmares like the ones she used to have but had never told anyone about—and...and she just couldn't take any more of it.

Oddly, her father was home when she got in. 'Have you told Dad?' she asked her mother, finding her alone in the kitchen.

'I think we can leave him in blissful ignorance for a day or two,' her mother answered incorrigibly. 'Though, given he went to the firm early this morning to make up for time he's losing tonight, he seems to be making a bit of an effort since I told him I'm going to divorce him. He thought I might like to go to the theatre this evening.'

'Oh, that's nice,' Karrie said on the instant. 'What are you going to see?'

'Oh, I'm not going!'

'You're not?'

'If he thinks he can neglect me year after year, while he's busy making money he'll never need, and then, when the comfort of his home is threatened—I can't see him cooking himself bacon and egg every morning—think I'll change my mind for one night at the theatre, then he can jolly well think again.'

'Oh, Mum.'

'Besides which, I'm not leaving you alone while you're so upset.'

'There's no need…' Karrie went to protest.

'There's every need.'

'But I'll be busy on the phone tonight anyway. I'll have to ring round and tell everybody that the m-marriage is cancelled and won't be taking place. And…'

'I've been thinking about that, and it seems to me that, since Farne doesn't know of your decision yet, it would be kinder to him if, instead of saying that the wedding is cancelled and that it will not now take place, we say it has been postponed.'

'Postponed? But I'm not going to…'

'I know, love. But in all fairness you'll have to tell Farne before anyone else that you've decided not to marry him. And since we can't leave it until after he's home on Friday night to start ringing people who've accepted the invitations, I thought I could make a start tomorrow and say that, because Farne is delayed in Australia, the wedding is postponed for a short while.'

Her mother was right, of course, she realised. 'I've been a bit muddle-headed, haven't I?' Karrie owned. 'I'll take some time off in the morning, and work late in the evening to make up, and...

'I can do all the telephoning,' Margery Dalton said stoutly.

'I couldn't let you.'

'Yes, you can. With most of the guests being couples, it will only mean sixty or so phone calls. And don't forget tomorrow is your last day at Irving and Small. They won't expect you to work overtime on the day you finish with them. That is—if you're not thinking of rescinding your notice now that...'

Karrie shook her head, gave her mother a kiss, and went up to her room. How could she stay working at Irving and Small? Apart from anything else, she would be on pins the whole of the time in case Farne walked by on one of his irregular visits. No, she would leave tomorrow, as planned, and on Friday evening she would call Farne's number every half-hour until he was back, and tell him that she must see him. Then she would drive to his house and return his engagement ring, tell him that she had made a mistake and that her mother had announced that the wedding was postponed, but that, if he wished to later tell everyone that the engagement had been broken by mutual agreement, that was fine by her.

Karrie felt not a bit better about any of it when she drove to Irving and Small on Thursday. She had asked her mother to allow her to ring Farne's parents when she got in that evening—but she was not looking forward to making that call.

Nor was she looking forward to lunchtime today. She was supposed to be going for a parting drink with several people from her office, but talk was certain to be of her intended marriage, and she just didn't know if she could face it.

Salvation was at hand, however, in that Heather phoned

in to say she had broken her wrist playing netball the previous evening and would not be in for some days.

'I know this is your last day with us, Karrie.' A fraught Pauline Shaw came to see her. 'But you know Heather's work better than anyone—I know I've got an awful cheek but, could you short-cut your lunch hour, do you think?'

'I won't take one at all,' Karrie smiled, ready to kiss Pauline's feet. And, feeling mean suddenly that she'd got nothing whatsoever to do tomorrow now, 'Actually, I could come in for a few hours tomorrow if it's of any help.'

'You wouldn't! Oh, you lovely thing!'

Karrie drove home that night wondering if she would ever get Farne out of her head. His wonderful eyes, his wonderful smile—they seemed to haunt her the whole time. And yet, her father was home again early—chalk it up. Karrie was convinced she had made the only decision possible.

'How did things go?' she asked, seeking her mother out.

'Everyone was most understanding—including the vicar. And you don't have to ring Farne's parents. His mother rang to see if she could help with any last-minute problems that might have cropped up, so I told her what we agreed on.'

'Was Mrs M-Maitland...' Karrie stumbled at the name she would have been so proud to have as her own '...all...?'

'She was fine. Extremely sympathetic. And just a mite cross with her son, by the way, but...'

'Oh, I didn't want Farne to be blamed!'

Her mother looked at her sharply, and Karrie knew that she had just revealed in her exclamation that she still loved Farne. 'Oh, darling,' her mother cried, and caught hold of her. 'I don't know what's gone wrong between you, but—' She broke off, as if realising that they were both close to tears. 'Anyhow,' she said bracingly, letting go of her, 'Adele Maitland won't be at all cross with Farne once she's had a chance to talk to him.'

And that will be either tomorrow night or Saturday morning, Karrie guessed, and would liked to have phoned her cousin for a chat, but wasn't sure she could hold back from telling her some of the truth—that way lay tears.

Karrie slept better that night, from sheer exhaustion, but she got up the next morning with thoughts of Farne going round and around in her head. She wished now that she had pocketed her pride and rung his PA for his Australian phone number. But it was too late now. Right at this very moment he was flying home.

She went to work still wearing her engagement ring— there were too many sharp eyes among her work colleagues; someone would have spotted its absence had she taken it off, and doubtless have commented on it. She wasn't up to equivocation or explanation just then.

But someone she did owe an explanation to was Farne. Karrie sat at her desk, trying hard to concentrate, but was finding it extremely difficult. Because she knew that tonight, when she saw Farne, when she took that beautiful ring off and handed it back to him, whether she was up to it or not, she was just going to have to explain. And the trouble was, she did not have an explanation to give him.

Mr Lane came by her desk, and stopped and smiled. 'We're most grateful to you for coming in this morning, Karrie,' he beamed. 'Especially when tomorrow is such an important day for you.'

Oh, grief! She had thought she'd work up until one o'clock, but she didn't know how much more she could take. She felt as if she was cracking up fast. 'My pleasure,' she smiled, and he went on his way and she struggled to keep herself in one piece.

She wouldn't think of Farne and her meeting with him

that night; she wouldn't, she wouldn't. For the next hour she made desperate attempts to close her mind to all but her work—and found it impossible.

Oh, heavens, at this very moment Farne was winging his way home, anticipating that tomorrow he would be going through a wedding ceremony with her—and she had not one single solitary explanation to give to him as to why that ceremony was not going to take place. There was no way she was going to tell him the truth—that she loved him, he didn't love her—and talk about all that followed from this basic fact: the result had to be a marriage of disaster. But she would have to tell him something.

All at once she became aware that someone was near her desk. Absently, she assumed that whoever it was would go on by. But they didn't. She looked up enquiringly, vaguely suspecting that it was Darren. But—it wasn't Darren! And, as her heart started to hammer, Karrie was suddenly very much aware that she was going to have to find an explanation to give her ex-fiancé sooner than she had thought.

'Farne!' she gasped, her head a nonsense. It couldn't be him! He wasn't due home yet!

'Karrie,' Farne replied, seeming taller than ever as he stood over her, a very tough kind of look in his piercing blue eyes.

'Wh-what are you doing here?' she stammered witlessly.

'Funny you should ask,' he answered, not looking the smallest bit amused—in fact, looking the sternest she had ever seen him. 'A very peculiar story has reached me. I thought I'd better come and check it out.'

She swallowed, and as her brain started to function again so did her hearing—everyone, it seemed, had stopped work and was tuned in! 'It—er—isn't so much p-peculiar as true,' she replied as calmly as she was able, and saw a muscle involuntarily jump in his temple.

'I—see,' he answered. But, as she might have known, he wasn't likely to let her get away with that—and, in fairness, she saw it was no kind of an explanation. 'Then may I suggest we go somewhere a little more private and discuss it?' he requested evenly.

Oh, help her, someone. She knew she owed him that at least. But knowing without seeing him that they must discuss the matter of their broken engagement was an entirely different matter from seeing Farne now, in the flesh. She had so longed to see him, yearned to… Stop it. 'There's little to—hmm—discuss.' She tried for an off-hand note. And lost it completely at his reply.

'My dear Karrie, the last time we were together, you were in my arms—most willingly, I recall. I do think we have everything to discuss.' And, while she was going all shades of crimson, yet still refusing to budge, he continued, 'We were upstairs in my home. We were, if *you* recall—' He broke off when she grabbed her bag from her desk drawer and shot to her feet.

Farne stood back to let her go in front, and Karrie felt she hated him. She knew, without a shadow of a doubt, that he had been about to state—*in front of everyone*—how she had been as near naked in his arms as made no difference!

Ignoring the open-mouthed stares of her work colleagues, Karrie stormed past him on her way out of the building. Farne was right there to open the door for her, and she caught the determined glint in his eyes. She knew then that there was no escape. Whether she had an explanation ready or not, he was insisting on knowing why, when his back was turned, while he was out of the country, she had jilted him.

From the resolute look of him, Karrie had an idea that he would accept nothing but out-and-out honesty. She was glad to hate him, needed to hate him—she envisaged a very difficult time ahead!

CHAPTER EIGHT

KARRIE saw his car right outside the main door, parked where it shouldn't be, of course, but left there as though Farne had entered the building in some haste. She went to march on by, her emotions in chaos, but her hate of him still strong.

'We'll go in my car!' he clipped, catching a hold of her arm, plainly uncaring of her hate.

She halted, because she was forced to. 'I'll follow you,' she snapped. 'There's no need for strong-arm tactics!' He ignored her hint to let her go and held on to her. She wished he wouldn't because she had so yearned for his touch, to be this close to him this past fortnight, and just his hand on her arm was weakening. 'I give you my word I'll follow you,' she told him coldly.

'You gave me your word you would marry me! My car!' he repeated.

Someone she knew came out from the building and looked over at them. Karrie realised that even if it was unlikely that she would see anyone from Irving and Small again—and no way could she ever go back in the building after this—if she didn't want a blow by blow account of any slanging match she and Farne might have circulating—and by the look of it he wouldn't give a damn who heard it—then she'd better do as he wanted.

Unspeaking, she got into his car. He started up the engine and without another word drove away from Irving and Small, and Karrie was so stewed up inside it seemed ages before she could get any thoughts together.

By that time it was plain to her that Farne was heading in the direction of his house. And that was when she realised how entirely illogical she was. Because she had planned to call and see him at his home that night, but now, now that he was taking her there, she didn't want to go.

She took a sideways look at him—he seemed grim, determined. Oh, heavens—determined! Determined to have the truth about why she wouldn't marry him! The basic truth was that she loved him too much to marry him.

They arrived at his home and he helped her out of his car, and Karrie tried to drum up that brief spasm of hate again. She didn't want to go inside his home with him. Even when common decency if nothing else demanded that she gave him some sort of explanation, she didn't want to go inside his home.

Karrie took another quick glance at him. He eyed her steadily back. Something there in the depths of his piercing blue eyes assured her he was relentless enough to pick her up and carry her in if she wasn't prepared to walk. She looked from him and went towards his front door.

In no time they were in his drawing room. Karrie was still searching desperately for some kind of explanation when, Farne invited shortly, 'Take a seat.'

It seemed a good idea. But she was afraid to relax so much as a muscle. Farne looked tough. Boardroom tough. Her knees felt shaky. 'I'm not going to marry you!' she stated bluntly. Oh, how she loved him. Oh, how she'd missed him.

Farne looked at her through narrowed eyes. Coldly, coolly, he looked at her. 'Would it be impolite of me to enquire why?' he asked.

And that gave her a little of the backbone she so desperately needed. Sarcastic swine! 'How did you find out?' she prevaricated. 'You obviously knew when you came to the office.'

'Rachel—my PA—told me.'

'Your PA? But—but my mother wasn't going to contact her!'

'She didn't. Rachel, on my instruction before I left for Australia, yesterday contacted her to enquire if there were any problems she might need help with. To her surprise, your mother told her that everything had been cancelled and that the wedding would not now take place.'

Cancelled! Not postponed? Karrie wondered why her mother had told Rachel 'cancelled', and then realised that since Rachel was the one person who was likely to know better than anyone that Farne had been in no way delayed, her mother must have realised it too, and could not give Farne's delayed return as a reason for the postponement.

'So Rachel phoned you…?' Karrie began. 'No, she couldn't have,' she contradicted. 'You'd have been on your way back from Austral… You're not due home until tonight, when—'

'I arrived last night,' Farne cut in. His look of determination was still there. 'No way was I prepared to suffer a flight delay and miss my wedding—stupid of me—you should have let me know your plans!' he said curtly.

'I would have done had I known where to contact you!' Karrie erupted.

'When did you decide?'

'Not to marry you? Tuesday night—er—Wednesday morning.' Her spurt of temper fizzled out. 'It wasn't an easy decision.'

Farne's expression all at once softened, and Karrie found that far more weakening than when he had looked all set to toughly get to the answer he was insisting upon. 'Wasn't it?' he asked gently.

Oh, Farne, don't, don't. His gentleness was undermining. She turned her back on him and went over to one of the sofas. 'It—wasn't an impulsive decision,' she said slowly, belatedly accepting his earlier invitation to take a seat. 'I worried and worried about it for hour after hour.'

Farne came over to her, but though she feared he might come and take a seat on the sofa next to her he seemed to change his mind. She was a little relieved to see him move one of the chairs around and place it opposite her.

'I'm—sorry you've had such a worrying time,' he said kindly. 'I wouldn't have wanted that. But—' his tone was firm '—I need to know why you've come to the decision you have. It's—important to me, Karrie.'

Oh, Farne! She so wanted to be truthful with him, but feared she could not be. And she supposed it was important to him. She supposed it would be a blow to any man's pride to have the woman they thought they were going to marry say no at the last minute.

'I'm sorry to have hurt your pride,' she began—and soon found she had got that wrong.

'To hell with pride!' Farne suddenly rapped. Then he took what seemed to be a steadying breath before, leaning forward, he caught hold of her hands in a warm but gentle hold. 'Karrie,' he said, 'Karrie, my dear. I know, thought I knew, that you had some sort of a—for the want of better words—a hang-up about the bedroom.' Her eyes shot wide and she stared at him. A hang-up about the bedroom! 'You said you didn't want to give up your virginity without first being married. And I didn't press you or question you on that because—apart from anything else—I felt you were responsive enough to me that, if there was any problem, with a little patience and understanding we would be able to overcome it once we were married.' Karrie was still staring at him wide-eyed when he went on. 'Two weeks ago, here, upstairs in one of the bedrooms, we kissed, touched and intimately held each other, and I thought from your response that I could forget any notion of your having a problem—other than a sweet and natural shyness—when it came to sharing a bed with me. But, little one, did I get it wrong? If there is a problem, I'm sure we…'

'Farne, no!' She stopped him, snatching her hands away from him. He was being so wonderful—she'd had no idea he'd thought that way. And she wanted above everything to marry him. But she could not—for both their sakes.

'No?'

Oh, heavens—he wanted more than just no. She looked from him, and realised she could prevaricate no longer. She knew he wanted honesty, and she now felt she wanted to be honest with him—as much as she could possibly afford to be.

'I don't have—um—any hang-up of—er—that kind,' she began, feeling a tinge pink because Farne above anyone else had first-hand knowledge about that! 'I do want to—that is, I don't want to have made love with anyone before I'm married. Not for any—' She broke off, and came up against the shyness he had spoken of, because when it came to talking and taking part in the most intimate of communications she still, in talking about it, seemed to be having problems. 'It—this—isn't easy,' she stated, a touch exasperated.

'There's no rush,' Farne said quietly. 'And, if I didn't think it has some bearing on the decision you've laboured over about us, then I'd say leave it. But, as I mentioned, it's important to me.' Important to him—but had it nothing to do with his pride? She supposed she was too muddled already to take in any more confusion. 'So tell me, Karrie, in your own time why it's important to you to be able to wear white in the true tradition on your wedding day?'

She supposed it did have some slight connection with why she couldn't marry him. 'It's—part me, partly because of my upbringing, I think.'

'Your upbringing?' he prompted when she hesitated.

'I—I've never mentioned it because it seemed like breaking my mother's confidence. But my father has a thing about duty, and married my mother when she told him she was pregnant.'

'With you?'

Karrie shook her head. 'My mother miscarried a week after their wedding and my father never forgave her for what he saw as her trapping him into marriage.'

'So you decided that no way were you going to risk becoming pregnant until you were safely married.'

'No man was ever going to accuse me of trapping him into marriage,' she answered. 'And it was never a problem—until I met you. Oh—!' She broke off, panicking madly inside. She'd have to watch her tongue; she was saying too much, much too much.

'You never had a problem—until us?' Farne refused to leave it there.

Karrie, her feelings of guilt for breaking off their engagement really getting to her, began to think that she owed him answers to everything he asked—he wasn't likely to ask her if she loved him.

'No,' she answered. 'Not that I've ever been seriously involved with anybody to that extent. But, well, when you and I started—well—the other Friday when I was here and—well, until then, until you really...' Oh, shut up, Karrie, do! Your tongue's running away with you. But Farne was quietly watching and waiting for more. 'Well, I didn't want to go home. I wanted to stay.'

'You wanted to stay—the night here—with me?'

She wouldn't look at him. 'Oh, I know you didn't. Want me to stay, I mean. You couldn't have been more casual about it. But—'

'Oh, sweetheart, what utter rot!' Farne cut in softly. And had her full attention when her eyes shot to his face.

'Rot?' she questioned.

'Rot,' he confirmed. 'I wanted you so badly that night, it was all I could do not to break into a sprint when you indicated I was trespassing far too far.'

'I…' She stared at him thunderstruck.

'Is that what all this is about?' Farne asked. 'You think I don't want you with every fibre of my being?'

Good heavens! 'You're saying you do?'

'Oh, Karrie. I know you're inexperienced. But believe it. Why else do you think I took myself off to Australia for two weeks?'

'"Business calls", you said.'

'It did—but I could have got out of going,' he confessed, and while Karrie continued to stare at him, wide-eyed, he said softly, 'My dear, Karrie. There was nothing for it after that night but for me to disappear. When you showed every sign of wanting to be mine that night I realised that the strong feelings you held about being a virgin bride were in no way connected with any particular hang-up. Other than, of course, your shyness with the unfamiliar that communicated itself to me—at a very late stage.' He smiled the smile she loved and reached for her hands again, and she let him keep them in his warm hold. 'Only at that moment did I vaguely remember what was so essential to you. I got us out of there as quickly as I could and took you to your home, not daring to breathe easily again until I'd seen you safely indoors.' Karrie's mouth fell slightly open. 'And it was then that I knew I had to keep you safe from me for two weeks more,' Farne went on, adding softly, 'In case you don't know it, you have the power to drive a man demented.'

'I do?' she questioned faintly.

'You do. I knew as I drove home that the only way I could be absolutely certain you would get your wedding day wish was if I didn't see you again until we met in church.'

He'd done that—for her! He'd gone away—for her! Surely—didn't that mean—he cared? And not just sexually. A smile started to tremble on her lips. Then she remembered—and her smile didn't make it. Farne was still a workaholic.

Again she pulled her hands from his, and took off her engagement ring. 'You'd better have this,' she said, extending her hand to give him the ring.

'No!' he refused fiercely. 'Put it back on!' he ordered. When she declined to obey, he said grimly, 'Whether we end our engagement or not, the ring is yours. But it won't come to that. I refuse to release you from our engagement without some sound and solid reason.' He took the ring from her—but only to push it back home on her engagement finger. 'So far,' he stated firmly, 'you haven't given me one.'

'I—did,' she attempted to argue, to bluff it out.

'No, you didn't!' he denied, not allowing her to get away with it. 'We've just agreed that—given your last-minute reserve, your shyness, which I fully understand—physically together we have no problems. So—what is it, Karrie?' he insisted on knowing.

Karrie took a shaky breath. The secret of her love for him he would never know. But she could tell that he was never going to give up. There was that steely look of intent in his steady unflinching blue eyes that told her so. And didn't she owe him some sort of an explanation? Yes, she did. She had known that since her decision last Wednesday. Hadn't she been trying to come up with an explanation since then?

That she hadn't been able to find one which avoided the truth was a problem. But—the time had arrived. 'I—didn't want the same sort of marriage that my parents have.' She owed him an explanation and reluctantly decided to stick to the truth as much as she could.

Farne was still eyeing her carefully, taking in every word, every nuance, every look. 'There's something the matter with your parents' marriage?' he enquired calmly.

It was difficult for her to discuss her parents in this

way. But she loved Farne, and knew that she could trust him with anything she told him. 'To the outside world, no,' she answered. 'But behind closed doors they row endlessly.'

'What about?'

'It doesn't have to be about anything in particular. My father has always resented—it's his belief—that he was trapped into marriage with my mother. While my mother has grown increasingly embittered that he's a workaholic and, neglecting her and any social life, he spends as much time as he can out of the house working.' She looked away as she added unhappily, 'They rant and rave at each other over the smallest thing.'

'And you think our marriage will be like that?' Farne asked quietly.

'No,' she answered, 'because I'm not going to marry you. I'm not going to have my mother's life, or end up as embittered as she has become.'

'You'll never become embittered, Karrie. I wouldn't let it happen,' Farne assured her.

'It's already happening,' she replied sadly. But when she looked at him her wide velvety brown eyes unknowingly revealed her depth of happiness. Farne, as if unable to prevent himself, leaned forward and placed a tender kiss on her cheek.

'Don't be sad,' he said softly. 'We'll make it right, I promise.' She shook her head, looking away from him, tears so near. He was being so sensitive, and she adored him, but it was not to be. 'Tell me, little one, what is it that's already happening?' he urged. 'I can't put it right if I don't know what it is that upsets you so.'

Karrie swallowed on a hard knot of emotion. 'You can't put it right. It's a fault in me. I'm already getting uptight that you work so much. That you're a workaholic too.'

'You think I'm a workaholic?' He seemed genuinely

surprised. 'I'm not,' he assured her, going on, 'I admit I get tremendous satisfaction from the work I do, but it's not the be all and end all of my existence.' He paused, seemed to hesitate a moment, and then, causing her to stare at him, startled, he clearly said, 'At the great risk of ruining everything that is most important to me, I have to tell you, Karrie, that is what *you* are.'

Karrie's eyes were enormous as she stared at him. There was a roaring in her ears, a commotion in the region of her heart. Had Farne just said what she thought he had just said—that *she* was the be all and end all of his existence? She couldn't believe it! And when all her senses had quietened down, she still didn't believe it.

'It looks like it!' she snapped, plummeting from the heights to the depths. 'You've spent every spare moment working, you've broken dates with me in order to work—' she charged, and would have gone on, only Farne butted in.

'Only for you!' he stated—but she wasn't having that!

'How for me?' she flared—she had never asked him for anything.

'You had stated it was essential to you that you were chaste on your wedding day, and, given a panicky moment or two, I've always respected your wish—hell on earth though it's sometimes been.'

Hell on earth! Desperately did she feel in the need of some backbone, because she had gone all weak again. 'You're lying!' she accused. But the accusation came out sounding more than a mite feeble to her own ears.

Farne took her accusation on board, however, and had never looked more serious when he moved determinedly from his chair and came and sat on the sofa beside her and, turning, again taking both her hands in his, said, 'I have lied; I admit it. But not any more. Everything I've said today is the truth—my lies before...' He seemed to need to take a steadying breath. 'Those lies seemed to

justify the end—until now. But not any more, Karrie.'
His eyes were fixed on hers as he went on. 'Now I insist
on only the truth between us.'

You're on your own there, Farne! Karrie knew she
would lie her head off if he came anywhere close to discovering so much as a hint of how much she loved him.
'You're the one who's been telling all the lies.' She gave
him the floor—and spoilt it all by adding, 'You're the
one who isn't a workaholic but always seems to be working.'

'Oh, my dear—I hadn't realised you felt neglected,'
Farne soothed.

Oh, my word, keep your mouth closed, Karrie. 'Neglected, pfff!' she scorned. But her mouth refused to stay
closed. 'Forgive me for gaining the impression we'd be
taking your briefcase with us on our honeymoon! Not that
there's going to be any honeymoon,' she tacked on hastily. And, since she didn't seem able to keep a guard on
her tongue, now seemed as good a time as any to get out
of there. She stood up, but so did Farne. 'I'm sorry,' she
said, and went to walk away.

She walked maybe three steps. *'Don't go!'* Farne's
voice halted her, such a note of anguish there that she
spun about. 'Karrie, don't go,' he said more quietly, and
actually seemed to have lost some of his colour. Stunned,
she stood there, not moving. She saw him swallow. Then
she felt riveted to the spot when Farne reminded her, 'You
said you love me a bit. I think I'd like you to know
something of how much I—care—for you.'

Karrie eyed him uncertainly. She wanted to go. Knew
she should go. And yet, even while it was firmly estab-
lished in her head that Farne was a workaholic like her
father, Farne only had to hint that he had some kind of
caring for her, and she was having the hardest job in the
world to remember why she wanted nothing to do with

any work-dominated male. Love for him was turning her world upside down.

'As I remember it, you loved me "some"!' she offered coolly, not leaving, but determined she wasn't staying.

'I take great comfort from the fact that you remember my vast understatement,' Farne replied—and her resolve to depart vanished that instant. 'Come and sit with me while I explain,' he urged, and, coming forward, he took a hold of her arm and led her, unresisting, back to the sofa. And when they were once more seated he again turned to her. 'I came to the offices of Irving and Small almost three months ago on one of my occasional management morale visits to Gordon Lane. But no sooner did I enter the purchase and supply office than I was blinded by a cloud of blonde gold-threaded hair.' Karrie stared at him.

'It was a Tuesday,' she said without thinking.

'Tuesday it was,' he agreed. 'And there was I, feeling positive the face wouldn't match up to the beautiful hair, when, as I drew level, you stood up—and I saw that it did match up, that you were exquisitely beautiful—and I was lost for words.'

Oh, Farne—she was feeling all wobbly inside again. 'I thought you'd never have noticed me if I hadn't bumped into you,' the person within her who had an uncontrollable tongue spoke.

'Don't you believe it.' Farne shook his head. 'I came out from Gordon Lane's office just knowing I'd got to speak to you. Your voice matched up to the rest of you. You, Mr and Mrs Dalton's daughter, had literally almost knocked me off my feet in more ways than one. I had to see you outside of work.'

'And I said no.'

'You lied and said you were washing your hair,' he said, with that dizzying smile. 'But I wasn't leaving it there. I got hold of your phone number and rang you, and we had dinner together.' He paused, and then added, 'And life, for me, Karrie, was never the same after that.'

'Oh,' she murmured, wanting to know more, much more. The question just refused to be held down. 'Er—why was that?' she asked.

'I'd enjoyed being with you so much. And I knew, before you held out your hand to shake hands at the end of the evening, that you were different. I couldn't wait to see you again.'

Karrie stared at him. 'Truly?' she gasped.

'Truly,' he confirmed. 'I'd said to you that evening that I wouldn't lie, but everything—the uproar caused by my emotions—seemed to be happening so fast that I was totally thrown.'

'I—think I'm getting a tiny bit confused,' she owned.

'It can be nothing to what I felt in those early days of knowing you,' Farne confessed—and Karrie was glued to his every word.

'Don't—um—leave it there,' she invited huskily, and saw that Farne looked encouraged by her invitation.

'So there was I,' he took up, 'honest as I'd always been until then, having parted from you only the night before, feeling all thrown off balance, as I said, and vulnerable with it, knowing only that I felt quite desperate to see you again—and soon.'

'Farne!' she gasped. He had been desperate to see her again! She swallowed. Even though he'd admitted to lying in the past, only a short while ago he'd said 'not any more' and that he insisted on only the truth between them. Was it really true that, for all she'd seen no sign of him being desperate to see her, he had been? That he had managed to hide his feelings? Karrie swallowed again—his—*feelings?* 'You were desperate, you said?' she questioned huskily.

'Believe it,' he answered. 'The next morning, Sunday, I remembered having attended a function at a hotel near you. In next to no time, and hoping against hope that you'd be in, I casually called at your home and lied my head off, saying I was passing your way *en route* to lunch at The Feathers, and asked if you were free to join me.'

He hadn't been passing! He'd made a point of calling—she doubted her heart would ever beat normally again.

'I was all scruffy in the garden,' she recalled dreamily. 'And after, down by the river, you kissed me with a beautiful kiss, and I—' She broke off, coming to abruptly as it suddenly dawned on her what she had been about to say—that she had known then that she loved him!

'And you…?' Farne prompted.

No way! 'And I went home, and you went off in your casual way.'

'Casual! It seems I've been a master at hiding the turmoil that's been going on inside me.'

Turmoil! Him? She knew turmoil inside out. But Farne! 'What turmoil would that be?' she asked politely.

'May I kiss you? I haven't seen you for a fortnight. And I'm going to marry you—if you'll have me. And, to be blunt my darling, I'm aching to hold you in my arms.'

Her mouth went dry again. But this time she didn't swallow. Something was happening inside her. Some happiness was trying to burst forth—if she'd let it. She wanted to trust in Farne, in the fact that he seemed to care, perhaps a little more than 'some'—and besides, didn't she ache to be in his arms, ache to be held by him? She hadn't seen him for a fortnight either.

'Farne, I…'

'What is it—you're struggling?'

'To be honest, I could do with a h-hug myself, but I can't marry you only for it to go all wrong.'

'Come here,' he soothed, and, not waiting, he put his arms around her and held her close. 'Nothing's going to go wrong.'

'You're going to spend for ever working.'

'Certainly not!' he assured her. 'Had I known anything at all about your home background I'd have looked for a different kind of antidote to your—charms.'

'My charms?' Farne placed a tender kiss to her mouth, smiled a giving smile. 'Antidote?' Her head seemed to be in wild disarray. She pulled out of his hold, needing a clear head.

Farne released her, but looked gently at her as he explained, 'My dear, I very soon knew that I wanted to marry you. But just when I was starting to believe that, incredibly, everything was going my way, and that, within a month of meeting you, I *was* going to marry you, you were giving me heart failure by phoning and saying not to get the special licence!'

'I—er—guessed you were a bit put out to have your plans altered for you,' she somehow managed to remember.

'A bit put out! Understatement!' Farne declared. 'I thought at first you were telling me that you weren't going to marry me at all. Then, while you went on to state your mother's view that we had to wait six months, and I was recovering, all I knew was that there was no way I could wait that long.'

'You—couldn't?' she queried, striving her level best to keep hold of her reasons for not marrying Farne. But those reasons were not so easy to hold on to now that she was with him, now that he was this close.

'I could not,' he said emphatically. 'The thought of waiting six months was not to be considered. I was having a hard enough time already not to take you in my arms every time I saw you.'

'You wanted to…'

'Every time,' he confirmed. 'Two months of not kissing and holding you as I wanted was going to be bad enough—six months was totally out of the question.'

'Because…' Her voice faded, an upsurge of relief starting to invade that Farne hadn't felt as cool and remote as he had often seemed. He had, like her, just yearned to hold and be held.

'Because,' he took up, 'while I was unsure that you might have some kind of a hang-up, as I explained, I was at the same time aware of my need to embrace you—yet afraid most of the time to touch you. I'm only human, my dear, but I knew I had to respect your essential wish for your wedding day.' Karrie stared at him speechlessly, and Farne, looking into her stunned face, went on. 'There were times when I felt I'd go crazy if I couldn't kiss and hold you, just once. Which was how I realised very early on that if I was going to cope in any way at all until we were safely married I was going to have to avoid situations where you and I would be alone together, that I was going to have to limit the times I saw you.'

Karrie was still staring at him, stunned. Though she did manage to find her voice. 'You—deliberately—broke dates with me? Deliberately…'

'Deliberately, when the waiting started to get more than I could handle, saw you only in the company of other people. And, yes, not knowing about your workaholic father and your mother's unhappiness because of it, I deliberately picked on work as an antidote to try and stop myself craving to be with you the whole of the time.'

She was astonished! She'd no idea it had been like that for him! 'S-so you're—not truly heart and soul into work?' she asked when she found her voice. And discovered, at his reply, that her astonishment wasn't over.

For, taking her hands in his, he replied softly, 'What I am, Karrie, is truly, heart and soul, in love with you.'

Her mouth fell open, her eyes saucer-wide, 'You're not!' she whispered. 'Are you?' she asked.

'"Some",' he answered softly, 'was the biggest understatement of my life.'

'No!' she denied faintly.

'Oh, yes,' he contradicted. 'I've loved you from almost the first. Certainly from that first night we dined together.'

'Since then!' she gasped.

'I knew it then, when I took you home. I sat in the car after you'd gone in. And, with the car empty of you— you were no longer there—my life, too, suddenly seemed empty.' Karrie's heart was racing, her mouth dry again.

'I—can't believe it!' She felt winded. Farne loved her! Had loved her all this while!

'Nor could I,' he smiled. 'It wasn't logical. I didn't know you. And yet I did. I saw you the next day and kissed your cheek in parting, but didn't want to go. I wanted to hold you and go on holding you, and beg you not to see my rival, Travis, that night.'

'Travis w-was never your rival,' she said a little tremulously, not surprised that her voice sounded a little shaky, it was the way she felt.

'Any man who wants to marry you is my rival,' Farne stated. 'I was ragingly jealous of that man.'

Oh, this was all too too wonderful. Farne *loved* her! 'Ragingly?'

'Ragingly, illogically,' he confirmed. 'I tried to tell myself that this man couldn't be that important to you or you'd never have broken a date with him to go out with me the previous night. But logic has nothing to do with love, I discovered. Can you blame me, sweetheart, that, for my sanity's sake, I decided I was going to keep away from you?'

'Oh, er—' She was still feeling very shaken, but Farne had said he loved her, and she just had to hear more. 'You—um decided that on that Sunday?' she asked.

'I did,' he confirmed. 'You enchanted me, sweet darling. I wanted to see you every hour of every day.'

Oh, it got more and more wonderful, and a belief in all that Farne was saying, that he did, as he'd said, love her, was starting to get a firm foothold in her mind. 'So—you decided you wouldn't,' she smiled, and, because it was all too fantastic, she gave a delighted laugh.

Farne grinned. 'Just you wait—I'm going to kiss you breathless.'

Bliss, pure bliss. 'Go—on,' she invited softly.

'You're not going to tell me how you feel about me, I suppose?'

She wanted to. But perhaps shy all at once; she didn't know, but she wasn't ready. Perhaps she just needed to let this new-found knowledge that Farne loved her sink in a little first. 'I...' she said helplessly.

'All right, little love,' Farne relented gently. 'Let it come naturally. But—' he placed a loving kiss to the corner of her mouth '—make it soon.' And then, as she'd requested, he went on, 'So I decided, for heaven's sake, I'd only known you two minutes—not even a week yet. It just wasn't right that some slip of a woman could make such a nonsense of me. Ye gods, I *enjoyed* being a bachelor.'

'You weren't—even *then*—thinking of not being a bachelor?' she questioned incredulously.

'Not consciously—though I knew I was before the week was out.'

'We got engaged the following Sunday.'

'Oh, so much happened that week,' Farne murmured.

'Your determination not to see me again didn't last long,' she recalled dreamily.

'Neither it did. Two whole days I held out,' he admitted. 'But after a dreadful struggle all through Tuesday night I woke up on Wednesday knowing that I was just going to have to see your lovely face again.'

'You came to Irving and Small, and...'

'And was near to panicking when I got to the door, in case you weren't in that day. But there you were. I saw the back of your lovely head and, just as though my heart

wasn't racing nineteen to the dozen, stopped for a word—
and then felt as though my heart would stop altogether
when, my eyes going straight to your desk on the way
out, I saw you weren't there.'

'I'd gone to the cloakroom—but got scared you might
have left the building and almost ran back in case I
missed you.'

Farne eyed her steadily for long, long moments. Then,
'You love me don't you?' he questioned quietly.

'I…' The words got stuck.

'More than a bit?' He helped her out.

'Like—I've never known anything like it,' she answered shyly.

'Like—it consumes you, and turns your whole world
upside down?'

'All of that,' she said.

'Come here.'

She didn't have to go very far because Farne met her
more than halfway. He looked deeply into her eyes, and,
as if satisfied at last with what he saw there, he gathered
her into his arms, and for long, long, heart-healing seconds he held her close. Then he kissed her, and, willingly,
Karrie kissed him back.

'Say it,' he said, even though she knew he knew she
loved him still needing to hear her say it.

And this time, the time right, she could. 'I love you,'
she said. 'With all of me, Farne Maitland, I love you.'
And Farne kissed her again, a long, wonderful, most satisfying kiss. And held her, and seemed as if he would
never let her go.

But, after a long, blissful moment of just holding each
other, he pulled back to look into her face. 'When, my
darling?' he wanted to know. 'When did you know?'

'That day. Down by the river,' she whispered.

'Since then! You've loved me since then?' He seemed
amazed.

'I can't help it if I think you're wonderful,' she laughed.

'Keep saying that. You've no idea of how I need to hear it.'

She smiled a loving smile, feeling something very similar. 'It was all so sudden, wasn't it? Meeting each other, two arranged dates—and one that was accidentally on purpose.' She laughed—she felt she wanted to keep on smiling, there was such joy breaking in her. The joy of knowing, and at last believing, that she was truly loved heart and soul by the man she loved. She strove to concentrate on what she'd been saying. 'Then we were going to Milan, and came back here that Sunday night—'

'Don't remind me of Milan!' Farne cut in with some feeling.

'It was fantastic! That Saturday...'

'It was special,' Farne smiled. 'Never had a day been more perfect. I wanted more days like that with you. How the blazes I managed to let you go to your room alone that night I shall never know!

'You didn't want... I didn't know...!'

'You weren't supposed to. And had I not given my word to your mother that—'

'My mother? What...?'

'Ah!'

It seemed as if he intended to leave it there. 'Please?' Karrie requested. 'I've only just got clear of one lot of confusion—I'm getting fogged up again.'

'I love you,' he said.

'Oh, I love you,' she sighed, and they held each other and kissed. Karrie could only wonder at the sublime, heady yet contented feeling she felt, knowing that Farne loved her. In fact, so at one was she feeling with the man she loved that she forgot for a moment that she had asked him to tell her what he had given his word to her mother about. 'My mother?' she reminded him, some ageless minutes later.

'Milan,' he answered. 'You phoned my office before we went and left a message with Rachel that you urgently needed to contact me.'

'You said "non-urgent" when you mentioned it in Milan,' Karrie recalled.

'Rachel wrote down everything you said—but I was afraid to mention it until we were on Italian soil in case your message had been that you weren't going to come with me after all!'

'Oh, Farne!' she sighed. If she was dreaming she never wanted to wake up. 'I—er—lied about my reason for that phone call,' she felt honour-bound to confess.

'You said you'd rung to say you'd managed to get the Friday off work. That wasn't the reason?'

How could she feel shy about telling him when he loved her and she loved him? She took a brave breath, and began, 'It hadn't occurred to me that you might be thinking in terms of our—um—sleeping together that weekend. Not that you were,' she added hastily. 'But my mother, when I told her my weekend plans, was very upset and called me unworldly and…and…'

'And so you rang to check?' he helped her out.

'I thought I might have accepted your invitation under false pretences.'

'Oh what a delight you are!' Farne pulled her to him and just had to kiss her.

'But I need not have worried, because…'

'Because your mother got there before you.'

'I am *totally* fogged,' Karrie confessed.

'And I lied too, when I told you I almost came to your home in response to your message,' Farne owned.

'You lied?' she questioned, staring at him.

'My love, I asked you to come to Milan with me be-cause I genuinely wanted to spend more than just a few hours in your company. To have you with me for a whole weekend would, I thought, be little short of perfect. But in response to your message I drove over to see you...'

'On Thursday night, when I was out?' she gasped.

'The very same, and, as you said, you were out—with that diabolical Travis.'

'I love it when you're jealous.'

'Shut up, woman,' he growled, 'and let me continue.' She kissed him. 'So there I was, having the temerity to ring your doorbell only to receive a frosty reception from your mother, who started off by stating that she hoped I planned that you and I should have separate rooms in Milan.'

'She didn't!' Karrie didn't know whether to be embarrassed, appalled, or what to be.

'She did,' he answered with a smile, kissed her and said, 'Now don't be upset. It's all over now. Anyhow, your mother then went on to tell me that you were a good girl and innocent-minded—and that she hoped I would return you in the same state.'

'Oh, Farne, I'm sorry.'

'Don't be. You're everything your mother said. And she was just trying to protect you. Though I'll admit that at that time I was of the opinion that mothers didn't know absolutely everything about their daughters. But by then I knew that if I had the smallest chance, that I was going to marry you. Which meant this woman—who was asking that I wouldn't violate your innocence, that I would sleep alone—would, if everything went well for me, be my mother-in-law. So I gave her my word—never knowing what hell keeping my word was going to be.'

Questions rushed to her lips to be answered. 'My mother said nothing of your visit that night to me! No wonder I thought she was a little distant with me—it wasn't that. It was her deception in...'

'In trying to protect you from the wicked likes of me,' Farne grinned.

'And it worked,' Karrie laughed.

'Only just!' Farne smiled. 'I went to my room that first night just aching to hold you. Having earlier that day let my jealousy over your friend rule my head, and only just managing to change "you're my love, my life" to "you're my guest".'

She remembered. 'Oh, Farne!' she sighed blissfully.

'Don't "Oh, Farne" me, you temptress,' he teased. 'I knew after my conversation with your mother that I should have booked us into a hotel. But—I simply wanted to be with you, just you and me, with no one else around. And so I went to bed that second night, again, for my sins, lying sleepless with you in the next room. I got up on Sunday morning breathing a sigh of relief that I'd been able to keep my word to my future mother-in-law—and made the mistake of walking into the kitchen. My second mistake was to take you in my arms. You'll never know the desperation in me or from where I found the will-power to let you go. I'd planned to return to London some time during the late afternoon, but after that I couldn't get us out of that apartment quickly enough. I was half afraid to speak for fear I might blurt out how much I wanted to marry you.'

'No!' she gasped, amazed.

'Yes,' he contradicted. 'Afraid to speak, afraid to touch. Vulnerable as I'd never been. My confidence in tatters, I had to get you out of there. But my attempts at conversation dried up when that foul monster jealousy got to me again. It was only as we landed back on English soil that I realised that if I didn't buck my ideas up I was going to lose what small chance I had with you before I started.'

'It didn't occur to you that for me to have gone to Italy with you in the first place meant you were in there with one very big chance?' she asked impishly.

'My dear, while I own I'm confident about all else, you, and the great love I feel for you, had me so shattered I didn't know where the blazes I was. All I knew was that I had to marry you—and soon.'

'Dear Farne,' she whispered chokily, and kissed him. 'We sort of—got engaged that night.'

'I couldn't believe it,' he confessed. 'I'd barely recovered from the shock of knowing that you were actually as innocent as your mother believed when—my promise to her kept in Milan—just when I believed I could be forgiven for thinking that you, my wonderful darling, were going to be with me the way you have been with no man, you cried out that fiendish word ''no''.'

'Have you forgiven me yet?'

'I'd forgiven you within seconds of hearing you state that you couldn't, not until you were married.'

'You seemed to be having difficulty coping with it,' she recalled.

'I was stunned,' he owned. 'Stunned, and then my heart started to crash against my ribs as, incredulous, I began to see a possibility that marriage to you might, just might, be within my grasp. It didn't matter to me why you couldn't give yourself completely to me then. I could sort that out later. What was more important was that I didn't miss this unexpected but most marvellous opportunity.'

'You said, ''In that case, Karrie, we'd better get married'',' she remembered dreamily.

'My heart was in my mouth as I said it,' he revealed. 'I was afraid to tell you of my love for you, of the way my heart aches for you, of how much I adore you. Afraid to begin telling you how it is with me in case once I got started I wouldn't be able to stop. Afraid I might alarm you—frighten you away. I was afraid to even look at you. And when you didn't answer, I was scared of saying another word about you and I marrying for fear you would tell me no.'

'I was terrified of saying anything at all—in case you were joking,' Karrie admitted.

'Oh, sweet love,' Farne crooned, and kissed her, and held her close up against him. 'And there was I hoping, since you hadn't rejected me outright, that you might love me a little so that I could build on that once we were married.'

'Darling, Farne,' she whispered. 'All that was going on in your head and I never knew!'

'As I mentioned, I was terrified of scaring you away. Yet I wanted our engagement to be a concrete fact.'

'Which is why you went to see my father the very next day?' she smiled.

'I wasted no time,' Farne agreed. 'But I seem to have spent all my time since then trying to avoid the ever-present urge to take you in my arms.'

She laughed joyously and just had to tease, 'I believe we both gave in to that urge two weeks ago.'

'When you rattled me beyond bearing by hanging on to Vaughan Green's every word.'

She laughed again; she had to. Oh, she did love Farne so. 'If we're talking jealousy, you didn't seem in any great hurry to shake off the limpet Eleanor.'

'You were jealous!' Farne exclaimed in obvious delight.

'Swine!' she becalled him, and he gathered her in his arms close up to him.

'My darling,' Farne murmured softly. 'Is it any wonder after that night that I decided to take myself off to Australia?'

'Because of…'

'I was losing control,' he admitted. 'I'd lain with you near naked for a second time—Lord knew what control I'd be able to find should it happen a third time. Yet it was still of paramount importance to you that I should

keep control. But, against that, there were still two un-
bearably long weeks to be got through.'

'You went—because of me?'

'I had to,' he admitted.

'It's been a miserable fortnight.'

'Tell me about it!' he agreed. 'There was I, desperate
to phone you, to hear your voice, but scared to call you
for fear the longing I feel for you might have come rushing out.'

'Was that the reason why you never phoned?'

Farne nodded. 'I ached to hear your voice, but was sure
just hearing you would set off my longing to be near you,
and it would become too much for me to remain in
Australia.'

'Oh!' she sighed blissfully. 'As it was, you came back
a day early.'

'I always intended to return when I did.'

'For shame,' she chided him lightly. 'And there was I,
forever thinking how open you always were!'

'It's only since falling in love with you that I've had
to go in for a little deception.' He smiled that devastating
smile, continuing, as she went all weak inside, 'Can you
blame me, after what happened the last time we were
together, for wanting to ensure that I wouldn't see you
again before we stood together at the altar and exchanged
our vows?' He paused, and then asked. 'When, by the
way—assuming I didn't arrive home until tonight—were
you going to tell me you'd decided you weren't going to
marry me? You *did* intend to tell me?'

'Oh, Farne, don't think that of me. Of course I was
going to tell you. I'd had to tell my mother because of
all the planning that's gone on. And I intended ringing
round to everyone saying that our marriage would not
take place, but my mother said it would be kinder to you
to say that the wedding had been postponed because you

were delayed, and that she would phone round everyone and let them know not to go to the church.'

'I think I'm going to like my mother-in-law,' he smiled. 'Do my folks know?'

'I was going to ring them, but your mother rang my mother before I could, to ask if she could offer any help, and my mother told her of the postponement.' Karrie said softly, adding apologetically, 'I'd intended to come over tonight to tell you when you returned. I'm sorry you had to learn it from your PA.'

'No more than I,' Farne replied. 'I was absolutely shattered. I'd only gone to my office to drop off some information about my trip and to clear up any last-minute loose ends before I took a long honeymoon. I was on my way out when Rachel let me into the little secret that I'd be spending my honeymoon on my own.'

'I'm so sorry,' Karrie apologised. 'It must have been something of a shock.'

'Bombshell!' he corrected. 'I came the nearest to panicking that I ever have in my life. It was all of a minute before I could even begin to think at all clearly.'

'And when you could, you decided to come and embarrass me out of Irving and Small.'

'I was prepared to do what I had to so that we could start talking,' Farne admitted. 'Though at first, when I was trying to decide where I might find you, I was of the view—since you were supposed to have finished work yesterday—that you were either at home or, ye gods, gone off somewhere.'

'We were short-staffed at Irving—'

'So Gordon Lane told me.'

'You rang him?' Oh, heavens!

'I was desperately trying to keep a lid on my emotions while at the same time trying to think logically. Since it seemed you'd cancelled our wedding, had you also cancelled your resignation? I rang Gordon Lane, and before

I'd got started on my pretext for ringing him he was saying how he hoped I didn't mind that my fiancée had generously come in that morning.'

'Clever clogs,' she told Farne lovingly.

He smirked; she kissed him. 'So I knew three things. No one at Irving and Small was aware of your cancelled wedding, you still intended leaving the firm, and—best of all—I knew where you were.'

'You came straight over.'

'I stopped only to ask Gordon Lane not to tell you I'd rung, that I had a surprise for you.'

'You certainly had!'

Farne kissed her.

'Then I instructed Rachel to wait half an hour and then to ring the vicar and the caterers and tell them that the wedding was back on again. Then…'

'Rachel was to wait half an hour?'

'I wasn't having either the vicar or Dawson's phoning your mother for confirmation, only for your mother to ring you when for all I knew you might bolt.'

'Did I say clever?' Karrie said, and Farne grinned. 'Then…?' Karrie prompted.

'Then I started to get angry as well as panicky, and felt as though I was fighting for my life. Nobody had the right to do that to me. I came looking for you.'

'I love you,' Karrie said quickly. 'And I'm glad you found me.'

Farne smiled, and gently touched his lips to hers. 'I didn't say it right the first time. So—' he kissed her gently again '—will you, my darling, marry me?'

'Oh, yes, my love,' she sighed.

'Will you, sweet Karrie, marry me tomorrow?' he asked.

'Oh, I will, I will,' she replied, and Farne brought her once more into his arms, and kissed her deeply, and ardently.

'Oh, I've missed you so,' he breathed. 'These past two weeks have been hell.'

'Oh, Farne,' she cried. She had known something of that two weeks of hell too, and as he kissed her, and that kiss deepened, all past unhappinesses vanished. She loved him and, wonder of wonders, Farne loved her. Was there ever such joy? He held her close in his arms and she put her arms around him as kiss for healing kiss they exchanged, until suddenly Farne pulled back from her—and moved a little away.

'Karrie, Karrie, you are making a nonsense of my head!' he scolded adoringly.

'Am I?' she asked innocently.

'Just wait until you're Mrs Farne Maitland!' he threatened, and, when she laughed delightedly, 'Come to my study, young woman. You can use the desk phone and I'll use my mobile. Starting with our parents, we've a lot of telephoning to do.'

Her wedding day dawned bright and sunny. Karrie was awake and sitting up long before her mother brought her breakfast in bed. 'How do you feel, darling?' her mother asked as she placed the bed tray over her knees. 'Did you get any sleep at all?'

'Happy, excited, nervous, and I slept a little,' Karrie answered honestly, but, glancing down to the tray, 'What's this?' she exclaimed at the Cellophane-wrapped red rose that lay beside a teacup.

'It plopped through the letter box and on to the hall carpet when I went down an hour ago,' her mother smiled. 'There's a card attached.'

Karrie picked up the lovely rose and took the card from its envelope. 'I'm waiting for you, my love,' she read. 'It's from Farne,' she said chokily, emotional tears pricking her eyes.

'I know,' Margery Dalton smiled. 'I saw the tail-end of his car disappearing down the drive.'

'He delivered it personally?'

'Like you, he probably couldn't sleep. Now don't cry, or you'll make me start.'

They both laughed, and Karrie received a quick hug before her mother left her to her breakfast. Karrie wasn't hungry, but stayed there holding the rose to her cheek. Oh, how wonderful of him to come all this way to deliver her a red rose of love with his message. She wished she had seen him—not that her mother would have allowed it. The next time she would see Farne would be at St James's church. Karrie's heart suddenly swelled with the wonder of it.

Her father came to see her a short while later, and warmed her heart by saying, 'Hello, poppet'. She couldn't remember the last time he'd called her poppet. 'Feeling a little bit jittery?'

'Just a little,' she smiled.

'Farne will look after you,' he assured her confidently.

'I know,' she answered, and wanted as much to look after Farne as she was sure he would look after her.

There seemed to be a lot of coming and going that morning; her cousin Jan arrived, the flowers were delivered—including her wedding bouquet of pink rosebuds intertwined with trailing cream Singapore orchids—and all the while her parents spoke amiably to each other. They weren't rowing, or shouting and yelling, or not speaking at all, but talking to each other as if they were friends.

Whether her mother had changed her mind about the divorce, or whether they were both making a special effort, Karrie had no idea. But it all helped to make her day especially perfect.

Karrie bathed, and shampooed her hair and styled it

back from her face and on top of her head, ready to place the pearl coronet. Then it was time to get into her dress.

'Oh, darling!' her mother cried, her voice all wobbly. 'You look beautiful!'

'Don't!' Jan cried. 'Or you'll have my mascara running. 'Oh, Karrie, you look out of this world!'

Karrie looked at her reflection in the mirror, the full-length dress even more beautiful to her eye now that she was wearing the veil that went with it. Her decision to discard the other dress, extravagant as she knew she was being, had never been more right. She wanted to look beautiful. For Farne, she wanted to look like a bride worthy of him.

'The car's here for you, Margery!' Bernard Dalton called up the stairs. 'Are you going with your aunt, Jan?'

Jan, looking elegantly lovely in lemon silk, whispered, 'See you soon,' and went quickly.

Margery Dalton held her daughter's hands. 'Everything all right?' she asked, clearly not ready to leave her.

'Couldn't be better.'

'You'll be all right with your father?'

'I'm sure I will.'

'Bye—then.'

Karrie did not want to be late, and went downstairs where her father, looking as smart as new paint in his morning suit, was waiting and would, in a short while, as part of the marriage service, be 'giving her away' to Farne.

'I'm blessed if I want to give you away,' he teased, and smiled, and escorted her out to the waiting car, following his wife's instructions to the letter, seeing to it that Karrie's dress was not crushed.

It took only about five minutes to get to the church, where a host of well-wishers stood. 'Oh, doesn't she look lovely?' reached Karrie's ears. But her nerves had peaked and she was starting to tremble.

Her mother and Jan were waiting for them in the church porch. Then her mother was leaving them to take her place inside, and Karrie vaguely realised that the organist must have received a signal from someone, because the strains of Wagner's 'Wedding March' began. Then Jan was falling in behind, and her father was placing Karrie's hand on his arm, and they began their walk down the aisle.

As the music swelled with every step, and although the church was crowded to capacity, Karrie was aware of no one save the tall and handsome tail-coated man who stood at the chancel steps, and who, as she drew near, turned. He looked strained, as though waiting was getting to him. But as she went to take her place next to him he suddenly smiled a most wonderful smile.

'I'm so glad you're here,' he murmured.

'Oh, so am I,' she whispered back.

Jan relieved her of her bouquet. 'Dearly beloved,' said the Reverend Thompson, and the marriage service was underway.

Farne vowed to love and to cherish her in firm, clear tones, and Karrie made her responses in a quiet, sweet voice, only just managing to hold back emotional tears as she became his wife.

As man and wife they went up to the altar, and then to the vestry where, her veil now back from her face, Farne whispered, 'I can't wait any longer,' and bent and reverently placed his lips over hers. 'You're trembling, my darling,' he stated gently as her nervousness communicated itself to him.

'I've never been married before.'

'You never will be again!' he promised, and made her laugh, and her shaky world suddenly started to steady itself.

Then they became aware that the small vestry was full with her parents and Farne's parents, her cousin Jan, and

Farne's best man, Ned Haywood—with the vicar presiding as the marriage register was signed.

Afterwards they went out into the sunshine, and as they posed for photographs and were showered with confetti it was truly the happiest day of Karrie's life.

She and Farne were able to snatch a few moments alone together before everyone joined them at the wedding reception. 'You're beautiful,' Farne said tenderly as they stood together. 'Breathtakingly beautiful,' he murmured as he held her hands and looked down at her. 'I thought my heart would stop when I saw you coming down the church aisle to be married to me.'

'I saw only you,' she confessed.

He smiled, raising her right hand to his lips. 'Are you really mine?' he asked, as if he was having the same difficulty Karrie was having in actually believing it.

'Oh, I am,' she whispered, and started to feel more secure in that knowledge when Farne put his arms around her and kissed her.

Then Farne was breaking his kiss and looking into her wide, shining velvety brown eyes. 'I love you with all my heart, Mrs Maitland,' he said softly. 'Thank you for being my wife.'

Mrs Maitland, Farne's wife. Oh, how wonderful that sounded. 'Oh, Farne,' she murmured tremulously. And tenderly they kissed once more. Then the guests began to arrive.

THE NINE-MONTH BRIDE

by

Judy Christenberry

Chapter One

"What's wrong with the old-fashioned way?"

Susannah Langston could feel the heat rise in her cheeks, but she kept her chin up. She was an intelligent woman, an educated woman. She wouldn't allow this…this scientific discussion to embarrass her.

"In case you didn't know, Doctor," she began crisply, "it takes two people to create a child the old-fashioned way."

The elderly medical man gave a rusty chuckle. "Well, I reckon they explained that in my first class. Not that I didn't already learn that lesson in the back seat of my—never mind." He cleared his throat. "Now, Miss Langston, I don't know where you came up with this crazy idea—"

"Doctor, artificial insemination isn't crazy, nor is it new."

"Hell, I know that. We've been doing it to the animals for years. But it seems a shame—"

"I'm sorry, but I'm not asking for your personal opinion," she said gently but firmly. "All I want to know is where do I have to go to have it—to get the procedure performed."

He leaned back in his chair and rubbed his chin. "You're all-fired set on this, aren't you?"

"Yes. My decision is not a whim. I've carefully thought out the complications, and I believe the reward will far outweigh the difficulties."

"You realize a pregnant woman without a man around will draw some talk even today? We're still a small community."

Susannah squared her shoulders. "If gossip becomes a problem, I can move to a new community after the birth of my child and pass myself off as a divorcée." In this day and time, single motherhood shouldn't carry a stigma, but she realized what should be and what was were sometimes two different things.

With a gusty sigh, the doctor leaned across the desk. "I believe I could do the job right here, Miss Langston. We don't have the capabilities of a major hospital, but, assuming you have a donor in mind, I could impregnate you with his sperm."

Damn! Susannah closed her eyes. Then her determination surged, and she stared at the doctor. "I don't have a—a donor. I assumed I'd go to a sperm bank."

She'd read articles in the magazines at work, in the library in Caliente, Colorado, where she spent her days. Sperm donors weren't in big supply in the library. Males weren't in big supply in the library. Only books. And dust.

The library was quite large for such a small town. It, and the money to hire her, had been a gift to the town from one of its late citizens who died with no heirs. Only books. Like her.

"Well, of course, that's how the normal person would go about it if we had a sperm bank. But we don't. And it'll be real expensive if you go into Denver."

She tried to hold his gaze, but there was a speculative look in his eyes that bothered her. "I've saved a lot of money."

"Hmm. If there was someone locally..."

He was staring beyond her shoulder now, his eyes almost glazed over in contemplation. Susannah wanted the interview to be over.

"Doctor, can you tell me the name of a group in Denver, or a hospital, where I can begin the process? That's really all I wanted. I want to go to the best facility for this...procedure." She should have done research and not bothered with this interview, but Abby, her best and dearest friend, had suggested Doc Grable.

"I think I know a donor," the doctor abruptly said, bringing his gaze back to her.

Susannah's eyes widened, and she blinked several times as she took in his bizarre statement. "What?"

"I think I know someone locally who would be a donor. And a damn good one, too. Good blood. Make you a fine baby."

"I don't think—"

"You go talk to him. I think he'll be willing. It'll help him, too."

"What do you mean?" Help him? How could donating sperm help a man? "I don't want someone from around here. It would cause all kinds of problems."

"None that I can see. And it would save you a bundle of money. Unless you've got more money than the city's payin' you, that has to be a concern. Having children these days, even the old-fashioned way, isn't cheap."

Susannah chewed on her bottom lip, a habit from her childhood she'd tried to rid herself of. Money was a concern, since she was alone in the world. But—

He shoved a piece of paper across the desk. Picking it up, she read a name and directions. Lucas Boyd. She didn't know the man, but she did know he had a large ranch in the area. Certainly he didn't visit the library. And she'd never seen him at church.

"Why?"

"Why what?" the doctor asked in return, his eyebrows rising.

"Why would this man want to—to be a donor?"

"I can't discuss why. That would be breaching a patient's confidentiality. All I can do is tell you to discuss your, ahem, needs with Lucas. What can it hurt? And it could save you a lot of money. Plus time."

"Time? I have two weeks' vacation coming. I thought that would be—"

"Lord have mercy. These things don't always take

right away. You're not going to the supermarket doing your weekly shopping, my dear. Sometimes it takes months.''

"Yes, but—"

"Go see Lucas. I'll tell him you're coming. Can you go right now?''

"Yes, but—no, I—well, all right, I suppose I could but—surely it would be better if I waited until you talked to him, gave him some time to think about what—'' Susannah had never felt more flustered in her life.

"Naw. Right now. I'll call and tell him you're on your way.'' He waited, watching her until she finally nodded.

"If Lucas won't solve your problem, then I'll draw up a list of the finest doctors in Denver. There are only a couple I'd trust with such a delicate matter, you know.'' He stood and came around the desk to pat her shoulder as she rose. "I'm glad you came to me with your problem, Miss Langston. One way or another, we'll take care of it.''

Suddenly she found herself on the other side of the door with it closed firmly behind her. She stared at the piece of paper. What had come over her? To agree to discuss such a personal thing with a stranger? To ask this—this stranger to be the father of her child?

The trembling that seized her almost took her legs from under her. She reached out for the wall.

"Are you all right, Miss Langston?'' the rosy cheeked nurse who'd worked for Dr. Grable for thirty years asked. She was a frequent visitor to the library.

"Yes, I'm fine," Susannah hurriedly said. "Miss Cone, do you know—know Lucas Boyd?"

"Well, a'course I do. He's lived here all his life. He's a good man."

Without meeting her gaze, Susannah smiled, hoping her lips didn't wobble on the ends as much as her knees were doing. "I—thanks. I'll see you later—at the library, I mean."

"Sure. I'll be in Saturday, as usual. Those last books you recommended were wonderful." With a big smile and a wave, she headed down the hall to another patient's room.

Susannah drew a deep breath and hurried from the office before someone else noticed her shakiness. She certainly didn't want to find herself back in the doctor's office.

Once she was behind the wheel of her car, she looked at the piece of paper the doctor had given her. It was damp and wrinkled, but she could still read the directions.

Directions to certain embarrassment.

She squared her shoulders. *You promised yourself you'd go through with your plan, no matter how embarrassing it might be.* And it would be embarrassing. But no more so than being the oldest living virgin in the entire state.

With a sigh, she started the car. Yes, she'd promised herself. She refused to continue to limit her life to rows and rows of books. Beloved books, but still only books.

She wanted more out of life. She wanted a child

to nourish, to shower with love. With whom she could be a family. Even if it meant embarrassment.

Lucas Boyd's housekeeper, Frankie, a cowboy injured by a bull a few years earlier who found riding more painful than sweeping floors, chased him down in one of the big barns beyond the house.

"Luke? You in here?"

"Yeah, Frankie. What's up?"

"The doc wants you to call him. Now. He said it's important."

Lucas patted the mare as he moved around her, his heart suddenly racing. "Did he say why?"

"Nope."

"Thanks, I'll be right there."

He stood still until he heard the slam of the door, signifying Frankie's return to the house. Drawing a deep breath to calm the excitement and fear that rushed through his veins, he began a slow, steady walk to the house.

Nothing to get excited about. Probably had nothing to do with the request he'd made when he visited Doc last week. Doc couldn't have found someone so fast, could he?

Hell, he'd been so unenthusiastic, Luke had figured he wouldn't hear from Doc at all. But Lucas had come to his decision logically. Three years was long enough to mourn his late wife, his beautiful Beth, and the tiny baby boy delivered stillborn.

Lucas knew he couldn't risk his heart again. That was too painful. But he needed a son to carry on the tradition of the family ranch. And to make the future worthwhile.

Doc Grable didn't agree with his decision to find a surrogate mother. The old geezer thought he had a right to interfere in Lucas's plans because he'd delivered him into this world. But it looked as though he'd changed his mind. Maybe Lucas owed him an apology.

Instead of using the phone in the kitchen, where Frankie could always be found, Lucas passed through to his office.

"Doc? It's Lucas Boyd. You wanted me to call?"

"Yep. I've sent one out to you. It's up to you, now. I still think it's a fool idea, but I've done what I can for you."

He wasn't going to have that argument again. "Thanks, Doc. When?"

"She should be on her way now, if she doesn't get cold feet. Name's Langston."

Before Lucas could ask for any more information, Doc's gravelly voice said, "Gotta go. Patients." Then the dial tone rang in Lucas's ears.

His hand was shaking when he hung up the phone. There was no going back now. He stood, then realized he wasn't prepared for a social visit. He smelled of the barn.

"Frankie!" he shouted as he rushed toward the stairs. "I'm hitting the shower. If—if I have a visitor, ask them to wait."

Because his future was right around the corner. And he didn't want to miss it.

* * *

"Luke, there's a lady to see you," Frankie shouted up the stairs.

A lady.

Lucas took one last look in the mirror, feeling foolish. He seldom studied himself, but it was important that he make a good impression on the lady downstairs.

After all, she was going to be the mother of his son.

Drawing a deep breath, he smoothed back his hair and then hustled down the stairs before nerves could get the best of him. Knowing Frankie would've put the visitor in the seldom-used living room, he paused on its threshold to take his first view of her.

She looked up as he appeared, then stood. Not a beauty, like his Beth. Her features were bland, and she was tall, lanky, almost. Somehow, those differences made what he was about to do easier. That, and the fact that he'd never seen her before.

"Mr. Boyd?"

"Yes, ma'am. Are you Mrs. Langston?"

"Miss Langston," she said, correcting him.

He frowned. In his mind, he'd assumed whoever agreed to his terms would be married, a mother already. From what he'd read, that was the typical profile. "You're not married?"

"No."

She added nothing to her blunt reply, but her gaze continued to meet his. He liked that. His son shouldn't have a timid mother.

Suddenly realizing they were both still standing,

he crossed the room and gestured toward the sofa behind her. "Please, be seated."

As she sat down, he noticed her skirt was long, hiding her legs. Probably has fat ankles, he speculated. Doesn't matter for a boy, he assured himself. Dark hair, like his. Beth had had pale blond hair, spun gold, an angelic halo. And a beautiful smile.

This lady wasn't smiling.

Of course not. Having a baby was serious business. He cleared his throat. "I assume you have no health problems."

She stiffened and then frowned. Dark brows rose and she tilted her head as she stared at him. "No. Do you?"

"None."

Tense silence fell, and Lucas tried to think of what he needed to say. "You understand that afterward…I mean, there'll be no contact between us?"

Her reaction was curious. A sigh of relief moved through her and a hopeful smile formed on her lips. Even that half smile made him reevaluate his impression of her. Her brown eyes warmed and a touch of color enlivened her pale cheeks. The severe style of her hair, pulled back into a bun low on her neck, didn't change, but she looked younger somehow.

"How old are you?"

She blinked several times. "Thirty-two. And you?"

"Thirty-three." He studied her. Yes, she looked that old. He might even have said a year or two older. "You're sure you're young enough?"

"I don't think that's any of your business," she replied, her jaw squaring.

One eyebrow slipped up in surprise as he stared at her. Not any of his business? She was going to have his son. "I want this...our agreement to be successful."

"My age is not a problem," she said firmly, looking away.

"Okay." He'd take her word for it since Doc had sent her. What would be the point of sending someone who couldn't have a baby? "Do you have any questions?"

"I—I know why I'm doing this, Mr. Boyd, but I don't understand...what are your reasons? Is compensation involved?" As she finished, she looked around the room, as if evaluating his worth.

"Didn't Doc explain the terms?"

She shook her head. "He said it would be a breach of confidentiality."

"Well, it's pretty simple. I want you to have my son, and I'm willing to pay." He leaned forward, his elbows on his knees, waiting for her response.

"*You'll* pay? But—but why?"

His eyes narrowed as he studied her. She was willing to go through the pregnancy gratis? Something wasn't right. Was she some kind of freak?

"I'd expect to. I'm asking a lot."

"I assure you, Mr. Boyd, payment isn't necessary on your part. I'm even willing to pay you." She raised her chin, as if expecting him to take her up on her offer.

He stood and shoved his hands into his back pockets. "Let me get this straight, Miss Langston. You're willing to get pregnant, have my son and then disappear, for free?"

"If you feel that my leaving the community is necessary, yes, I'm even willing to do that. The baby and I will find another home."

"You and the baby?" he gasped before responding to her in hardened tones. "The baby stays here, Miss Langston. We're agreed on that." He glared at her, wondering what her game was.

She rose, alarm on her face. "No, of course not, Mr. Boyd. The baby is mine."

"Damn it! What would be the point? I want my son! Why else would I go through the embarrassment of—"

"You thought I would give you the baby?" she demanded, her features tightening.

"Isn't that what a surrogate mother is? Someone who gives birth to the baby and then hands it over?"

"But you're supposed to be a sperm donor. Not a—you can't keep the baby."

"You think I would allow anyone, *anyone*," he repeated for emphasis, "to take my child away? I've already lost one son. I'm not about to lose another one."

They were almost nose to nose now, his hands on his hips as he challenged her. She was even taller than he'd thought, only a few inches shorter than he was. Beth had been a petite doll, not even as high as his shoulders.

His visitor reached down behind her for the large shoulder bag she'd left on the sofa. "Clearly we have both—*I* have made a mistake. Dr. Grable suggested you as a sperm donor for my pregnancy. I apologize for wasting your time."

"You mean you're not willing to be a surrogate mother?" Lucas demanded.

"No."

Again she didn't waste any words. As she moved to step around him, he caught her arm. "I'm offering a lot of money."

Tugging at his hold on her arm, she didn't meet his gaze. "That's wonderful. Now, if you'll excuse me?"

"You're not interested?"

Her brown-eyed gaze flew to his eyes briefly before she stared at his hand clutching her arm. "No."

"You haven't even asked how much."

Again she stared at him. "Which should tell you I have no interest in your...intentions."

"Then why did Doc send you?" he demanded in frustration. From the moment he'd gotten Doc's message, he thought his problem had been solved. He'd almost imagined himself holding his child.

"You'll have to ask Dr. Grable that question, Mr. Boyd. I also have some questions for the good doctor." Her lips tightened, and he noticed their fullness for the first time.

Again she tugged at his hold, and this time he released her, stepping back, his cheeks flushing in embarrassment. "You can name your terms, Miss Langston. I'll be generous." His jaw tightened as he waited for her to ask for some outrageous sum. But he was so close to having his dream. He was willing to pay.

Her response wasn't what he'd expected. Instead of a calculating stare, he received a soft smile, gentle almost, as she said, ''My dream is just as important to me as yours is to you, Mr. Boyd. I can't do what you're asking, for any amount of money. I'm sorry I took up your time.''

Without waiting for an answer, she walked out of the room, taking his dream with her.

Chapter Two

Someone had to bear the brunt of his anger, and it seemed only fair to Lucas that that someone be the doctor.

"Doc, what the hell game are you playing?" he demanded over the phone.

"Now, Luke, calm down. Did you talk to Miss Langston?"

"Yeah, I talked to her. But she wasn't willing to be a surrogate mother. She intended to keep the baby!" He couldn't have sounded more horror-stricken if he'd been talking about infanticide. "Why did you send her here?"

"It seems crazy, I know, but with both of you wanting a baby, I thought—hell, I'm sorry, Luke, but I don't like either of your choices. I was hoping to kind of jolt the two of you, if nothing else."

"Well, you succeeded. I've never had such an embarrassing conversation in my life. Who is the woman? I've never seen her before.''

"You might've seen her if you'd stop living like a hermit. You don't even come to church anymore, much less the few social occasions we have around here."

"Who is she?" he repeated, ignoring the other comments.

"She's the librarian...hired six months ago."

"Why doesn't she get pregnant the old-fashioned way?" If she'd done that, she wouldn't have raised his hopes and then dashed them to the floor.

"I asked her the same question. Seems she doesn't have any candidates around."

Lucas frowned. She wasn't a beauty, but she didn't put out any effort to attract the opposite sex with her concealing clothes, lack of makeup and severe hairstyle. But, hell, they were in Colorado. Single women, outside the big cities, were scarce.

"Why does she want a baby?"

"She didn't explain her reasons. All she wanted was information about how to go about it, not a discussion of why or why not." There was a pause and then Doc said, "You could ask her if you want to know."

"Has nothing to do with me!" Lucas snapped, irritated by the curiosity that filled him. "Find me a real surrogate mother, Doc. Okay? I'm ready to get this done."

"I'll do what I can. But you know it's not going to be easy. Or fast. That's why I thought—oh, well. I'll see what I can do."

* * *

"What are you reading?" Abby asked.

Susannah jumped as if someone threatened her very existence. With a protective arm over the article she'd been studying, she shrugged her shoulders. "Nothing much."

Abby McDougal, one of the volunteers who helped Susannah with the various chores of running the library, and her best friend, narrowed her gaze.

"You're working on getting pregnant, aren't you?"

"Abby, shh!" Her cheeks flooded with color as Susannah looked around to be sure no one had overheard Abby's remark.

"You are. I can tell."

"I'm reading an article. That's all."

"What's the title?"

"'Options.'"

"Aha! I knew it."

"So? I tried it your way. I spoke to Dr. Grable, but he told me I'd have to go to Denver for what I wanted." She fought to keep the blood from her cheeks because of the lie. After all, it was almost the truth. Without a local donor, she'd have to go to Denver.

She hadn't returned to Dr. Grable's office after the debacle of the interview with Lucas Boyd. She was no masochist. She figured she'd do the research herself. And she had. This article was the last she intended to read before she contacted a particular clinic in Denver. She already had the number written on a pad by her phone.

All she had to do was work up the nerve to make the call.

Heck, that would be a breeze compared to confronting that cowboy. That tall, sexy, handsome cowboy. Her emotions had gone on a roller-coaster ride that afternoon.

Exhilaration that her child would have this man for a father. Confusion when he told her he would keep the baby. Actually the son. She didn't think he had considered the possibility of a daughter.

Anger and disappointment when she realized he wouldn't cooperate. And forgiveness when she heard his admission of having lost a son. No one should have to suffer such pain.

Even though she'd been curious about his past, Susannah decided it would be best if she didn't ask anyone about Lucas Boyd. How could she explain her interest?

Instead, she concentrated on her desire to have a child. It would be easy to chalk up her decision to her internal clock. But she knew better. She didn't need a child for fulfillment. She loved her work and believed in the need to encourage reading.

But she wanted a child. A family. A way to pass on the important things she'd learned from her loving parents. A personal connection to the future. She actually ached with longing when she saw a young woman carrying a baby.

"Susannah, you need to find a man."

"It's not necessary these days, Abby. I can manage just fine without that added complication." She kept her voice calm, swallowing the tremor that ran through her.

Abby frowned. "Some man must've really done a number on you, Susannah. They're not all bad."

Turning her head away, Susannah tried to think of another subject that would engage Abby's interest. She didn't want to discuss her insignificant experience with men. The one time she'd thought she'd fallen in love, the man had dumped her because she hadn't accepted his advances with open arms. He'd labeled her frigid.

Susannah wondered if the newest shipment of books would distract Abby. "Did you see that we received the latest Nora Roberts romance? Have you put your name on the list to check it out?"

"I don't want to talk about books. What you're thinking of doing—"

"Morning, Abby, Miss Langston," a deep drawl interrupted.

Susannah almost passed out. She didn't have to turn around, or wait for Abby's greeting. That voice told her who was standing in front of her counter.

"Why, Lucas! I haven't seen you in a dog's age. What are you doing in the library?" Abby asked, a big smile on her face. "Have you met Susannah— well, I guess you have or you wouldn't have greeted her by name."

Susannah avoided looking at Abby, but she heard the curiosity—and speculation—in Abby's voice. "Hello, Mr. Boyd. Is there something in particular you're looking for?"

"Yes, Lucas, just what are you looking for? I've never seen you in the library before."

"Well, Abby, I'm looking for a private conversation with the librarian," Lucas said, a grin on his face.

Abby's interest sharpened. "Oh, really? Now, isn't that interesting?"

Susannah had no idea what the man wanted, but she knew she didn't want to deal with any more comments from Abby. "Could you please watch the counter while I talk with Mr. Boyd, Abby? I shouldn't be long."

"I'll be happy to."

Ignoring Abby's grin, Susannah looked at Lucas Boyd for the first time and drew a deep breath. The man oozed sex appeal. "Shall we go into my office, Mr. Boyd?"

He nodded and came around the end of the counter, then waited for her to lead the way.

Her back ramrod straight, Susannah stalked into her small office, wishing she'd cleaned her desk this morning. She wasn't compulsively neat, but she didn't want the man following her to think badly of her.

Almost laughing at that ridiculous thought, as if this man's opinion mattered, Susannah straightened her features and sat down behind her desk. She paused as he removed his hat and hung it on the antique hat stand. A shiver ran down her spine. The conversation must be important if he took off his hat.

"Won't you be seated?" she asked politely, gesturing to the small narrow chair across from her, the only other seat in the room.

He eyed the chair suspiciously, as if he didn't think it would hold him. He could be right. He was a big man, several inches over six feet, his body a solid mass of muscle.

"I think I'll stand. That seat doesn't look any too stable." He smiled but didn't wait for her response. Instead he turned away and looked out the small window. Since she knew the view encompassed the parking lot, a few scraggly buildings and the mountains in the distance, she didn't think it was that compelling.

"How may I help you, Mr.—" She broke off as she remembered their last meeting. Somehow her question seemed inappropriate. "I mean—why are you here?"

His intense blue eyes lightened slightly as he turned around, a grim smile on his face. Clearly he understood her change of question. "I think I owe you an apology."

He took her by surprise.

"I—I can't think of any reason."

"I can. I was angry when you—about the misunderstanding we both suffered two weeks ago. I don't think I was much of a gentleman about it."

She waved a hand in dismissal, but she couldn't trust herself to say anything.

"You see, I'd made a difficult decision. And I wanted to get on with it. When Doc said you were coming, I assumed he'd explained my offer and you'd accepted. I could already see my son—" He broke off and turned back to the window.

Tense silence filled the room, and Susannah sought to ease it. "I guess an old-maid librarian was a bit of a shock, too."

He turned and stared at her attempt to smile.

"If you're an old maid in Colorado, it's got to be your choice, Miss Langston. We don't have all that many available ladies to choose from except in the cities."

Color filled her cheeks and she looked away. "I don't meet any men at the library."

"Why?"

"I guess they're not big readers."

He stood with his hands on his trim hips, watching her intensely. "No. I don't mean why don't you meet men. Why do you want a baby?"

She swallowed, her throat suddenly dry, then nibbled at her bottom lip. She wasn't about to bare her soul to this stranger. "Why do you?"

He frowned, as if surprised by her turning the tables. Well, she had as much right to ask questions as he did, she decided, raising her chin.

"For the obvious reasons."

"Me, too."

Frustration filled his handsome features. "That doesn't tell me anything!"

"But it's the answer you gave," she reminded him.

"Yeah, but I'm a—"

"A man?" She finished the sentence when he didn't continue.

A sideways grin only made him more attractive. "So I'm dealing with a feminist here, am I?"

To avoid looking at him, she picked up a pen and doodled on the pad of paper on her desk. "You're dealing with an educated woman, Mr. Boyd. Not one who's going to accept stereotypes and limitations because she's a woman."

He gave a disgruntled chuckle. "You're not like Beth at all."

"Beth?" She suspected the woman's identity, but she waited for him to confirm her thought.

"My wife. She—she and my son died in childbirth," he murmured, looking away. "Three years ago." He swallowed, as if forcing down emotion.

"I'm sorry. But no, I'm probably not like her."

"She was little...and sweet and beautiful." His voice was dreamy and sad. Then it changed as he added firmly, "And she always agreed with me."

"Well, that confirms it. I'm definitely not like Beth." She was ready to end the conversation. He didn't owe her an apology, and she didn't want to discuss beautiful women whose husbands adored them. Or little boys who died before they could even live. "I appreciate your apology," she said, rising, "but it wasn't necessary."

"Wait! I—you never explained why you want a baby."

"Neither did you," she said pointedly.

"I told you about Beth and the baby!" he returned. When she said nothing, he added, "I'm trying to work something out here!" He put his hands back on his hips, a scowl on his face.

"What?"

"Well, you see, there aren't—Doc hasn't been able to find a surrogate mother for me."

He looked at her, as if he expected a response, but she had nothing to say.

"I wondered if—I'll have to have someone take care of the baby when it's born."

Why would he tell her that...unless he thought she'd like the position? With a shrug of her shoulders, she said, "Yes, but I'm not looking for a job. You'll need to hire a nanny."

"Why? You could have the baby, and I'd hire you as the nanny. The baby would have the best care in the world, from his own mother." As if he'd finally made his case, he relaxed and smiled at her.

A beautiful smile. Too bad.

"And at night I would go home?"

"Yeah, I could handle things at night. After all, I'm his father."

"And the neighbors would think I'd had your child—probably as a result of a careless one-night stand—and I've given it up to you to raise, but I'm receiving payment to take care of it."

"I don't care what my neighbors think!" he growled.

"You may not, but what they think would harm your child. Do you care about him?"

"Of course I do!" he roared. "That's the reason we're in this mess in the first place!"

She moved from behind her desk, passing dangerously close to him, and reached the door.

"Don't open that door!" he rapped out, an order that he apparently assumed she would obey.

"Mr. Boyd, you are *visiting* my office. You do not give me orders." She opened the door. "Thank you for stopping by."

He stared at her as if she'd slapped him. Finally he took a step toward her. "You're not even going to consider my suggestion?"

"No, thank you."

"But we'd both get what we want."

"No, Mr. Boyd. You would get what you want. I would get crumbs, not even a piece of the cake. And I would lose my good standing in the community. Does that sound like I would get what I want?"

She could sense Abby's birdlike gaze flicking back and forth between them and wished she hadn't been so stubborn about opening the door.

He continued to glare at her, as if expecting her to explain herself further. Instead she stared at him, holding onto the door, hoping he didn't realize she might've fallen without its support. Finally, when she wasn't sure she could remain standing much longer, he smashed his cowboy hat on his head and strode from her office, not even responding to Abby's good-bye.

"What got stuck in his craw?" Abby asked, staring at her as she took her place behind the counter.

Susannah sighed, "I love you, Abby, but I'm not going to discuss what was said in there. It's private." She added a warm smile, which wasn't easy when she felt like crying.

Something must've alerted Abby to her fragile

condition. "Enough said. Why don't you go back in there and work on those orders. I can handle everything out here."

With a whispered thanks, Susannah fled into her office, closing the door behind her. She returned to her chair, where only moments ago Lucas Boyd had stood over her.

Great! Now he'd invaded her workplace. She already had trouble getting him out of her head from their one meeting. Seeing him as the father of her child had been a mistake.

As foolish as those thoughts were, she had dreamed of creating that child the old-fashioned way, as Dr. Grable had put it. Strange reaction from someone who was frigid. Those intense dreams had left her unsettled and wanting what she couldn't have.

Lucas's description of his wife, and the longing and love that filled his voice, had gouged a hole in her heart. Why hadn't she found a man to love her the way he'd loved his wife? Why was she alone?

And the biggest question of all: Why was it so difficult to have a child, so she *wouldn't* be alone? She'd faced the fact that part of her longing for a child was selfish. But she also knew that she would care for and love her child, provide for him or her, be a good mother.

Her child.

His son.

They couldn't be the same baby, in spite of his ingenious proposal.

It would never work.

* * *

It could work.

If only the woman wouldn't be so difficult. He was offering her what she wanted!

Her words replayed in Lucas's head. Well, almost. Couldn't she settle for what he wanted? The desire to hold his son in his arms was overpowering. He could see himself teaching the boy about the ranch, about his heritage. They would share the past and the future.

And Lucas would love him, his child, as he'd loved Beth and that other little baby boy. With all his heart.

He slung himself behind the wheel of his truck and drummed his fingers on the steering wheel. What now? Doc didn't seem to think he'd be able to find someone willing to have his baby.

The old man had suggested he go into Denver and find some poor woman who needed money desperately. Hell, he didn't want his child's mother to be a street person. She had to be strong, healthy, upstanding.

A dry chuckle surprised him. He couldn't say Miss Langston was weak. Or meek. Or agreeable. She was tall, too. He'd worried about his future sons with Beth. She was so little. What if—such a thought seemed like a betrayal of their love. But—

He turned the key and slammed the truck into Drive. He wasn't going to think about such things. Didn't matter anyway. Beth was dead. They wouldn't have children together.

When he stopped the truck at the streetlight, he

realized he was half a block from Doc's office. He'd make a detour and fill him in on the latest discussion with Miss Disagreeable Langston.

"You did what?" asked Doc, a comical look on his face, after Lucas revealed his conversation with the woman.

"I just told you. I offered—"

"I heard you. Lord'a'mercy, boy, don't you have any more sense than that?"

"What's the matter with what I offered? She'd get to have a baby, take care of it and get paid for the job, too."

Doc grinned. "And what was her answer?"

"She wouldn't even consider it."

"That doesn't surprise me."

"So why did you suggest such a disagreeable woman?"

"Disagreeable? Susannah Langston? Everyone loves her. She's patient with the elderly, gentle and loving with the children and extremely knowledge-able about her job. What's not to like?"

"She wasn't gentle, loving or patient with me."

"And were you any of those with her?"

"Hell, no! I just met the woman."

"Then why expect anything different in return?"

"You're turning the tables on me, just like she did," Lucas complained, frowning fiercely. What was wrong with everyone today?

"Lucas, you're spoiled. You've been running a huge operation for about eight years now, and every-one jumps to your command. Your wife was a sweet lady, beautiful, but she would've jumped off a bridge if you told her to. When was the last time someone told you no?''

"Today," he replied grimly.

"Exactly, and you're upset that she didn't see everything your way."

Lucas sprang from his chair and paced the office. "Okay, okay, maybe it isn't the best deal for her. But—but I need my son, Doc," he whispered, his head bowed. "I need a reason to keep going, to look to the future."

Dr. Grable stood and came around the desk to put an arm around Lucas's shoulders. "I know you do, son. And I'm going to help you."

Chapter Three

"How?" Lucas asked hoarsely. He hadn't intended to break down in front of Doc—or anyone for that matter. He was embarrassed and anxious to get back in control.

"It's simple. You marry the woman."

He stared at the old man. Doc must've lost his mind. "I can't do that, Doc, and you know it!"

"'Course you can."

He jerked away from Doc's touch. "No, I can't. I can't let myself—I loved Beth!"

"I know you did, son. But that doesn't mean you can't marry again. Lots of men do." Doc moved back to his chair. "Come sit down and let's talk about it."

"No! When I lost Beth and my baby boy, I vowed I'd never—I can't do that, Doc!" He clenched his jaw. A man didn't cry, especially not where someone else could see him.

"You took a few hits that year," Doc said calmly. "After all, your father had been dead only a few months. And your friend Billy died in that car crash in Denver. A rough time."

Lucas shook his head and stared out the window. He'd been doing a lot of that lately. But it was easier than facing Doc's pity.

"But that doesn't matter, because I'm not asking you to love Miss Langston. Just to marry her."

Lucas turned to stare at Doc. If he'd thought him crazy before, now he knew it. "Come on, Doc. She wouldn't even consider what I offered today. If I tried that idea on her, she'd slug me."

"Why?"

"*Why?* No woman would consider that kind of marriage proposal! It's an insult."

"It's my belief there are a lot more marriages based on practical reasons than there are based on love. And if you look at it from a practical angle, it meets all of your and her requirements."

"I don't see how," Lucas said, but he took the chair in front of Doc's desk, listening intently.

Doc raised his hand and began counting off his reasons. "You get your son *and* someone to take care of him. And no gossip. She gets her baby and someone to support both of them. And no gossip."

Put that way, Doc's idea seemed simple. But Lucas didn't think a female would think the same way. "I don't believe Miss Langston would agree with you. In fact, I'm sure she wouldn't. She hasn't agreed with anything *I've* said!"

"Maybe you haven't approached her right. You gotta give her a little romance, take her out to din—''

Before he could finish, Lucas jumped up from his chair. "Wait a minute! You said no romance!"

"Nope. I said no love. Women set a lot of store by romance. You know the things—flowers, gifts… All that takes is a little money and a little thinking."

"I'm not going to mislead her," Lucas muttered as he stared at the calendar on Doc's desk. He didn't realize his mistake until he looked at Doc and discovered a big grin on his face. "I haven't agreed to it!" he hurriedly said.

"Just think about it, son. Just think about it."

Susannah pulled herself together after a few minutes. It was foolish to wish for what she couldn't have. She'd learned that lesson a long time ago when the petite, pretty blondes, girls like Beth Boyd, took the roles of cheerleaders, homecoming queens and popular dates, while the tall, gawky, plain girls sat home, waiting for the phone to ring.

It was no surprise that Lucas Boyd still loved his dead wife. And mourned his baby boy. His pain had touched her again. She could understand why he wanted a baby, even if *he* didn't comprehend *her* reasons.

But she couldn't give up her baby any more than he could.

She squared her shoulders and picked up the phone. She was going to have her baby.

She dialed the number written on the pad. After a

conversation with the fertility clinic in Denver, she felt a little better.

Life was strange. Lucas Boyd had had all the things she wanted. Now, he was no better off than she was. Indeed, he was worse off, because he couldn't have his child.

She emerged from her office and Abby immediately searched her face.

"I'm fine." She even added a smile.

"If Luke insulted you, or hurt you, you tell me, girl. I love that boy, but I won't tolerate him not treating you with respect."

Susannah chuckled. Abby's normally serene eyes were agitated and her lips were pressed together. It would be fun to see her take on Lucas Boyd. But Susannah couldn't lie. "He didn't hurt me, Abby. It was a misunderstanding, and he came to offer his apology."

"An apology that made you cry?" she asked skeptically.

"I—I felt sorry for him. It's so sad that his wife and child died."

Abby didn't look convinced but she didn't ask any more questions. Unfortunately she turned to the one subject Susannah wanted to avoid more than Lucas Boyd. "What are you going to do about this baby thing?"

"Exactly what I planned to do. I called the clinic in Denver and I have an appointment next Friday for my initial examination."

"You're going to close the library?"

Friday was their second busiest day, but Susannah

didn't want to postpone the appointment. "No, I'm hoping to talk you and another volunteer into covering for me. Would you, please, Abby? I don't want to wait."

Since today was Friday, she already had to wait seven days. Seven long days. What if she discovered she couldn't have children? Then she'd be just as bad off as Lucas Boyd.

Stop thinking about that man.

Easier said than done. He would be many a woman's dream of Prince Charming. Prince Charming with an attitude. He was one of those men who thought women should be barefoot and pregnant.

"I still think you could find a man around here interested in settling down if you'd just make a little more effort," Abby insisted. "Are you coming tomorrow night?"

"I don't think so, Abby. I don't know how to dance, and I won't have time to bake something."

"I'll bake double. You promised me you'd come to the next social." Abby had the determined look of a dog after a bone. "It seems a fair trade for keeping the library open for you next Friday."

"That's blackmail, Abigail!"

"Yep. Well? Is it working?"

She had promised. And she did need Abby's help. "Yes, I suppose so. But I'll do my own baking."

"Just as well. The only thing I ever bake is a pecan cake. If you brought one, everyone would know I made it. Then folks would think you couldn't cook. Can't catch a man that way!"

"Abby! I'm coming to be sociable, not to find a

man. I've already made my decision." She stared at her friend, trying to make her position clear.

Abby turned limpid hazel eyes on her and said with a sugary voice, "Why, of course, Susannah. Just what I had in mind."

Patting her gray hair, Abby slid off the stool behind the counter. "I'd better hurry home if I'm going to get my cake made tonight. Don't you work late, either."

"No, I won't." She had too much to do, what with baking a dessert for the church social and preparing herself, mentally at least, for next Friday's date.

"Oh," Abby said as she paused by the front door, "wear your prettiest dress, too."

"Abby!" Susannah warned, but her friend was out the door with a wave.

Abby never gave up. At least she believed someday a man might be attracted to her friend. That was more than Susannah believed. But Abby's faith was comforting.

Lucas surveyed himself in the mirror. Since he'd made his decision, he'd spent more time looking at himself than he had in years.

Was he dressed all right? His jeans were clean, his shirt pressed. The sports coat, kind of tweedy, still fit, though it wasn't new. Beth had picked it out for him.

He ran his fingers over its lapel, his mind turning once more to his wife. They'd only been married a little over a year. She had been ten years younger than he, just a kid, when he'd fallen for her. Her folks lived on a farm close to town. She'd loved the ranch, the big house, lots of money to spend.

That was what he missed most. The way she'd enjoyed life. His dad had been sick the past two years, and Lucas had forgotten how to smile. When Beth came into his life, suddenly sunshine was everywhere.

For the past three years, it felt as if he'd been living in a cave.

Well, tonight was his coming out party. Doc had persuaded him to try his plan. Lucas still wasn't convinced he could go through with it. But it did make sense.

He turned away from the mirror. His looks didn't matter. And neither did memories. He needed to be practical.

When he entered the kitchen, Frankie was sweeping the room. "Did you fix a dish for me to take, Frankie?"

"Yeah, boss, but you know you don't have to take anything. It's the womenfolk that bring the food." While he spoke, Frankie's gaze was running up and down him.

"Is something wrong with the way I look?"

"Naw. You look real purty!" Frankie assured him with a chuckle.

"Watch it, you mangy coyote, or I'll tell Mrs. Appleworth that you're longing for her company."

Frankie shivered with fear. Mrs. Appleworth, already having married five times, was known for her interest in cowboys. "That lady would have me hightailin' it out of the county, boss. And then who would cook and clean for an ornery cuss like you?''

"Okay, point taken. I'll see you tomorrow,'' he assured his cook and picked up the large bowl filled with potato salad. At least he'd gotten by Frankie without him commenting on his boss attending the party. Lucas hoped his entry would be noticed as little.

He'd timed his arrival for after the party had gotten into full swing, figuring he'd slip into the room while no one was looking.

Instead the music had just ended and suddenly it seemed everyone was staring at him. Then there was a concerted rush forward to greet him. Damn! You'd think he'd been in hibernation for a century.

"Luke! Good to see you! Didn't know you were venturing out,'' one neighbor said. Another commented on the last time he'd seen him, then hastily broke off his words because it had been the occasion of Beth and the baby's funeral.

Someone else hurriedly asked about a problem on the ranch. One of the ladies took his bowl from him with a gracious smile, and then Doc took him by the arm and drew him into the big room.

He wanted to run the other way. Small talk was beyond him tonight. He had too much on his mind. Doc seemed to realize how he felt.

"You did fine, boy. First step's the hardest. She's already here, and lookin' real nice. See her? On the other side of the room with Abby.''

He saw her. Susannah Langston did look nice. She wore a blouse that fitted her curves, surprising him, and a full skirt. And he'd been wrong. She didn't have fat ankles.

The music started up again.

"Go ask her to dance," Doc urged in a whisper.

"I just got here, Doc."

"Never mind. It's too late now."

His head whipped around and he stared at the cowboy who was leading the librarian onto the floor. Max Daingerfield. He was a wiry cowboy from north of town who considered himself to be the life of the party. Sometimes he was a little too lively for the other guests.

Lucas clenched his teeth as he watched the man's arm snake around Susannah's waist and haul her up against him. Then he relaxed with a smile as the lady removed the cowboy's hand from her hip, took a step away from him and made a brief remark.

At least Susannah was no more compliant with Max than she'd been with him.

"Hey, Lucas, heard you bought a new stallion," one of his neighbors said, drawing his attention from the couple on the floor. Soon he found himself drawn into ranch talk, almost forgetting his reason for attending the party.

"Aren't you gonna dance with her?" Doc finally whispered, as he dug his finger into Lucas's side.

"What'd you say, Doc?" Joe Springer asked, standing beside Lucas.

"I was just suggesting Luke have a dance. If he can still remember how."

Joe laughed. "I reckon it's like a few other

things,'' he said with a wink. "Once you learn, you don't forget.''

Lucas didn't want to follow Doc's suggestion. But he'd promised himself he'd give it the old college try. He surveyed the room and found Susannah leaving the dance floor with another partner. Had she danced every dance? Why was she looking for a donor if she could have her pick of men?

That thought didn't make him too happy. He stomped across the room and hauled up in front of her. "Evening, Susannah. Want to dance?''

"Thank you, but I imagine I've mangled enough toes this evening.'' She smiled but it wasn't with the same warmth as he'd seen earlier.

He couldn't believe she was turning him down.

The music started and he reached down for her hand. "I think my toes can handle the torture.''

"Mr. Boyd, I don't want to dance with you!'' she whispered as he pulled her to her feet.

"I kind of gathered that when you said no. But it'll be a little too embarrassing to face everyone now. So I reckon you'll dance whether you like it or not.''

She looked over his shoulder and then back to his face. "Everyone's watching us.''

"I know. Unfortunately for you, this is the first time I've danced with anyone since—in a long time. That's why I couldn't just walk away. Sorry.''

His voice was gruff, but she didn't seem to take offense. She tentatively put her hand on his shoulder as he began to move to the waltz.

"I'm not going to bite you," he growled and pulled her a little closer.

"I didn't think you would, but I don't like to dance so close," she informed him in a schoolteacher voice.

He grinned. "I know. I watched you straighten Max out."

She leaned back and caught his grin. "Is he a friend of yours?"

"Nope."

"Ah."

Neither spoke for several minutes. Lucas noticed how small her waist was, how neatly she fit into his arms, the top of her head right next to his cheekbone. He even noticed how good she smelled. Like springtime in the mountains.

Beth had always worn a heavy scent, too sophisticated for—he'd promised himself he wouldn't think about Beth. Not tonight.

"You haven't managed to stumble over my toes yet," he muttered, pulling her just that little bit closer, so that her breasts brushed against his chest when they turned. His groin tightened and he was suddenly very conscious that he was a man…and that Susannah was a desirable woman.

"I guess you're lucky," she said, her voice breathless, as if she'd been running a race.

"You tired?" he asked, frowning down at her. If she was in such bad shape, how would she handle having a baby? But she didn't look weak.

She took a step back from him. "No, I'm fine. And the dance is almost over."

"Counting the minutes, huh? Maybe I should tell you *some* women around here are eager to dance with me." He hadn't meant to sound so cocky, but she'd damaged his ego with her reluctance.

She lifted her chin and met his gaze. "How would you know, Mr. Boyd? According to you this is your first dance in three years. Maybe local taste has changed."

He gave a cynical chuckle. "Money never goes out of style, Susannah, so I reckon I'm safe."

"Is that why Beth married you?" she retorted and then gasped. "I'm sorry. I shouldn't have—I let my temper—I'm sorry."

He'd stiffened in rage, but her immediate apology had made it impossible to vent his anger. So he clenched his jaw and continued to dance.

"Mr. Boyd, that was horribly rude of me. I'm sure your wife loved you very much. I—"

"You don't know anything about Beth, Miss Langston, so keep your comments to yourself."

And she did.

They circled the room, in each other's arms, not speaking. Lucas regretted his rough words, but he was still angry. When the music ended with a flourish, the leader, Red Jones, stepped to the mike. "Grab your partner, fellas, and head for the tables. There's good food awaitin'!"

Susannah acted as if she hadn't heard the man's words. She started away from Lucas as if walking away from a car she'd parked. He grabbed her arm.

"Didn't you hear the man?"

She looked as pale as when she'd first stood in his

living room, but her gaze was harder. "I assumed that was a suggestion, not an order."

"Well, we're going to follow it, whatever it was. You'll eat with me," he said sternly, urging her on.

She came to a complete halt. "Mr. Boyd, you have a distressing habit of issuing orders and expecting me to comply with them. In case you haven't noticed, servitude has gone out of fashion. So has manhandling a woman in public. Now, excuse me." She jerked her arm from his hand and gracefully crossed the room to Abby's side behind one of the tables.

In the rush for food, Lucas didn't think anyone noticed his partner abandoning him in the middle of the floor, but he was still angry. He casually strolled over to several of the men talking and joined the conversation. But he watched Susannah Langston out of the corner of his eye.

Which is probably why he didn't notice Abby approaching.

"Lucas Boyd, I want a word with you!"

"Uh-oh, Luke," Joe said, "you'd better watch out. I think Abby's on the warpath."

"You'd better be scared, all of you, since I remember changing your diapers!" she said, glaring at the four men. Then she grabbed Lucas's arm and tugged him in the direction of the open door.

He was reminded of Susannah's words when he'd tried the same thing with her, but he didn't think Abby would pay any attention. "What's wrong, Abby?"

"Wait till we're outside. I don't want anyone overhearing us."

They stepped out into the clear, crisp October night. After they'd gone past several parked cars, she turned to face him. "What did you say to hurt Susannah?"

"Me? She's the one who said something! Hell, she said Beth married me for my money, Abby!" He hadn't intended to repeat the idiotic words, but he hadn't realized how deeply they'd cut him.

"Susannah wouldn't do that, Luke. Why, she's the gentlest, kindest—"

"I'm tired of everybody saying that. She's not gentle or kind with me." He crossed his arms over his chest. Saint Susannah didn't exist as far as he was concerned.

"You must've said something mean for her to try to hurt you. What did you say first?"

"I asked her to dance. Is that a crime?"

"No. But you must be wanting something she can't—"

"Abby, this is ridiculous. I didn't do anything."

"Then what did you want from her? When you came to the library yesterday, you did something to upset her then, too. She was almost in tears."

Lucas's nerves were stretched tight, what with his appearance among his neighbors this evening, and his plans for the future. Suddenly he couldn't stand Abby's prying any longer. With a roar, he said, "I want her to have my baby, Abby. That's what I want!"

Unfortunately, several other couples had also come outside for the cool air. They all froze as his words rang in the air.

Then there was a concerted rush back inside, each hoping to be the first to pass on the delicious gossip they'd just overheard.

Chapter Four

Susannah stood near one of the serving tables, chatting with several ladies who frequented the library. Even so, she kept her eye on the door, watching for Abby and Lucas's return.

It didn't take long for her to realize something had happened outside that was causing a lot of excitement. Three or four people rushed in and immediately began whispering.

When everyone who heard the gossip turned to stare at Susannah, she knew she was in trouble.

"What's goin' on?" Mrs. Wilson wondered, staring across the room.

"I have no idea," Susannah said, then fell silent. Abby and Lucas Boyd entered the room.

"There's Abby. I bet she'll know. Yoo-hoo, Abby!" Mrs. Wilson called across the room.

Wishing the floor would open and swallow her whole, Susannah stepped away from her acquain-

tance. Suddenly she didn't want to know what was
causing all the ruckus. Because it involved her…and
Lucas Boyd.

Whether it was in response to Mrs. Wilson's call,
or something else, Abby started across the room, determination in her every step.

Followed by Lucas Boyd.

And the gazes of everyone in the room.

Susannah stood frozen, unable to escape or think.
She never liked to be in the spotlight, but when Lucas Boyd was involved, she became absolutely paralyzed.

Abby reached her and clutched her hand, as if to
comfort her. "Lucas didn't mean no harm, Susannah."

Considering her friend's words, Susannah looked
at the handsome cowboy, surprised to discover his
lean cheeks filled with color. "About what?"

Vaguely, out of the corner of her eye, she noticed
Mrs. Wilson whispering with another woman. Before
either Abby or Lucas was able or willing to answer
her question, Mrs. Wilson turned to her.

"Oh, I'm thrilled. I mean, I had no idea! Why
didn't you let on, Susannah? Why, you've caught the
most eligible man in the county!"

Dread filled Susannah. She'd been right to be
afraid. Taking a deep breath, she said, as calmly as
possible, "I haven't caught anything, Mrs. Wilson.
There must be some mistake."

With an arch laugh that grated on Susannah's
nerves, Mrs. Wilson said, "Well, I hope you've
caught him if you're going to have his baby!"

Susannah let her eyelids sink, shutting out everything. When she opened them again, she had no clue what she should do or say. Especially when she still didn't know exactly what had been said. But now wasn't the time to be asking. A quick glance at Abby and Lucas Boyd showed them frozen. ''There's been some mistake, Mrs. Wilson.''

She couldn't go on. How could she explain about *her* baby, without everyone thinking it was *his* baby? They'd never believe the scientific arrangements she'd made. It would be so much more fun for them to speculate on her sleeping with Lucas Boyd. The man had ruined everything!

The plate she was holding, filled with various samplings of the delicious food, held no interest for her now. With a rigid smile, she set it on the edge of the table. ''Excuse me, please,'' she murmured and turned to head for the rest room.

''Susannah—'' Abby called.

Susannah didn't turn around, but she heard footsteps behind her and hoped they were Abby's, not the cowboy's. She thought if he touched her now, she'd scream.

She slipped into the small rest room and entered a stall, closing the door, hoping Abby would allow her some privacy. No such luck.

''Susannah, he didn't mean to embarrass you. It's partly my fault.''

''Abby, could this discussion wait—''

''No. I'm trying to tell you it was an accident. He didn't mean to announce that you were going to have his baby.''

"He did what?" she gasped, unable to remain silent.

The stall next to her opened. "Who did?" a quavery voice asked. "Is someone pregnant?"

"Now, Gertie, I didn't know you were here. This is a private conversation," Abby hastily said.

Susannah leaned her head against the door, trying to hold back a moan. Gertie Lumpkin was probably the only one who hadn't heard what happened. Until now.

"Don't seem too private if he announced it. I just want to know who he is."

"Abby, don't—"

The door squeaked as two women entered. "Oh, here you are, Abby. Where's Susannah?" one asked with a giggle.

Abby remained silent but Gertie didn't. "She's in there, I think."

"Susannah? Come on out. We want to congratulate you!"

"You're supposed to offer best wishes to the bride and congratulate the groom," Gertie instructed.

The second voice, which Susannah couldn't identify, either, protested, "Honey, if she's getting Lucas Boyd to the altar again, she deserves congratulations!"

"Is she in here?" someone called as the door squeaked again. There was a rush of footsteps, telling Susannah more than one lady had swelled the ranks.

Lifting her chin, Susannah opened the stall door. "Sorry, I didn't mean to keep everyone waiting.

Whoever's next," she said and waved to the stall behind her.

"Is it true?" a young woman asked, a pout on her lips. "Have you lassoed Lucas Boyd?"

"I don't think so. I don't even have a rope," Susannah said with a smile. A weak smile, but still a smile. "I only met the man a couple of weeks ago. If he's looking for a wife, you know he's going to choose one a lot prettier than me."

With a nod, she began to push through the women, ignoring their startled looks. Abby was right behind her.

As soon as they were in the hall, Susannah whispered, "Is there a back way out of here?"

"No. And you got no reason to hide, Susannah. But tell me, is what he said true? Are you going to have his baby?" Abby was watching her anxiously.

She covered her face with her hands and then looked at Abby. "Are you sure that's what he said?"

"Well, he said he *wanted* you to."

"No. I'm not going to have his baby. Dr. Grable...Lucas thought...never mind. The answer is no."

When she walked back into the large room, everyone stood clustered in groups, talking. Until they saw her.

Silence filled the room.

She felt the heat building in her cheeks, but she pretended all was well. Pausing by one of the committee members who organized the social, she offered her thanks for a lovely evening, shaking the woman's hand.

"Are you leaving?"

"I have to be up early for Sunday School, so I think I'll call it a night," Susannah said.

"Lucas already left."

Susannah licked her dry lips. "Lucas? Oh, you mean Lucas Boyd. Did he? Maybe he's teaching a Sunday School class, too."

There was a ripple of laughter at her words, indicating more than a few were listening. She maintained her friendly smile with some effort and started toward the door, bravely meeting the stares and nodding.

Abby plucked at her sleeve when she reached the door, almost free to hide in the darkness of the night. "Don't be mad at Lucas, Susannah. It was partly my fault. I wish you'd stay a while longer."

Susannah looked down at her dearest friend. "I don't think so, Abby. But thank you for inviting me." She pulled free from Abby's grasp and hurried down the stairs. Her car was parked along the side of the building, out of sight. She breathed a sigh of relief as she turned the corner.

Until she caught sight of her car.

And her nemesis leaning against it.

Lucas feared she was going to run in the opposite direction when she saw him. He wanted to talk to her, but he wouldn't be able to chase her here. Everyone would be watching them.

But instead of running, the woman started walking toward her car again, her gaze on the ground.

"Susannah," he began, keeping his voice quiet.

"Please move," she ordered.

He'd blocked her door on purpose. He wasn't about to abandon his position of strength before he'd had his say. "I want to apologize. I lost my temper."

"Did someone refuse to follow your orders?"

He couldn't believe her cool challenge. He'd been prepared to grovel because he figured he'd upset her, maybe made her cry. A gentleman didn't cause a lady grief. But her cool voice, challenging him, didn't inspire him to wallow in remorse.

"No," he responded through gritted teeth. "But your behavior certainly didn't help."

Her chin rose slightly. "My behavior was exemplary."

"Oh, yeah? You walked off and left me standing like a fool on the dance floor!" His fists went to his hips and he glared down at her. Not too far down.

"The last I heard, a woman has a choice about her dinner companion."

"There was no call to embarrass me."

"Is that why you said what you did? To pay me back? You certainly accomplished your goal, Mr. Boyd."

He felt a few inches shorter at her words. "No! No, I wasn't trying to embarrass you, Susannah. I promise. Abby was pressing me about—about upsetting you. Did I upset you?"

"I don't find it charming to be the object of gossip, Mr. Boyd."

"Before that. While we were dancing. Abby said she thought I'd upset you." He watched her face carefully, seeing changing emotions reflected in her eyes. Her full bottom lip trembled slightly. He'd never have noticed if he hadn't been watching so closely.

She looked over his shoulder. "I was embarrassed that I had behaved so rudely. I never meant to insult your wife or imply that your marriage was—was less than a love match. Abby interpreted my embarrassment as something else." She brought her brown-eyed gaze back to him. "I suppose I owe you an apology also."

She amazed him. He'd never expected her to apologize. In his experience, women accepted apologies well. But they weren't in the habit of owning up to any guilt for an argument. Some of the tension flowed out of him.

"Thanks, Susannah. I guess neither of us showed our best social skills this evening. I don't know about your excuse, but I'm a little out of practice." He tried a smile, curious to see if she'd give him one back.

She didn't.

"Now that we've finished our discussion, could you move so I can get in my car?" She stared at his boots.

"Well, I would," he drawled, watching her, "but I don't think we're finished."

His words drew a flash of her brown eyes filled with questions and not a little alarm. "What do you mean? Of course we're finished."

"Nope. We have to decide what we're going to do about my little mistake." He crossed his arms over his chest, as if he intended to remain in place for the next century.

Any softness, or sympathetic feelings, he'd thought he'd seen in her apology disappeared. "We're going to do nothing, Mr. Boyd. Absolutely nothing."

"Don't you think you could call me Lucas? After all, since everyone thinks we're already sleeping together, being formal seems a mite silly."

She gasped. "All the more reason to remain formal. And to avoid each other. All we have to do is go back to our normal routines. You avoid the library. I'll avoid your ranch. Problem solved."

Rubbing the back of his neck, Lucas asked her another question. "You still going to have a baby?"

"Of course I am!"

"You know people are going to say it's mine." This time he held her gaze, waiting for her reaction.

"If—if we continue to deny it and aren't seen together, I'm sure that rumor will disappear… eventually."

Again there was that slight tremble of her bottom lip. He wanted to reach out and stroke its softness. Reassure her. "Maybe."

"I need to go home. I'm cold."

Now he had no choice but to move aside. Any other woman, he might offer to warm her up. But Susannah had suffered enough tonight at his hands. He wouldn't make things worse. But he was surprised at the disappointment that filled him.

He must've been too long without a woman.

But thoughts of Beth had made the idea of seeking physical relief impossible. He couldn't imagine holding another woman in his arms.

Turning, he opened the car door and held it for her. She slid past him, leaving as much room as possible between them, murmuring a thank-you.

Before he closed the door, he said, "I have another idea, Susannah. I'll explain it to you tomorrow."

"No! We're supposed to avoid each other."

The panic on her face gave him pause. Maybe she wasn't as calm about all this as she pretended to be. He grinned. "Don't worry, sugar. I'll be discreet."

Her only response was to slam the door and gun the engine, her tires spraying gravel, and shoot out of the parking lot.

Luckily Lucas was fast on his feet or he might have had tire tracks on his boots.

Discreet? The man didn't know the meaning of the word. It was because of his indiscretion that she had a headache now.

That and his sex appeal. She'd almost lost her footing when her breasts had pressed against his chest while they were dancing. She'd never experienced such a flood of wanting in her life.

Susannah clenched her teeth as she drove to the small house she leased from Abby. When she got out of the car, she unlocked her door and entered, throwing her purse and keys on the sofa. Then she paced the room, suddenly wishing it were larger.

What was she going to do now?

If she went ahead with her plan, everyone would assume she was having Lucas's baby, as he'd said. If she didn't, she'd miss out on the one thing she longed for.

As she strode around the room, she discarded several different ideas. Then the most logical response filled her head.

Of course! The best answer would be to find someone else for Lucas Boyd. Every woman there tonight had shown an interest in the wealthy, handsome rancher. All she, Susannah, had to do was turn one, or even two, loose on him. Soon she'd be completely forgotten.

Relieved that she'd come up with a solution, she sat down at the small desk her grandmother had once owned and took out the elegant cream stationery she seldom used. After writing a careful note, she reread it.

Yes, this should do the trick.

But she'd have to work fast before he turned up at the library again.

Sunday afternoon, Lucas was putting in time at his desk, trying to catch up on the mountain of paperwork involved in running a ranch.

Someone knocked on his door. "Come in," he shouted, his gaze glued to his paperwork.

Frankie walked in.

"Yeah?" His housekeeper seldom interrupted Lucas when he was doing the books.

"Sam Jenkins stopped by. Wanted me to give you this letter. Said someone asked him to drop it off after church."

He took the envelope, studying it curiously. "Thanks," he muttered and laid it aside.

He didn't remember the envelope for several

hours. Then, as he finished paying the bills for the month, he noticed the envelope he'd put to one side.

Frowning, he picked it up. His name was on it, but nothing else, no address. Sam Jenkins? His neighbor didn't seem the type to use such nice stationery, but maybe his wife was having a party. Lucas supposed his emergence into local society last night might draw a few invitations.

Inside, he didn't find an invitation. His gaze flew to the bottom where Susannah Langston's signature grabbed his attention.

Dear Lucas,
I think I've come up with a plan to solve our little difficulty. Could you meet me for lunch tomorrow at The Red Slipper? At noon, please.

She didn't know much about ranchers if she thought they went to town for lunch in the middle of the day. But he'd make an exception for her. Later, he'd explain that you didn't interrupt a man's day for little things.

A smile settled on his lips as he thought about the meaning of her note. There was only one solution, as far as he was concerned, but he'd be glad to listen to Susannah's version. After all, he was flexible.

Now he could make real plans for his son. And he could forget Doc's scheme. He hadn't been comfortable with the idea of marrying anyone, much less Susannah Langston. True, she was more attractive than he'd first thought. A lot more attractive. But she always argued with him.

She wouldn't be a good wife because of that, but she'd make a damn fine baby for him. A tall, strong son, determined and courageous. Yeah, she'd be a great mother.

He could hardly wait until tomorrow.

Lucas came in from the pastures at about ten-thirty the next morning. He felt pretty silly showering in the middle of the day, but you couldn't have lunch with a lady when you smelled of horse.

All morning he'd thought about Susannah's note. Celebrated it. And ignored the small worrisome nudge that the sweetness and light routine it projected wasn't like her. That had occurred to him just before he went to sleep last night, and it had taken him a while to put it aside.

She was probably happy because she was going to have a baby. That's all it was. Her dream was going to be achieved, just like his. She'd probably decided to accept his offer of taking care of his son after he was born.

His son.

Those two words danced in his heart, giving him such pleasure. He almost forgot the woman who would make his dream happen. Almost.

She'd been pretty angry Saturday night. But her note showed that she'd gotten over her anger. He liked that, someone who didn't hold a grudge.

He dressed with extra care. At this rate, he'd have to go shopping for some new shirts and jeans. His social life seemed to be on the upswing.

With a grin, he grabbed a jacket and headed down

the stairs. When he passed Frankie, he said, "I'm lunching at The Red Slipper with a lady, Frankie. I'll be back later."

The man was too stunned to say anything, and Lucas left with a smile on his face. Wait until he could tell Frankie about his son!

It was a short drive into Caliente, and he quickly parked the truck among the many others around The Red Slipper. There weren't too many dining choices in town. The Red Slipper was the best of the lot.

The hostess met him at the door with a grin. "Howdy, Luke. I heard you were coming today."

"Oh, really? Word travels fast." He didn't mind. Soon he'd be able to tell everyone his secret.

"Just follow me."

He took off his hat and weaved between the tables, searching for Susannah. When he couldn't see her anywhere, he assumed the hostess was taking him to an empty table to wait for her. Instead the woman stopped unexpectedly and Lucas almost ran over her.

"Here you go, Lucas. Enjoy your meal, ladies."

Lucas stood there as if he'd been poleaxed. Staring up at him with eager faces were three blondes, all waiting for him to sit down beside them.

Chapter Five

Susannah was feeling quite satisfied with herself.

Not only had she figured out how to end the speculation about any baby she might have, but she'd also managed to pull it off quickly.

It hadn't been easy to locate three petite blondes in Caliente. Since Lucas Boyd had fallen for that type the first time, it made sense to Susannah that he'd most likely follow the same pattern now. With Abby's help, she'd located the three most attractive ladies.

But that had only been the beginning. Then she had to convince them to share their moment with Lucas Boyd with each other. None of them liked the idea.

In the end, however, they'd all agreed, because they wanted first crack at a wealthy widower who'd finally come out of seclusion.

"Did you hear?" Gertie asked as she tottered up

to the front desk in the library, two books clutched against her sagging bustline.

"I beg your pardon, Gertie? Did I hear what?" Susannah asked, somewhat distracted by her thoughts.

"Lucas Boyd. He's eatin' at The Red Slipper with three women," the little lady said, as if she were revealing a secret liaison between China and Russia.

"Really?" Susannah said nonchalantly. "Well, I guess my heart is broken."

Gertie peered at her. "You don't look too upset."

"I'm a great actress. I hide my feelings well." Susannah added a grin so the old lady would realize she was teasing.

"Humph. Lucas is a good catch."

"Yes, I believe he is, but I'm not fishing." She held out her hand for the lady's choices and proceeded to stamp them and then hand them back. Gertie was known for her gossiping. If she believed there was nothing between Lucas and Susannah, the entire town would know it at once.

"Well, you ought to be trying to catch someone. Ladies need husbands," Gertie muttered, ignoring the fact that she'd been widowed twenty-two years ago and managed just fine.

"Maybe you should go after Lucas, Gertie. He'd make you a fine—"

Susannah's teasing smile was wiped from her face as the library's front door, an antique in oak with flawlessly etched glass, was slammed against the outside wall.

Even more disturbing was the angry man standing

just inside. His cowboy hat was jammed low on his forehead, shadowing his face, but Susannah had no difficulty identifying him. Or the mood he was in.

"Oh, my," Gertie whispered, staring.

Susannah fought the urge to run. She'd known that Lucas Boyd might initially have been unhappy with her scheme, but she'd counted on the ladies to charm him.

She'd miscalculated.

He strode up to the checkout counter and gestured behind her. "In your office!" Then, without waiting to see if she complied, he marched around the counter and through her office door.

Gertie's eyes were wide as she swung her gaze back to Susannah. "What's going on?"

"Um, I think Mr. Boyd has an overdue book," she offered, though she knew her answer was nonsensical. She gestured to one of her volunteers to come take her place at the front desk. "Excuse me, Gertie. I hope you enjoy your books."

The little lady didn't take the hint, not budging one inch from her front row stance. "You going to go talk to him?"

"Well, yes, as librarian, I—"

"Susannah, get in here!" Lucas roared.

That did it! She didn't often lose her temper, but if that man thought... Without finishing her response to Gertie, she slid from the stool and crossed the short distance to her small office.

After carefully closing the door, she whirled around. "How dare you?"

"How dare *you!*" he returned.

He was standing with his fists cocked on his hips, his lips pressed tightly together, a frown on his brow. And his hat was still on. Susannah felt her heart racing wildly and wondered if it was his anger…or his potent virility that caused all her senses to quicken.

"All I did was arrange a luncheon so you could meet some nice ladies," she said, primly, and perhaps not quite truthfully.

"All you did was feed me to three female barracudas in front of the entire town!"

"That's not a gentlemanly remark," she protested. As he opened his mouth to respond, she hurriedly added, "They are all beautiful blondes. I thought you liked blondes."

"Two of them aren't blondes. Lisa's been bleaching her hair since she was fourteen, and it looks like straw by now. Belinda bleached hers when she got her first divorce."

Susannah blinked in surprise. "I didn't know you were such a purist, or knew the ladies that well."

"Hell, of course I know them. They've lived here all their lives. Now, you tell me what kind of game you're playing." He took a step closer to her.

Backing until she was plastered against the door she'd just closed, Susannah drew a deep breath. She wanted to avoid his touch at all costs—it would never do for him to realize the bone-melting effect he had on her. "I thought the debacle Saturday night would be best handled by your showing some interest in—in other women."

"And you didn't think it necessary to inform me

of your little plan?'' he asked, his soft tones more threatening than his earlier yelling.

Susannah wished she had more room to maneuver. ''N-no. I didn't think you'd cooperate.''

''Damn right I wouldn't cooperate. Those women thought I was going to marry one of them,'' he growled.

''Wouldn't that solve your problem?''

His hands shot forward to trap her against the door. ''No, ma'am, that wouldn't solve my problem.''

''I don't see why not. You would have your son—''

''And a wife I don't want.''

Susannah nervously chewed on her bottom lip as she tried to come up with another answer, but her mind was blank. It was hard to think with two hundred pounds of sexy, angry cowboy hovering over you.

''Damn! Stop that!''

Her eyes widened and she stared at him, at a loss. ''What? Stop what?''

''Chewing on your lip,'' he informed her as he turned his back on her and took several steps away. He tried to relax the muscles that had tightened in his gut when he saw her nibbling on those soft lips. A softness he had wanted to test with his own lips.

She didn't really understand his concern with her lip, but if it convinced him to give her some breathing space, she wasn't going to complain. ''I'm sorry if—if you had a difficult time at lunch. I did pay for it.''

He whirled around to glare at her. "Yeah. That really made me feel good. A woman paying my way!"

"You really are a macho man, aren't you?" She didn't think he'd be under any illusions that she was paying him a compliment. "Of course I paid. I extended the invitation."

"A bogus invitation. I thought you were going to agree to—you know."

His gaze shifted away from her, but not before Susannah caught a glimpse of the sadness and hurt inside him. She hadn't intended to be mean. Without thinking, she reached out to pat his shoulder. He jerked back as if he'd been stung.

"I wanted to say I'm sorry," she explained stiffly. Okay, he didn't want her to touch him. She could certainly understand that reaction, but she'd only meant to be gracious. "I didn't intend to hurt you."

"Yeah, right."

"Really. I thought you might like one of those ladies. I tried to find some who looked like Beth because—"

"Don't you mention her name with those three! You know nothing about Beth. She was—was perfect! I'll never love anyone like I loved Beth. And don't you forget it!"

Susannah jumped aside as Lucas rushed out of her office. He didn't pause to greet any neighbors in his flight from the library. Even Gertie.

Who was still standing next to the front desk, watching Lucas's exit.

"Gertie. I didn't know you were still here," Susannah said, forcing her voice to sound normal. "Were there some other books you were interested in?"

With a sly grin, the little old lady shook her head. "Nope. I was just passing the time of day with Louisa, here," she said, gesturing to the volunteer who'd replaced Susannah.

"Ah. Louisa, could you hold down the fort a while longer. I have some paperwork I need to take care of."

"Of course, Susannah. I'm here for another hour. Take your time." Then the woman exchanged a look with Gertie.

Unable to deal with anything else at the moment, Susannah murmured her thanks and retreated into her office, closing the door behind her. She felt like an animal who needed privacy to lick her wounds. The cowboy's pain echoed in her heart. And she didn't know what she was going to do now.

Time to reevaluate her plans. Lucas Boyd wasn't cooperating.

Word spread like wildfire through the small community. First, Lucas's unexpected luncheon with three blondes. Then his visit to the library. When the men of Caliente came to their dinner tables that evening, their wives were primed to entertain them with the excitement of the day.

Lucas's hopes that other, more exciting developments would occur to dismiss his antics were dashed when his phone rang after dinner.

"Boy, what are you up to?"

He didn't need the caller to identify himself. "Hi, Doc. What do you mean?"

"You interested in one of those women? They're all wrong for you."

Lucas sighed. "I'm not playing the dating game, Doc. Calm down."

"Then why—"

"It's all your fault," Lucas assured him, a grim smile on his lips.

"What are you talking about? I didn't have anything to do with it."

"No, not directly. But Susannah Langston, that sweet, angelic lady, did. She trapped me without me having any idea what was coming."

Heavy silence followed his words. Finally Doc said, "What do you mean?"

"She wrote me a note, saying she had a solution to our difficulties, asked me to meet her for lunch at The Red Slipper today. When I arrived, those three were waiting for me. And the lovely Miss Langston even paid the bill."

"Oh, my. I guess that explains the second part of the gossip. You went to the library to tear a strip off her hide, didn't you?"

Lucas sighed again. He regretted his impulsive behavior, but after an hour fending off the blatant seduction of three women at once, he'd been ready to vent. "Yeah, I'm afraid so."

More silence.

Finally Doc asked, "So, are you abandoning our plan?"

Groaning, Lucas shook his head, then realized Doc couldn't see his response. "I don't know, Doc."

"Hell, you knew it wasn't going to be easy."

"Easy? True, but I didn't expect to have to survive anything like that lunch today. Those women were in a feeding frenzy. I was a big fat lunch ticket, and they were willing to do anything to seal the bargain. I've never been so embarrassed in my life."

"What did they do?"

"Other than run their hands all over me under the table? Of course, Doreen, since she was seated across from me, had to use her toes, but that didn't slow her down. Let's see, they offered some comfort in the dark, without the others, in various ways."

He closed his eyes as he thought of their blatant overtures. "They all expressed sympathy that I'd been without a woman for such a long time." As if sex were nothing more than a creature comfort.

"And you weren't tempted?"

That question stopped Lucas cold. Because he had been tempted and he'd tried to forget that part.

It wasn't the blondes who had tempted him, however. To his amazement, Susannah with fear in her eyes and chewing on her soft lip, had aroused desire. His gut had clenched and he'd fought the temptation to reach out and stroke her face.

"Those ladies didn't tempt me," he finally said.

"So what are you going to do?"

Lucas had given that question a lot of thought. He still wanted a son. His disappointment had been immense when he'd realized the local librarian had tricked him. But he couldn't abandon his plan. Or rather Doc's plan.

"I've got to do some more thinking, Doc. I don't know if I can carry your idea off."

"All you have to do is be honest, boy. Explain what you're offering, pure and simple. That shouldn't be so hard."

Lucas's gut tightened again, but it wasn't from fear of being honest. No, it was from fear of losing control, of being too attracted to the woman, of wanting too much. He had to stay focused on his child and forget Susannah.

The next day, Susannah knew her plan had backfired on her by all the curious stares of the patrons of the Caliente Library. Some of the visitors had never darkened the library's door before. They all wanted to see the woman who had spit in the wind, trod on Superman's cape and messed with Bad Leroy Brown. Or, in this case, Lucas Boyd.

In other words, instead of making people forget she was connected to Lucas, she'd only reminded them. Or rather, Lucas's reaction to her plan had done so.

With a quickly subdued sigh, she smiled at the old rancher who requested books on Colorado history and led him to the proper section. She supposed she should be grateful. The increase in usage of books would impress the city council.

"My, we're busy today," Abby said as she rounded the counter. "Haven't seen this many people here since we opened the place."

"Yes. The people of Caliente are certainly eager to learn today," Susannah said, unable to keep a touch of sarcasm from her voice.

Abby smirked. She'd warned Susannah that her plan might go awry. So far she hadn't said the fatal words, "I told you so," but Susannah was expecting them at any moment.

"They're just showing a little interest in their community," Abby assured her with a wider grin.

Susannah remembered Lucas's words of disbelief and used them herself. "Yeah, right."

Unfortunately for her, she hadn't been able to forget a single word the man had said. She supposed it was only fair that she use a few of them in her defense.

She turned away to go into her office when the sound of the front door opening was followed by a rush of feet and a whispering that seemed to go around the main room as if it were an electrical connection. Whirling around, Susannah braced herself.

Lucas Boyd, with all eyes upon him, walked into the library...again.

Lucas realized, as soon as he entered the building, that he should've chosen someplace a little less public. But he didn't feel right turning up on her doorstep at home. That seemed too personal.

A hell of a thought about the woman he was going to— He broke off his thoughts and approached the front desk.

"Hello, Susannah. I wonder if you'd spare me a few minutes to chat."

She looked all prim and proper today, her hair pulled back in that unflattering bun, a sober dress, though its chocolate color did complement her eyes. He almost believed his coming didn't matter to her, but then he noticed her fingers trembling as she tried to insert a card in a returned book.

"It's a busy time," she muttered, never meeting his gaze.

He scanned the big room. "You folks mind waiting while I talk to Susannah?" After receiving encouraging nods, he returned a triumphant smile to his quarry. "I think everyone will be patient. And what I have to say is kind of important."

Kind of important? He thought what he had to say was earth-shattering. Mind-bending. Cataclysmic.

Without another word, she turned and walked into her office. He followed, his gaze unconsciously enjoying the sway of her hips until he realized what he was doing. He jerked his look back to her bun.

"Look, Lucas, I don't intend to apologize again about what happened yesterday. I may have not…you may not have been pleased, but I had good intentions."

"I'm not here to talk about yesterday…except that I think you owe me for that little trick." He watched the fluctuating color in her cheeks, wanting to touch her, to feel the heat.

"It wasn't that big a deal," she said dismissively, shifting papers around on her desk as if she had business on her mind.

But Lucas wasn't fooled.

With a change of tactics, he said briskly, "You're

right, it wasn't. And it didn't make a hill of beans difference to our situation. If you have your child alone, everyone will still believe it's mine. Both of our reputations will be damaged.''

"I'll move.''

His heart clutched, and he took a deep breath before he could speak. "That would be a shame. You're well liked here.''

She almost turned her back to him, shielding her eyes from his gaze. "Yes, I like it here, too.''

"So I have a better solution.'' He took a step closer, instinctively believing this conversation would be easier if he could touch her. When he reached for her hand, however, she snatched it behind her.

"Wh-what solution?''

This time she faced him squarely, her chin up, ready to do battle. When he'd swept Beth up in plans she didn't vote for, she'd pouted, or tried coyness. Not Susannah. She faced her adversary with every ounce of her, ready to go down for the count.

He swallowed, his throat suddenly dry. It wasn't easy to say those words he'd never thought to utter again. "Marry me.'' His voice cracked with emotion.

"Wh-what?'' she asked faintly. Her face was pale, and he feared she was going to pass out.

"It makes sense, Susannah. I'll get the baby I want, and you will, too. You won't have to worry about supporting it. I'll do that. And I won't have to worry about someone to take care of it.'' He'd summed it up just like Doc said. But she wasn't impressed. Taking a step back, she gnawed her bottom lip, color returning to her cheeks.

"You shouted at me yesterday for trying to arrange a marriage for you," she reminded him, her gaze fixed on his. "In fact, you assured me marriage was out of the question. You didn't want a wife."

He remembered those words he'd shouted at her. Too bad she did, too. "Uh, I was angry."

"That still doesn't explain your change of mind."

He turned away from her and paced across the small office. "Look, Susannah, those ladies didn't understand. They thought—I mean, you led them to think I was interested in—in a love match." He snuck a look at her, but he couldn't read the expression on her face.

"And you're not. You're just interested in a baby."

He'd known she'd understand if he explained it properly. Sighing with relief, he nodded and offered a smile. "Exactly."

"Thank you for the offer, Mr. Boyd," she said calmly, "but I'm not interested."

Before he could recover, she reached for the door, prepared to end their discussion.

Just as he'd done before, he ordered, "Wait!" Unlike their previous discussion in the office, this time she halted, but she kept her back to him.

"Susannah, think about what you're throwing away. You could have it all…a good home, a family, whatever you need to make you happy." He was pleading for his own happiness, but he didn't think she'd be persuaded by his needs.

"I can have it all without your help, Lucas," she said gently, turning to face him. "I have an appointment Friday with a sperm clinic in Denver."

His heart skipped a beat as he saw his dream escaping. "No!"

"Lucas—I can't discuss this anymore today. My mind—"

"Don't say it! Give me one more chance, Susannah. Let me have one more shot at—at persuading you." He didn't know what he'd come up with that would change her mind, but he wanted some time to think.

"Lucas," she began in protest. "I can't—"

"Yes, you can. This is only Tuesday. Come out to the ranch tomorrow night for dinner. It won't interfere with your schedule for Friday…unless you change your mind. If you do, you can call them Thursday and cancel the appointment." He held his breath while she considered his words.

She lifted her head and stared at him with those big brown eyes that could be warm and laughing, or cold and formal. He couldn't read her answer there.

Drawing in a deep breath, she turned away. "All right."

Her voice was so soft, he wasn't sure he'd heard her answer or had supplied what he wanted to hear. "Did you agree?" he asked, stepping to her side, putting his hand on her shoulder.

"Yes, but I'm warning you. I don't think I'll change my mind. I understand why you want to convince me, but I can have my child without your help, Lucas."

"I know. I know, Susannah," he replied, squeezing her shoulder. "But I appreciate your giving me a chance."

Chapter Six

What did one wear to reject a marriage proposal?

Susannah didn't know the answer to that question as she studied the contents of her closet Wednesday night. Why had she ever agreed to this meeting?

She knew why. It was impossible to look into Lucas's pleading blue eyes, to know the pain he'd suffered and deny him something that would cost her nothing but embarrassment.

Embarrassment that she would suffer when he asked her why she wouldn't marry him. And he would ask. Then she'd have to explain how painful it would be to be married to a man who could only marry her because he had absolutely no interest in her.

And that would be embarrassing because she'd discovered a growing interest in *him*.

He couldn't consider those three blondes she'd set him up with, because they might tempt him from his mourning. After all, whether he admitted it or not, they were all quite like his Beth.

Unlike her.

And, as he'd said several times, he had nothing to give any woman ever again. Not since Beth died.

With a sigh, she pulled out a matching plum blouse and skirt, then searched in her top drawer for a silver concha belt to accent it. She left her hair down for the first time, pulling the sides back with barrettes, the rest curling down her back. Perhaps it was an unconscious attempt to feel prettier, more womanly, in the face of Lucas's businesslike proposal.

Okay, so she was human.

With a shuddering breath, she finished her application of makeup, also an unusual occurrence, and gathered her purse and keys. She was to pick up Abby on her way to Lucas's ranch. After consideration, she'd insisted on Abby's presence, and Lucas had agreed.

"Are you sure you want me to come?" Abby asked as soon as she got in the car.

"Yes, Abby," she replied quietly, softly. Inside, she screamed her need of Abby, a third person, someone who wouldn't be swayed by startling sexual feelings. Someone whose presence would keep Lucas from touching her. Because his touch, even with a friendly intent, made her crazy.

Nothing more was said on the short drive. Lucas's ranch house was located only a couple of miles outside the city limits. Of course, his acreage, large even by Colorado standards, spread out behind the house for miles.

Susannah parked her compact car beside a navy blue Cadillac. "Is that Lucas's car?" Somehow she'd expected a pickup truck.

"No," Abby replied, frowning, "that's Henry Grable's car. Did you know Doc was invited?"

"No. But I suppose it's logical. After all, Dr. Grable started this...I don't know what to call it."

"You know I'm going to support you, whatever you decide, Susannah. But I hope you'll give Lucas's idea some thought. He has a lot to offer a woman."

Susannah bit down on her bottom lip. Maybe she'd made a mistake inviting Abby. It sounded as if Abby was on Lucas's side. "He's—he's not offering what I want."

And she was a fool for even thinking about a real marriage. She didn't think she could make Lucas happy, even if he loved her. Her one venture into a relationship had ended badly, with her fiancé blaming her frigidity for their difficulties. And giving him license to do what he wanted with her best friend.

But she couldn't help the feelings that Lucas Boyd had aroused in her, in spite of her supposed frigidity. As inexperienced as she was, she didn't know how to handle those feelings. And that's why she needed Abby by her side.

The front door to the house opened and Lucas stood silhouetted in the doorway.

With another sigh, Susannah opened her door. "Let's get this over with."

* * *

Lucas heard the sound of a car. His nerves went on alert.

She was here.

His wait would be over. He'd have the answer to his question. Tonight, he'd know if he'd one day soon hold his son in his arms, or whether he'd have to find someone else.

To his surprise, his hands began to shake.

"You okay?" Doc asked, stepping toward him.

"I'm fine. If this—this plan doesn't work out, I'll come up with something else. I *will* have my son."

"'Course you will, Lucas. You almost sound like you don't want Susannah to agree."

"What? Don't be ridiculous," Lucas admonished his friend gruffly. Turning his back on Doc's prying eyes, he walked to the door and opened it.

Doc was wrong, of course. Why would he want her to refuse him when he'd gone to such lengths to persuade her? That was a ridiculous idea.

But one he couldn't deny.

"Evenin', Luke," Abby called out, stepping from the shadows into the porch light.

He returned her greeting, but his gaze searched the darkness for his other guest.

When she finally moved into the light, he stared. With her hair loose and flowing down her shoulders, her body outlined in flattering clothes, she was a far cry from the plain, frumpy librarian he'd first encountered.

Which explained his troubled stomach.

He wanted nothing to do with emotion, with wanting. And yet, in his efforts to convince Susannah, he'd noticed in himself a renewed interest in life, an eagerness to face a new day.

Feelings long dead. Three years long.

They scared him.

"Come in, Abby, Susannah. Welcome to my home."

Even as the two women approached, Lucas drew a deep breath and shored up his determination. It was the hope of his son that was causing the blood to race through his veins once more. Not a woman.

And he was going to win. Susannah was going to agree to give him his son. Because he'd figured out the weak link in her armor.

"I'm glad you could come. Let me show you around the house."

Susannah fell in love.

With the house. Only the house, she assured herself. If she'd planned it herself, she couldn't have been more satisfied.

Oh, not with the decor. It had an air of neglect, of a half-finished project, that reminded her too much of Lucas's past. The furniture was a mixture of sturdy, pioneer furniture, meant to last through the ages, and touches of modern, inexpensive pieces that appeared incongruously beside the rest.

It was a house that needed love to turn it into a home.

You're an idiot, she scolded herself. A sentimental fool. Even worse, she knew Lucas sensed her reaction. If she didn't know better, she'd consider his expression one of gloating.

Abby and Dr. Grable had acted as Lucas's own personal Greek chorus, affirming every advantage he'd pointed out. Financial security. A home. All the time she wanted to care for her child.

"Dinner was delicious," she said politely as she wiped her lips with her napkin.

"I'll tell Frankie you appreciated it. He's a good cook."

"Yes, excellent," Abby hurriedly agreed. "He'll be a big help. Most new mothers don't have enough help." She elbowed the good doctor as if she feared he'd forget his role.

"Absolutely," he hurriedly agreed, putting down his fork. "Most new mothers have to do too much too soon. Frankie will be a big help."

Susannah tried to hide her smile as the doctor looked longingly at his last bite of coconut custard pie. Keeping his eye on Abby, he slowly picked up his fork. Then, with his prize in hand, he hurried it to his mouth.

"I think Frankie would make it hard to regain my figure, don't you, Doctor? That pie was impossible to resist."

"It was mighty good," he agreed with a grin that disappeared as Abby elbowed him again. "I mean— um, I'm sure Frankie has some low calorie recipes."

Several remarks about the likelihood of a man cooking for a bunch of hardworking cowboys even thinking of calories passed through Susannah's head, but she said nothing.

What was the point? In spite of all the advantages on display, Frankie included, she couldn't accept Lucas's offer. She would pay the price of a loveless marriage, daily rejection of the feelings she might develop.

Work had never bothered her. Coldness. Loneliness. Those were her fears. And even among the crowd of people on Lucas's ranch, she would be lonely.

The object of her thoughts, her host, settled back in his chair at the head of the table. "Well, Susannah, have you thought about my idea? Have we convinced you?"

Something in his look, his tone, made her leery. She'd earlier thought she'd detected a self-congratulatory smirk, but something was different now.

"No, Lucas, I'm sorry. I still have to refuse your—your gracious offer."

It took some courage to meet his gaze, but she did, hoping she hid the turmoil inside her. Instead of looking disappointed, he regarded her steadily, seriously.

"So, the idea of wealth and comfort didn't move you?"

She swallowed, her throat suddenly dry. "No, thank you."

"You have beautiful manners, Susannah."

His non sequitur puzzled her. She looked at Abby and the doctor to see if they understood his meaning, but they looked as nonplussed as she felt.

"I bet your mother was from the South."

She nodded hesitantly, then said, "From Texas."

"Ah. But your parents are both dead, aren't they?"

"Yes."

"No extended family, cousins, aunts and uncles?"

Growing more and more uneasy, Susannah shook her head, confirming his words.

He leaned forward, staring at her intently, "What will happen to your baby if you fall ill? Or, God forbid, die in a car wreck?"

She closed her eyes even as she heard Abby gasp. She wanted to hide the pain that filled her.

"Lucas Boyd, shame on you!" Abby protested.

Even the doctor protested. "That's hard, Lucas."

"No, it's the truth. While Susannah may not need my wealth, my home, her baby does. If he's my son, I'll be there for him if she can't. And she knows I'll love him. If something happens to me, she'll have the financial means to carry on. But—" he paused, but Susannah didn't open her eyes "—if she has her child alone, he could end up in a foster home, if something should happen to her."

She prayed she'd open her eyes and discover she'd been having a bad dream. That she was home in her solitary bed. That she'd never met Lucas Boyd.

"Is that what you want, Susannah?"

That low, almost whispered question echoed in her heart. She opened her eyes and stared at her tormentor. Her bottom lip trembled as she tried to speak, to respond to his question.

She couldn't.

"Oh, my poor dear," Abby moaned and leaped up to come around the table to her side.

"Boy, I think you may have gone too far," Dr. Grable protested, standing also.

Lucas remained seated. "I didn't mean to hurt you, Susannah. I just wanted to make you think about what's best for the baby. Our baby."

Chills coursed through her body. She wanted to get up and race out of his house, away from his words. But she didn't think her legs would hold her.

Finally she composed herself enough to whisper to Abby, "I want to go home."

"Of course you do, dear. Come on. We'll get away from these nasty men," Abby agreed, taking Susannah's arm to help her up.

"Hey, I didn't do anything," Dr. Grable protested.

Now Lucas stood. "You promised you'd answer my question tonight," he reminded her, again drawing Abby's ire.

"Haven't you done enough?" Abby demanded. "The poor girl is shaking like a leaf."

"Please, Abby, let's just go," Susannah insisted as she tried to pull herself together. "My answer—"

"Never mind," the cowboy abruptly said, cutting her off. "Think about what I said. Tell me tomorrow."

She wanted to scream no at him. But she couldn't. The reason his question had shaken her so was that he'd found her Achilles' heel. He'd struck at the one weakness to her plan.

If she had a child, it would be totally dependent on her.

So now she was faced with her selfishness, or giving up her hope of having a child.

Or marrying Lucas Boyd.

Lucas felt like a wolf that had savaged an innocent lamb. The stricken look on Susannah's face as she'd hurried from his house, quite possibly from his life, would stay with him for a long time.

His secret weapon had certainly shaken her, he admitted as he paced the bedroom floor. He'd been right. He'd discovered her weakness. After he'd seen her tender heart, seeing how much she worried about hurting even him, he'd known she would never be able to deny her child.

But he'd found himself shaken, too. The urge to beat Abby to her side, to sweep her into his arms and promise never to hurt her again, had almost paralyzed him.

It was because he'd felt responsible. Felt, hell! He *was* responsible. His daddy had always taught him to protect women, to care for them. Instead he'd hurt her.

That was the only reason he'd reacted so powerfully. He'd done something his daddy wouldn't have approved of. It had nothing to do with Susannah.

But he'd repeat it a thousand times if it would bring him his son.

He paced across the room again.

For Colorado in the fall, it was a mild night. But Susannah shivered beneath the blankets on her bed.

Lucas Boyd had forced her to face facts. Her child, if she had a child by artificial insemination, would be totally dependent on her. If something happened to her, the baby would go into foster care, as Lucas had said.

Could she take that risk? Could she selfishly give life to a child so she wouldn't be alone, knowing that if she died, the child would face the same difficulty?

But could she give up her unborn child?

She rubbed her hand over her flat stomach as if a child were already growing there. She'd longed for this child, prayed for it, planned for its care. Loved it.

Tossing and turning, she debated her options until early in the frosty morning. Finally she fell asleep without coming to a decision.

But when she woke, the questions were waiting, lurking in the shadows. What would she choose?

"Dang it! What's wrong with you today?" Frankie asked as his boss paced through the kitchen for the fourth time that morning. "I kin hardly make one pass with the mop before you muddy the floor again."

"What?" Lucas asked, staring at Frankie with a bewildered look on his face.

"Never mind. Just get along."

Lucas rubbed his forehead, unsure where he was heading when Frankie interrupted him. He couldn't concentrate on anything this morning…other than Susannah's decision. He'd stopped her last night because he thought she needed time for his argument to sink in.

But he didn't understand why. He was offering her everything she could want.

Except himself.

And she had no more interest in that kind of relationship than he did. If she did, she wouldn't be considering a test tube in Denver.

The phone rang and he almost leaped across the kitchen to the extension on the wall. "Hello?"

"Luke? This is Mike. I noticed some fencing down on your western boundary, just below Culligan's Pass. Thought you'd want to know."

"Oh. Thanks, Mike. I'll send a couple of the boys over right away." His heart rate settled back to normal.

"Maybe you should go, yourself," Frankie suggested, as Lucas got off the phone.

Lucas frowned at him. "Me? Why?"

"To get you out of my kitchen," Frankie said with exasperation, leaning on his mop.

"I'm going to town," Lucas abruptly said. He'd borne the suspense long enough.

"You comin' back for lunch?"

"No." If Susannah agreed, he'd take her to lunch. If not...well, he wouldn't have an appetite.

"Yes, I understand. I'm sorry for the inconvenience," Susannah said with a shaky voice. She put down the receiver and covered her face with trembling fingers.

"What inconvenience?"

Her head whipped up, and she stared at Lucas Boyd, who was leaning against the doorjamb to her small office. She'd hoped for some time to compose herself before she had to face him. Time to let her raw emotions retreat, find protective cover.

"What inconvenience?" he asked again, staring at her with passionate eyes.

"My canceling the appointment with the sperm bank." She didn't offer any explanation.

A spark of hope fired up in his gaze. "Because?"

No patient waiting on his part. Lucas Boyd wanted his trophy at once.

"Because I realized you were right. I couldn't have a child alone, with no safety net in case—no one to care for my child."

He left the doorjamb and sauntered closer. She knew it was her imagination at fault, but his movement seemed like that of an animal closing in for the kill.

"I'd make a great safety net, Susannah."

Her chin lifted. She wanted to deny his words, to tell him she'd found another way. A way that wouldn't involve putting her heart, her soul, at risk.

But she hadn't.

Slowly she looked down at the pile of papers on her desk. "I know."

He stepped closer and lifted her chin with his big, callused hand. "Tell me, Susannah. Spell it out plain and clear. Are you going to marry me, have my baby?"

Moisture filled her eyes, but she wasn't a coward. Meeting his stare, she nodded.

His reaction only underlined their future together. He released her chin as if she'd burned his fingers, and he took a step backward.

"Have you changed your mind?" she asked, her voice shaking. Was she failing again at a relationship before it had even begun? Had he already realized she wasn't...wasn't good with the physical side of love?

"No!" he protested hoarsely. "No, I haven't changed my mind. But I've been afraid I couldn't convince you. It's just taking me a little time to figure out that I've won."

"Won? You make it sound like a game, a challenge. We're talking about a life, a—a child."

"I know that! Damn it, I know that better than anyone. I stood there and watched my baby boy die," he shouted, suddenly pacing her little office. "Don't try to tell me what we're talking about!"

The deep breath Susannah drew shuddered its way through her. Had she made a mistake? Could she handle close quarters with this man, with his past, his pain, his memories?

"Sorry," he apologized even as she worried. "I—I'm thrilled with your decision, Susannah. But it's a lot to adjust to. Even though we talked about it before, it—it seems more real now."

"You can still change your mind."

A smile slowly grew on his firm lips, reaching his eyes. "No, sweetheart. I'm not going to change my mind. I'm going to be a daddy. I couldn't be happier."

She looked away. Too much exposure to his happiness would damage her heart for sure.

"Come on. Let me take you to lunch to celebrate," he said, moving toward her again.

She pressed against the back of her chair. "But everyone would see us."

"That's okay. We're going to be married. They might as well get used to the idea." Without leaving her any choice in the matter, he seized her hand and pulled her from her chair. "Hurry up. Suddenly I'm starving."

Susannah spent her energy trying to get her feet underneath her before she fell on her face. Which made it impossible to protest his action until they were out the door and in the main room of the library.

"Lucas, please—"

"You don't want to go eat?" he asked, frowning, coming to an abrupt halt.

"It's not... Lunch isn't necessary."

One eyebrow slid up over his sparkling eyes. "Sweetheart, it's sure necessary where I come from. Don't you eat?"

"I mean you don't have to buy me lunch."

He blinked at her, as if he didn't understand her words. Then, a trifle grimly, he muttered, "I think the occasion warrants it."

Without any more conversation, he led her across the street to The Red Slipper.

She didn't want to go in, but with Lucas's hand gripping her arm, Susannah didn't think she had a choice. It seemed to her, as they stepped through the door, that the entire room grew still, silent, watching.

Her cheeks heated up and she discovered a strange urge to hide her face against Luke's strong shoulder. Great! Nothing would confirm the gossip faster.

Lucas seemed at ease. "Morning, Molly. We need a table for two."

The hostess grinned. "You cuttin' down, Luke? Last time you had three ladies waiting for you."

"Yeah, I'm cutting down. Permanently." He added a big grin, and conversation picked up at once, everyone abuzz with this latest tidbit of gossip.

"Lucas!" Susannah protested hoarsely.

He buried his nose in her hair and whispered, "You can't keep secrets in this town. And I won't have anyone thinking I'm ashamed of my baby's mother."

Stunned, unable to move as fast to acceptance as he, Susannah stared.

"Sit down," he said gently, as if realizing her difficulty.

She flopped into a chair, aware of Molly's stare. When the hostess handed her the menu, she buried her face behind it.

"Enjoy your meal."

"We will," Lucas said.

Susannah peeped over the top of her menu to find him smiling. "You're enjoying this, aren't you?"

He settled in his chair before he answered. The smile left his face and he shrugged. "We're both going to achieve our dream. What's not to enjoy?"

With a jerky nod of agreement, she returned to the menu. When the waitress arrived at their table, an old friend of Lucas's, of course, Susannah was able to order her lunch without stumbling.

Maybe she could get through this...this arrangement. What was important was the baby, her child.

Their child.

"Lucas, you do realize the baby could be a girl, don't you?" She'd meant to mention that possibility before now.

The grin returned to his face. "Not a chance. Boyds have boys."

As if she were talking to herself, she said, "I was hoping for a girl."

He reached across the table to take her hand. "Maybe we can have more than one. Surely there have been some girls somewhere in my family tree."

She gasped, staring at him. How had he known? Had he realized how much she hated the idea of having an only child? Like herself? Or was it a lucky guess?

He seemed to recognize her surprise. "Sorry, Susannah. I know we haven't talked about more children, but I'm not against the idea. Are you?"

"No."

"So, we need to set the date. Can you be ready by next Saturday?"

Before she could answer, the waitress set their plates in front of them, giving Susannah a breathing space.

"Next Saturday?" she repeated after they were alone.

"Yeah. I'll talk to the pastor, and we can get a license."

"I thought we should wait until—until after I'm pregnant before we actually marry."

Chapter Seven

Lucas shook his head, wondering if he'd heard correctly. What was wrong with the woman? He offered marriage and she suggested an affair?

"Why?"

She didn't meet his gaze. "It makes sense. The purpose of our marriage is to have a child. If I can't get pregnant, we'd both feel foolish, wouldn't we?"

"Is there any reason you can't get pregnant? Did Doc find something when he examined you?" He watched her closely, wondering what was going on.

"No. He said everything was fine."

"Then we'll go ahead and marry. I want my son conceived *after* the wedding, not before." Feeling he'd settled the matter, he turned his attention to the food in front of him. Not that he was as calm as he hoped he looked. But he didn't want Susannah to know about the jitters in his stomach.

She didn't respond. When she picked up her fork

to begin her meal also, he relaxed somewhat. Before she ate anything, however, she lowered her fork to her plate.

"Maybe you should go ahead and...and give Doc some, uh, some specimens. That way we can get the process started as soon as possible. I'll—"

"I should do what?" His voice was low, almost guttural, but if he'd understood what she said, no one would blame him. He waited for her explanation.

"I know you said you wanted us to be married, but surely, a couple of days won't—"

"What does Doc have to do with anything?"

That blasted bottom lip of hers was trembling. The urge to comfort, to touch, to kiss—nope, he didn't really want to do those things. It was her distress, not her sex appeal, that moved him. Wasn't it?

"Dr. Grable will perform the procedure."

A coldness settled around his heart. Leaning forward, he said, "Lady, the only one performing will be me, and I promise you won't call it a 'procedure,' like canning tomatoes, when we're finished."

He watched her cheeks flash fire and then go deathly pale. Clamping her lips tightly together, she didn't say a word as she hurried from the table in the direction of the ladies' room.

What in the hell was going on? She thought they'd marry and not have sex? Had he missed something here? Knowing he couldn't enter the ladies' room, he summoned the waitress to the table.

"Something wrong with the special?" she asked, looking at his plate.

"No, but Susannah left the table in a hurry. Would you check the rest room to see if she's okay?"

"You think the food made her sick?"

"No, she hasn't eaten anything. Just check on her for me." Right after he'd spoken the words, Susannah reappeared. Both Lucas and the waitress watched her progress back to the table.

"You okay, hon?" the waitress asked, studying her.

"I'm fine."

"Your boyfriend here thought you were sick. Maybe you're pregnant," she suggested with a chuckle.

Lucas glared at her and, if possible, Susannah turned even more pale.

As if suddenly realizing her teasing had gone awry, the waitress hurriedly apologized and dashed off to another table.

"Susannah, what's going on here?"

"Nothing," she whispered. Since she picked up her fork and took a bite of the meat loaf she'd ordered, Lucas ate, too, but he couldn't shake the feeling that something was wrong.

"Are you sure you're healthy?"

Woodenly, without looking at him, she replied, "Do you want Dr. Grable to write out a certificate of health for me?"

"No, I didn't mean—"

"It's all right, Lucas. I understand what is at stake, what kind of commodity I'm offering. If I can't produce a child, I realize—"

"Damn it! Stop it, Susannah. You make it sound like we're bartering pigs for chickens, here."

For the first time since their arrival at the café, her gaze met his. "We are. I'm trading a part of my child for the security you've promised. You're trading a promise to love and protect in return. Love and protect the child, I mean," she added hurriedly, embarrassed again.

Why did something feel wrong? He frowned. "I will protect you as well, Susannah. After all, you'll be my wife."

She straightened her spine and replied crisply, as if she was once more in control of herself, "I can take care of myself, Lucas. All I'm asking is that you keep your word to our child. And I know you will do that."

"I promise, Susannah."

She nodded and took another bite. They finished the rest of their meal in silence. She left at least half of the meat loaf and vegetables on her plate. It took effort to control the urge to press her to finish her meal. But he managed.

As soon as he'd eaten the last bite of his food, she said, "I need to return to work, Lucas. I have a lot of things to do."

He frowned again. She seemed extremely anxious to get away from him. "Okay, but we're decided on next Saturday?" At her nod, he said, "I'll call the preacher and see if the church is available. And I'll bear the cost of the wedding. After all—"

"No! That's my responsibility. Besides, it won't

cost all that much. There'll just be my dress…and—and a ring for you. Do you mind wearing a ring?"

He considered his response. Oh, not about the ring. Of course he intended to wear a ring. But if she thought they were going to be married secretly, as if he were ashamed of her, she had another thought coming. "I'll be glad to wear a ring. We can go into the Springs Monday and pick something out. And you can shop for a gown there. I'll take care of everything else."

"What else?" she asked with a frown, pausing in her movement to leave.

"A few minor details. Don't worry about it." He stood and came around the table as she shoved back her chair.

"But I want to—"

He stopped her words with a kiss. He'd intended it to be light, a notice served to the community of his intentions. But that damn lower lip, both lips in fact, were soft, surprised and downright inviting. Even the slightest physical contact between them seemed to arouse in him long-dormant sensations. She made him aware of his masculinity as no other woman did.

When he finally lifted his head, she stared at him with tragic eyes, as if he'd just broken her heart. "What? It was only a kiss, Susannah. What's wrong?"

"Nothing," she said hurriedly, ducking her head and turning away. "I have to get back to the library."

He let her go alone. That seemed to be what she

wanted. But he was puzzled…and worried. Why should his kiss upset her? Did she think they wouldn't touch just because they weren't marrying for love?

If that was her idea, it was a good thing he'd kissed her. He might not love her, and have no intention of loving her, but a man has needs. And he'd just discovered one of his most urgent needs was kissing Susannah.

Susannah felt like a mouse scurrying back to her hole after the big, ferocious cat had pawed her. Lucas Boyd was dangerous. Not because he would ever intentionally hurt her, but because his careless touch could destroy her.

She'd thought he understood that touching, sex, lovemaking, wouldn't be a part of their marriage. When he'd dismissed Dr. Grable as a part of their pregnancy plan, she'd known she was in trouble.

When her fiancé had condemned her as frigid, she hadn't argued. After all, she had felt no urge, no heat, no impatience for her wedding bed. He'd blamed her for his affair with her friend.

Books were Susannah's living. She'd read enough self-help books to know she was not to blame for his behavior. But her lack of interest in sex with him, the distance she felt when he touched her, had coincided with his condemnation.

She wished she could feel as distant when Lucas kissed her.

He wasn't being dishonest with her. No, he'd told

her up-front that there was nothing personal about his interest in her. He wanted a baby.

The old-fashioned way.

Impossible to do without touching. And Susannah was finding it difficult to deal with her response when he touched her. When his lips met hers, she lost all rational thought. But he brought her to earth with a *thunk* when his words underlined his concept of their marriage.

They had only shared one kiss and she was already out of control. How was she going to protect herself? How was she going to hide her response?

The last thing she wanted was for him to feel sorry for her, to realize how needy she was. They couldn't live together, coexist, if that happened. He'd be embarrassed and disinterested. She'd be miserable.

The only comfort she could find was that it was one of the busiest days at the library. Once she entered the building, her work pulled at her, tugging her thoughts from the disaster of her personal life.

At least she would have her work, giving her an air of normalcy during the day.

At night, she was in big trouble.

"Doc, did you examine Susannah when she first visited you?" Lucas asked over the phone.

"Of course I did. Why?"

"Did she discuss any, uh, her past?"

"No. Didn't say much. What's the problem, boy? Did she turn you down?"

"No, she agreed."

"Hallelujah! When?"

"Next Saturday. Will you stand up with me?"

"I'd be delighted."

"When she agreed, she thought we should wait until after she got pregnant to get married. I thought maybe she was afraid she couldn't, you know, conceive." Lucas wrapped the telephone cord tightly around one finger, watching it grow pale as the blood flow was cut off.

"I didn't see a problem. She's very healthy."

Lucas unwrapped his finger and let out a sigh. "Okay. Well, I've talked to the preacher and the wedding's set for four o'clock next Saturday. We'll have the reception here afterward. Pass the word along, will you?"

"The entire town?"

"Every last one of them. We're going to celebrate."

Susannah waited until she got home that evening to call Abby. Though they weren't having a formal wedding, she'd need someone to stand up for her, and she wanted Abby.

"Abby? It's Susannah. I wondered if—"

"It's about time you called. You are going to ask me to stand up for you, aren't you?" Without waiting for Susannah to speak, she continued, "A'course, I'll understand if you want someone younger, but—"

"Of course I want you to stand up for me. But how did you know?"

"Lord'a'mercy, child, it's all over town."

"You mean Lucas's behavior in the café?"

"Aw, he's kissed women before. But the wedding

is the big news. We've got lots to do before then. Mark next Thursday evening off your schedule. That's when we're giving you a shower. And Friday night you'll spend here with me. Since the wedding's at four, we'll—''

"What? The wedding's when?'' Susannah couldn't believe it. The entire town knew when her wedding was scheduled before she did?

"At four. With a big party at the ranch afterward for the entire town. There'll be a big cake, lots of food and Jed Roy is over the moon with the order for flowers. Didn't Lucas tell you?''

"I have to go, Abby. I'll call you later.'' Even though Abby was still protesting when she hung up the receiver, Susannah didn't hesitate. This might not be a real marriage, but Lucas Boyd had another thought coming if he thought he could run roughshod over her.

Rage filled her as she marched out of her little house to her car. She only hoped her rage wouldn't disappear by the time she reached his ranch, because she knew she'd need its energy to deal with the ornery man who *thought* he was about to become her husband!

To her relief, her anger was still simmering when she jerked to a stop in front of his house. By the time she reached the door, she'd stoked it with the reminder of how little she figured into his plans.

Only her baby.

After her knock he opened the door with a smile. "Susannah, I just tried to call you.''

How dare he? He acted as if he was pleased to see

her. The pain was so acute, her prepared speech went out the window. Without warning, she slapped him. "The wedding's off!"

Then she ran.

He caught her before she reached her car.

"What the hell's gotten into you, woman?"

She couldn't answer him. Tears filled her eyes and she was choked up. All she wanted was to get away, to hide in the dark until the panic eased.

In spite of her pushing and pulling, she couldn't get away. He held her tight. He even tried to force her face up, so he could see, but that at least she could prevent. Finally, in a surprise move, he threw her over one of his broad shoulders and headed for the house.

"Put me down! I want to leave!" She choked out the words, flailing uselessly at his back.

"Not until you explain," he said, his voice grim with determination.

"All right, put me down. I'll explain," she assured him with almost gleeful anger. She was glad she had an excuse to break off their six-hour engagement.

Because she was afraid.

With a sigh, she hung limply, no longer struggling. She was afraid. It hurt to admit her cowardice, but that was why she had become so enraged.

He opened the door and stepped inside, into the light, just as Frankie entered the hallway.

"Uh, everything okay, boss?"

"Yeah, Frankie. There'll be one more for dinner. Okay?"

"Sure, boss. There's plenty of food." Then he

scurried back down the hall and into the kitchen as Lucas let Susannah slide down his body to stand beside him.

Susannah closed her eyes. Could she embarrass herself more? Probably her behavior would be fodder for the gossip chain that existed in the small town before breakfast the next morning.

"What happened?" he asked.

She opened her eyes, suddenly weary. And heartbroken. "It doesn't matter. It's over. I never should've agreed."

Dully she tried to move around him, to walk away.

Catching her shoulders in his strong hands, he held her firm. "Come on, Susannah, tell me what made you mad, made you change your mind."

"Why ask me? Probably within the hour the tomtoms will be beating across the mountains, detailing our argument, just as they detailed our wedding. You can wait until then to find out." She knew she was being unfair but she was desperate.

"What are you talking about? You're not making any sense."

"No, I'm not. I'm being overly sensitive, melodramatic, demanding, expecting to be consulted about our wedding before the entire town is informed. It's a good thing you discovered I'm outrageous before you actually married me." She kept her spine straight, her shoulders back. But she couldn't look him in the eye.

Finally she raised her gaze. The silence had gone on too long. Why didn't he say anything?

* * *

Lucas was too busy cursing his insensitivity.

When he'd married Beth, he remembered the weeks before the marriage, the details that consumed her, the way she'd gotten irritated with him because he didn't care about what color the bridemaids' gowns were going to be.

Why had he thought Susannah wouldn't care? She was a woman, and this marriage would be her only opportunity to indulge in sentimentality.

No wonder she'd gotten angry.

''I'm sorry, Susannah. I should've called you and told you the only possible time was four o'clock next Saturday. But since it was the only time the preacher could make it, I assumed it would be all right with you.''

His apology didn't solve anything.

She tugged futilely on his hold. ''Please, let's just forget it. We've made a mistake.''

''No, we haven't. *I* made a mistake. I was insensitive. But there's no need to call off the wedding. Our reason is still valid.'' He ducked his head, trying to see her face. ''Susannah?''

She kept her head lowered, but tears trailed down her pale cheeks. ''Please, let me go,'' she whispered.

''I can't.'' Without thought, he wrapped his arms around her, pulling her against him. ''You're going to take away my dream because I didn't think? I promise I won't do it again.''

Almost as if in slow motion, she laid her head on his shoulder, her face buried in his neck, letting her body rest against his.

His reaction boded well for their marriage bed.

Even as his manhood swelled and surged, his lips sought hers, his hands stroked and coaxed her participation. When her arms slid around his neck, her fingers weaving through his hair, along his neck, her mouth opened to him, he thought he was going to lose control and embarrass himself right there.

Not that he stopped, or let her go. In fact, he pressed her tighter against him, loving the feel of her breasts' tight buds rubbing against his chest. He deepened the kiss, pushing his tongue past any barriers, encouraging her to join him.

And she did.

When one of his hands sank to the front of her blouse and began unfastening the buttons, she returned the favor, pulling his shirt aside and stroking his chest.

He let his lips leave hers, seeking new treasures, but he couldn't stay away from their luscious softness. His hand cupped a neglected breast as his mouth plundered hers again. He thought he'd eat her alive. And still be hungry for her again.

He'd never felt this way before.

Not even with Beth.

Such a betrayal jolted him out of his sensual haze, and he stumbled back, shocked.

He didn't have long to dwell on the traitorous thought, however, because Susannah turned and ran again.

"No!" he yelled even as he caught her.

The kitchen door swung open almost simultaneously and Frankie opened his mouth to announce dinner. "Dinner is— Uh, sorry." He hastily re-treated.

"We'll be right there," Lucas called out.

Then he turned his attention to the mass of nerves in his arms. Even as she buttoned up her blouse, she was trembling like a leaf.

"He didn't see anything, sweetheart. There's nothing to be embarrassed about."

He supposed he could count it a good thing that she looked him in the eye. Except for that glow of anger.

"I can't stay to eat. I have to leave."

"Come on, Frankie's already fixed everything. It will give us a chance to talk."

"In front of Frankie?" she asked, scandalized.

"No. I'll, um, I'll suggest he eat in the bunkhouse tonight. He won't mind."

"No, I have to go."

"Susannah, I'm not letting you go until we work out our problems. I'm not giving up my dream."

She went completely still in his hold, and he feared he'd said the wrong thing. To his surprise, however, she drew a deep breath and stopped pulling away. "No. I guess not."

Without another word to him, she finished buttoning her blouse, tucked it into her skirt, smoothed back her hair, caught in its usual bun and turned to walk to the kitchen.

"Susannah—" he called out and she turned to stare at him.

"Didn't you want to eat?"

Hell, yes, he wanted to eat. He'd had a busy day.

But his head was all ajumble. He didn't want her to leave. He didn't want her to stay. How could he face what had popped into his mind when she was still there?

Still tempting him.

What was he going to do?

Chapter Eight

Her wedding day.

Susannah lay in Abby's guest room bed, staring at the ceiling. Abby had ordered her not to get up before ten this morning...8:47 and counting.

She should be exhausted. There had been a hundred chores to accomplish before her wedding. Including packing. She'd considered keeping her little house, but coward that she was, she couldn't face either Abby's or Lucas's reaction.

She and her fiancé had come to a silent agreement at their last meeting. They would stay as far apart as possible until the ceremony. At least, Susannah assumed that was what Lucas wanted since he'd avoided being alone with her.

She knew it was her preference.

In fact, she was surprised that Lucas was willing to go ahead with the ceremony. Especially since she'd already revealed how inadequate she was in…in certain areas. The expression on his face when he'd pushed his way out of her arms had confirmed her worst fears.

The click of the door snapped her from her thoughts. Surprisingly she almost chuckled to see Abby's kind face peeking through a narrow slit between the door and the wall.

"Come in, Abby, and give me permission to get up. I'm tired of lying here."

"Land's sake, child. You were supposed to sleep late this morning."

"But I always get up by seven, Abby. It's habit. I did sleep until almost eight this morning. Will that do?"

"Why, of course, child. I was going to serve you breakfast in bed. But you can come to the table if you want."

"I want," she replied succinctly and shoved back the covers. "I've never been much for eating in bed."

She slipped on a robe and followed Abby to the kitchen. Her day had begun.

He'd been up since before sunrise.

What in hell was he doing? He couldn't marry again. If he did, he'd face the pain of loss, as he'd lost Beth and his little boy.

He'd thought he could protect his heart by not loving a woman. But his child? Didn't he intend to love his child? He'd promised Susannah he would. Of course he would. He couldn't help himself.

And the fear of losing that child, as he'd lost his first child, scared him to death.

After hours of pacing, he knew he couldn't give up the hope of a son. But he'd gird his heart, keep it locked away, until that child lived and breathed in front of him. Until he could hear its heartbeat, watch it take a breath of sweet air.

Lucas drew a shuddering breath. He'd hold his unborn child at a distance as he intended to hold his wife at a distance.

Except for making love to her.

Having sex.

"Boss, breakfast's ready," Frankie called up the stairs.

As if escaping from a torture chamber, Lucas rushed out of his bedroom and down the stairs to the kitchen.

When Doc arrived that afternoon to escort him to the church, Lucas had put on his best suit, a crisp white shirt and a silver-and-blue tie. His mirror told him he looked the part of the eager groom.

Except for the pallor beneath his tan.

"Ready, boy?"

"Am I making a mistake, Doc?" He wanted to grab the older man by the neck. It was his fault, after all.

"No, Lucas, you're not making a mistake. It's time for you to enter the human race again."

Lucas stared at him, afraid he was right.

"Come on. It's too late now." Doc took him by the arm and led him out to his Cadillac.

Doc remained at his side as he entered the church

where he'd married his sweet Beth. She'd looked like a delicate doll in her white gown, all innocence and eagerness.

It took all his courage to face the filled church. But, with Doc at his side, he walked down the aisle to greet Pastor Collier who was waiting at the altar. The people quieted and the pastor signaled the organist to begin to play.

Though he'd organized most of the wedding and all of the reception at his ranch, Lucas had meticulously informed Susannah of each event, giving her every choice, during the week. He didn't want a repeat of the night she'd heard of his plans secondhand. But he'd consulted with her from a distance. He hadn't seen her since their confrontation.

Since neither he nor Susannah had parents, the only person to precede his bride down the aisle was Abby. When the organ music swelled and the guests stood and faced the front of the church, Lucas closed his eyes, unwilling to face his future.

He hadn't seen Susannah's gown. He'd given Abby strict instructions and she'd promised to keep Susannah from choosing a sensible suit. Even though their marriage wasn't romantic, he felt he owed her a real wedding.

A murmur ran through the audience and he snapped open his eyes. And understood why she'd gained their attention. She wore a white satin gown that draped her tall, rounded figure, sweeping the floor. The white drifting veil gave her a fairy princess air, only heightened by her brunette curls touching her shoulders.

He drew a deep breath. *You don't care about her. You don't care about her. You're just going to make love to her. That's all.*

Susannah's hands trembled as they clutched the huge bouquet of pale pink rosebuds and baby's breath Lucas had sent her. In spite of the distance they'd maintained this week, he had gone the extra mile to provide a beautiful wedding.

She was grateful. Really she was. But she was so worried over what would happen after the reception that she could scarcely concentrate.

Raising her eyes, she stared at the tall, handsome man waiting for her. Soon to be her husband. When she reached his side, she lowered her gaze to her trembling flowers and waited.

The music stopped and the minister began the ceremony.

They should've discussed the vows, she realized as Lucas repeated the words. He was promising to love her and she knew his words were a lie. Again she looked at him, but his gaze was fixed on the minister.

Then it was her turn. Like Lucas, she mouthed the words, knowing that in her heart she was promising no such thing. Not that she hated him. But she wasn't promising to love him. It was too frightening. Her gaze flashed to his, panic filling it.

He frowned and squeezed her hand, as if to offer support.

She turned back to the minister and Abby handed her the gold band she'd purchased for Lucas. Dr.

Grable did the same for Lucas. When he slid a ring on her trembling finger, she started, surprised by the diamonds. She'd tried on a plain gold band on Monday. Now she was wearing at least three carats of diamonds—an incredibly beautiful ring.

After Lucas had received his ring, the minister informed them they were now man and wife and added the words she'd been dreading. "You may kiss the bride."

Lucas lifted the veil, then drew her into his arms and lowered his mouth to hers. Every time he'd kissed her, she'd lost control, her body responding to his touch no matter how much she'd intended to remain distant. This kiss was no exception.

"Ahem. Mr. and Mrs. Boyd, I think we're ready for the reception," the minister said, breaking into the passion they were sharing.

Susannah's cheeks flamed as Lucas turned her toward the doors of the church and the crowd cheered, some of them laughing, she supposed, at the length of the kiss.

"Ready?" Lucas whispered, his arm around her waist.

She nodded, though she had no idea what she was agreeing to. She was still lost in a haze of passion. How could she respond to Lucas that way when no other man had ever aroused her?

Lucas took his arm from around her and laced his fingers with hers, pulling her from the altar down the aisle. A lot of well-wishers patted them on the shoulder or stopped them for a handshake as they made their way out of the church.

"Looks like everyone made it," Lucas whispered when they stepped outside in the late-afternoon sunshine. "We'll have a full house at the ranch. There hasn't been a party there since...I mean—there'll be a crowd."

"I haven't helped prepare anything," she returned, feeling guilty.

"No problem. Half the town has dropped off food and Frankie's been cooking for three days. We'll have leftovers into next week."

How mundane to be discussing leftovers after leaving the church. If she could hold on to such practical things, maybe she'd be able to handle this liaison better than she thought.

Doc and Abby stepped out after them. "Let's get a move on," Doc ordered. "We're going to be surrounded in ten seconds."

His Cadillac was waiting by the door and Lucas helped Susannah get her gown into the back seat and then slid in after her. Abby joined Doc in the front.

They were back at the ranch in five minutes, not enough time to worry about conversation. Halfway there, however, Lucas realized he was still holding Susannah's hand and jerked his away, as if she'd been trying to trap him.

She missed the warmth of his touch. But she wasn't surprised.

"All right, now," Abby said over her shoulder. "You two stand by the front door so you can greet everyone. I'll check on Frankie. He was in the back of the church and scooted out just ahead of you."

For the next hour, Susannah greeted everyone

she'd ever met, and a few strangers, too, as Mrs. Lucas Boyd. It was a strange experience. And draining. When she sagged against Lucas briefly, he immediately called a halt to the line.

"My wife needs to eat something. Did you skip lunch?" he demanded.

Susannah couldn't believe he sounded as if he were her keeper, not her husband. "I ate something."

"What?"

Her mind was buzzing with the day's events. "I don't remember. I'm fine."

Ignoring her protest, he pulled her into the living room and found her a place on the sofa. "I'll bring you some food."

"No, I can—" She didn't finish her protest because he'd disappeared. "Well, really!"

"Let him wait on you, honey. It won't last long," one older lady assured her, laughing.

"True," another chimed in. "When I was pregnant with our first baby, Walter waited on me hand and foot. By the time the third came along, he'd plop down in a chair and ask me to wait on him."

Several other ladies had stories to tell, and Susannah relaxed for the first time that day. And felt more married than she had up till then.

Lucas returned with a plate piled high. "Eat quickly. We need to cut the wedding cake in a few minutes," he warned. "Do you need anything else?" He set a cup of coffee beside her.

"No, I'm fine."

"Go on, Luke, go out to the barn and man-talk. We're taking care of everything here."

He walked away and Susannah looked at the woman who'd spoken. "The barn?"

"At these parties, the men always end up in the barn, having some beers and talking about sports or cows or something else we don't care about."

"Oh. But the cake—"

"There's no rush. Eat up. You'll need your strength for tonight. That boy's all man."

Her ribald comment brought the blood to Susannah's cheeks again, and she tucked into her food. She didn't want to think about tonight, after everyone left. But the image of Lucas, all two hundred hunky pounds of him, was uppermost in her mind.

Abby came over. "Want to remove your veil? Is it bothering you?"

"Yes, thank you, Abby." She hadn't intended to have a veil but according to Abby, Lucas insisted. In fact, she'd intended to buy a plain business suit, one that she could wear again and again. Lucas had nixed that idea, if she believed Abby.

Abby unpinned the veil, careful not to disturb Susannah's hair. She'd felt a little silly curling it to fall around her face, as if she were a teenager trying to impress the boys. But Abby had insisted it looked more bridal than her normal bun.

"You look beautiful," Abby whispered and kissed her on her cheek.

"Are you ready for some cake?" Lucas asked, stepping in front of her a few minutes later. "You took off your veil?"

"Yes, it was giving me a headache," she replied.

"You look beautiful," he repeated Abby's words

without the kiss. It bothered Susannah that his words meant more to her than Abby's. The husky catch in his voice sent an unwanted shiver down her spine.

Taking her hand, he helped her to her feet and escorted her to the formal dining room where she'd dined last week. The chairs were all pulled back from the lace-covered table, and in its center was a magnificent wedding cake.

"Where…?"

"Frankie made it," Lucas whispered.

The man was standing by the door to the kitchen and Susannah left Lucas's side to kiss Frankie's cheek. "Thank you so much, Frankie. The cake is absolutely gorgeous. I'm so amazed."

He beamed at her. "My pleasure."

"All right, stop flirting with Frankie and come back over here," Lucas called, amid much laughter. As if he were really a jealous groom.

She moved back to the table and he slipped his arm around her waist, pulling her close, then handed her the knife and covered her hand with his. The flash of a camera startled her and she almost dropped the knife.

"Hey! I don't want to lose any toes," Lucas joked. Again, everyone gathered around the cake laughed.

She gulped, not bothering to smile.

He guided the knife to the middle tier of the cake, sliding the knife through the creamy icing and cake beneath. Abby held out a plate for the first piece. Once they'd put down the knife, Lucas took the plate and turned to Susannah. "Ready?"

"You're not going to—" she began, fearing he

meant to smear her face with cake as she'd seen some bridegrooms do. She'd always thought it was childish and cruel, but she'd forgotten to discuss this with Lucas. Because she hadn't realized they'd have such a big reception, or a wedding cake.

He stopped her question by taking a small bite of cake and feeding it daintily into her open mouth. "Chew," he ordered. As she automatically followed his order, he bent over and surprised her with a kiss.

"Hey, Luke, we're never gonna get cake if you don't stop kissing your woman!" some male called out.

Susannah, again lost to his touch, jerked back. She stared at Luke, unsure what to do next. He lifted the plate of cake he was holding just a little higher, catching her attention.

"Oh. It's your turn." She took a larger piece between her fingers, and he opened wide. But as he took the cake into his mouth, he captured her hand. Staring at her, he drew each of her fingers into his mouth, licking the icing from them, one at a time.

"Damn, someone get a water hose. They're going to set the house on fire."

The laughter was even louder, increased by a few cheers, and Susannah thought she'd never been so embarrassed in her life.

"All right, you two. Move aside so we can serve this hungry bunch some cake," Abby ordered, as if nothing unusual had occurred.

And maybe it hadn't. If this had been a usual marriage. But Susannah knew it wasn't. Lucas had assured her it wasn't. So why was he acting as if he'd been in love with her forever?

He pulled her aside and answered her unspoken question at once. "I think we fooled 'em," he whispered in her ear, his arm around her waist. At his touch she felt a familiar current of longing travel through her.

Of course, she should've known. Lucas Boyd would be too proud to let people know his marriage was one of convenience. Probably, in the barn, he'd been telling everyone how crazy she was about him.

The sad thing was, it might be the truth. It would help explain her reaction to him. But he didn't know. Or want to know. And, if she were smart, she'd make sure it wasn't true.

After the cake was served, people began leaving. The crowd thinned out enough that Susannah noticed the huge pile of presents they'd brought. She'd already had a shower Thursday night, receiving some lovely, thoughtful gifts. It had surprised her that many of them were personal. She now owned an array of beautiful nightgowns and underwear.

One of which she would wear tonight.

Quickly she shifted her thoughts. She'd never make it through to the end of the reception if she started thinking about what was to come.

Lucas couldn't focus on the conversations going on around him. All he could think about was tonight.

When the reception was over, he and Susannah would go upstairs and consummate their marriage. And make a child.

"There he goes again," one of his cowboys said, punching his friend with his elbow. "He drifts off, with that look on his face. Think maybe he's worried about the herd?" Then he laughed uproariously as if he'd made a witty comment.

"What are you talking about?" Lucas asked.

"Don't mind Mike. He thinks you're thinking about what's going to happen after we leave," one of his neighbors explained.

"Yeah," Mike chimed in, "and we ain't talking about the cleaning up!" He laughed again.

Several others joined him as Lucas felt his cheeks redden. Hell, he hadn't realized he'd been so open.

Another neighbor, older, made a big production of looking at his watch. "It *is* getting late. Probably we should all pack it in."

"Late? Hell, it's only eight o'clock," Mike protested. "I think we should make another run at the food. You've still got enough to feed an army."

Lucas considered telling him to have all the food he wanted—to go. He didn't want to be inhospitable, but he was ready for the reception to end. He looked over the guests' heads, searching for Susannah.

Fortunately for his patience, some of his neighbors decided an early departure was called for and began a general movement toward the door. Which meant, of course, that Susannah would come to tell them bye.

So he didn't have to search for her anymore.

Instead they reversed the procedure for the afternoon, staying by the door to tell their well-wishers goodbye.

By the time the last of them, Doc and Abby, had left, it was closer to ten than nine. He thought Susannah looked even more tense than she had earlier.

"Why don't you go on up and get ready. I'll help Frankie straighten the furniture for a few minutes." He thought it was a tactful way to give her some time alone.

She didn't even smile. With a stiff nod, she hurried up the stairs, as if escaping.

He stared after her, frowning. What was wrong? Everything had gone well. They'd convinced the entire town that they were in love. That they were eager for their wedding bed.

Well, maybe that last thought hadn't taken much work. There was some kind of chemical reaction every time he touched her. It wasn't love. He was sure of that, but his body responded to that lady like a stick of dynamite to a match.

"Hey, boss, I don't need no help. Most of it can be left until tomorrow," Frankie assured him.

"It's okay. The groom is supposed to give the bride a little time to herself."

"Oh. It's a good thing I never married. I woulda messed up good, 'cause I wouldn't be able to wait. She's some looker, Mrs. Boyd. And nice, too."

"Yeah. I didn't think she was pretty at first, but she kind of grows on you."

They moved the chairs back around the table in the dining room. When they finished there, Frankie started into the living room, assuming Lucas would follow.

He stopped and stared up the stairs.

"Uh, Frankie, I think I'll go on up, now, if you don't mind."

"Right. I'll go to the bunkhouse for tonight, but I'll cook breakfast for you in the morning."

"Uh, okay, but probably not till eight."

He figured his wife could sleep in the day after her wedding. Hell, Beth had slept in most of the time, especially when she was pregnant. She said she wasn't a morning person.

Suddenly realizing he didn't know if Susannah was a morning person or not, he hurried up the stairs. Not that it mattered, but...he felt funny, knowing so little about his bride.

Except that he wanted her more than he'd ever wanted a woman in his life.

But it was only because of that strange chemistry.

Unexplainable but true.

He took the last two steps in one and reached the door to his bedroom. Mindful of her possible shyness, he rapped before he opened it.

With a smile on his face, he stepped in and came to an abrupt halt. There was no sign of Susannah here. No suitcases. No bed turned down. No scent of perfume in the air.

He crossed the room to the bathroom door. Another knock before he impatiently opened it. Nothing. No feminine clothes, no makeup, or the usual clutter a woman left in the bathroom. He hadn't realized, until that minute, how much he'd missed that feminine presence.

Where was she?

The thought that she had changed her mind and

returned to town was enough to take his breath away. He charged through the bedroom, throwing open his door, preparing to shout at Frankie, when the door across from his opened.

Chapter Nine

She stood there, pale and trembling, in a simple silk gown in shell pink that brought out red highlights in her long hair. Her teeth sank into her bottom lip and troubled eyes met his.

He looked over her shoulder. There were her bags. The wedding dress was laid across the bed. White pumps were beside it. "Frankie must've put your things in the wrong room. Our bedroom is across the hall."

"No. I didn't think you'd want to share a room, since—" She broke off and stared at her feet. When he said nothing, she added, "So I took this one, if you don't mind."

He stared at her blankly. What could he say? *No, I want you in my bed every night.* That made him sound like a demanding, insensitive male. "Okay."

When she didn't move, he slowly reached out and took her hand. She didn't resist, so he tugged her toward him. "But we'll, uh, you'll come to my bed. My son is going to be conceived in my bed, okay?"

To his relief, she didn't refuse.

But she also didn't exhibit any enthusiasm for what lay ahead. He didn't understand why. He might be distracted by his reaction to her every time he touched her, but he knew she responded, too. In fact, it was that response that put him over the top.

He'd loved Beth with all his heart. But the physical side of marriage hadn't interested her. She "did her duty" but found pleasure in other things.

Unaware of his thoughts, Susannah stepped into his room. Her gaze focused on the king-size bed, and she stopped. He frowned, unsure what to do next. Was she afraid of making love?

He touched her arm and found it icy cold. As if— if she were a virgin. That thought slammed into him with all the strength of an earthquake.

"Susannah, you're not—I mean, you have—damn it, this isn't your first time, is it?"

Her cheeks flooded with color and she barely nodded.

"You are?" He hadn't believed any woman over the age of twenty was inexperienced.

"I'm sorry."

Her soft apology awakened him from his surprise and brought a frown to his face. "You have nothing to apologize for, Susannah. I wasn't aware— It makes no difference."

She swallowed convulsively. "I—I don't know how—" She broke off and looked away.

All her concern, her nervousness was suddenly explained, and Lucas breathed a sigh of relief. With a smile, he added, "That's okay. I do know how. Everything will be fine, Susannah."

She nodded but said nothing, still not looking at him.

"I like your nightgown," he said softly, running a finger up her bare arm to slip beneath the strap. She shivered and shot him a quick glance before dropping her gaze again.

He moved closer.

"Is it new?" he asked, both hands now caressing her arms.

It had been a long time since he'd seduced a woman. An inexperienced woman. He hadn't run across one of those very often. Usually he'd moved on.

But he found the need to seduce Susannah incredibly attractive. And he couldn't quite extinguish a feeling of satisfaction that he would be her first. And her last. Bending over, he kissed her on the corner of her sexy lips. "You smell good, too."

"So—so do you."

"I haven't had my shower yet. You won't go away if I take a quick one, will you?"

It bothered him that she seemed to welcome the respite his shower offered. Her shy smile almost had him changing his mind. But it was her wedding night. He wanted everything perfect.

"Just make yourself at home. I won't be a minute." He backed to the bathroom door, relief flooding him as she walked to the bed and sat down on its edge.

* * *

She'd almost melted.

When he'd touched her, she'd had to fight to keep from throwing her arms around his neck, pressing her body against his, begging for his kiss.

Thank goodness she'd been able to control herself, to keep him from knowing how needy she was. They were going to make a baby, not love. And he would be embarrassed to know that she wanted his touch, craved his caress. She still couldn't quite believe her reaction to him.

She closed her eyes and concentrated on control. On pretending to be blasé about what was about to happen. On pretending.

True to his word, Lucas opened the bathroom door in no time. She gulped as he stood before her, a towel wrapped around his waist.

His broad, hairy chest tapered to slim hips and muscular legs and she couldn't stop staring. She'd been an only child and her limited experience with her fiancé, much to his disappointment, hadn't involved disrobing.

"Am I embarrassing you?" he asked, moving toward her, a grin on his face. "I could get dressed, but then I'd have to take it all off again. It didn't seem worth the effort."

His relaxed air was a novelty, one that eased Susannah's tension. She didn't know lovers could find amusement as well as possible passion. With a hesitant smile, she said, "I'd hate for you to waste all that energy."

"My thoughts exactly. I'd much rather put it to better use."

She shivered, her eyes growing wide.

"You look like Little Red Riding Hood when the Big Bad Wolf said he wanted to eat her. Do I scare you?"

No, I scare myself. "No, of course not."

"Good." He reached the bed. "Want me to turn back the covers?"

"Oh! I can—can do that." She stood, glad for something to do, and pulled back the bedspread and sheet. As she straightened, strong arms slid around her waist and his lips lightly caressed her shoulder.

She held herself still, not sure what her reaction should be. When he did nothing else, she looked over her shoulder.

"Look, Susannah, let's make a pact."

Turning to face him, she waited for him to explain. Had he changed his mind? Was he going to suggest they turn to Doc, as she had suggested earlier?

"This is an awkward situation. So I think we should be honest with each other. If I do something you don't like, that makes you uncomfortable, just tell me."

"And you'll tell me if I do something wrong?" she asked, relief filling her.

He pulled her close against him and she was startled to feel his arousal through the towel. "I think that's highly unlikely. I haven't been with a woman in a long time, sweetheart, and I'm liable to embarrass myself at any moment."

It hadn't occurred to her that he might be nervous

or concerned about his performance. Immediately she yearned to set him at ease. Her lips planted butterfly kisses on his face, as she'd dreamed of doing.

As if she'd detonated a bomb, their lovemaking exploded. His mouth devoured hers even as his hands urged the gown up her body. Her hands roamed his chest, delighting in the hard muscles.

Before she knew it, her gown and panties and his towel had fallen to the floor and the two of them were stretched out on the bed. He covered her body with his as he intimately stroked and caressed her skin, and she met him at every turn.

When he entered her, his lips returned to hers, urging her to join in the frantic pleasure, but she needed no encouragement. She'd never experienced such joy, such oneness, even though there was a temporary discomfort. She hadn't even known making love could be so pleasurable.

Everything seemed to explode at once, and Susannah wasn't sure if she lost consciousness or not. When she opened her eyes, filled with incredulous joy, Lucas's eyes remained closed. His body slid from hers, and he slumped beside her. His mouth moved, mumbling something, but she couldn't understand the words.

And he slept.

She lay beside him, her gaze tracing the strength of his body. It occurred to her that, had she been asked, she would never have agreed to make love with the light on. But she hadn't even remembered to be self-conscious once Lucas touched her.

Had he realized? Had it been obvious that she'd been overwhelmed by his lovemaking?

Strangely enough, her thoughts turned to Beth, his wife. Poor Beth. She had had Lucas as her husband, had shared his bed, had conceived his child, had owned his heart.

Now Susannah would have all but the last, if she was lucky. Her emotions changed from remorse for Beth to sadness for herself. Because owning Lucas's heart suddenly seemed a prize beyond belief.

Enough, Susannah. No feeling sorry for yourself. You've made your bed, so lie in it. She almost giggled. Not many women would complain about the bed she'd made, as long as Lucas Boyd filled it.

And he'd given her an incredible gift. She wasn't frigid. In fact, she had to fight herself now to keep a distance between their two bodies.

So she had nothing to complain about.

To ensure that she maintained control, she'd have to go back to her bedroom. Otherwise, she wouldn't be able to keep her hands off him. Even now, she wanted to stroke him all over, to learn his body, every indentation, every muscle. To meet his lips with hers.

And he wanted to sleep.

With one last, long, greedy look, she slid from the bed. Picking up her nightgown and bikini panties, she returned to her sanctuary.

And dreamed of Lucas.

Lucas opened one eye, a smile on his face. Why was he feeling so wonderful? Then he remembered.

Susannah. And the incredible lovemaking they'd shared.

He reached out for her warm body. And found nothing. Both eyes popped open and he sat up. The lights were still on. He had no difficulty seeing that he was alone.

He sprang from the bed and hurried to the closed door. Crossing the hall, he eased open the door to the room across from his. It was dark, but he could see the faint outline of her body under the covers. She was alseep.

Frowning, he closed the door. He didn't want her in that room. He wanted her in his bed. Had he upset her? Done something wrong? Disgusted her with his uncontrollable passion?

The last few moments with her in his arms had gone by incredibly fast. He hadn't spent much time holding her before he'd taken his pleasure.

Damn! He hadn't meant to be so selfish. But it had been so long for him, his body had taken control. He thought Susannah had received some pleasure, because he remembered a sweet moan that had urged him on. And her lips touching him as he'd kissed her incredible body.

He opened the door again, his gaze tracing her outline. He wanted to scoop her up in his arms, carry her back to his bed and tell her she could never leave. He even took a step toward her.

His conscience stopped him. They'd agreed to make a child. He'd warned her there would be no emotion. She'd chosen a bedroom separate from him.

She wanted her privacy.

He wanted her.

He closed the door again. Okay, so he'd give her privacy. For a while. They'd ease into this marriage business slowly. Maybe they could become friends.

As long as they continued to be lovers. For whatever reason, Susannah gave him more pleasure than he'd ever experienced. A pleasure that he longed to repeat as soon as possible.

But she didn't want to wake up beside him. She didn't want more lovemaking tonight. She didn't want him to touch her, to hold her against him.

Even thinking about such actions caused a reaction in him. He backed across the hall into his room and shut the door. It was the only way to ensure that he didn't spoil everything.

And the next time he made love to Susannah, he would take it slower, give her pleasure before he took his own.

He couldn't wait.

After a shower the next morning, Susannah dressed in slacks and a shirt and made the courageous trek to the kitchen. She wasn't sure how she would be able to face Lucas this morning.

She didn't have long to wait. He was leaning against the kitchen counter, talking to Frankie as he rinsed some dishes.

As soon as Lucas saw her, he crossed the room to greet her. With a brief kiss, before nodding in Frankie's direction. "Frankie thought maybe you'd like some cinnamon rolls for breakfast this morning."

She understood his meaning. Thankfully her lips

hadn't clung to his, as they'd wanted to. He was kissing her for Frankie's benefit. She cleared her throat.

"That's very thoughtful of you, Frankie, but really, it isn't necessary to go to so much trouble."

"No trouble. How about some coffee, too?"

"I'd love some."

To her surprise, it was Lucas who brought her coffee as she sat down at the table. "You shouldn't wait on me, Lucas. I could've—"

"Hey, it's your first day in your new home. I think that deserves a little pampering," he said and sat down beside her.

Frankie brought a plate of warm cinnamon rolls to the table and then added a bowl of fresh fruit from the refrigerator.

Nervous, Susannah smiled at the man. "Won't you join us for a coffee break, Frankie? You must've been up early to make these rolls."

A smile broke across his face. "I don't mind if I do. Boss, you want more coffee before I sit down?"

Lucas shoved his cup forward as an answer. After pouring more coffee, Frankie joined them. Susannah struggled to eat, under two pairs of eagle eyes, while the men didn't hesitate to finish several rolls.

"When you're through, we probably need to start opening gifts," Lucas told her. "We got a delivery this morning from the church. Seems a lot of people left presents there, as well. You're going to be writing thank-you notes for months."

Susannah turned to look at him. "What's this *you*, Tonto? I thought we were in this together."

It was Lucas's turn to stare. "What do you mean?"

"I mean *we* will be writing thank-you notes. Not just me." She smiled at his reaction.

"But that's woman's work," he protested, rearing back in his chair.

"Come into the nineties," she suggested dryly.

"Susannah, I mean Mrs. Boyd, is right, Lucas. Men are supposed to do lady things these days. It says so in the magazines," Frankie assured him.

"When did you read a ladies' magazine?" Lucas demanded, glaring at his cook.

"At the dentist's office in the Springs last year. You wouldn't believe what they put in those magazines."

"Thank you for your support, Frankie. And, please, call me Susannah. It will take me a while to remember to respond to Mrs. Boyd." She blinked several times as Lucas turned his glare on her. Was he upset that she expected him to help with the thank-you notes?

"All right. I'll do it, but you've got to help, too, Frankie," he suddenly said.

"Me? I can't write no thank-you notes."

"No, but you can help open the presents. You and I will do the grunt work and Susannah can make a list of who gave us what."

Susannah downed her last sip of coffee and rose. "That sounds like a good plan. Let me rinse these dishes and—"

"Here now, Susannah, that's my job," Frankie

protested. "You're not thinking of doing me out of my job, are you?"

"Of course not, Frankie. I couldn't do it half so well as you. But I don't need to be waited on."

Frankie seemed pleased with her response, even as Lucas stared at her, frowning. She didn't know what she'd done to upset him this morning, but she was pleased that Frankie would be with them. It eased the awkwardness a little.

She'd thought the matter of opening presents would be quickly resolved, but when she entered the living room, the pile she'd seen last night seemed to have multiplied like rabbits.

"Good heavens! I didn't expect—this is too much."

"Yeah," Lucas agreed, rubbing his nape in embarrassment. "Seems folks were real happy about me marryin' again."

She watched him, her gaze greedily following every movement. She wasn't surprised. For this man to be a hermit would be an incredible waste.

"Here's paper and a pen," Frankie said, entering the room.

"Well, let's get started," Lucas ordered.

They worked for several hours, sharing laughter and appreciation for the various gifts they received. A handmade quilt almost brought tears to Susannah's eyes, and she stroked the soft material as it lay across her lap.

Lucas followed the movement of those hands, remembering how they'd touched him last night. And hungered for them to do so again.

His instincts had been right. Susannah would be a wonderful mother. Her gentle hands would console and love a child.

The bootjack, in the shape of a big frog, brought a different reaction. Amid giggles that felt like champagne bubbles in his stomach, she stared at the metal creation.

"Show me how it works," she insisted, pulling on Lucas's arm.

"Haven't you used one before?"

"No. I don't own any boots."

He eyed her slender feet. "We'll correct that situation real soon."

"Why would I need them?"

"Darlin'," he drawled, "you're living on a ranch now. You're the rancher's wife. Of course you'll need boots."

She stared at him but offered no argument. He put one foot on the jack and the heel of his other boot in the notch and pulled. The boot slid off.

"Oh, I like that," she said, clapping her hands.

He raised one eyebrow, but a smile tugged at his lips. She liked a lot of things. He hoped one of them was his lovemaking.

After lunch, organized by Frankie with the leftover food from the night before, Lucas put an end to their work. "We'll finish later. I need a break."

"But we could—"

"Nope," he returned to Susannah's protest. "You could use a nap. Yesterday was pretty stressful."

"A nap? I never—"

"I'll go check on the bunkhouse," Frankie said and left the room. At least one person had understood his intention. Unfortunately, it wasn't the one he was interested in.

"Did we offend Frankie?" Susannah asked, looking at him curiously.

"Nope. He was just getting out of the way."

"Out of the way of what?"

"Our going upstairs to my bed."

He'd shocked her. That much was clear.

"But—but it's the middle of the day." Her lower lip was trembling again.

"I know, but it takes real dedication to make a baby. Night and day." When she looked doubtful, he desperately asked, "Want to call Doc to ask him? I'm sure I'm right about this."

"Of course not!" she exclaimed, her cheeks reddening. "I just—I didn't—"

"Hell, sweetheart, if it makes you uncomfortable we can confine our efforts to darkness, but it may take us a little longer." It hurt that she wasn't as eager as he was, but that wasn't going to stop him. He was too hungry for her. Unless she said no.

"No, of course I'm willing—I didn't know—I mean—" She broke off, as if she couldn't figure out what to say.

He took her hand and pulled her to her feet, sending the duly recorded list to the floor. Then he scooped her up into his arms and headed for the stairs.

"Lucas, I'm too heavy. You'll hurt yourself."

"I'm gonna hurt myself if I don't get you in my bed, lady," he assured her as he climbed the stairs. By the time he reached the top, his breathing was heavy. But he wasn't sure if the exertion caused it, or if her body pressed against his chest was the reason.

After pushing past the door and shutting it behind him, he looked into Susannah's eyes. To his relief, she smiled at him.

"I wouldn't want you to be injured," she assured him softly and held her lips up for his kiss.

Chapter Ten

Susannah prepared for work the next morning, her cautious heart wondering if she could really be happy living with the man she had developed a craving for…but didn't love, she hurriedly assured herself.

She'd learned a lot yesterday. That sex was as good in sunlight as moonlight with Lucas Boyd. That pillow talk provided an intimacy she'd never experienced, one that brought smiles to the bedroom, another new experience. Even though Lucas's gentle teasing held nothing significant and didn't mean he cared about her, it represented a closeness new to her.

And she learned that she was no more frigid than the hottest salsa served south of the border. She didn't know why, except perhaps that incredible chemistry between them. Or maybe he was a superlative lover. But he could melt her bones with a look. When he touched her, she had no resistance at all.

So, all in all, she descended the stairs that Monday morning with a good feeling about the future. When she entered the kitchen, she headed straight for the coffeepot, needing caffeine to substitute for the lack of sleep their lovemaking had caused.

"Morning," Frankie called.

"Good morning. I could get used to you having a pot of coffee ready every morning, Frankie. I'm being spoiled."

"You got to have more than coffee. Sit down and I'll fix you breakfast."

"Just a piece of toast, please. I'm running late."

"Where are you going?"

It wasn't Frankie who asked that question, but her husband, Lucas, standing just inside the back door.

She raised her eyebrows. "To work, of course."

"Nonsense. You're my wife. You don't need to work," he asserted firmly as he stepped forward to the coffeepot.

Shaking her head to clear it, she waited until he had his first sip of coffee before she answered. She kept her response mild, not wanting to argue. "Really?"

He must've thought that word indicated amazement at his generosity. With a smile, he leaned forward to brush her lips with his. "Of course, sweetheart. I told you I'd provide—" He halted to glance at Frankie. "We're okay financially."

Anger rose in her. He thought he could simply dictate her life? Without saying anything to him, she turned to Frankie. "I'll be back a little after five,

Frankie. If you have something to do, I can fix dinner."

Then she turned to leave, only to be stopped by Lucas's hand on her arm. "Didn't you hear me?"

"Of course I did," she responded, struggling to hold on to her control.

"Then why are you going to work?"

"Because I want to. Because I committed myself to the job before I ever met you. Because a librarian is who I am. Because you're going to work today, so why shouldn't I?" She finished by drawing the breath she'd suspended during her rapid-fire response.

"Because you don't have to," he countered, his voice more forceful.

With a coldness she wouldn't have believed possible when she'd shared his bed the night before, she only said, "Excuse me."

Her effort to move past him failed.

"Damn it! Why won't you listen to me? We had an agree—" Again he halted and looked at Frankie. "Uh, we'd better go to my office to discuss this."

"I don't have time. I'm going to be late as it is." She tugged at his hold on her but was unable to break loose.

Lucas appeared stunned that she didn't fall in with his suggestion at once. "You are my wife!" he roared. "You'll do as I say!"

It was just as well she hadn't gone into the marriage with rose-colored glasses on, she thought. The honeymoon was definitely over. "I will do as I think best, Lucas Boyd, and nothing you can do will change that. Now, turn loose of my arm.''

''You promised to obey me Saturday!'' he reminded her.

''No, I didn't. The pastor asked me if I objected to that wording just before the ceremony. He left it out. You should've listened.'' She gave a powerful jerk on her arm and escaped out the door. Wasting no time, she hurried to her car and drove off.

Lucas stood there fuming.

He could've caught up with her, of course, but what would he have done with her then? He had no idea. After yesterday, he'd thought the marriage idea had been a brilliant move. Now he wasn't so sure.

''Boss, you can't talk to her like that. That women's magazine said—''

''Frankie, I will not allow your afternoon in the dentist's office to rule my marriage.''

''I don't know why not. It lasted almost as long,'' Frankie muttered as he sidled out the back door, escaping his boss's temper.

When Lucas finally returned to the barn after ranting in solitude about the contrariness of a certain woman, he discovered that his difficulties were well-known. His men, apparently thrilled with the changes in him since Susannah came into his life, offered several hints to help him get along with his bride.

''You gotta sweet-talk women.''

''Flowers are a good thing.''

''It don't hurt none to have a working wife.''

''You oughtta apologize.''

He finally exploded. "Mind your own business! I'll take care of Susannah. She's *my* wife."

The cowboys slinked away to their various jobs, leaving him alone again, feeling lower to the ground than a pig's belly.

And the only thing that would make him feel better was for a certain contrary woman to return home that evening.

In spite of their disagreement about her work, something they never discussed again, Susannah found a satisfying routine in her new life. She spent her day doing the work she loved. Then she returned home to her husband. That word never ceased to thrill her.

Each night, after she went upstairs, he would knock on her door and lead her to his bed. There was no discussion, only a desire that enflamed them when they touched.

After their lovemaking, Susannah, in spite of Lucas's requests for her to stay, returned to her own bed. It was her only protection from complete submission to his powerful presence. But she longed to wrap herself in his strong arms, to snuggle against him, listening to the rise and fall of his breath. Feeling his hands as they roamed her body, feather touches that sent shimmers across her skin.

But she denied herself those pleasures.

She dreaded the arrival of the wrong time of the month for their lovemaking. She was becoming addicted to his touch. In a normal marriage, the husband and wife might still cuddle, whisper in the dark, hold each other as they fell asleep. But Lucas had no interest in those things.

So she waited with dread.

Only her period never came.

When she was a week late, she drove on Saturday all the way into Colorado Springs to an anonymous drugstore to purchase several pregnancy kits.

Lucas protested the trip without knowing the reason for it. He'd made plans to show her around the ranch. While she would have loved the attention, she felt an urgency to discover if she was pregnant.

She waited another week. Then, the next Saturday morning, she took the test. It was positive.

Now she faced a true dilemma. If she told Lucas she was pregnant, he would be thrilled. But he also wouldn't see a need for them to continue to make love.

While Susannah was thrilled, also, at the idea of a child, her child, she mourned the loss of intimacy with Lucas. Her mood that day, as he gave her the postponed tour of his beloved land, alternated between despondency and exhilaration.

"Are you all right?" Lucas asked her after a couple of hours.

"Yes, of course!" she gasped. "What do you mean?"

"You seemed distracted," he said pointedly, reaching over to cover her clasped hands. "Are you sure you're not wearing yourself out with the job?"

It was the first time he'd mentioned her job since their argument. "No. I enjoy my work."

With a grunt he accelerated, leaving the south pasture behind. "Want to see my prized Black Angus bull? We call him Rocky, but that's not his registered name." He rattled off a scientific-sounding name.

"Is he big?"

"He's huge. But he's as tame as a baby." His gaze drifted to her stomach and she sat up straighter. Had he guessed her secret?

It was the first time they'd spent so much time in each other's company since the Sunday after their wedding. Susannah found herself charmed all over again with Lucas's gentlemanly behavior, his teasing. He might not love her, but he was kind.

They shared a picnic lunch that Frankie had prepared. Lucas urged her to eat more when she picked at her food. But she was discovering a queasy stomach with her pregnancy.

Before Lucas could wonder at how little she ate, he was distracted by the weather. It was November now, and the clouds had built up suddenly.

"We'd better pack it in and get back to the house."

"Why?" Had she displeased him?

"I think we're going to have our first real snowstorm of the winter. We don't want to get trapped out here."

He'd been right. The snow closed in on them as they pulled in near the barn. He sent her into the house. That night, when he came in, Frankie had built a fire in the fireplace for them, and she snuggled in his arms before a dying fire, contentment filling her.

"You don't mind the snow?" he asked, his arm wrapped around her.

"No, I like cold weather." The man would have to be blind to think she was unhappy, she decided with a smile. In fact, she'd never been happier.

When he led her upstairs to his bed, she was glad she hadn't shared her news with him. She wanted more days like today, more possibilities to share their inner selves with each other. Somewhere, in the back of her mind, hovered the idea that their marriage might become a true one, filled with exchanges and togetherness.

December. Lucas emerged from his room at his normal time, even though he wouldn't start work quite as early. The days were growing shorter and the chores lighter with the wintertime.

But hell, why not get up at his regular time? He had no reason to linger under the warm covers. His wife refused to share his bed. Oh, she'd let him make love to her. In fact, she'd met him more than half-way. Her innocent joy in his touch, the sweet moans that slipped out as he loved her, her utter contentment afterward, made his control problematic.

He'd blamed his need for her on the three years he'd remained celibate, but after six weeks of love-making almost every day, he had to admit he wanted her. More and more.

He paused as he passed Susannah's door. Some noise had distracted him. Leaning closer, he thought it sounded like someone throwing up.

Was Susannah sick? He almost bolted through the

closed door before a thought struck him. *She might be pregnant.* Some women experienced morning sickness, he knew, though Beth never had.

Exhilaration filled him. His son. The child he needed. The reason he'd entered a loveless marriage. The reason he and Susannah—his joy came to a screeching halt. If Susannah was pregnant, there would be no need for those nights in his bed. She might refuse to ever let him touch her again.

He turned to stone, his mind frantically dealing with those revelations. He didn't want to give up the intimacy he'd found with Susannah.

What was the hurry? If she didn't tell him she was pregnant, he didn't have to admit it. He could continue making love to her. Maybe she didn't know, yet. She probably thought she had the flu.

Or maybe she did have the flu. He was no doctor. Only her lover.

He tiptoed down the stairs, pretending he never heard her physical distress. She'd have to tell him before he'd give up those incredible nights with her in his bed.

Christmas Day. Last Christmas Susannah had been in the throes of decision-making. She'd been living in Denver, alone, after her mother's death, trying to decide what to do with herself.

Alone. Unhappy.

Then, she'd taken the job in Caliente. And decided to have a child.

She rubbed her still flat stomach. She'd noticed a slight thickening of her waist, a sensitivity to her breasts, that confirmed the pregnancy test. She was going to have to see Dr. Grable soon.

But not before she told her husband.

She'd decided today was the day. His gift, along with a fine leather wallet and some new cologne, would be his child. Today, beside the Christmas tree she'd decorated with her family's special ornaments, she would tell Lucas that his wish had come true.

Abby and Dr. Grable were joining them for Christmas dinner. Susannah spent the morning in the kitchen helping Frankie prepare the meal.

"Susannah, I can't thank you enough for that Cuisinart. I've been wantin' one of those things for a long time," Frankie told her as he operated the new machine.

"But why didn't you tell Lucas? He would've bought you one." She knew Lucas appreciated Frankie's work and wouldn't have hesitated to provide him with anything he requested.

"Aw, I didn't *need* it. The boss was feelin' so bad, it seemed low-down to bother him."

Susannah was touched by Frankie's concern. She kissed him on the cheek. "You're a good man, Frankie."

"Hey, what's this? You trying to seduce my wife, Frankie?" Lucas called from the doorway. He laughed when Frankie turned red in the face and jumped away from Susannah.

"Shame on you, Lucas Boyd," she reprimanded. "I was expressing our appreciation to Frankie."

He crossed to her side and casually slid an arm around her shoulders. More and more, he touched her freely, making her feel he was more comfortable with her as each day went by.

"Sorry, Frankie. But I figured that expensive machine told him we appreciated him. I hate to see the bills come in after Christmas. You bought every cowboy on the ranch a present. They're all calling you Santa Claus."

He was grinning at her, so she didn't think he really minded her gifts. Besides, there would be no bills. She'd paid for everything herself.

"They work hard" was Susannah's only comment.

"So do I. Is there something for me under the tree?"

"Aw, boss, you know there is. I caught you looking at the tags on the boxes the other day," Frankie said.

"Quit giving away my secrets," Lucas protested. Then he pulled Susannah under the mistletoe hanging over the door and kissed her.

Maybe she was going to get her wish for Christmas, too. She wanted a real marriage, a real husband, because she was discovering she couldn't do without Lucas Boyd. And she was afraid that feeling was called love.

Dinner had been served and greatly appreciated. The dishes had been cleared and Frankie had gone to join the other men at the bunkhouse. Then presents were opened. Susannah had taken special care in gifts for Abby and Doc.

After all, they'd had a part in the changes in her life.

As she rose to gather the wrapping paper and throw it away, Doc got up to help.

In the kitchen, he asked softly, "You feeling okay?"

Susannah jumped in surprise. "What do you mean?"

"You've changed a little. I just wondered—"

"I'll be in for an appointment next week," she admitted, unwilling to say the actual words before she told Lucas.

"Ah. Good." He said nothing else, and Susannah knew he wouldn't reveal anything to Lucas. But she was on needles and pins the rest of the evening. Lucas had to be the first to know.

After Abby and Doc had left, Lucas drew her down on the couch in front of the glowing Christmas tree. With his arm around her, her body pressed to his, he smiled at her.

"I want you to know I appreciate your efforts for Christmas. The whole place is happier. Those idiotic cowboys tell me every day how lucky I am to have you around here. Every last one of them would do anything you asked."

"They're sweet."

"Come on, Susannah, they're men. No one ever called them sweet before." He pulled her a little closer.

"I'm glad everyone was pleased. Did you like your presents?"

"Of course. I've been needing a new wallet and the—"

"I haven't given you your real present." She held her breath, excited but afraid.

"You haven't? But I don't have anything else to give you," he said with a frown.

She fingered the diamond ear studs he'd given her. She'd never owned such expensive jewelry. "You gave me more than enough. My earrings are beautiful."

"So what's my other present?"

She hesitated and then whispered, "Your child."

Unsure what his reaction would be, she waited as he grew absolutely still, not moving. Wasn't he happy?

He removed his arm from her shoulders and slewed around to almost face her. "You're sure?"

She nodded.

"When?"

"I think around the first of August. I'll go see Doc next week."

"He knows?"

"I haven't told him. He asked about my health today, so I think he suspects."

"Are you feeling all right?"

He looked worried, a frown on his brow. Susannah couldn't resist smoothing it away with her fingers. "I'm fine. I get a little sick in the mornings, but that's all."

"You should stop work at once," he ordered.

"No."

"Susannah, be sensible. I don't want you to take any risks. This baby—"

Her heart sank. She'd hoped for an avowal of love. Instead she'd received what she should've expected. Concern for his child.

Unable to bear the disappointment, she rose to her feet. "I'm going to bed now. Thank you for my earrings."

"Susannah—" he called but she ignored him. The tears sliding down her cheeks wouldn't allow her to stay near him. She would hide in her room to lick her wounds. Alone.

No, not alone. She and her child would be together.

Lucas sat on the couch alone. He'd upset her, but he wasn't sure how. He'd suspected for several weeks that she was pregnant, but it had suited him not to know.

Now, he no longer had a choice. He couldn't pretend a need to plant his seed in her. To hold her in his arms, to revel in the sensations she aroused in him every time he touched her.

But in exchange, he had knowledge of his son. His child. His reason for the future. He lost himself in dreams of the child with whom he would build the future. But the picture wasn't as bright as he'd once thought it would be.

Because of Susannah. He didn't know what to do about Susannah. Tonight, he'd climb those stairs, as he had every night since his wedding. But would

Susannah be receptive to his touch? Would she willingly come to his room, melt into his arms?

He paced the floor, debating what he should do until the hour had advanced more than he'd realized. Finally creeping up the stairs, he opened her door without knocking. She lay in her bed, the covers pulled snugly around her, her back to the door.

With a grieving that shocked him, he quietly closed the door and turned to his own room, alone. She had no interest in him anymore. He'd given her what she wanted, a child.

He slid into his bed, prepared to dream of his child. Instead, he found himself mourning his loss of Susannah.

Chapter Eleven

Susannah awoke the next morning at her normal time. But that was the only thing normal. She hadn't visited Lucas's bed last night. He had let her go to her room, and he hadn't disturbed her.

Because he had what he wanted.

Oh, how she'd hoped he would still want her. She should've known. After all, she was inexperienced. While he'd never complained about her lovemaking, she'd feared he might not enjoy it as much as she.

Tears seeped from her eyes, as they'd done last night. She hadn't realized how much she'd counted on their marriage being real. But she had. Because she'd fallen in love with that ornery man.

The father of her child.

She dressed and went downstairs. She couldn't hide in her room all day because her dreams hadn't come true. Even after the baby was born, she still had to face Lucas each day, pretending not to love him. Pretending not to want him. She might as well learn to hide her feelings today.

Besides, the library was closed both today and tomorrow. She wasn't sure what she was going to do with herself, but she'd find something.

Frankie was in the kitchen and greeted her with a cup of coffee and toast.

"Where's Lucas?"

"He went to the barn half an hour ago. Didn't seem in a very good mood. Hope he's not catching the flu that's going around," Frankie said, frowning.

Susannah's heart leaped in spite of her warnings to herself. Maybe he was missing the lovemaking. Maybe he'd bring her back to his bed. Maybe…she'd better think of something besides the bedroom.

When the door opened as she was finishing her coffee, however, she couldn't help searching his face eagerly for some telltale sign that he'd missed her last night.

He ignored her completely, concentrating on the coffeepot rather than her. "It's cold out there."

"Yeah," Frankie agreed. He, too, studied Lucas. "You coming down with something, boss?"

Lucas turned to stare at his cook. "Coming down with what?"

"The flu. Heard it was goin' around."

Lucas shot her a look but she couldn't read his expression. "No, of course not. I'm fine. Slept great last night."

Susannah felt her stomach clench at his words. Drawing a deep breath, she fought to keep her breakfast down. Misery and coffee weren't a good mix for a pregnant woman.

"How about you, Susannah? How did you sleep?" Lucas suddenly asked, staring at her.

Unexpected anger invaded her misery. Was he taunting her? Did he think she would beg for his touch? Did he think he could reject her and she'd still want him? With a control that surprised even her, she smiled at him and said, "Like a baby."

The temperature seemed to drop in the kitchen. Frankie looked up suddenly, his gaze going from one to the other of the pair at the table. "Uh, I gotta put in a load of laundry. Back in a minute."

If she'd hoped for tenderness in their first moment alone, she had to be satisfied with a gruff question. "Are you feeling all right?"

"Fine," she returned.

"No throwing up?"

After successfully battling nausea, she was surprised by her sudden response to his question. She leaped from the chair and just made it to the kitchen sink in time to rid herself of breakfast.

When she felt his hands on her, trying to ease her distress, Susannah couldn't help the shiver that coursed through her. She'd longed for his touch. Straightening, after washing her face, she tried to smile, but she wasn't very successful.

Especially when Lucas immediately dropped his hands and stepped away.

"Have you talked to Doc about throwing up?"

She took a deep breath. "I will when I go to his

office next week, but I understand it's perfectly normal.''

''I think you should call him now. The baby is—''

''I know, Lucas. The baby is all-important.'' Wearily she sank down onto the seat at the table. She already loved this baby with all her heart, but it hurt to be reminded over and over again that, for Lucas, she was nothing more than a means to an end.

After a hesitation, he didn't respond to her words. Instead he asked, ''Do you want anything more to eat?''

Nausea roiled in her stomach again. ''No!'' Out of desperation, she rose and turned toward the door. ''I'm going back to bed.''

Lucas watched the door swing behind her, depression filling him. He hadn't helped her at all. If anything, he'd made her feel worse. What was he going to do?

He thought of his hopes this morning. Somehow, after tossing and turning all night, he'd wondered if Susannah might have missed their lovemaking. If she'd given him any indication that she'd welcome a return to his bed, he'd have carried her upstairs and made glorious love to her. Instead, she'd thrown up.

Did that mean he shouldn't touch her again?

Could he live in the same house with her and not have any contact? He groaned. He'd lived three years without making love to a woman. In mourning for Beth, he couldn't imagine touching another woman.

Then along came Susannah. So different from Beth. But stirring him to even greater heights. He craved her warm body next to his in bed, her arms wrapped around him, her mouth meeting his.

Maybe after the first few months of pregnancy. He'd heard sex was possible almost up until the birth of the baby. He'd talk to Doc. He wouldn't take any chances on the safety of his baby, but he wanted Susannah in his bed.

He strode to the phone and dialed Doc's home number. When Doc's gruff voice answered, he got right down to business. "Doc, should Susannah be throwing up?"

"Is she?"

"Yeah. She lost her breakfast this morning."

"That's fairly normal. Be sure—"

"But Beth didn't."

"Susannah isn't Beth, Lucas," Doc said gently.

"I know that!" he snapped, then apologized.

"I'll give her a thorough checkup next week, boy, but the main thing you need to remember is give her what she wants, be supportive. It's important for the mama-to-be to be happy."

Lucas bowed his head, resting his forehead against the wall. He didn't need to ask his other question. Doc had just answered it for him.

"Thanks, Doc."

"You bet. And congratulations, boy. You did it!"

But it wasn't joy that filled Lucas. When Beth had been pregnant, she'd lost what little interest she'd had in sex. And since Susannah had already indicated she preferred to be left alone, Lucas would have to comply with her wishes.

* * *

Lucas insisted on accompanying Susannah to her first appointment with Doc. Susannah appreciated his concern for his child. She just wished his feelings would extend to her, too.

Since he never touched her now, however, she had to believe it was the baby that caused the continuous frown on his forehead. Her fingers itched to smooth his skin, but she didn't dare touch him. She might break down and plead for him to hold her again.

"Maybe Doc can give you something for your nausea," Lucas suggested.

"I'm doing better since I followed Abby's advice about the crackers by my bed."

"Yeah."

"And I'm sure he'll prescribe vitamins, so the baby will be healthy."

"Doc said to give you whatever you want, to keep you happy, so if there's anything I can do, let me know," he said, keeping his gaze on the road.

Susannah closed her eyes, afraid he'd read the hunger in her gaze. What she wanted was for him to love her. To want her more than life itself. The way she wanted him. But she knew better.

"Okay?" he prodded, still not looking at her.

"Of course. But there's nothing. I'm fine."

He parked the car next to Doc's office and came around to help her out of the pickup, as if she were a precious treasure.

But it wasn't her. It was the baby. At least her child would benefit from his love.

After Doc's examination, with Lucas waiting in his office, the three of them sat down to talk.

"You're perfectly healthy, Susannah, and the baby seems fine. I'm giving you a prescription for vitamins, and I want you to get plenty of rest. These first three months are exhausting."

"Should she quit work?"

Susannah stared at Lucas. She thought they'd settled that question.

"That's up to Susannah, Luke. If she gets too tired, she might. More than likely, though, it would be better if she cut her hours a little. Could you get someone to take over about two or three o'clock, Susannah? That way you could nap before dinner."

She was tempted to assure Doc as well as Lucas that she could work twelve hours a day if she chose. But she buried her obstinacy and said calmly, "Possibly...if I need to. Right now I'm not too tired."

And she'd go crazy sitting in the house longing for Lucas's love.

"Susannah!" Lucas protested.

When he would've said something else, she noticed Doc's frown and shake of his head. Aha, an ally!

They were almost ready to leave, having stood up, when Doc added one more thing. "Oh, and, of course, there's no reason to stop relations. You won't hurt the baby." He smiled as if what he'd just said would make them supremely happy.

With her cheeks flushed, Susannah hurried from the office. Did Doc think their marriage was real? He should know better since he orchestrated it.

Lucas thanked Doc for his words of wisdom and followed his wife from the office. Doc had no idea he'd upset the mother-to-be, but Lucas knew. Susannah couldn't wait to get away from him.

Even helping her from the truck had made her uneasy. He had to remember she'd been a virgin on their wedding night. She wasn't used to a man's needs. And since she was pregnant, her needs took precedence over his hungering for her.

He'd just have to wait until after the baby was born.

Surprisingly, since he'd longed for that moment, the birth of his child, he skipped right over that significant event. All he wanted to know was how long he'd have to wait before he could persuade a non-pregnant Susannah back to his bed.

The first Saturday in March, Susannah slept a little later than usual. After all, she wasn't working today. And Lucas would be out on the ranch working.

She'd taken Doc's advice and cut back on her hours at the library. Each afternoon, she returned to the ranch and crawled into bed for an afternoon nap. Even if she awoke before dinner, she remained in her room until Frankie summoned her for supper.

It was easier that way, because it seemed to her that Lucas was returning to the house earlier and earlier each afternoon. She'd hear his booted step on the stairs, pausing by her door, as if he considered knocking.

She'd hold her breath, wishing he would, knowing he wouldn't. Then he'd continue on into his room.

They'd meet at the dinner table and he'd meticulously ask about her health and that of the baby.

Then they ate in silence. Miserable silence.

Occasionally, when she could bear the silence no longer, she'd come up with some anecdote about her day at the library, but more often than not, she remained silent, too.

Since Christmas Day, when she told him about the baby, it was as if someone had dropped a plastic shield between them. No talking, no touching, no lovemaking.

And she hadn't slept as well. Perhaps it was the naps, but she didn't think so. She'd lain awake in her bed each night, hoping and praying Lucas would seek her out once more.

With a sigh, she dressed and wandered downstairs. Frankie had left the coffeepot ready, but he'd gone to tend to other chores. She'd finally convinced him she could make her own piece of toast.

Downing her glass of milk first before she poured the one cup of coffee Doc allowed her, Susannah rinsed the glass in the sink. Then she got her coffee.

Before she could reach the table, however, she felt something strange. With a gasp, she put her free hand to her stomach.

"What's wrong?" Lucas demanded urgently, from the door.

For the first time since she told him she was pregnant, Susannah smiled naturally at him, excitement erasing all the awkwardness. She couldn't wait to share this moment with him.

"The baby moved. Come quick."

He reached her side and she pressed his big hand to her stomach.

A look of wonderment filled his face as the slight fluttering made itself felt. She looked at him, love and excitement filling her eyes.

Without a word, he scooped her into his arms and headed for the stairs.

He carried her straight to his bed, his lips covering hers before their bodies reached the mattress. The strength of his need was overwhelming. He'd missed her.

When, after an incredible coming together, he began to recover his breath, he wondered why they'd waited so long to be in each other's arms. He could feel the contentment emanating from Susannah as she snuggled against him. There was no murmur of objection as he held her, warm against his heart.

They should have been making love every night, he decided fiercely. What they shared was a gift that not every couple had. Making love. No, he meant having sex— Suddenly he couldn't breathe.

No, he meant making love.

He had done the impossible, the one thing he'd promised himself he wouldn't do. He'd fallen in love with Susannah. No! his heart protested. No, no, no!

Without thinking, he pushed himself away from her, staring at her with horror on his face. He couldn't have made himself vulnerable to such pain again.

Susannah couldn't believe what had just happened. After two months of loneliness, Lucas had renewed her hope, filled her with love, brought her joy about the child together with her love for him.

Smiling, she opened her eyes even as he moved away from her. Before she could stir, she saw the expression on his face. What was wrong?

All her insecurities came rushing back. From the look on his face, he was rejecting her all over again. Not just ignoring her, or avoiding her touch, as he'd done the past two months, but denying any feelings. Regretting what he'd just done.

Regretting the love that filled her.

Sure she had betrayed her feelings, she slid from the bed, grabbing her clothes to press to her body along the way. He hadn't loved her before. He certainly couldn't now that her body had changed, grown larger. She wanted to hide from his gaze.

And she wanted to hide her heart from his rejection.

She ran to her room, slamming the door behind her.

He rapped on the wood almost immediately. "Susannah? Susannah, I'm sorry. I can't—"

No, he couldn't. He couldn't love her as she wanted to be loved. He could only love his child.

With her dreams shattered, her silly, ridiculous dreams of love, she crawled under the covers and wept into her pillow.

He called her name one more time. When she didn't answer, she heard his boots as he walked away.

She couldn't blame him. He'd never promised her he would love her. Only her child.

After telling herself the difficulty was her, not Lucas, the tears finally stopped. But the pain only grew worse. Unable to stop herself, she got up and pulled a suitcase from the closet.

She would accept his behavior. It wasn't his fault, she reminded herself again. *She* was the one who had changed, whose needs were different. How could she have known that Lucas Boyd would melt her frigidity? But she needed some time to shore up her defenses, to hide her wants. Some distance.

Calling Abby, she explained that she would be gone the next week and asked her to take care of the library. Then she wrote a brief note to Lucas, telling him she was visiting a friend. She wouldn't give him the number or address. She needed total isolation. But she didn't want him to worry, either.

She remade the bed and left the note on her pillow. Then she carried her suitcase down the stairs and out to her car. Frankie wasn't around, so she was able to avoid explaining her behavior to him, too.

So no one told her goodbye, and no one saw her tears.

It was better that way.

Chapter Twelve

Lucas stood over his first wife's grave, traces of his earlier shock on his face.

He hadn't intended to love another woman. Just another woman's child. Beth would understand that. She knew how much he'd wanted their child.

He hoped Beth would understand how things had changed. He'd loved her with the heart of a young man: naive, tender, expecting everything to go right.

But it hadn't.

He was a different man, now. Seasoned with pain and sorrow. And able to love with a maturity and strength he hadn't known he'd had. Had Beth lived, his love for her would've grown to this strength, he was sure.

But she hadn't.

Now he loved Susannah. He'd missed her in his bed, but he'd told himself it was the sex he'd missed. When he'd returned her to his bed, he'd realized, shockingly, that it wasn't the sex, it was the love-making. The holding, the touching, the sharing.

He'd hungered for the sight of her, for the close-ness of their togetherness. He'd loved her. Only he hadn't realized it.

When had he begun to love her? From the first, when she intruded into his sad world, refusing to do whatever he asked? When she came to him with her agreement to have his child? Or had it been that first night he'd loved her, when she'd shown him, in spite of her inexperience, how much she needed him, too?

Because she did. He knew, with a joy that grew with each moment, that she loved him as much as he loved her. Susannah, with her generous heart, her determined spirit, wanted him as much as he wanted her.

He walked away from Beth's grave, after bidding her a final goodbye, and headed for the house. The day wasn't over, there was work to be done, but he needed to see Susannah, to hold her, to touch her. To tell her he loved her.

He drove his truck at a breakneck pace, thinking of how he'd left Susannah. She might refuse to let him near her, if he'd read her mood right. But he'd fight for his marriage, for his love, for his heart.

He'd make her listen.

After jerking the truck to a halt, and throwing up pieces of gravel, he sprinted for the house.

"Where's the fire, boss?" Frankie asked as he rushed through the kitchen.

Lucas grinned, the joy spilling out of him. "Gotta find Susannah."

"I think she's gone," Frankie said as he continued rolling out pie dough. "Her car's not here."

Lucas was halfway up the stairs before the man's words penetrated. He tumbled back down the stairs. "What?"

"I said I—"

Lucas ignored him and raced for the window that overlooked where Susannah usually parked her car. "When did she go?"

"I don't know. I came back to the house about half an hour ago to fix lunch and—"

Lucas ignored him and sprinted for the stairs again. He wrenched open the door to Susannah's room and stood on the threshold, studying the neatness. Then he saw the note.

"No, dear God, no," he prayed. God couldn't be so cruel as to give him a second love and then take her away.

But, then, God didn't know how stupid Lucas could be.

The note was simple. She'd gone away to visit a friend. But she'd given no phone number where she could be reached, no address. And she hadn't said when she'd be back. If she'd be back.

He called Abby. "Where's Susannah?"

"Don't you know? She's visiting a friend."

"What friend? Where?"

"I don't know. She hung up before I could ask. What's wrong?" Abby demanded, a growing urgency in her voice.

"She's left me," Lucas whispered, unintentionally

voicing his fears, covering his eyes with his free hand.

"What? What did you do?" Abby asked.

But Lucas couldn't answer. He hung up the phone and sank down to the mattress. What had he done? How could he have been so stupid as to walk away from her without explaining what had happened? He'd thought he'd needed some time.

Now he had more time than he wanted...a lot more time.

Susannah drove into Caliente on Thursday morning.

She'd intended to stay away for a week. But she couldn't. She'd missed the town, her friends, the ranch, Frankie and the cowhands. And Lucas. Dear God, how she'd missed Lucas.

But she punished herself by pulling into a parking space in front of the library. She had abandoned her responsibilities by leaving so suddenly. She needed to see how the library was doing.

Besides, Lucas wasn't expecting her. He probably didn't care when she returned, as long as his baby was well cared for. She might as well practice her resolution to treat him as the father of her child. And nothing else.

She entered the library to find Abby behind the desk.

"Susannah! You're back! Are you all right?" her friend demanded as she rushed around the desk to hug her.

"Yes, of course I'm all right," Susannah replied,

patting Abby's back, wondering what had caused her concern. "I told you I'd be away for a week, but I came back early."

"Does Lucas know?"

"Not yet. He's not expecting me."

"You can say that again," Abby replied.

"Hi, Susannah," Gertie called from across the room. "You're back!"

"Susannah!" Mr. Jones, one of her regular customers, boomed. "'Bout time you came back."

Several other frequent visitors greeted her with the same phrase.

"What's wrong with everyone?" she asked.

"They thought you'd left Lucas," Abby said succinctly.

"Why would they think that? I told you I was going out of town to visit a friend. I left Lucas a note." True, it had been brief, but it was a note.

"You'll have to ask Lucas about that. He pretty much came unglued. The whole town has been worryin' about the two of you. Especially since word got out about you being pregnant." Abby's cheeks actually flushed.

"How did that happen?"

"Well, Lucas and I were talking, and someone overheard. I didn't mean to let it slip, Susannah."

She hugged her friend again. "Don't worry about it. Everyone will know just by looking pretty soon. I'm getting as big as a house." Which would keep Lucas away from her even more, she reminded herself. As if she needed any reminding. She'd spent all the time she was gone preparing herself for his lack of interest. Perhaps even distaste.

"Well, if everything's all right here, I'd better go on to the ranch. I need to unpack and then maybe take a nap. Driving tires me out these days."

"Need me to drive you to the ranch?" Abby asked anxiously.

"Don't be silly. It's not that far. Thank you for taking care of everything here. I'll be in tomorrow."

She turned and headed back for her car.

When she pulled up beside the ranch house a few minutes later, Frankie was already beside the door. He had her suitcase out of the car before she could get out.

"You all right?" he asked, his brow furrowed.

"Of course I am. Did Abby call you?"

"Yeah. We sent for Luke. He'll be here anytime."

Her stomach clutched, and she rubbed it. "There was no need for that. He wasn't even expecting me today."

"Nope. Today's the first time he's given up trying to find you. I don't think he would'a stayed out long, anyway."

Susannah frowned. Trying to find her? She'd left a note. Didn't he read it?

With a shrug, she followed Frankie and her suitcase into the house. He didn't stop until he reached her room, setting the bag down on the floor.

"You hungry? I'll have lunch ready in a few minutes."

"Thanks, Frankie. That would be nice. I'll rest until you call me."

"Want me to call Doc? He could come right out."

"Frankie, I'm fine. Driving tires me out, that's all. I'll rest and then be down for lunch."

He closed the door behind him, and Susannah looked around the neat room. She'd even missed this room. But the one she'd missed most of all was across the hall.

Stop it! You won't be sharing anything in that room anymore.

With a sigh, she sank down onto the bed, slipped off her shoes and put her head on the pillow. She was home.

Lucas was a long way from the barn when one of his cowboys finally caught up with him. He was riding a fence line, doing the most hated work of all, hoping to escape his thoughts. And not having much success.

He saw the rider from a distance, noting his all-out gallop. Uneasiness filled him. Something was wrong. Without hesitation, he urged his horse toward the rider, increasing his speed as he moved.

"Boss, she's back!" the rider gasped as he pulled his horse to a stop.

Lucas's heart leaped. His horse danced, eager to run again, but he paused to ask, "She's okay?"

"Frankie said she's fine."

He didn't ask any more questions. Instead he raced flat out for the house...and his wife.

Sleep had been in short supply this week. Most of the nights he'd paced the floor, worrying, longing for her. Finally, he'd turned to work today, hoping to distract his mind…and she'd come home.

It took almost half an hour to reach the house. News had evidently spread, because several of his cowboys greeted him with broad smiles as he flew from the saddle.

"We'll take care of your horse, boss."

He threw a thanks over his shoulder and ran the rest of the way to the house. She was in the kitchen with Frankie, sitting at the table as if everything were normal. Standing as he entered, she looked apprehensive.

As well she should. She'd scared him to death.

Without speaking, he pulled her to him, wrapping his arms tightly around her. "Don't you ever do that again!" he warned, his voice tight.

"Now, boss, you should talk nice—" Frankie began.

"We're going upstairs," Lucas announced, interrupting his cook's advice.

"But I got lunch almost fixed," Frankie complained.

Susannah had said nothing.

He loosened his grip, staring into her beautiful face. He intended to talk, only talk, but he couldn't help himself as he lowered his mouth to hers. He'd talk in a minute. As soon as he tasted her, made sure she was real and not a figment of his imagination.

He was encouraged as her arms stole around his neck. Then applause and several cheers disrupted the most precious moment in his life to date. Susannah gasped as she looked over his shoulder and saw a number of the staff on the back porch, watching them.

"Shoo, now!" Frankie said, rushing to wave the audience away with a cup towel.

"You, too, Frankie. Go with them," Lucas ordered.

"But, boss, lunch—"

"Turn the stove off and go." His order was stern, and Frankie did as he asked.

When the door closed behind the cook, Susannah looked at him, her eyes wide. "What did you do? Tell everyone we had a fight? The people in town acted as if I'd run away. I—"

"Isn't that what you did?"

She stiffened under his touch, and he knew he'd said the wrong thing. Before he could apologize, she spoke.

"I needed some time away. I didn't mean to worry you." Her voice was solemn, quiet, almost sad.

"Sweetheart, you scared me out of a year's growth."

"The baby is fine. I took good care of it."

"And you? Did you take good care of you?"

"Of course." But her voice was still sad, and she didn't look at him.

"Look, Susannah, when we—the last time—I realized—I loved Beth!" he finally said, unable to figure out exactly how to explain his awakening.

She pulled from his arms and turned her back to him. "Of course. I understand completely."

Instead of turning her, he walked around to face her. "You do?" But the tears streaming down her face told him she didn't. Or she didn't want to hear that he loved her.

She nodded her head.

"Susannah, I want us to have a real marriage. I want—"

He stopped as she turned her back to him again, wiping her tears.

"I can't," she said faintly.

This time he turned her around. "What? Why not? We were getting along just fine. I don't see—"

"I haven't been honest with you."

Her words stopped him cold. What was she talking about? Had she found someone else? Was she going to leave him? His heart ached with fear. "What do you mean?"

"I—I have to tell you something. Then, if you— you still want us to have a real marriage, then—"

"I do!" he insisted, with more fervor than he'd used in his marriage vows. But Susannah meant more to him now.

"I broke our agreement."

"What do you mean? Damn it, Susannah, you're killing me. Tell me what's going on."

She dropped her chin down on her chest, and he leaned closer. "I—I love you."

Her softly whispered words stunned him. Filled him with joy. Worried him. He finally connected them to her earlier explanation that she hadn't been honest.

Lifting her chin, forcing her gaze to his, he said, "Are you telling me you left this week because you love me?"

She nodded.

He closed his eyes and leaned his forehead against hers. "Thank you, God." Then he lowered his head and kissed her. He kissed her to tell her he loved her, to tell her he'd missed her, to tell her he'd never let her go again.

But just in case she didn't understand all those things, he stopped kissing her to tell her in words. He wasn't going to walk away from her again until she understood just how much he loved her.

"Sweetheart, I reacted the way I did last time because I realized I loved you. Completely, totally. More than life itself."

Her tears increased, and she sobbed as she lay her head on his shoulder.

"I promise it's true."

"You...you didn't look like you loved me," she reminded him.

"I was in shock. I'd told myself it was because you were so good in bed that I climbed those stairs earlier and earlier." He tightened his arms around her. "But the truth is, I love you, and I don't ever want you to go away again."

"I don't want to," she assured him, caressing his cheek. "But I was afraid if you saw how much I love you, you'd—you'd want me to go away."

"Never. And I want you in my bed every night, the entire night," he added fiercely. "I hated it when you'd leave me."

"But—"

"I know it's my fault," he admitted, not waiting

for her to speak. "I was an idiot. I was so afraid of being hurt, I was afraid to hold you close."

"I promise I'll try never to hurt you."

He kissed her again.

"I know that, Susannah. And I promise to hold you close forever."

He scooped her into his arms and headed for those stairs that led to heaven. "Mind waiting a little while for lunch?"

She tucked her face into his neck. "I'm more hungry for you than I am for Frankie's cooking."

Satisfaction and eagerness filled him. Susannah was back, to stay, and they'd never be apart again. God had blessed him a second time, and he'd never forget to be grateful.

Epilogue

"Damn it, Doc, get in here!" Lucas exploded, entering an emergency room cubicle.

"Settle down, boy. I'll be there as soon as I sew up Jaimie, here." Doc was bent over a three-year-old, with the boy's mother holding him still.

"But Susannah's in pain," Lucas protested. He'd promised himself he'd be calm, but the moment she went into labor, he'd been out of control. He knew it, but he couldn't stop. He was so afraid something would go wrong.

"Nurse Cone will call me if things change. Susannah is going through the normal stages of labor. It's only been a few hours," Doc said calmly, finishing his work. "There now, Jaimie, I suggest you avoid that toy in the future. Okay, young—"

"Doctor, you'd better come," the nurse said from the door, just behind Lucas.

It wasn't a fair contest since he had a head start,

but Lucas beat Doc to Susannah's side by a long shot. "Sweetheart, are you all right?"

Susannah, in the throes of another pain, couldn't answer at once. It was the nurse's calm voice that reassured him. "Of course she is. But I don't think it will be much longer."

Doc settled at the end of the table and examined Susannah. "You're faster than I thought, young lady. Or maybe this baby is impatient, like his daddy."

Susannah drew a deep breath and smiled. Lucas kissed her forehead, then stroked her cheek. "Hold on, sweetheart. Doc's going to take care of everything."

"Don't you believe him for a minute," Doc contradicted. "I'm just along for the ride. You and Junior here are the ones doing all the work. It's time now. I want you to push," he urged.

Susannah, clutching Lucas's hand, followed directions. Only a few minutes later, Doc held the next generation of Boyd men in his hands.

"He's a fine, healthy boy, Susannah," Doc assured her.

Lucas glanced at his son, but his attention was focused on his wife. "Are you okay, sweetheart? Can I get you anything? Does it hurt?"

"You can bring our son here," she said. When her baby was laid in her arms, Susannah beamed at her husband. "See, I told you everything would be fine."

His hand trembling, Lucas touched first his child and then his wife's face. "Yes, you did. And you were right, as always. I love you."

He gently kissed her soft lips.

"So next time I can have a daughter?" she teased.

They'd had several arguments over the topic of more children. Susannah wanted them, but Lucas wasn't sure he could risk losing her again. She'd made him promise to change his mind if she came through this delivery without difficulties.

"We'll see. Doc can—"

"Lucas, you promised," she reminded him, cuddling her infant against her. "Besides, we make beautiful babies together. How could you say no?"

He stared at his beloved wife and child and only shook his head. He'd been truly blessed when Susannah came into his life. He never wanted to chance losing her.

But he also knew he could never deny her anything. And he suspected he'd have difficulty doing that with his children, too. His son grabbed hold of his finger, trying to carry this new object to his mouth.

Lucas tucked Susannah's head against his shoulder. "I suppose we could consider a little girl. In a year or two. If you're sure."

Smiling at him, her love filling her eyes, Susannah nodded her head. "Yes, in a year or two."

"But only if you promise she'll look just like you," he added.

"Okay, but only if *you* promise you'll love me when I'm fat and lumpy again."

She'd worried about losing her figure, but Lucas had delighted in every change, holding her close each night, giving thanks for her.

"Done," he agreed, with no hesitation at all. And with another loving smile, he kissed her again, a kiss that communicated all the husbandly devotion that swelled his heart.

*   *   *   *   *

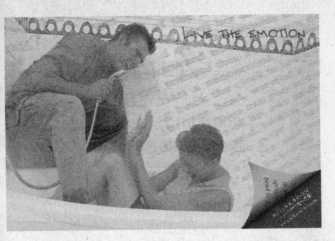

MILLS & BOON

Strictly Business

When the fun starts...
after hours!

PENNY JORDAN

Liz Fielding

Hannah Bernard

On sale 3rd September 2004

Available at most branches of WHSmith, Tesco, Martins, Borders,
Eason, Sainsbury's and all good paperback bookshops.

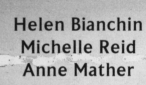

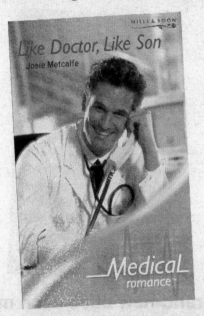